First Cut

J. T. Bishop

Eudoran Press LLC

Dallas, Texas

Eudoran Press LLC
6204 Frazier Dr
Plano, TX 75024
www.jtbishopauthor.com

Publisher's Note: This is a work of fiction. Names, characters, places, and incidents are a product of the author's imagination. Locales and public names are sometimes used for atmospheric purposes. Any resemblance to actual people, living or dead, or to businesses, companies, events, institutions, or locales is completely coincidental.

First Cut/ Eudoran Press LLC. -- 1st ed.
Paperback ISBN 978-1-7325531-2-5
Paperback V2 ISBN 978-1-955370-02-8
Hardback ISBN 978-1-955370-11-0

Original Book Cover design by betibup33 design
Book Cover Update by JT Bishop

Other Books by J. T. Bishop

The Red-Line Trilogy

Red-Line: The Shift

Red-Line: Mirrors

Red-Line: Trust Destiny

The Red-Line Trilogy Boxed Set

The Red-Line Sister Series: The Fletcher Family Saga

Curse Breaker

High Child

Spark

Forged Lines

The Fletcher Family Saga Boxed Set

The Family or Foe Saga with Detectives Daniels and Remalla

First Cut

Second Strike

Third Blow

Fourth Strike

The Family or Foe Saga Boxed Set

Detectives Daniels and Remalla

Haunted River

Of Breath and Blood

Of Body and Bone

Coming soon…Of Mind and Madness

The Redstone Chronicles

Lost Souls

Lost Dreams

Coming soon…Lost Chances

To my Mom…we may bump heads sometimes, but you’ll always be my mom. I’m lucky to have you, thank you for all you do, and I love you.

Acknowledgements

Thank you to my family, friends, coworkers and fans, all of whom make this possible. I wouldn't write if it weren't for you and your continued support and encouragement. I hear it, I see it, and I thank you immensely.

CHAPTER ONE

The body stared up with vacant eyes, the garish lipstick smeared across the lips, and the cheeks streaked with harsh red. Blood pooled on the carpet and stained the walls. Large drips dried as they slid down the walls. Detective Aaron Remalla recalled the TV show he'd watched the previous night. The one with the demonic clown wreaking havoc in a small town, and wished this scene could be just as fictional, only it wasn't. Compared to this, the TV show was tame. He took a breath to settle his stomach.

"Seen enough?"

Rem looked up to see his partner, Gordon Daniels, standing beside him. The light from above silhouetted his long, powerful frame, and Rem squinted. "I saw enough about three years ago." He stood.

"I hear you," said Daniels. He crossed his arms, and his leather jacket crinkled with the movement. "I'd thought we'd seen the worst of it."

Rem grunted. "There's always another sicko in the works to take the last one's place."

"Don't you think at some point, we'd reach the limit for psychopaths?"

The front door was open, and Rem noticed two police officers who kept a small crowd at bay. One of them held police tape. "Is that Delgado?"

"It is."

He shook his head. "How is it he always gets these scenes?"

"Maybe he's a fan of the macabre."

"I should give him my job."

"He'd take it in a second."

Rem raised a brow. "You want a new partner?"

Daniels rubbed his neck. "I finally got you trained. I've been tortured enough."

Rem snorted. "Trained? I taught you everything I know."

Daniels uncrossed his arms. "The location of every gas station bathroom and fast-food chain between home and the station is helpful, but not exactly necessary."

"It is when you need a couple of Taco del Fuegos after a twelve-hour shift."

Daniels sighed, his face strained. "Nothing's stopping you from eating a banana."

"My sanity is. Nobody's eating a banana after a shitty day."

"Speak for yourself."

"I usually do. Who else would I speak for?"

"Really? You want me to answer that?"

Rem shrugged.

"Detectives?"

Rem looked to see Officer Delgado standing at the doorway. "Stay put, Delgado. Crime Scene is still working." He stepped away from the body and toward Delgado, and Daniels followed. Once outside, he pulled off the shoe coverings and gloves he wore. Daniels did the same. "What is it?" asked Rem.

"You need me to take pictures of the crowd?"

"Why?" asked Daniels. "You like photography?"

"The light is especially good right now. Don't you think?" asked Rem.

Daniels pointed. "Yes, especially on that particularly large gentleman in the front. You could get a great shot of him eating his sandwich."

Delgado rolled his eyes. "I've heard that serial killers sometimes revisit the scenes of their crimes. I just thought…"

Rem raised a hand. "Serial killer? Who said anything about a serial killer?"

Delgado's eyes rounded. "Come on, guys. You know what this looks like." He gestured toward the door.

"I also know what that looks like," said Daniels, motioning toward the street as a press van pulled up. "Until we confirm anything, you know nothing. You got it?"

Delgado set his chin but nodded. "I got it."

"And don't worry about the pics. Crime Scene will handle it," said Rem.

Delgado stared out at the growing crowd. "I guess I'll go help Parsons."

"I'm sure your partner would appreciate that," said Daniels.

With a last, almost sad, look at the house, Delgado turned and walked down the front stairs.

"You should be nicer to him," said Rem. "He could be your partner someday."

Daniels started to leave. "I'd rather eat a Taco del Fuego."

Rem followed. "You know, we could pick one up on the way to the station." He raised a brow as Daniels groaned.

**

Captain Frank Lozano stared at his computer monitor. The information coming in unsettled him. What he'd most feared appeared to be true. He sat back in his seat, put his hands on his midsection, and sighed.

A knock on his door made him turn. His two detectives, Remalla and Daniels, stood outside the glass. He motioned for them to enter.

Remalla came in with a coffee cup and a paper bag, wearing his usual worn jeans and a T-shirt with a long-sleeved, red checkered shirt over it. His thick, shoulder-length brown, almost black hair, ruffled by the wind, gave him the appearance of a teenage kid after an impromptu game of touch football. Daniels wore slim khakis and a long-sleeved ironed shirt, unbuttoned at the collar. His shorter, sandy colored hair was gelled in the latest men's style, and he held his leather jacket and a water bottle. He threw the jacket over a chair and sat.

Rem put his cup on Lozano's desk and, still standing, pulled a hot dog out of the bag. Lozano stared at the apple next to his stapler and the picture of himself and his third wife from early in their marriage. His blue suit and canary yellow shirt had complemented his brown skin and his then slimmer physique. Since becoming a cop and eventually a captain, he'd been divorced twice and gained ten pounds. He missed his younger days, although not his first wife. That marriage had lasted only two years and his second only four. Being a cop did that. Eyeing the picture, he was happy to say he felt the third marriage would stick. He and Sheila would hit their ten-year anniversary next month.

"What you got, Cap?" asked Rem through a mouthful of hot dog.

"Talk to me about the crime scene first. Same M.O.?" asked Lozano.

"The same," said Daniels. "Female. In her mid to late twenties. Stabbed multiple times. Body was staged. Makeup on her face. Just like the last one."

"Any writing on the walls?" asked Lozano.

"Nothing," said Rem, wiping his face with a napkin.

Lozano rubbed his face. "Press?"

"They were there," said Daniels. "They're sniffing around. It won't be long before they put two and two together."

"I hate to ask, but you think we're dealing with the same guy?" asked Rem. He took the last large bite of his hot dog and crumpled his napkin. Detectives could eat faster than a busy mom.

Lozano eyed his apple again. He marveled at how Rem could stuff down food like a horse but still maintain his trim physique. It was the only thing his detectives seemed to have in common. Remalla ate like crap, dressed the same, and was a serial dater. In high school, he'd been a star athlete in track and field, and he still ran and occasionally sparred at the local ring for exercise, which helped maintain his long and lean frame. Daniels watched what he ate and what he wore, lifted weights at the local gym; he'd won the arm-wrestling competition at the policeman's picnic last year, and his longtime girlfriend was seven months pregnant with their first child. Daniels had a college degree and had almost gone to law school. Rem had street smarts and had barely avoided going to jail in his youth. Despite their differences though, they made a formidable team and shared a tight bond. They'd worked with Lozano in Robbery/Homicide for the last four years, and they were his best detectives. Lozano studied his monitor again.

"What is it, Cap?" asked Daniels.

"A report from Seattle. I talked to a Sergeant Merchant who led the case up there. Based on that conversation and what I'm reading, we're dealing with the same guy."

Rem and Daniels made eye contact and Rem sat in the seat next to Daniels. He picked up his cup. "You sure? Couldn't be a copycat?"

"The details are too similar," said Lozano. "The make-up, the staging, the stabbing. The press didn't know all of that."

"They knew most of it," said Daniels. "Plus, there's no writing on the walls. I thought the killer left messages in Seattle. This guy isn't doing that." He took a swig of his water.

"I just got pictures from Seattle. The press reported about the makeup but not the specifics on how it was applied." Lozano flipped his screen to show his detectives. They leaned closer to look.

"Shit," said Rem.

Daniels narrowed his eyes. "Hell. They look the same. The lipstick. The blush."

"Based on this, and my conversation with Merchant, I'd say the Makeup Artist is now hunting in our backyard." Lozano swiveled the screen back around.

"The Makeup Artist," said Rem. "That's catchy." He sipped from his cup and grimaced. "This coffee sucks."

"Maybe you shouldn't drink it when it was made yesterday," said Daniels.

"I put it in the microwave," said Rem, taking a last gulp and crumpling the cup in his hand. "This doesn't make sense, Cap. Why would a serial killer come here? Seattle is one thing, but this is a small suburb outside of San Diego. What's here that's caught his interest?"

"Merchant has a theory about that. His department searched long and hard for this guy. He killed seven people in an eight-month span. Five women and two men. Then he stopped. Nothing for the last two years."

"Two men?" asked Daniels. "That's unusual. They're sure about that?"

"They are. They had the same MO. Makeup, stabbing, staged corpse. And writing on the walls."

"Huh," said Daniels. "I wonder why."

"You'll have to go over the files. They're sending copies. Profilers have their theories. Merchant has his own," said Lozano.

Rem leaned forward. "That sounds interesting. Do his views differ from the profilers?"

Lozano pulled a notepad and pen from his desk. He flipped over to his email and wrote a name and address down. He tore off the paper and handed it to Daniels. "I want you to go talk to her."

Daniels read the paper. "Jill Jacobs. Who is she?"

"She has a connection to the case. Worked on it in Seattle until she couldn't do it anymore. Took a leave of absence but never went back. She moved here about six months ago. Merchant says you should speak to her. She might be able to help."

"Help?" asked Rem. "She burned out? Sounds like she's the last person we should be asking for assistance."

"We've got a serial killer on the loose in our city," said Lozano. "Not to mention these recent bank robberies that we've been trying to foil with little success. We're a little thin right now, and this Artist, if that's who he is, has killed two people in a six-week span, which means we don't have long before he kills again. If this woman can shed some light on this case, I don't care if she's crispy fried, we need to try. So, go out there and use what little charm you have to get her to work with us. We're going to need all the help we can get."

Daniels stared at the paper. "Okay." He stood. "You ready?"

Rem stood and tossed his cup in the trash. "You know, Cap. You're a pretty charming guy yourself. Have I ever told you that?"

"Get out of here," said Lozano, waving his arm. "And for the millionth time, get your hair cut. It's too long."

Rem smiled, tucked his hair behind his ear and followed Daniels out of the office.

CHAPTER TWO

Daniels pulled up in front of the RV park. A rusty sign and rickety, leaning wooden fence stood outside the weed-infested property.

"Is this it?" asked Rem.

"According to the address."

Rem scanned the area. "This looks like something out of a zombie movie."

Daniels killed the engine and opened the door. "Don't worry. I'll protect you."

Rem smirked and exited the car. They paused in front of the open, sun-bleached wooden gate that would have crumbled with a good kick. "Jeez," said Rem. "How long has this place been here?"

Daniels walked down the driveway. "I don't know. Why don't you ask Google?"

Rem followed, checking each RV as they passed. "Which one is it?"

"I have no idea."

"Then where are you going?"

"Thought I'd just take a stroll. Maybe look for a few zombies."

Rem made a dubious look.

Daniels pointed. "I'm going to the office." He pointed to an RV with chipped siding and a banged-up sign marked "Office" on the front. "I figure they might know something."

"Oh, good idea," Rem huffed. "You'd make a great detective."

Daniels reached the RV and opened the door. "Thank you."

They stepped into a small room with a desk and not much else. The walls needed new paint and the windows were so dirty, they barely let in enough light. A TV was playing from one of the back rooms, but no one was present.

"Hello?" asked Daniels. "Anybody here?"

Rem stepped up close to his partner. "I swear. If a zombie walks out of that room, it's every man for himself."

Daniels offered his partner a side glance. "You watched that horror movie the other night, didn't you?"

"It was last night."

Daniels shook his head. "Hello?" he asked again, only louder.

"Keep your shorts on. I'm coming," said a scruffy, deep voice from the back.

Rem moved closer to Daniels.

"Would you step back?" whispered Daniels.

An older woman, wearing a worn and at one point, maybe pink, bathrobe, appeared. Her short hair stood up in crazy tangles and it was silver at the roots and the rest was a dull faded brown. Her face was wrinkled, and she smelled of cigarettes. Rem thought she was maybe sixty, but he didn't know if that was her true age or just the results of years of smoking.

"What do you want?" she asked, looking over the two men.

"I told you," whispered Rem to Daniels. "Zombie."

Daniels pulled out his badge. "Excuse me, ma'am, but we're looking for a woman. She has an RV here. Her name is Jill Jacobs. Would you happen to know where we might find her?"

The woman studied his badge. "You a cop?"

"Yes, ma'am. I'm Detective Daniels and this is Detective Remalla."

"What'd she do?"

Rem finally spoke. "Nothing ma'am. We just need to talk to her."

The woman looked around Daniels and gave Rem an appraisal. She smiled, and Rem could see some missing teeth. "You're a good-looking one, aren't ya?" She put a hand on her hip, and her robe partially opened, revealing a long nightgown equally as worn as the robe. Rem kept his eyes on her face. "If I were twenty years younger," she said, her gaze never leaving Rem's.

Daniels gave Rem a flat look, and Rem shrugged.

"Uh, ma'am?" Daniels asked, as the woman stalked Rem with her eyes. "Jill Jacobs?"

Rem squirmed and pointed to his partner. "He's talking to you."

The woman blinked and finally answered Daniels. "She's down at the end. Last RV on the left. Good luck talking to her though. She doesn't say much."

"I can't imagine why," said Rem, under his breath. He pulled on Daniels' arm. "Thank you."

"Come by after, if you want," she said, cocking her head to the side. "I got some potato chips and onion dip I don't mind sharin'."

"That's your favorite snack," said Daniels as Rem pulled him out of the trailer. "You sure you don't want to…"

"No, thank you." Rem waved at the woman. "We're pretty busy today."

Daniels smiled and spoke to the woman. "Thanks for your help, ma'am."

They closed the door behind them, and Rem walked at a brisk pace away from the trailer.

Daniels jogged up beside him. "You sure you want to walk alone? I thought you were scared of zombies."

"She just cured me."

Daniels chuckled. "I bet she's free if you're looking for a date on Saturday, you good-looking man."

Rem frowned. "Funny."

They walked past several other trailers until they reached the end of the lot. Heavy trunked, green trees dotted the landscape, and, in the distance, they could hear the beach. A chain link fence listing to the side ran through the back of the property and to their left stood the last RV. It was painted white, but it looked more like a dirty taupe after years of neglect. There was a small porch, with a table and chair that looked out over the trees. The leaves had been raked and there were two potted, healthy plants on each side of the entry.

They took the short set of stairs up to the door and knocked. Daniels leaned over and touched one of the leaves on a leafy potted plant. “It’s healthy, so she can’t be a total monster.”

Rem scanned the area, making sure that the woman from the office wasn’t lurking somewhere. “Who says monsters aren’t capable of watering plants?”

Daniels peered through a window. “She used to be a cop. Let’s cut her some slack.”

Rem couldn’t argue with that. He knocked again. Another minute passed but there was no answer. Rem tried the knob, but it was locked. “Wonderful,” he said. “We’re here and she’s not.” He walked to the end of the porch and looked around. “What do you want to do?”

“I wonder if Lozano has a phone number for her,” said Daniels. He pulled out his cell.

“She’s not home,” said a male voice. Rem startled and Daniels put his phone down.

Rem saw a man standing outside the adjacent trailer. He wore denim overalls and a hat, but no shirt. He pointed a bony finger. “She likes to go in the woods.”

Daniels and Rem glanced toward where he pointed. Beyond the fence was a wooded area thick with foliage.

“Which way?” asked Daniels.

“Hop the fence. Head toward the water. You’ll find her.” He tipped his hat and walked into his RV.

Rem raised his hand, as Daniels stepped off the porch. “Thanks,” said Rem. But the man had already gone inside. “This place is straight out of 'American Horror Story.'" He joined Daniels and headed toward the fence.

"I told you not to watch that show," said Daniels. He put a hand on the chain link and jumped over it. Rem did the same. Seeing an overgrown trail, they followed it and walked into the woods. An eerie silence enveloped them. But as they walked, the sounds of the shore grew louder, and within a few minutes, they saw the cove. The ocean surf met soft sand dotted with dunes and a few rocky patches. Rem could not have imagined a more idyllic spot to come and sit. He pictured a campfire, a six pack and a beautiful woman by his side. How that rundown RV park held on to what had to be expensive property was a mystery to him.

"Not a bad place to hang your hat," said Daniels.

Rem saw a beach chair sitting in the sand. Next to it was a bucket of ice with three bottlenecks protruding from the top. An empty bottle lay on its side beside the chair, and down near the waves, facing away from them, holding a half-filled beer while her hair blew in the breeze, stood a woman. From a distance, Rem could see she was tall. Her denim cutoffs revealed trim legs, but her oversized shirt divulged little else. Water splashed over her feet and the only movement she made was to take a swig of her drink.

"I'm guessing that's her," said Daniels.

They stood for a moment. "You want to make the introductions, or should I?" asked Rem.

"Go for it, Tonto."

Rem snorted. "Thanks, Kemosabe. And you get on me for watching horror flicks."

"The Lone Ranger is a classic. You should watch it some time."

"I have. John Wayne is far superior."

Daniels waved a hand. "Then go for it, Duke. I got your back, in case any Indians show."

Rem frowned at Daniels as he walked down the beach, muttering about westerns vs. zombies. Approaching the waves, he stopped just as the woman made a sudden turn. Her beer bottle dropped into the water as her other hand came up, and he saw the glimmer of the gun.

CHAPTER THREE

Seeing the gun, Daniels pulled his weapon, aiming at the woman. He stood at a diagonal to Remalla, so his partner was not in the line of fire. His heart rate tripled, and he watched Rem hold up his arms.

"Drop the gun!" he yelled.

The woman glanced at him, but she held the gun on Rem. "Who are you? What do you want?"

Rem kept his hands visible. "Take it easy. We're cops," he said. "I'm going to take my badge out." He slowly moved his hand toward his back pocket, making it obvious so the woman could see he wasn't going for his weapon.

The woman, eyes wide with uncertainty, kept looking between Rem and Daniels. "You, too," she said to Daniels.

Daniels didn't move. "Take that gun off my partner."

Rem pulled out his badge and opened it. "I'm Detective Remalla and this is my partner, Detective Daniels. Are you Jill Jacobs? Sergeant Merchant told us where to find you. All we want to do is talk." He kept his hands up and spoke in a soothing voice.

The woman hesitated. "Talk about what?"

"Drop the gun first," yelled Daniels.

Remalla took a small step forward, and Daniels held his breath. "We didn't mean to scare you. We want to talk about the Makeup Artist."

Even from a distance, Daniels could see her face pale. She stared for a second, her forehead furrowed, and then she relaxed her stance, lowered her weapon and tucked it into the waistband of her shorts.

Rem dropped his hands and glanced back at Daniels, who let go of a lungful of held breath and holstered his gun. He debated arresting her, but realized she wasn't a threat and they would need her cooperation. He walked over to his partner but stayed on alert.

"You okay?" asked Daniels to Rem.

Rem took a shaky breath. "That'll wake you up."

"Still scared of zombies?"

Rem didn't answer as the woman approached with wariness.

"Jill Jacobs?" asked Rem.

She walked past them and toward her beach chair. Reaching it, she grabbed another bottle from the bucket. "That's me."

They followed. "You want to tell us why you pull guns on strangers?" asked Daniels.

She twisted the cap off. "You came up behind me," she said, taking a healthy swig.

"It's a public beach," said Rem.

She waved. "Does it look public?"

"You go around waving guns, you're going to get arrested," said Daniels.

"I'll take my chances," she said, and sat in the chair. She removed her weapon and put it beside her, careful to do it slowly to not alarm Rem or Daniels.

"Well, we don't mean to interrupt your 'me' time, but we'd like to ask you a few questions," said Rem.

"Can't promise I'll answer." She took another swig.

Rem raised a brow at Daniels. "You were a cop in Seattle, right? Worked on the Makeup Artist case?"

"That was a long time ago. In another life," she said, resting her head back.

Daniels nodded. "Been in the RV park long?"

She watched the waves. “A while.”

“It’s a charming place, but a little crazy.” Rem paused. “It matches your personality.” She gave him a quick appraisal but didn’t respond. “Your sergeant thought you’d be helpful to us. We’re working on a case you might have some insight on.”

She took another pull, and Daniels wondered how often Jill Jacobs drank. It was a lot based on how fast she was draining her beer.

“He wasted your time. I can’t help you,” she answered.

“You worked on the Makeup Artist case in Seattle, didn’t you?” asked Daniels.

She hesitated, picking on the bottle’s label. “I did.”

“Then I’m pretty sure you can help us,” said Rem. “We’ve—”

“You don’t get it,” said Jill. “I don’t want to help you.”

Rem crossed his arms and set his jaw, and Daniels knew his partner was getting agitated. He could be cool and calm with a gun pointed at him but could lose his temper with an uncooperative stranger in a heartbeat.

“Fine,” Daniels interjected, before Rem could say something less fruitful. “We’ll go back and let our captain know that the two victims who were slaughtered in the last six weeks and their families are no closer to finding justice and the madman who did it. Even though he’s already stalking his next victim and will continue to enjoy the same freedoms as you and me. We’ll be sure to let your Sergeant Merchant know that his suggestion was a waste of our time.”

Her face pinched, and she picked off a chunk of the label. Daniels saw her swallow.

“Merchant gave us your name for a reason,” said Rem.

“He did,” she said. Daniels could barely hear her over the waves.

“Listen,” said Rem. “We don’t know your story. I don’t know why you’re sitting on a beach, drinking alone, and living in an RV in Horrorville, but you were a cop. You worked on a grisly case and you must have been good, or your Sergeant wouldn’t have sent us.”

“I know why he sent you,” she said, before taking another swig.

"So why not help us?" asked Daniels. "Look over—"

"No," she said, standing and wobbling slightly. "I'm going to pick up my gun. Don't shoot me." She leaned over and picked up her weapon and tucked it back in her shorts. "Good luck with your case." Turning, she walked back toward the waves, never looking back, and assumed her former position with the waves crashing over her feet.

"Son-of-a…" said Rem, turning toward Daniels. "What the hell's the matter with her?"

"A lot," said Daniels. "I think a lot is the matter with her. She's done. Like we thought. Burned out."

"It's more than that," said Rem. "Did you see her when she pulled her weapon?"

"Quite vividly," said Daniels.

"Did you see her eyes?"

"I was more focused on preventing her from shooting you."

Rem paused. "I could see it. I think she's terrified."

Daniels watched Jill, standing in the surf and drinking her beer.

"Whatever happened, it wasn't good," said Rem.

"That's probably why she threatens to shoot strangers."

Rem put his badge back in his pocket. "I don't think she was expecting us. She was expecting someone else."

Daniels shook his head. Rem patted Daniels on the arm. "Let's go."

**

Lozano stared at his apple for the hundredth time that day. He'd had his roasted chicken, cauliflower potatoes and grilled veggies for lunch, but his stomach rumbled. This low-salt, low-sugar diet his doctor had recommended was going to kill him before this job ever would. But his high cholesterol and higher blood pressure were saying otherwise. He needed to lose about twenty pounds. So far, he'd lost seven. Rem had invited him to the gym to spar, and Daniels had offered to take him to lift weights, but he'd declined both offers. He saw his detectives enough as it was. He didn't need to work out with them. Lozano opened his drawer and saw the loose change. The vending machine beckoned down the hall.

A knock on his open door made him close the drawer. Remalla stood there grinning. "What you doin', Cap?" He pulled a candy bar out of his pocket and started to open it.

Lozano's stomach rumbled again. "Mind your business, Remalla."

Daniels walked up behind Remalla. "You got a sec, Cap?" He saw the chocolate in Rem's hands and rolled his eyes.

"I do. Have a seat. How'd it go with Jacobs?"

The detectives sat, and Daniels pointed at the apple. "You gonna eat that?"

Lozano eyed the fruit and his detective. He sighed, picked up the apple and tossed it. "It's all yours."

"Thanks," said Daniels, and he took a bite.

"Jacobs was a total bust," said Rem as he licked the chocolate off his thumb. "She has no interest in helping us."

"She's a recluse," said Daniels. "She lives in a run-down RV park, drinks a lot and waves guns at people. I'm not sure why Merchant recommended her."

Lozano sighed and sat back in his seat. "I know why. I talked to Merchant and got her file."

Rem paused before taking the next bite of his candy. "Really? Now I'm curious."

Lozano tapped on his keyboard and the monitor came to life. "I'm going to send you the info, but in a nutshell, she's the youngest female promoted to a detective on the Seattle force. She rose quickly in the ranks. Scored high in every area. She was book smart and street smart. Her father is a Federal judge. Did you know that?"

Daniels leaned forward. "That didn't come up in the conversation."

"The honorable Thomas Jack Jacobs. Known as—"

Daniels raised a brow. "Jailtime Jacobs?"

"The one and the same," said Lozano.

"I've heard of him," said Daniels.

Rem shot Daniels a puzzled look. "Since when are you familiar with the Seattle judicial branch?"

"You remember when I took that course on criminal law? They mentioned him. His harsh sentences are legendary. He's famous in Seattle law enforcement." He studied his apple. "Jill's his daughter?"

"She is," said Lozano. "Probably why she was so impressive on the force."

"Like father, like daughter," said Rem, as he took another bite of his candy bar.

"Anyway, when the killings started in Seattle, the city was in an uproar. Merchant had a slew of detectives on it. But he was dealing with the same issues as us. No prints, no DNA, nothing. The guy was a ghost."

"Wonderful," said Rem.

"Jacobs was a policewoman, but her ideas and observations about the killer caught Merchant's attention. Said she was like a profiler. She could almost predict the killer's next steps. By then, they had three victims and Merchant needed a plan, so he promoted her to detective and put her on the case. At that point, they were keeping the press at bay, but Jacob's had her own ideas. She wanted to use the press to draw him out. Merchant wasn't convinced. Not long after her promotion, Jacob's took it upon herself to hold a mini press conference outside one of the victim's homes. Called the killer…" he studied the screen, "…frightened, disturbed, with a slew of sexual issues." He sat back. "You get the gist."

Daniels chewed and swallowed another bite of his apple. "I don't know if that makes her brilliant or incredibly stupid."

"It certainly makes her fearless," said Rem. He popped the last bit of candy in his mouth. "How'd that go over with Merchant?"

"Not well," said Lozano. He laced his fingers together and put his hands behind his head. "It pissed off the higher-ups, and Merchant took the heat. But that's when the writing on the walls started."

Daniels' eyes widened. "Really?"

"Really," said Lozano. "After the next victim, the first message appeared, written on the bathroom wall in the victim's blood. It said, 'I see you.' There was also a rose."

"A rose?" asked Rem. He licked chocolate off the rest of his fingers. "What rose?"

"At the crime scene. The killer left a rose in the tub, and on the wall above it, written in blood, were the words 'For you.'"

"You got to be kidding me," said Daniels. "I didn't hear that."

"Seattle PD never released it to the press, for obvious reasons," said Lozano. "They kept it under wraps. Once we get the files from Seattle, you'll read all about it."

"And they think the killer was referring to Jacobs?" asked Rem. "Those messages were for her?"

"I guess her portrayal of him got his attention," said Daniels. "What exactly was she hoping to accomplish by pushing his buttons?"

"Probably exactly that," said Rem. "Get the guy to do something stupid. Something different from his routine and pray he makes a mistake."

"It worked," said Lozano. He opened his top drawer and pulled out a granola bar. His planned foray to the vending machine would have to wait. "Problem is, it worked too well."

Rem wiped his fingers on his jeans. "It got him to change his routine, but he didn't make a mistake. Only now, Jill's in his crosshairs."

"Right," said Lozano, as he opened the granola bar. "According to the file, not long after, Jill started receiving mail, flowers, phone calls, all from the killer."

Rem leaned forward and put his elbows on his knees. "Wow. He started contacting her?"

"And following her. He sent photos, too," said Lozano.

"Shit," said Daniels.

"And with all of that, they still couldn't catch this guy?" asked Rem. "It seems she gave Merchant exactly what he needed. Between the contact and photos, they couldn't nail him down? If nothing else, they could follow Jacobs."

"They did it all," said Lozano. "The phone calls were too short to trace, and if they weren't, the killer was long gone before they got there. No prints or DNA on the letters. Following Jill led nowhere. It was like he found a new way to taunt them, and he was having fun with it."

"And torturing Jacobs at the same time," said Daniels. He took a last bite of his apple and tossed it in the trash.

"Merchant said she handled it pretty well at first. She thought like most of them that it would lead to his capture. If she could just keep up the game, he would screw up. She played her part, talking to him, and trying to get him riled enough to slip up. Merchant put a detail on her to keep watch even though Jacobs argued with him about it. Said it would be hard to lure the murderer out if she was being followed all the time. Merchant argued back that he didn't need a dead cop on his hands."

Daniels let out a sigh. "Brave lady."

"I'm sensing this didn't end well," said Rem.

"You should be a detective," said Daniels.

Rem smirked.

"You're right, it didn't," said Lozano. He held his granola bar. "The murders continued, as did the messages. More notes to Jill at the crime scene. More photos and phone calls. Crazy thing is, Jill had an uncanny sense about the guy. Merchant said she knew when he would strike again and could almost sense the killer's and victim's pain. She lost weight, spent sleepless nights working, and yelled at other cops when they didn't keep the same regimen. The respect she'd garnered through all of this began to wane. Merchant said after a while, the stress on the department began to cause fractures. There were grumblings that maybe Jill knew the killer all along. Maybe she was in on it, which is why she could predict his actions. Maybe she liked the attention, so she strung everyone along, not telling them everything she knew."

Rem rubbed his face and stood. A strand of hair fell in his face and he pushed it back. "That's great. She's killing herself to find this guy and her department's turning on her." He leaned against the wall and crossed his arms.

"What did Merchant do?" asked Daniels.

"He defended her. Did his best to protect her. Most knew none of the rumors were true, but the squad was just tired and fed up. They wanted a scapegoat."

"They couldn't get the killer, so they had to blame somebody," said Daniels.

"It seems so. But according to Merchant, the more he told Jacobs to slow down and take a break, the harder she worked. She ignored the rumors, but at some point, the cracks showed. Arguments broke out on the job. She became less and less tolerant of her fellow officers and more belligerent with him. She even lost it with the killer. He'd called her, and she'd let loose, daring him to come for her, saying he didn't have the balls to kill her. Merchant took her off the case after that."

Rem cursed under his breath. "This story just keeps getting better and better. How'd she handle being taken off the case?"

"About as well as you can imagine," said Lozano.

"Merchant was right. She was in too deep," said Daniels.

"Is that when she left?" asked Rem.

"No," said Lozano. He paused and stared at his granola bar. He'd yet to take a bite. "Three days later, a policeman was killed." He studied his monitor. "Officer Rick Henderson. They found him in a bathtub, stabbed, his face painted. There were notes written on the walls to Jacobs, telling her it was all for her."

Rem stared at the floor, and Daniels leaned back, rubbing his eyes. "Holy shit," he said.

"That's when Jacobs left the force, and hasn't been back," said Lozano. "That was the last murder. The killer went silent afterwards. It was as if he'd had his fun with her and when she left, he did too. Until six weeks ago."

Neither detective spoke.

"So, if you're wondering why she's not too social, drinks a lot, and pulls guns on people," said Lozano, "now you know."

Daniels nodded and sighed. "And now the killer's back and he's picked our little corner of the world to prey upon," said Daniels. "Lucky us."

Rem raised his head. "But now we know why."

Daniels shared a look with Rem, and his brow furrowed. "He's come back for her."

CHAPTER FOUR

Jill tossed her shorts and a pair of shoes into her suitcase. Glancing around the room, she spied another pair of shoes and a pair of jeans hanging over a chair. She grabbed those, added them and started to close the case when she caught sight of herself in the mirror. She couldn't help but stare and wonder what had happened to her. Her long uncombed hair hung in tangles down her back. It had turned a lighter shade since she'd spent some time in the sun. *Honey-haired angel.* It's what her mom had called her when Jill was very young. It was one of the few memories Jill had of her.

Still staring, Jill noted her deep-set brown eyes with the dark circles beneath, the hollows beneath her cheeks and the haunted look she held. She couldn't remember the last time she'd had a good night's sleep. Her stomach growled, and she considered what she had in her sparse kitchen to eat. Some peanut butter and maybe some graham crackers. Her neighbor had given her a banana some days ago, and she wondered if it was still edible. Probably not.

She could get something on the road, then find the nearest hotel and liquor store, and drink till she slept or passed out, whichever came first. A memory surfaced of her on the beach at a different time and place, only she was laughing…and kissing… Jill closed her eyes. A wave of emotion crashed down on her and she fought back the tears. She breathed deeply, regaining her control. Opening her eyes, she saw the picture on the nightstand. She picked it up and stared at it, wishing she could throw it away. But she tossed it into the suitcase and began to close it when the doorbell rang.

She froze, the familiar fear coursing through her, and told herself to relax. It was probably Lou from next door or the strange landlord Annie with the crazy hair. Those were about the only two visitors she ever received.

Despite that, she still picked up her gun and tucked it into the back waistband of her jeans. She walked to the door and peered through the peephole and cursed when she saw who stood there. The two cops were back. What were their names? Daniels and Renata? Something like that. She wished she'd taken that shot of Vodka earlier, but she'd held off because she knew she would be driving.

The doorbell rang again, and she saw the dark-haired one knock. Reluctantly, she opened the door. "What is it?"

They glanced at each other before the one with long, dark hair—*Renata, Remata*—she couldn't recall, spoke. "Well, first, thank you for not greeting us with a gun. I feel we've made progress."

She studied him. *This guy is used to women liking him,* she thought to herself. It was understandable. He was a nice-looking man. They both were. "What do you want?"

Daniels answered. "Can we talk?"

Definitely the more pragmatic one. But also used to being well-liked. Standing there, she felt that same rush envelope her and she tuned in. *Good cops. Trustworthy. Loyal.* The feeling surprised her. It had been a long time since she'd met anyone she could trust. Merchant was the only one who came to mind, other than…the memory pierced her thoughts, but she ignored it and stepped back. "What the hell…come on in."

Daniels held a look of surprise. "Thank you," he said as he entered with the other detective behind him.

She shut the door. "I'm guessing this isn't a social visit."

"No, it isn't," said Daniels.

"Good, because I'm all out of French Roast," she said. "In fact, I'm out of everything." She walked back to her suitcase and shoved it down to zip it.

"Going somewhere?" asked the dark-haired one.

She successfully closed it and put it on the ground. "I'm leaving."

The detectives eyed each other. "Leaving where?" asked Daniels.

The other one held up his hands and looked around. "I mean this place is so nice."

The paint had almost peeled away, the dilapidated shades were falling off, and her linoleum floor was cracking. "It is nice, isn't it?" she answered. "But unfortunately, my time in this pleasure palace is over. And to answer your question," she looked at Daniels. "I'm going wherever the road takes me."

She walked to her small, banged up kitchen table, and started throwing away trash.

"So, you're running?" asked Daniels.

She stopped and turned. "Excuse me?" She pushed her hair off her face. Something stirred in the pit of her stomach, and she had the fleeting need to vomit, but she breathed through it. She was skilled at it. "What are your names again?"

"Detectives Daniels and Remalla," said the dark-haired one. "Or just Rem and Daniels will do."

"Well, Rem and Daniels," she said. "I don't recall asking your opinion. Nor do I care what you think or why you think it." She turned toward the sink, walked over, and flipped on the faucet. There was a mound of dishes, and she started cleaning.

They were quiet for a second. "Listen," said Daniels. "Our captain talked to Merchant. We know what happened."

The nausea returned, and she gripped a plate. "Good for you. You know my history." A cold sweat broke out on her skin. "But that doesn't change a thing. I'm still leaving."

Remalla spoke. "You sure that's what you want to do?"

She placed the plate in the drainer even though it wasn't clean. "That's none of your business."

"You know he's killed again, don't you?" asked Daniels. "Two in the last six weeks."

The sick feeling in her belly reared up again, and she swallowed. She picked up a glass and rinsed it. "You mentioned that before."

"We'd like you to help us catch him," said Remalla.

A glass slipped from her hand and fell into the sink where it cracked and broke. "Shit."

"You okay?" asked Remalla.

Sensing him behind her, she whirled. "What the hell do you two want?"

Remalla sputtered. "Uh, like I said, we'd like your help—"

Her anxiety rising rapidly, her voice rose. "You come in here, asking me to do something you know nothing about. I don't care what Merchant told you. I don't know either of you. But you want me to sacrifice everything again to help you? This case… this case…," she couldn't get her breath, and everything started to spin. She put her hand on her stomach and tried to suck in air, but nothing would come. Her belly turned on her, and she couldn't stop it and ran for the bathroom. Once inside, she slammed the door behind her and vomited into the toilet. Little came up because she'd had nothing to eat that morning, but it didn't stop the retching. Cold sweat trickled down her back and she was shaking. *God,* she thought. *I've lost it. I've completely lost it.*

The retching slowed and came to a stop, and she flushed the toilet and sat on the floor, still shaking, her skin cold and clammy. There was a soft knock.

"Yeah," she said, her voice shaky.

The door opened, and Daniels poked his head in. He held a glass of water. "You want something to drink?"

She considered telling him to get the hell out of her house and never come back, but she nodded instead.

Remalla came in behind Daniels with a damp washcloth. She didn't know where he'd found a washcloth. "Here," he said handing it to her.

She took it with trembling fingers, drank a sip of the water, and dabbed her face. The coolness felt good against her skin.

"Better?" asked Daniels.

She put the water down and covered her face with the cloth. Taking long, slow, deep breaths, she told herself to relax. The last thing she needed was to have a full-on breakdown. Merchant thought she'd already had one, but she knew she was still holding on by a thread. It was worn and frayed but it hadn't broken yet.

"We know you've been through a lot. But would you consider it?" asked Remalla. "Helping us?"

She chuckled, put the cloth down, saw how serious they were and chuckled more. "I'm sitting on a bathroom floor after just throwing up because you mention a case to me I haven't worked on in two years. And you want to work with me?"

Daniels shrugged and cocked his head at Remalla. "You should have seen him when we cracked the Fast Food Burglar case. He was a hot mess."

Remalla leaned against the sink. "It was devastating. Every time we investigated, we got free food. That was hard to give up."

Jill rubbed her eyes. "This might be a little different."

"We know it is," said Remalla. "We're not making light of it. But I'll be honest. You're sitting on the floor of a junky RV, in a city you barely know, with no company other than a strange neighbor, and a stranger landlord. You drink alone on the beach and are obviously still haunted by a case that was never solved and which has now come home to roost again."

Jill started to stand, and Daniels held out his hand. She took it, and he helped her up. She used a second to steady herself. "I realize my situation is unorthodox, but it's my life. Excuse me." She walked past them and out of the bathroom.

"Is this the life you want?" asked Daniels as he followed her out. "To be haunted by a killer for the rest of your life?"

"Who said it was for the rest of my life?" She went to the kitchen sink and rinsed her mouth out. "I left Seattle two years ago and I have no plans to return." She wiped her face with a towel. Her stomach was still a little unsettled, but her breathing was normal. "I'm not a cop anymore."

"But he's killed again," said Daniels. "Two more victims."

"And I'm sure the Seattle police department can handle it," she said. "That's not my job anymore."

The detectives went quiet.

"Do you read the papers, watch the news?" asked Rem.

"I avoid it," she answered. She picked up the shards of the glass in the sink.

"The victims were murdered here. Not Seattle," said Daniels.

She froze, staring at her hands, dropping the shards. "What?" She turned. "They were here? I thought…you aren't from Seattle?"

"No," said Rem. "We're local. We realized we were dealing with the same guy which is how we found you."

She stood open-mouthed, trying to fathom this new information. *He'd found her.* She stepped away from the sink and grabbed her suitcase. "Then it's good I'm leaving." She put it by the front door.

"Leaving won't help," said Daniels. "He'll only follow."

"He'll have to find me first." She grabbed a small bag and went into the bathroom and started throwing toiletries into it.

"Is that the best idea? To keep running from this guy?" asked Remalla. "Don't you want your life back?"

She tossed her shampoo and conditioner into the bag and stepped back into the front room. "You gonna give me the whole 'we can catch this guy' talk? The 'rah, rah rah' speech? Well, spare me. I heard it a million times in Seattle. Said it to myself repeatedly. It's bullshit though. It's a load of crap."

"You think he's uncatchable?" asked Daniels.

She stopped. "I know he's uncatchable. We did everything we knew how to do. He was always ahead of us. I thought he'd make a mistake. Counted on it. I believed in it so much that I put my life on the line for it. Others, too. And I paid a high price for it. I won't do it again."

"What happened in Seattle wasn't your fault," said Rem.

"You're my therapist now?" she asked. "Please. I've been through enough psych evals to gag a horse. I should have left the case long before I did. Everyone tried to get me to back off. But did I listen? No. I bulled through like I knew everything. And what happened? A cop is dead." Her voice trailed off as her emotions rose. She spoke in a whisper. "That's on me." Her eyes watered, and she blinked the tears back.

"You didn't kill him. You didn't stab him and leave him in a bathtub," said Daniels.

"I might as well have," she said. She went back to the sink and tossed the shards of glass into the trash.

"That's exactly what the killer wants you to think," said Rem. "He wants you to blame yourself. He's counting on it."

"You got in his face," said Daniels. "Challenged his masculinity. Didn't back down when he tried to intimidate you. The cop's murder did exactly what he wanted. He wants to see you low and emasculated. He wants to put you in your place."

"And he won," said Jill, wiping her face with her arm. "He got what he wanted."

"So why is he back?" asked Rem.

"Why kill again?" asked Daniels. "Why come to the city where you live and start again, when he won already?"

Jill sniffed and rinsed a dish, thinking of the shard in the trash. She could so easily slash her wrist with it. But she'd never had the guts to do it. "Because he likes the game. He's bored, and he wants to play again."

"And he likes to play with you," said Rem.

She nodded. "He does."

"But why you?" asked Rem.

She shut off the sink. "I could give you a laundry list of reasons, but it doesn't matter, because the game is over for me. He can't play if I don't participate." She wiped her hands on her jeans and turned, looking to see what else she needed to do before she left.

"Yes, he can," said Daniels. "He's taken two lives."

"And he'll take more," said Rem.

"Not if I'm gone," she answered.

"He'll follow and find others. He'll keep going until you agree to play the game," said Rem.

She went back to the table and threw away the rest of the trash. "I have to go. You two are welcome to hang out. The rent is paid for the rest of the month." She grabbed the trash bag, tied it and hauled it up. "I don't suppose one of you would want to take out the trash?"

"We're serious," said Daniels.

She dropped the bag. "And you don't think I am?" Anger flared. "I haven't slept in three years. I drink myself to unconsciousness to forget the hell of that case. I go over and over everything I did, second guessing everything, wondering 'what if' this or 'what if' that. I've distanced myself from my friends and family to keep them safe. Most of the people I worked with won't talk to me because they blame me for… Henderson's death." She bit her lip and refused to cry. "I got in that psycho's head, and I couldn't get out of it. I'm still not sure I am. Sometimes I see flashes or feel so much hatred, and I have to push it back. It happens less and less now, and the thought of letting him back in is terrifying." She pointed. "So, don't presume I'm not serious. I'm very serious. I'm not going back." She went to the door and opened it. "I think this conversation is over. You need to leave."

Standing there, Daniels nodded, and Rem sighed. They walked to the door.

At the threshold, Daniels stopped. "I didn't mean to imply you weren't serious. I apologize if it came across that way."

She sniffed and wiped a blurry eye.

"We know you've been through hell. We can't change that," said Daniels. "But consider this. This isn't Seattle. We aren't your former colleagues. We know what we're dealing with here. There are no surprises, and we're going in head first. Because of what you did in Seattle, we know this guy. We know what to expect. We can't promise it will go smoothly, and there won't be problems, but I can tell you this. If this guy wants to play the game, then you can be damn sure we're ready to play it too, and we'll back you up a hundred percent. And we play to win."

She shook her head, feeling weary. "And if it gets you killed in the process?" she asked. "Are you willing to pay that price?"

"We're cops," said Rem. "We signed up for this. I was never built for a nine to five." He paused. "Were you?"

She held his gaze. "Good luck with your case."

He offered a pensive glance, and she stepped away and closed the door.

CHAPTER FIVE

A week later, Rem poured himself another cup of coffee and sat at his desk, looking at his computer screen. Blinking, he rubbed his eyes. "If I look at any more reports, I'm gonna go blind."

Daniels, who sat across from him, sighed. "I hear ya. What happened in Seattle is nuts."

Rem yawned, and Daniels looked over. "How's it going at Uncle Martin's?" he asked.

"Better. I'm getting used to it. I actually slept a full, uninterrupted five hours last night."

"Good," said Daniels. "You were starting to look like one of those zombies in those movies you watch."

"It's a big house," said Rem. "I'm not entirely convinced there aren't zombies in the basement."

"Have you been in the basement?"

"Hell, no. I haven't been down there in years. Ever since Martin's brother, Uncle Joe, told me he'd heard stories of a grave down there. Aunt Audrey chased him out of the house when she heard that. He thought it was hilarious though. I went down one time to get an extra chair for dinner, heard a squeak, and almost peed my pants. Never been down again since."

Daniels smiled. "I tell you what. Next time I'm over, I'll go down there with you. I'll even hold your hand."

"I may take you up on that," said Rem. "Can't promise what will happen though if I hear anything."

"I'll take my chances, but please try not to pee your pants." Rem snorted and Daniels put down the pen he'd been holding and sipped his water. "How's Aunt Audrey? Has she adjusted to her new place?"

Rem sighed. "About as well as any eighty-four-year-old who's just lost her husband of fifty-five years and moved into a retirement home. It's not easy."

Daniels nodded. "I'm sure she's relieved you're keeping the house. When we get a chance, we'll take her for dinner somewhere after our shift."

"She eats at four o'clock. It will have to be an early shift, and I don't see many of those in our future."

"Well, we can at least visit. Take her some soup."

"She'd like that. She loves to see you. Thinks you have pretty eyes." He scratched his head. "There's no accounting for taste."

"When you got it, you got it, brother."

Rem clicked over to the next file. A picture appeared on his screen. He read the name. Alana Stenham. She was the Makeup Artist's fifth victim in Seattle. He read the details of the case and couldn't help but shudder, even though it was like the first four cases. Female. Thirty years of age. Stabbed to death. Her face made up and body posed. She lived in an apartment and was a nurse at a local hospital. She'd come home after working a night shift and never left. Police found her body after her sister and coworkers reported her missing. Rem flipped through the crime scene photos. Nothing that stood out, but they were just as gruesome as the others. He stopped at one photo and studied it. It was a picture of words, written in a neat scrawl in blood on the tiled bathroom wall. "*I see you, JJ.*" He flipped to the next shot, and it was a zoomed-out picture of the same words on the wall. This one showed a rose on the floor beneath the saying. A crude heart, painted in blood, was above the rose, along with the words, "For you."

"Hard to believe," said Rem. He took a sip of his coffee. "Which vic are you on?"

"Just moved on to number six," said Daniels, "Craig Lester. Thirty-two. Owned a dry-cleaning business. Divorced, but had a seven-year-old son, although Mom had custody. Had porn on his computer, cocaine on his desk and a DWI conviction ten years prior. Nothing after that. Appeared to be well-liked by the neighbors. They found him in his bed. Same M.O. Stabbed and made up."

"And the bathroom?" asked Rem.

Daniels pushed his keyboard back. "Same. *I see you* was written in blood and one red rose was beneath it." He glanced at a photo. "Plus, he added *You'll see me too*.

Rem stood and added more sugar to his coffee. "I don't understand. Killing a man does not fit the profile. What made him switch gears?"

"I don't know." Daniels opened a plastic container filled with grapes. He popped one in his mouth. "It's definitely unusual. And why this guy?"

"And why did the words change?" asked Rem. "This is the first we see *You'll see me too*. What does that mean? Did Jacobs know Lester? Did they have any connection?"

Daniels leaned in and read some more. "Not according to this. She had no recollection of ever meeting him."

"And he had no social connection to any of the other victims?"

"Nope. Not that I can tell, but I'm still reading."

"He was a dry cleaner. Did any of them use his shop?" asked Rem. He sipped from his mug and, satisfied it was sweet enough, he sat.

Daniels hit some keys. "I don't know. I'm not seeing any information on that."

Rem rubbed his neck. "This is why it would be helpful to have someone who worked this case help us out. Even if it's not Jacobs."

"Cap says he's talking to Merchant about that. They're short staffed in Seattle, but hopefully they can send someone out soon. Someone who was involved in the investigation."

"That would be nice. It would be pointless if they sent somebody who was just as new to this as we are."

"Cap's got Garcia and Mellenbuhl checking out the latest victim, plus Titus and Georgios should be able to help in a couple of days. They're still helping on the latest bank robbery." He plucked another grape from the container. "Have you considered the possibility though, that he may not strike again?"

Rem looked up from his computer. "You think? Because Jacobs left?"

"It's possible."

"Either way, we still have two murders to solve." Rem flipped a file folder open on his desk. "Daniella Oberon, our city's latest victim. Twenty-five. Aspiring actress. Waited tables at the Wharf."

"Yeah. Garcia and Mell are talking to her family and friends."

"The more eyes the better," said Rem. "It's been three weeks since Oberon. If the timetable holds up…and assuming he's still in town…"

Daniels nodded. "I know. We'll have another victim soon."

The squad room door opened, and a police officer walked in. Rem groaned.

"What?" asked Daniels who faced away from the door.

"Your favorite person," muttered Rem.

Delgado approached their desks. "Hi, Detectives." He was in uniform and held his hat.

"Delgado," said Rem. "How goes it?"

"Fine. Busy day. I ran down a drug store thief. They got him in custody downstairs."

"That's great," said Daniels. "Good for you."

"How can we help you?" asked Rem.

"I was wondering how the case was going, with the Makeup Artist. Have you had any leads?"

Rem made eye contact with Daniels, who raised a brow. "Not really, no," said Rem.

"But it's him, right? The same guy from Seattle?" asked Delgado.

Daniels hit a button, and Rem assumed he'd closed his screen. "It appears that way," said Daniels.

Delgado nodded, staring off. "That's unbelievable."

Rem leaned back in his seat. "You mind if I ask why the interest in this case? You seem very curious."

Delgado's voice quickened. "I don't suppose you know that I've put in for Detective. I'm hoping to do what you do. Robbery-Homicide is my goal. And this case would be incredible to work on."

"That's one way to see it," said Daniels.

"I didn't know you wanted to be a detective," said Rem. "How long have you been on the force?"

"This is my fourth year. I love working the beat, but I can't do it forever. I've always had an interest in forensics and crime solving. I studied the Makeup Artist in a course I took at a local community college not long ago. It was fascinating." He glanced at the desk. "Is that the latest victim?"

Rem closed the file on Oberon. "You studied the Makeup Artist?"

"I did," said Delgado. "And I'd like to offer my help in any way that I could be of service. I could go over what I learned. They talked about his profile."

Rem caught Daniels making a quick smile.

"Thanks, Delgado," said Daniels. "But believe me. We've got more than enough information in front of us to review. I think we've got it."

"Your offer is appreciated though," said Rem.

Delgado nodded. "The offer stands whenever you need it. If I get this promotion though, we might get to work on it together."

"Nothing against you getting a promotion, but hopefully we catch him by then," said Rem.

"If there is a God," said Daniels.

•

Delgado put his hat on. "Well, I don't want to take your time. I just wanted to extend the offer."

"We'll keep it in mind," said Daniels.

"And congrats again on the car thief," said Rem.

"Drug store," said Delgado.

"Right," said Rem with a wave.

Delgado smiled before turning and leaving.

"You think he really put in for detective?" asked Daniels, his eyes narrowed.

"Why would he lie?" asked Rem.

"Great," said Daniels. "I hope to hell we catch this guy soon. For the victims' sakes, and our own."

"He won't make detective," said Rem. "Not yet anyway." He sipped on his coffee.

"Why not?" asked Daniels.

"Because he's only four years in. It took us five. And I refuse to believe he can get there faster than us."

Daniels shot out a thumb. "Did you see him? He's brown-nosing. And we're probably the last ones on his list. God knows who he's already sucked up to. Plus, with this case, and the bank robberies, the department will need the help."

Rem flipped open Oberon's file. "Brown-nosing only gets you so far. Sometimes you just need a good word from somebody of importance to get you in the door. Like me with you."

Daniels punched his keyboard. "Oh, please. Don't even get me started on who helped who."

The office door behind Rem opened, and Rem turned to see their Captain step out. He held a newspaper in his hand, and his face was as dark as old coffee.

"Cap?" asked Rem. "Still mad about the blueberry muffin? I swear I thought it was for anybody."

Lozano slapped the paper on the desk between the two detectives. "The press has a hold of it. They know it's the Makeup Artist."

Rem and Daniels read the headline. "Makeup Artist Stalks City."

"Hell," said Daniels.

"It was bound to happen at some point," said Rem. "I'm surprised it took as long as it did."

"An unnamed source confirmed it," said Lozano.

"Welcome to law enforcement," said Daniels.

"Well, the shit is gonna hit the fan now. The city will be up in arms," said Lozano.

"We're going through the files from Seattle as quickly as we can," said Daniels.

"And we're going to have to get Garcia and Mell up to speed," said Rem.

"I'm putting in for more help," said Lozano. "Now that this is public, the mayor is going to be calling. I hope you two are up for some long hours."

"We'll do whatever it takes, Cap," said Rem.

"We're already putting in the hours as it is," said Daniels. "Marjorie's thrilled."

"Yeah, well. Tell her I'm sorry," said Lozano. "Ask her if she can wait on having that baby. We need you here."

"I'll ask, but somehow I think that baby may put a kink in our plans," said Daniels.

"He will if he's anything like his dad," said Rem.

"Watch it," said Daniels, pointing. "Or I'll ask Marjorie to get induced and you can have this lovely case all to yourself. Maybe you'll get lucky and get partnered with Delgado." His phone rang, and he answered. "Daniels."

Rem frowned. "You'd like that wouldn't you?"

"Who's Delgado?" asked Lozano. He frowned at Rem, who fiddled with his hair, which he'd pulled back with a ponytail. "And when are you gonna get that haircut, Remalla?"

Daniels turned serious and held up a finger. "What was that? Where?" he said. "He picked up a pen and wrote on some paper. "Got it. We're on our way." He ended the call.

"What is it?" asked Rem, standing.

Daniels grabbed his jacket. "We've got a third victim."

CHAPTER SIX

What have we got, Ibrahim?" asked Daniels. They stood in the front foyer of a small home in a tiny community only ten miles from the previous victim's location.

Ibrahim, a member of the crime scene unit, scratched his bald head with a gloved hand. "She's in the bedroom. Driver's license says she's Nicole Schein. Aged twenty-eight. Multiple stab wounds to the chest. Heavy blush on her cheeks and lots of red lipstick. Same pose. Not sure yet about time of death."

"Who found her?" asked Rem.

"Roommate. She'd been out of town."

"Where is she now?" asked Rem.

Ibrahim pointed. "Back porch. She's a mess. She's contacting immediate family."

"You been in the bathroom yet?" asked Daniels.

"My guys are focusing on the initial scene. Don't think we've checked the bathroom, but we can look."

"You mind if we join you?" asked Rem.

"After you," said Ibrahim.

Daniels and Rem put on gloves and covered their shoes. They walked through the living area seeing a small pile of unopened mail on the coffee table and passed the kitchen with flowered wallpaper where a dish with a half-eaten sandwich sat on the counter. There was a guest bathroom in the hallway, and Daniels leaned in and flipped the light on. The area was neat and tidy, and nothing looked disturbed. He flipped the light off and continued toward the back bedroom. The body was lying on the floor in a pool of blood as a technician snapped photos. The victim wore a long T-shirt, stained red, and she lay on her back with her arms crisscrossed over her chest. The crude make-up was smeared on her face, and her long blonde hair was fanned out behind her, as if it had been carefully brushed.

Rem stared at the body. "Jesus," he said.

Daniels' belly rolled, and he tried not to breathe. These scenes always made him nauseated. "It never gets easier."

"Let's hope it never does," said Rem, looking pale.

Daniels nodded and turned toward the master bathroom. The light was on and he peered inside. He saw the toilet and sink, but nothing out of the ordinary. A toothbrush sat in its holder and there was a tube of moisturizer and various toiletries on the small counter. A towel hung from a rack and there was a bra hanging from the doorknob. The shower curtain was closed.

Rem spoke from behind him. "Anything?"

"Nothing yet," said Daniels. He took a step and slid the shower curtain back. Crimson letters painted on the tile, glistening in the light, made him stop cold.

Rem saw them too. "Shit," he said.

I see you, JJ. Let's play was written in blood on the sides of the shower. Drips of blood carried the eyes down to the red rose on the tub floor where *I miss you* was written next to it.

Ibrahim saw the markings. "I'll get on this next," he said, and stepped out of the room.

"I guess this means he's sticking around," said Rem.

"Apparently," said Daniels, letting go of the curtain. "Maybe he thinks he can lure Jacobs out."

"How's he going to do that if she's left?" asked Rem.

Daniels shook his head. "I don't know. But you know how she said she could get in his head? Maybe he can get in hers too."

"He knows she'll be watching," said Rem.

"He's counting on it."

Rem shook his head. "What's he gonna do if she refuses to play?"

Daniels could only look and shrug. "Somehow I think he's a sore loser. He may up the ante."

Rem sighed. "Which means this isn't going away anytime soon." He sighed. "Let's go talk to the roommate."

"Yeah."

They stepped out of the bathroom and into the bedroom. Forensics was still working on the body, and they returned to the living room and walked onto the back porch. There was a wooden bench and coffee table and the roommate, her eyes red and holding a tissue, was sitting and talking to an officer beside her, who was taking notes with a notepad and pen.

Daniels dropped his jaw. "What in the hell?"

Rem stopped. "What are you doing here?"

Delgado lowered his pen. "Hi, Detectives."

**

Lozano punched the keys on the vending machine and the chocolate bar fell from its perch and landed below. Lozano pulled it out, eager for the sugar rush. The long hours and his cravings for his wife's homemade tamales were taking their toll, and he needed the energy.

"Hey, Cap."

Lozano turned to see Rem and Daniels enter the hallway. He shoved the candy bar into his pocket.

"You're not going off your diet, are you, Cap?" asked Daniels.

"What will you tell Sheila?" asked Rem. "She's worried about your blood pressure."

Lozano grunted. “My wife knows nothing. You got that? A man cannot live on fruit alone.”

Rem approached and leaned on the candy machine. “What’s it worth to you?” he asked eyeing the machine.

“One word, and I’ll make you a personal appointment with the barber across the street who charges ten bucks per cut. I’ll tell him you like it short,” he said, narrowing his eyes. “Better yet, I’ll bring my own clippers from home.”

Rem’s face fell, and he straightened. “Oh, well, that works too.”

“I figured,” said Lozano. “You two back from the crime scene?”

“We are,” said Daniels.

“Come on in, said Lozano, heading into his office. He pulled out the candy bar and threw it into a top drawer. “Anything new?”

Daniels and Rem took a seat. “Not much,” said Daniels. “Same M.O.”

“Crime scene on it?” asked Lozano.

“They were finishing up when we left. Should have more info soon, although I doubt they’ll find anything,” said Rem.

“Except for the writing in the bathroom,” said Daniels.

Lozano stilled in mid-sit. “There was writing?”

“Yeah,” said Rem. “Said ‘I miss you.’ Plus, there was a rose. Pretty much confirms he’s here for Jacobs. He’s trying to reel her back in.”

Lozano grunted, sitting back. “He’s putting on the pressure, isn’t he?”

“He is,” said Rem. “Question is, what do we do about it?”

“We’ve got no DNA, no fingerprints, no help from Seattle other than a slew of information to go through, and Jacobs is long gone,” said Daniels. “Now the press is all over this. They were there when we left. The pressure on this is going to go through the roof.”

“You sure Jacobs is gone?” asked Lozano. “How do you know she left?”

“She made it pretty clear. We can’t exactly lasso and bring her in,” said Rem.

Lozano huffed. "Then we do what we can with what we have." He sighed. "I talked to the chief. I'm taking Titus and Georgios off the bank robberies and putting them on this starting today. I'll ask for more help, but with everything happening, it will be tight. We're going to need a task force, and I want you two to lead it. Get some officers to assist." He reached for the phone but caught the glance between his officers. "What?"

Rem answered. "You know of a cop by the name of Delgado?"

"Never heard of him," said Lozano.

Daniels started to speak when Lozano's phone rang. He picked it up. "Lozano."

He listened, widening his eyes at his detectives, and responded. "Thanks. I'll take care of it." He hung up. "We may have a break in the case."

"What's up?" asked Rem.

"Jill Jacobs is downstairs. She wants to talk."

CHAPTER SEVEN

Jill sat on a bench, waiting. Anxious, she took a deep breath, but her heart pounded, and she was sweating. She made a concentrated effort to stay calm. Just being in a police station brought up memories she wanted to forget. She opened her small purse and pulled out the photograph. Sometimes, when it was bad, the photo would help to calm her. Other times, it only made it worse. Staring at it now though, she heard the quiet voice in her head, telling her she was doing the right thing. Putting the picture away, she stood and said a small prayer that she wasn't insane despite the inner voice. She stared out the window. It was taking all her strength not to run out the door.

"Jacobs?"

She turned to see Detectives Remalla and Daniels coming down the steps toward her. Something in her relaxed, although her heart still pounded.

"Hey," she said. "Surprise."

"You okay?" asked Rem. "Thought you'd be on another coast line by now."

She nodded. "Yeah, well…" She paused. "Can we talk?"

"Sure," said Daniels. "Come on up." He raised an arm for her to go first, so she headed up the stairs. At the top, they directed her to a small room to the right. It was an interrogation room. She'd seen enough of them to know.

"Don't worry. It's private," said Daniels.

She sat, putting her purse on the table. They came in behind her and shut the door.

Rem sat beside her. "So, we're curious. What's up?"

She pushed her hair back, wondering where to begin. "I didn't leave."

Daniels stood with his hands in his pockets. "Why not?"

She fiddled with the edge of her sweater. "I mean I wanted to. I planned on it. After you left, I wasn't far behind you. I'd gotten three hours outside the city when I realized I'd left my wallet at the RV. I had to turn back to get it. Once I was there, I ended up staying a few more days before I left again. But I got out to my car and saw I had a flat tire and no spare. Took me a couple of days to fix that. Then, I make another effort to leave, and literally, I'm going to my car and I hear someone yell, 'Stop!' I thought I was hearing a voice from God until I saw a kid running down through the RV park, carrying a small TV. He'd just ripped off one of my neighbors."

"Did you go after him?" asked Rem.

"No. Knowing my neighbor, he'd probably ripped it off from someone else."

"You think it was a sign?" asked Daniels. "The 'stop' part, not the TV part."

"The timing was uncanny. Plus, everything else. I haven't been much of a praying woman lately, but sometimes you can't ignore what's in front of your face. Something…or someone…is trying to get my attention." She tapped at the table.

"Maybe it's time you get this monkey off your back," said Rem.

Jill nodded. "Maybe. But despite all that, I still wasn't convinced. The thought of starting all of this again was terrifying. I drank a lot that night, trying not to think about it. That went on for several days. I couldn't bring myself to contact you. I just wanted it to all go away."

The detectives offered worried glances, and she realized what they were thinking. "Don't worry. If I were going to kill myself, I would have done it a lot sooner. Believe me."

"What got you here?" asked Daniels.

Her heart, which had slowed, picked up its pace again. Her throat was dry when she swallowed. "Do you have some water?"

"Sure. Hold on." Rem stood and stepped out for a second. He returned with a bottled water. He cracked it open and handed it to her.

"Thanks." She opened it and took a swig, noticing the tremble in her fingers. "Better."

"Take your time," said Daniels.

She took another calming breath. "I'm trying."

"There's a restroom down the hall if you need it," said Rem.

She remembered what had happened the last time they'd talked about this. "I'm okay." After a few seconds, she continued. "This morning I went to the beach, telling myself for the millionth time that I needed to do something. Either leave, despite the signs, or pick up the phone and call you. To be honest, my fear got the best of me. I walked back to my RV, intent on leaving no matter what the damn universe said, and I found this on my front porch." She reached into her purse and pulled out a clear plastic bag. Inside was one red rose.

"Shit," said Rem. "On your porch?"

"Yes." She handed the bag to Daniels, who reached for it. "That was the final catalyst, or sign, I needed."

Daniels took the bag. "You're sure it's him? It wouldn't be some cruel prank by some teenager who steals TV's?"

"No one I know here is aware of my history, other than you two," she answered. "I searched my place. It was undisturbed, but I know he was there. I could feel him." She took a shaky breath and rubbed her arms. Chill bumps ran down her skin. "On the way here, I heard on the radio that there had been another victim."

"There is. We were at the crime scene earlier," said Rem, taking the rose from Daniels.

"You should know. He left a note at the scene in blood. It said, 'I miss you, JJ,'" said Daniels. "He wants to play, and he's going to do whatever it takes."

Jill nodded. "Hell." She paused. "I know what he wants, which is why I'm here." She looked up. "I'm willing to help. I can't promise how long I'll hold it together. I can't even promise I'll stay. But I do know I have to try." She hesitated. "There's just one thing."

"What's that?" asked Rem, putting the rose on the table.

"You two have to understand that with my involvement comes risk. Your lives could be threatened."

"Our lives are at risk every day," said Daniels.

"That's not what I mean," she answered. "Associating with me can be dangerous. I learned that the hard way."

"No," said Rem. "Association with him can be dangerous. You're not wielding any knives. But we get what you're saying."

"We understand what's at stake. Everyone in this job does," said Daniels.

She studied the water bottle. "That's not necessarily true. Fear has a way of turning the tables against you."

"This isn't Seattle," said Rem. "We won't betray you. You work on this with us, then you're just as much a partner as we are," he said, cocking his head toward Daniels.

"Which begs the point," said Daniels. "You can't go back to that RV. It's not safe."

"Nowhere is safe. He knows where I am." She paused. "I think he always has."

"Certain places are safer than others," said Rem, making eye contact with Daniels. Jill caught the look and sensed a hidden communication between the two.

"Listen," she held up a hand. "I appreciate your concern, but I'm not staying in a safe house with a cop sitting in a car on the street. That's ludicrous. I had arguments with Merchant about this. It made zero difference and to be honest, I never saw the point."

"Who said anything about a safe house?" asked Rem. "I happen to know of a great place, with free rent, and a nice neighborhood. Not too far from the station. It's a steal."

Daniels continued to stare at Rem. "Be careful what you wish for."

Jill didn't know whether he was talking to her or Rem. "Where is this magical place of unicorns and fairies?"

Rem swiveled toward her. "You can stay with me."

"Excuse me?" she asked.

"It's perfect," said Rem. "I'm staying in my Uncle Martin and Aunt Audrey's house. Martin died recently, and Audrey is now in a retirement home. She wants me to have the house because she doesn't want to sell the home where they lived for thirty years. I agreed to move in. It's plenty big. You can have the master, which is downstairs. It's got its own bathroom and you can have plenty of privacy. I'll be in one of the three bedrooms upstairs."

She stood. "No. No way."

"Why not?" asked Rem.

"Because…because…," she sputtered. The thought was so ridiculous, she didn't know what to say. She paced, but he kept looking at her as if he really didn't get it. "Because, you moron, I'm being stalked by a serial killer. I think that's reason enough."

Rem relaxed. "Geez. I thought you were going to tell me you leave the toilet seat up or you're a slob."

"That would be you," interjected Daniels.

"This is not funny," said Jill. "There's no way I can do this. It makes you an obvious target."

"Why?" asked Rem. "We'll be roommates. We'll go to and from work together. There's been no indication from the files that he harmed your family or friends."

Jill's blood went cold, and she turned away.

"Jacobs?" asked Daniels. "Has there?"

Her stomach lurched, and she put a hand on the back of a chair. She wasn't ready to talk about this. "You're forgetting Officer Henderson.

He was a friend." The detectives went quiet behind her, and she turned. "I can't risk another officer's life." She caught Rem's gaze. "It would kill me if something happened."

Rem's face turned stoic, and he stood. "I understand what you're saying. You're worried someone else could get hurt. Don't think I'm not thinking about that. But you cannot stay by yourself somewhere. That's not any safer. You need a place where you can lay your head at night and not be alone. You're putting your life on the line every day. Besides, maybe you're right. Maybe this might help catch him. If we know he'll be watching, and we know he'll be curious, we prepare for that."

Daniels stood quietly, his arms crossed. "You'll need an alarm system," he said. "And we can put up some cameras outside the house."

Rem pointed. "Charlie," he said at the same time as Daniels.

Jill dropped her jaw. "I am not doing this."

"Yes. You are," said Rem. "If you're going to help us, then I'm going to help you. And relax. I don't plan on dying."

"None of us do," said Daniels.

"You don't know that," said Jill. "Henderson thought the same thing." She set her jaw.

Rem walked closer to her. "I know you're scared, but if you think about it logically, it's the perfect solution. You have a place to stay where you can feel relatively safe and you won't be alone. I have a big house with plenty of space—"

"And he needs someone who can go down to the basement for him," interrupted Daniels. "You can check the closets too."

Rem frowned and ignored Daniels. "We'll barely be there anyway except to sleep. Most of our time will be here where we'll be busting our butts to find this guy. We'll have cameras so if he does do something, we'll have it recorded."

She sighed. Sweat broke out on her skin and she drank some water.

"It's worth trying," he said. "You always have the option to move out."

She pulled her hair back, rolled it into a messy bun and tied a hair band from her wrist around it. "You like this idea?" she asked Daniels. "He's your partner."

Daniels straightened. "He is. I know him better than anybody. I know how stubborn he can be, so you might as well stop arguing because he's made up his mind. But if you're asking whether I like it, no, I don't like anything about this. But this is the hand we've been dealt. You deal with this every day of your life. I think we can both handle working with you and what it might entail."

"Henderson's partner hasn't spoken to me since the funeral," she said flatly.

Daniels' expression didn't change. "Every day we go out there, it's a risk. Talk to any cop on the street. It could happen to any of us. But I'll tell you this, if something happened, I sure as hell wouldn't blame you."

She bit her bottom lip, and her heart thumped. Was she considering this? She looked at Remalla, who slowly smiled.

"Let's go pack your bags," he said.

**

The rest of the day was a myriad of paperwork. Rem and Daniels talked to Lozano about adding Jacobs to the team to assist with the case. It was unlikely they could reinstate her as a police officer in such a short time, but they could hire her as a consultant which would allow her full access, but without the benefit of carrying a firearm, at least not one provided by the state.

As Jacobs met with Lozano, Rem sat back in his seat after flipping through yet another victim's file.

"You want to talk about it?" asked Daniels, as he wrote on a piece of paper.

"Talk about what?" Rem asked.

Daniels put down his pen. "Oh, I don't know. Maybe how you just invited a woman you barely know who's being stalked by a serial killer to live with you?"

Rem studied a paper on his desk. "It was the obvious solution. She can't stay in the RV. And you heard what she said about the safe house."

"She could have done either."

Rem dropped the pencil he was holding. "How would you sleep at night knowing she's by herself, unprotected, while she's trying to help us at the same time? It doesn't sit right with me."

"Are you going to sleep any better knowing a killer may be watching?"

Rem leaned forward and put his elbows on his desk. "Let him watch. That may be how we catch him."

"As long as that is all he does," answered Daniels.

Rem smiled. "You can always join us. Plenty of rooms upstairs. It'll be a slumber party."

Daniels snorted. "And risk my life too? Nah. Besides, Marjorie might take issue. She likes me next to her at night."

"That baby will be here soon," said Rem. "You guys pick a name yet?"

"You know we haven't and don't change the subject."

Rem nodded. "Okay." He paused. "Yes. I may be a little nervous, but it's the right thing to do. You'd do the same thing." He shifted in his seat.

Daniels considered that. "You're right. I would. And if Marjorie weren't in the picture, I'd join you. And don't get me wrong. I understand what you're doing and why you're doing it. But…" he leaned in, "my gut tells me there's something else."

Rem didn't answer.

Daniel's brow furrowed. "Do you like her?"

Rem looked up. "I admire her."

"Anything else?" Daniels waited.

Rem hesitated. "She sort of reminds me of…" He played with the pencil.

Daniels nodded. "Yeah. I know. She's a lot like her. Does that bother you?"

Rem thought about it. "No. Not really. Just brings back memories." He leaned back. "And now she's going to be living with me."

"You can still change your mind," said Daniels.

Rem shook his head. "No. I can't do that. You know I can't."

Daniels regarded his partner. "You're a good man. A brave one, too."

"Well, I have to put up with you every day."

Daniels smiled softly, but his tone remained serious. "You sure you're okay with this?"

"I am. Besides, I know I'll be safe."

"How can you be so sure?"

Rem went back to his computer. "Because I've got you to back me up."

Daniels nodded. "I'm just a phone call away." He paused. "Let's hope it's enough."

Rem glanced toward Lozano's office, seeing Jacobs through the glass as she spoke to Lozano. "It will be." He regarded the latest file. "It will be."

CHAPTER EIGHT

Rem opened the door to the master bedroom. "And this is your room."

Jill stepped inside to see a bed with two nightstands and a lamp on each. Green curtains covered a window and there was a bathroom to the left of the bed. "You sure I'm not taking your room? I can stay upstairs."

Daniels poked his head in from behind Rem. "He doesn't sleep in here. Never has."

Rem rolled his eyes.

"Why not?" asked Jill.

Daniels cocked his head at Rem, waiting for him to answer.

Rem hesitated but spoke. "Full Disclosure. My uncle died in this room, in that bed. It creeps me out. If you'd rather take a bed upstairs..."

Jill shook her head. "No. I'm fine with it. It feels good in here. Your aunt and uncle must have been happy together."

"If you see any ghosts, just send them upstairs," said Daniels.

Rem shoved his partner in the arm. "Don't you have somewhere to be?"

Daniels checked his watch. "Actually, yes. If I go now, Marjorie and I can catch a quick meal before I grab some shuteye. We've got a big day tomorrow."

"Yeah, well. Don't let the door hit your ass on the way out," said Rem.

"I won't," said Daniels. "You good, Jacobs? You need anything before I go? This guy eats like crap so don't expect much in the fridge."

Jill shook her head. "I'm fine. I'm not really hungry after our late lunch."

"Then I'll see you two in the morning, bright and early. Call me if you need me."

"Good night," said Rem and Jill, as Daniels waved and left.

Rem turned and brought Jill's bags in. "There are fresh towels in the bathroom."

"A hot shower sounds perfect. Thank you."

"I'll get you a key tomorrow. Charlie's putting in the alarm and video system in the afternoon, so we should be up and running by then."

Jill nodded. "Sounds great. Thanks." She rubbed her hands together.

Rem stood by the door. "You sure you don't need anything else? I'm gonna grab a couple of hot dogs and a beer. You're welcome to join me."

"No. I just want to take a shower and get some sleep. I'm exhausted." As if on cue, she yawned. She eyed the bed, looking forward to crawling into it.

"Okay. Well, just so you know, sometimes I'm not a great sleeper, so if you hear walking around at night or voices, it's probably me watching TV in the den, so don't shoot me."

She thought of the gun in her suitcase. "Good to know. Thanks." She paused. "The same goes for me, actually. I don't sleep well."

"Well, I'm a fan of old movies at around two or three a.m., so feel free to bring some popcorn."

"Do you have any popcorn?" she asked.

"No."

"Then we'll put that on the grocery list. What about coffee?"

"Got loads of that," he answered. "I have it trucked in."

She smiled. "Good. I'm not very civil until I've had my coffee."

"I hear that." He grabbed the doorknob. "Then I'll let you get some rest."

"Hey."

He paused before he closed the door.

"Thank you again for doing this. To be honest, this is the safest I've felt in a long time." She held up a hand. "But if you ever decide you want me to leave, please just tell me. I don't do well with beating around the bush." He leaned against the frame, and something about the way he held himself made Jill take notice. A fluttery feeling in her stomach surprised her.

"Got it," he said. "If I want you out, you'll be the first to know." His face softened. "And if we're being truthful, it's nice to have someone here. This big house gets quiet, and I don't always do well with quiet."

She reached for a suitcase. "I don't think you'll have to worry about quiet any time soon. After a few weeks of me here, you may want your quiet back."

He studied her, his eyes curious, and she wondered what he was thinking. "We'll see about that. See you in the morning."

"See you," she said, as he closed the door.

Turning, she stood thinking, wondering again if she'd made the right choice. She was in a house with a man she barely knew, preparing to track down another man who'd taken so much from her. Trying not to think about it, she put her suitcase on the bed and opened it. After seeing her purse, she unzipped it, took out the picture and placed it on the end table. The room was silent, and sitting on the edge of the bed, she closed her eyes, thinking back. It was something she rarely did, but now that her involvement had changed, her mindset would have to change too. She could no longer shut out the memories.

Allowing herself to drift, she returned to the Artist's case, remembering past victims, sleepless nights, arguments and unexpected betrayals by those she thought she could trust. A sudden weight came down like a blanket and her head spun. Glad she was sitting, she put her hands down to brace herself and opened her eyes.

It took a moment for her head to clear, and she sighed. The picture on the nightstand stared back at her, and for a moment, she considered closing her suitcase and walking out, but the photo told her otherwise. She had to find and confront the Makeup Artist and make him face his demons just as she was facing hers. Either he would die, or she would.

Standing, she placed the photo in the table's drawer and started to unpack.

**

Daniels walked into the station, carrying his orange juice and a wheat bagel. He checked his watch, happy to see he was on time.

Approaching the desk, he stopped when he saw Rem already sitting at his usual spot, a coffee in his hand and a donut in his mouth.

He looked up. "Mornin'," he said through a mouthful.

Daniels set his orange juice down. "To what do I owe this pleasure of you actually being on time?"

"I'm always on time."

"In what time zone?" asked Daniels.

The squad room door opened, and Jacobs entered. She sat at a vacant desk next to Rem and Daniels noticed the folders on it. They were the files of the three most recent victims. "Good morning," she said. She pulled a donut out of a paper bag and sipped on some coffee.

"Good morning," said Daniels. "Don't tell me he's pushing donuts on you."

She took a bite. "What's wrong with donuts?" she asked. "These are delicious."

Rem smiled, and Daniels moaned. "Great. Now there's two of you."

"You're so lucky," said Rem. He lifted a bag on the desk. "We got one for you too. Powdered. Your favorite."

Daniels sat and eyed his bagel, then considered the bag. "Fine." He took the bag and helped himself to the donut.

"I knew it," said Rem, taking his last bite. "Life can't be lived on bran muffins alone."

Daniels ignored the comment and enjoyed the donut. "What are you two early birds up to? You getting a head start?"

"Jacobs wanted to review the files on our latest victims. And I know we have some questions about Seattle," said Rem.

"Merchant sent us all of that info, if you want to review that too," said Daniels to Jacobs.

Jacobs flipped a piece of paper. "I won't need to review those."

Daniels glanced at Rem. "You sure? It's been a couple of years."

She took a sip of coffee. "I studied every one of those files incessantly for nine months straight. I know them like the back of my hand."

Rem cocked an eyebrow. "Really?"

"Really," she answered.

Rem hit some keys and studied his monitor. "The name and age of the second victim."

She didn't hesitate. "Alice Dumont. Age thirty. Cocktail waitress at O'Grady's and a single mom."

Daniels tipped his head. "Fourth victim?" he asked.

"Rebecca Molina. Twenty-nine. Married, but separated. Husband was out of town when she was killed. She worked as an accountant." She flipped another page in one of the folders.

Rem swiveled in his chair. "Seventh victim?"

"Craig Lester. Thirty-two. Owned a laundromat."

"What was his address?" asked Rem.

Jacobs looked up at that. Daniels figured they had her with that question.

"1225 Nashville Lane. Apt. 12." She shook her head and went back to her file. "Don't waste my time."

Daniels put down his donut. "You have a photographic memory?"

She closed the file and sat back. "I have a memory. Don't know what photos have to do with it. You could ask me what I did last week, and I couldn't tell you, but I remember everything about the victims and this case. It's branded on my brain." She touched a folder. "Just like these will be."

"You see anything in those files that stands out? Anything unusual?" asked Rem. He stood and helped himself to more coffee.

"It's interesting that he doesn't write anything on the wall until this last victim. If he wanted me back, why not write something sooner? Why wait?"

"Maybe he didn't know you were here?" asked Daniels, finishing his donut and wiping the powdered sugar from his fingers.

"He had to," she answered. "Him starting up again in the same city where I'm living is not coincidental. He knew I was here."

"Maybe he wanted to take his time. Start slow," said Daniels. "Maybe he knew you weren't watching the news."

"Or he wanted us to contact you first," said Rem. "He knew we'd come looking for you."

Daniels leaned forward. "When did you become involved in Seattle?" He looked at his monitor. "After which victim?"

Jill's eyes widened. "The third. April Denison. Age twenty-eight. Merchant put me on the morning after she died."

Rem held his coffee, thinking. "Is he re-creating the crimes?"

Daniels tapped his desk. "That's where we are now. We've got a third victim, and Jacobs is back on the case."

"But the writing didn't start until the fourth victim in Seattle," said Jacobs. "He jumped the gun."

"It's not a perfect recreation, but it got him what he wanted," said Daniels.

"So he's trying to duplicate what happened before?" asked Jacobs, rubbing her temples. "Shit."

"A metric ton of it," said Rem. "He wants to replay the events from Seattle. Like a scene from a play."

Jacobs stared off. "It makes sense."

"If that's the case, do we go along with it?" asked Rem.

"Hopefully not," said Daniels. "If we stick to his plan, that means four more victims."

Jacobs frowned. "And one dead cop."

Daniels went still. "You think he'd stick that closely to script?"

Jacobs faced him, her face pale. "This is a game to him. He won the first round. He wants to see if he can do it again. Sticking to the script is key. This is fun for him."

"Then we better catch him before that," said Rem, sitting back in his seat.

"We better, because I can't afford to lose again," said Jacobs.

Daniels nodded. "Then let's not waste time. Any questions on the files?"

She sighed. "They're pretty straight forward."

"We have some questions about Seattle," said Rem. "There's a lot missing from the files."

She stood. "We'll get to those." She grabbed her jacket.

"Where are you going?" asked Daniels. "Don't tell me you want another donut."

"No. We're going to the crime scenes. I need to see them."

"Now?" asked Rem.

"Now."

CHAPTER NINE

Jill stared at the small yellow house. Crime scene tape criss-crossed the front door. Standing at the bottom of the stairs at the front porch, she watched Daniels cut the tape and open the home. Until that point, she'd been going on pure instinct. Telling herself not to think, but just do. If she thought too much, then she would have talked herself out of doing any of this before she'd ever made it to the station that morning. She took a deep breath and prepared herself. By walking in that door, she knew everything would change. She'd successfully kept the killer out of her head for almost two years now, but this would be like ringing the dinner bell. The emotion and turmoil of entering the house would bring it all back, and he would be there.

But there was no other choice. Running was not an option. He would only follow and more would die. She steeled herself, erected a mental wall to provide some protection, and took the stairs up to the entry.

Rem stepped aside to allow her to enter. Daniels was inside, surveying the room. The first thing she saw was the pretty living area. Yellow paint and the bright sunshine streaming through the window gave the area a cheery look, masking the horrors of what had taken place here. Nothing seemed out of place, other than the fingerprint dust that dotted tables, pictures and door knobs.

She moved further into the room. The carpet was a soft beige and a small dining table sat just outside the kitchen.

Rem stepped inside and closed the door. "Vicky Smith. She was a bartender down at Sam's. Found her in the bedroom."

Jill nodded, not saying anything. Her stomach was already rolling, and she regretted eating the donuts. She closed her eyes, focused, and maintained the mental wall. *So far, so good*, she thought to herself.

"You okay?" asked Daniels. "You look a little pale."

"Hanging in there," she said. A stack of books lay on a small desk and a guitar case was leaning against the wall. "Did she live alone?"

"Yes," said Rem. "She rented the house. Her cousin owns it, so I'm guessing she got a good deal."

Jill peered down a hallway and saw a small bathroom and a bedroom at the end. Her body stiffened, and she knew she was getting close to the crime scene. She took tentative steps.

"You don't have to do this," said Rem. "You saw the crime scene photos."

Remembering the pictures, the mental wall crumbled a bit and Jill stopped and took a second to collect herself. "I know. But this is important."

She caught the glance between the detectives, but she ignored it. Preparing mentally, she pushed herself to keep going and walked toward the bedroom. Reaching the door, she stopped. A large bloody stain blackened the carpet on one side of the bed. The bed sheets had been stripped and there were streaks of blood on the walls and nightstand. Jill froze, her chest constricting. In that moment, her protective wall disintegrated. Images assaulted her. Screams of rage and fear bubbled up and she could see it in her mind's eye. Vicky's terror. The knife plunging. She heard an evil laugh in her head and knew it was him. She could hear and feel how he'd enjoyed Vicky's pain and torment. She fought the urge to be sick and tried to focus only on him. She tried to see his face, but it was only a blur. Colors swirled in her head, and she fought to catch her breath. Dizziness made her take a hold of the doorframe and she struggled to maintain control.

"Jacobs?" she heard Rem's voice, but she didn't respond. The colors brightened, as did the scene in her mind. Her belly rumbled as the sickness rose in her. Anger, madness, and pity replaced the disgust she'd experienced when entering the room. And then he was there, his mind connecting with hers, and she was no longer the compassionate detective who hated the killer; she was the killer himself. His fury and need to hurt assailed her, and she fought not to turn on Rem and Daniels, wanting to lash out, to hurt, to destroy.

Forcing herself to pull back, she searched to find the mental barrier she'd created, and he'd destroyed, hoping to reassemble it to protect herself. She needed to get him out. If he stayed too long, it would be a much harder recovery for her, so she fought to find herself again. As the wall grew, and her body and emotions became hers again, she sensed one last show of strength, and she heard him in her head, his voice a scratchy resemblance of the past. *Welcome back, Jill.* Opening her eyes, her stomach rebelled, and she ran for the nearby bathroom, pushing past Daniels and Rem, and barely made it before losing her donuts.

**

Sitting on the porch at the back of the house, Jill held her head and took long deep breaths. Her heart still raced, but her mind was her own again. Trying to relax, she let the sun warm her back. Her fingers shook, and she gripped them to keep them still.

"You sure you're okay?" asked Daniels. He squatted in front of her, and looking at him, Jill wondered if she was as pale as he was. "What happened in there?"

She squeezed her eyes shut but opened them when the dizziness returned. "I let him in."

Rem grabbed another chair, dragged it closer, and sat. "What does that mean? Can you see him?"

"No. I get images in my head, but no clear pictures. It's a feeling more than anything." She straightened and let the sun hit her face. "I can hear the screams, feel her terror, but the worst is his madness. If I get too close, I can sense his rage. He has so much anger and hatred. And I want to lash out and hurt too. I have to be careful not to engage too long, or the effects can be…difficult." She rubbed the bridge of her nose, feeling the dull ache of headache.

"That's obvious," said Rem.

"Sorry to keep throwing up around you. It's nothing personal," she said.

"Don't apologize," said Daniels. "Rem has that effect on women."

"Hey," said Rem. "Denise only threw up once on that date. And I blame the chicken."

"That's a record," said Daniels.

She knew they were trying to lighten the mood, and it was working. The faster she could relax and pull herself out of that dark place, the better it would be for her. She hadn't expected to connect as quickly and easily as she had in the victim's bedroom. It was as if the last two years had not existed and she was still in Seattle, playing mind games with the killer. If she continued to play this game, she would have to be careful. He'd been in her head so fast, and she'd been lucky to retreat as quickly as she did.

"Feeling better?" asked Rem.

"We can go back to the station. Let you rest for a bit," said Daniels.

She shook her head. "No. We have two more scenes to visit."

Rem's right eyebrow shot up. "Forgive me for pointing out the obvious, but I think you've had enough. You can't afford to throw up two more times. You've already wasted two perfectly good donuts."

"I won't be sick again. It was just because this was the first one. I'll be more prepared next time. It won't hit me as hard." She stood and stretched, taking a deep breath, thankful she didn't wobble.

"You're sure about this?" asked Daniels, standing with her.

"You want to catch this guy?" she asked. "Then let me do my thing. As hard as it is, each scene gives me another insight into his mind. And I have to believe, at some point, he'll slip up and reveal something that will lead to his capture. Crime scene photos won't do it." She stepped fully into the sunlight, feeling the warmth.

Rem stepped up beside her. "At what point does it become too much? I know you want to get inside his head, but how much of him gets inside yours? Whatever this connection is, you both have it. How far are you willing to go?"

She looked over. "You brought me back into this mess. I'd given up because I couldn't take anymore. That's not an accusation. He wanted me back, and if it wasn't you, it would have been someone else. But since I'm here and he's intent on playing this game, then I need to go all in. I have to do whatever it takes, or I'll never be free of him."

"And if it takes your sanity at the same time?" asked Daniels.

"It won't matter," she answered.

"Why not?" asked Rem.

"Because if we don't catch him, he'll probably kill me." A soft breeze blew her hair, and she tucked it behind her ear. "I think that's been his plan all along. Once he tires of the game." Feeling more stable, she walked down the steps and headed to the car. Looking back, she said, "You coming?"

**

Lozano signed his name on yet another form and, hearing voices, he saw his detectives return from their inspections of the crime scenes. He stood from his desk and walked to the open door.

Rem threw his jacket over a chair and immediately reached for his mug.

Daniels sat and rubbed his face. "Pour me some, will you?"

"You got it."

Lozano stepped out. "How'd it go?"

"About as delightful as you can imagine," said Daniels.

"Where's Jacobs?" asked Lozano.

Rem poured coffee into another mug and handed it to Daniels. "She stopped in the restroom."

"She's exhausted," said Daniels. "Drained."

"Me, too," said Rem, sitting in his chair.

"You learn anything?" asked Lozano.

Rem glanced at his partner. "Nothing yet. But it helped Jacobs reconnect to the case. Let's hope it leads us somewhere."

Two detectives, one black and tall and the other white and short, entered the squad room and approached.

"Titus. Georgios," said Lozano. "You learn anything?"

Titus, the shorter, rounder one, took out a notepad. "Not much. We talked to the family and coworkers of Schein, but they didn't have much to offer. Nobody could remember anything or anyone strange who aroused suspicion."

Georgios, the taller one, spoke. "Her routine was the same. Nothing different. She worked as a dental assistant. Nice girl, but shy and kept to herself. Not dating anybody but had a profile on an online dating service. The tech guys are checking her computer to see if there's anything there."

Lozano huffed and stretched his neck.

"You guys find anything on your ghost hunt?" asked Titus, smiling.

Rem lowered his coffee. "Excuse me?"

"Ghost hunt?" asked Daniels.

"You know," said Georgios. "We heard about the chick from Seattle. Did she pull out her crystal ball?"

Titus raised his hands. "Did she get inside his head? Talk to him with her mind?" He swatted Georgios. "Maybe she cast a spell." He spoke in a spooky voice. "Turn yourself in. Make yourself known. And I'll make you feel all better."

Rem stood. “You’re an idiot, Titus. Maybe if you two spent more time working instead of making fun of fellow cops, we might catch this guy.”

Titus stopped smiling. “Working? We’ve heard the rumors. We’ve been out there busting our butts while you two encourage a burn-out who got a cop killed in Seattle.”

Daniels rose from his seat. “You know, Titus, if you ran as much your mouth did, maybe you’d lose some of that weight you keep putting on.”

“That’s a lot of running,” said Rem. “But hey, maybe you’ll save on doctor bills.”

Georgios pointed. “You guys can joke all you want, but you’re the ones risking all of our lives.”

“Are you scared, Georgios?” asked Rem, stepping closer. “Worried you’ll be next? The only cops risking lives around here are you two. Talking about shit you know nothing about. That so called ‘burned-out cop’ has risked more than you can imagine to catch this guy. What have you risked lately? The last trade in your fantasy football league?”

Georgios’ face tightened.

“That’s enough,” said Lozano. “All of you. We’ve got enough to deal with. Georgios and Titus, if you can’t work together as a team with the people I’ve assembled, then I can happily send you to handle the ice cream shop burglary that occurred yesterday.”

“Titus would like that,” said Daniels.

Titus’ brow furrowed. “Shut up, Daniels.”

“I bet you’d get free ice cream,” said Rem. “You might want to reconsider.”

“All of you shut up,” said Lozano. He pointed at Titus and Georgios. “You two go check on Mel and Garcia. Find out if they learned anything on their canvas of the neighbors and report back to me. And check on the progress on the computer, too.”

“Cap,” said Titus.

"Go," said Lozano. "You have an issue with this case, you bring it up with me. In private. You got a problem with that?"

Titus paused.

Georgios glared at Daniels and Rem. "No. No problem." He tipped his head at Titus. "Let's go."

The two detectives turned and left the squad room.

Rem kicked his desk. "Motherfu—".

"Remalla," said Lozano. "That's enough."

"He's right, Cap," said Daniels, pointing. "They're assholes."

Rem started to complain but stopped. Lozano turned to see Jacobs standing by the squad door. Her eyes were weary from their long day, and she looked haunted. He wondered how much she'd heard. She stood for a second, but then seemed to shake off her melancholy and returned to her desk. Her eyes were puffy and red.

"You okay?" Rem asked her.

She opened a drawer and pulled out a bottle of aspirin. "I'll save you some time. You can stop asking me that question because the answer is no. I'm not okay. Your two cop friends are right. I haven't been okay in a long time. Maybe you should reconsider working with me." She dropped two tablets in her hand and swallowed them dry.

"Those two are idiots," said Daniels. "You could drive a bulldozer through the dirt in the rain and they still wouldn't understand why the ground was muddy."

"I'm sorry," said Rem, huffing. "I wish you hadn't heard that."

"It's not the first and it won't be the last. If you want me here, I've learned it comes with the territory. Those who don't understand, make fun." She rubbed her temples.

Rem picked up a mug and walked to the coffeepot. He filled it and brought it over to Jill. "We're not making fun." He held it out to her. "This is the best I got. Wish it was stronger."

She eyed the cup and took it, swallowing some coffee. "I know you're serious. But not everyone is."

Lozano eyed his fatigued and frustrated team. “It’s late,” he said. “You guys go home. You’ve had a long day, but longer ones are ahead. Go get something to eat and some rest. Everyone’s nerves are frayed, and you need it. Start fresh tomorrow.”

“I’m fine, Captain. I just need a few minutes,” said Jill.

“You didn’t hear me,” said Lozano. “Go home.”

Rem pushed his chair in. “You won’t hear this again anytime soon.”

“Best to take him up on the offer when we get the chance,” said Daniels, putting on his jacket. “Let’s go get something to eat. I’m buying.”

“You won’t hear that often either,” said Rem. “How about some steak?”

Daniels frowned. “How about burgers?”

“I’m not hungry,” said Jill.

“You barely ate lunch, you woofed up your donuts, and you didn’t have dinner last night. You’re eating,” said Rem. He opened a drawer, picked up her purse and handed it to her, waiting.

Jill eyed the three of them.

“Best not to keep him waiting,” said Daniels. “Especially if he’s hungry. It’s not pretty.”

“Fine,” she said, grabbing her purse.

“You want to join us, Cap?” asked Daniels.

Lozano patted his belly. “No burgers for me, plus I’ve got some paperwork to catch up on. But have a beer for me.”

“Will do, Cap,” said Rem.

“And Jacobs,” said Lozano. Jill stopped.

“I wouldn’t have you here if I didn’t believe in you. Merchant sung your praises. My detectives wouldn’t work with you otherwise. You’re needed here, regardless of whatever you may hear. Remember that,” said Lozano.

Jacobs’ shoulders dropped and the tension around her eyes eased. “Thanks, Captain.”

"You're welcome. Now go enjoy your burger and beer because you'll be working your ass off again starting tomorrow."

"That's the plan," said Jill.

"Don't be raiding that vending machine, Cap," said Rem, walking out. "Got to keep that ass small. Less to work off."

"Get the hell out of here, Rem," said Lozano. "Worry about your own ass. Not mine. And don't think I'm forgetting about your hair."

"Sure thing, Cap," answered Rem with a wave.

Lozano watched his people leave the squad room, grunted, and went back to his office, grabbing a bag of chips from the machine on the way.

CHAPTER TEN

The knife flashed, the cold steel glimmering in the darkness. Jill's heart raced, and she squatted low, listening. The footsteps encroached, and she did her best to not breathe, terrified he would hear. The door creaked as it was pushed open, and Jill braced. Before fear overwhelmed her, she sprang from her hiding place, ready to confront the madman who'd tormented her for so long. But she saw nothing and froze, her heart thumping and fingers trembling. The doorway was empty.

Cautiously, she took a step forward, barely able to make her limbs move, waiting for that flicker of steel's reflection. Peering around the door, squinting in the low light, she felt a hand on her shoulder and she whirled, falling backward. Cold, empty eyes stared down at her as she saw him raise the knife, and she screamed.

Jill sat straight up in bed, eyes open, a strangled cry in her throat. Breathing heavily, she clutched her chest, still seeing the knife arc toward her in her mind. Shaky fingers sought the lamp, and she clicked it on, illuminating the bedroom with soft light. There was a sheen of sweat on her skin, and she shoved the covers back, swinging her legs out, and sat with her head in her hands, trying to calm her breathing. *Jesus*, she said to herself. It was her first nightmare in months. Leaving the force and a steady and substantial alcohol intake had helped eradicate them, but now she had neither. She'd had a beer at dinner, but she'd stayed away from the hard stuff. She'd learned though that these nightmares were best handled with a shot of vodka, and a valium wouldn't hurt either.

Knowing the valium wasn't an option, she wondered if the vodka was. She'd seen some liquor in a cabinet in Rem's kitchen when he'd showed her around. Still shaky, she got out of bed and slipped on her robe. Glancing at the clock, she saw it was two-thirty in the morning. If she could calm down, she might get a few more hours in before the alarm went off. That's what she told herself, at least.

Quietly, she opened the bedroom door and after seeing the dark, the fear bubbled up. Thankfully, Rem kept a nightlight in the foyer, so she quickly made her way to the light switch in the kitchen, trying not to think of who might be behind her. She flicked it on and stood for a second, trying to collect herself. The nightmare still lingered, and she wanted to get those cold dead eyes out of her mind. She reached for a cabinet door.

"Can't sleep?"

The voice came from behind, and she jumped. If she'd been holding a glass, she would have flung it. Barely holding back a scream, she fell back against the counter and saw Rem standing in the kitchen door.

"I'm sorry." He held out a hand. "I didn't mean to scare you."

Breathing hard, she doubled over. She didn't know how she hadn't had a heart attack. She shook her head and straightened. "What the hell is the matter with you?"

"I didn't think…"

"No, you didn't." She turned and gripped the counter, knowing he hadn't done it on purpose, but pissed just the same. She took a deep, trembling breath.

He came up beside her. "Looking for something? Water? I'll get you a glass."

"I was looking for something stronger."

Grabbing a cup, he offered a surprised look. "We've got to be at work in five hours."

Still shaky, she walked over to one of the kitchen chairs and sat. "My mother died years ago. I don't need another one." She rubbed her head.

There was a pause. "What's wrong?"

Jill swiveled in her seat and put her elbows on the table, closing her eyes. "Nothing. I'm just great."

There was a movement and rustling behind her and then she heard him sit. Opening her eyes, she saw him holding two glasses and a bottle of vodka. He poured a small amount into each and handed one to her and kept the other to himself.

"It was a tough day yesterday," he said. "I get it."

She took the glass. "I could kiss you right now."

Smiling, he screwed the lid back on the liquor bottle. "Let's just stick to the drinking for the moment, but maybe later…" He wiggled his eyebrows.

She couldn't help but chuckle and some of the weight lifted. They clinked glasses and shot back their drinks. The liquid burned a path down her throat and her insides warmed. It soothed her, and her frayed nerves stopped chattering. She eyed the bottle.

Standing, he put it back. "We have school today."

Jill held her head and closed her eyes, hearing him sit down again.

"You want to talk about it?" he asked.

Those cold dead eyes. She could see them so clearly. "I had a nightmare."

"Not surprised, considering. Was he in it?"

She sighed and swallowed, wondering if she could sneak another drink after Rem went to bed. "I was in the dark. He was looking for me. I couldn't see, and he got behind me, grabbed my shoulder and I went down. All I saw was the knife coming toward me and his eyes. I screamed and thank God, woke up."

"Did you see his face?"

She looked up. "No. Just those dead eyes." She closed her own eyes and took a long deep breath, rubbing her arms. "Jesus. I need another drink."

"This happen a lot?" he asked.

"Not in a while. But now…"

"They're back."

"Seems so."

He nodded and glanced at his watch. "You like Bela Lugosi?"

She wasn't sure she heard right. "Who or what is that?"

Rem rolled his eyes. "The actor. Played Dracula."

"Oh, him. I don't know. Never seen any of his movies."

His eyes widened. "What? Well, you are in luck, my dear. Because in exactly ten minutes, his classic movie, *The Wolf Man*, is starting, so grab a seat and sit your butt, because this is going to be a treat." He stood and went into the kitchen.

Forcing herself to think of something other than the eyes, she answered. "I thought you said he was Dracula, and why am I grabbing a seat? Don't you have a sofa?" She swiveled to face him, when her robe caught on something. Reaching to pull it back, she saw a rough and rusty screw protruding from the back of one of the wooden rails that met the seat on her chair. "Do you know you have a screw sticking out here?" She poked at it, feeling its sharp edges.

Rem opened the fridge, glancing toward her. "Yeah. I know. Sorry about that. That's been there for years. It's sort of a running joke in the family."

"Running joke?"

"The chair broke a few years ago and my uncle tried to fix it. Needless to say, he wasn't an accomplished handyman which is why the window sill is painted orange and the knobs in the kitchen are all different. My uncle found extra paint in the garage even though it was the wrong color and bought all the various knobs at a garage sale. Didn't see the point of anything matching. My aunt and cousins made fun at his attempts, but in his mind, he fixed it, including the chair. He didn't see a problem. The nail stayed, and the jokes started from there." He grabbed two sodas and spoke in a lower tone. "You need a good screw? Just ask Uncle Mart." He smiled. "You get the gist."

"I do," she said. "Are you going to fix it?"

"Nah. It holds good memories. Just don't cut yourself." He kicked the fridge shut. "Now go sit your butt on the *sofa*, if you prefer. And to answer your question, Lugosi's known for Dracula, but he played other roles."

"This movie is supposed to be good?" She asked. "You wouldn't be joking about that would you?"

He stopped in mid-reach for something in the pantry. "I never joke about Dracula."

She frowned. "I can see that."

He grinned. "And I got you a treat."

His face made her think of an eager school kid who had something cool for show and tell. "What's that? Does it involve alcohol?"

He smirked. "Even better." He pulled out a flat bag. "Popcorn."

She stood and leaned against the table. "When the hell did you find time to get popcorn?"

"Never question my unique and rare abilities to find food at the most difficult of times. You can ask Daniels. It's one of my strengths."

"Apparently." She watched as he placed the popcorn in the microwave and turned it on and then filled two glasses with ice and added the soda. She had the distinct feeling that he was in his element. Seeing someone in distress, he'd found a way to redirect the energy, and it was working. Her shaking was gone, and her heart had stopped thudding. The alcohol had helped, but he'd done the rest. A memory flashed in her mind, and sadness threatened, but she wouldn't let it take hold. She couldn't help but appreciate Rem's efforts, nor the way his robe pulled against his narrow waist as he moved through the kitchen. Surprised that she'd noticed, she studied the floor.

The microwave dinged, and the smell of popcorn filled the house. Rem took it out, dumped it in a bowl and handed it to her. "You ready?" He grabbed the sodas and some napkins.

"As I'll ever be."

"Then let's go. We don't want to miss the opening scene."

Smiling, she popped a kernel of popcorn in her mouth and followed him into the den.

**

The next morning, Daniels munched on a banana as Rem talked on the phone with the lab and Jacobs worked on the computer, studying the crime scenes and profiles of the latest three victims. Daniels reviewed his own notes on the Seattle victims.

Jacobs stared at the monitor. "You're looking serious over there, Daniels. Something on your mind?"

He tapped his pencil. "What I don't get is this Craig Lester, who owned the laundromat. Why him? It doesn't fit the profile."

"That depends on your assumptions," she said. She sat back from the screen. "Our guy's been killing women, so the conclusion is he has an issue with them. He's a loner. Socially inadequate. Rejected in his sexually formative years. His mother probably did a number on him. If you look at the who he's killed, they're all strong females. Maybe not rich or powerful, but they've got jobs—some of them, two. They may or may not have boyfriends, but they are taking care of themselves. Paying their own way. They are not drug addicts or prostitutes. Based on that, the assumption is that he doesn't like women who are strong and confident. Women who have careers. Maybe they remind him of his mom or a female caregiver. If she was similar, it could be he rarely saw her. She left him alone, or with a dad or a guardian who maybe didn't take good care of him or abused him. Our killer resents her or blames her for whatever he's going through. Now years later, he's killing women that remind him of her. Enter Craig Lester. Did Craig stir memories of that abuser? Did he trigger something? Or is it a sexual thing? Does he harbor potential feelings for the opposite sex, or maybe the same sex, that are conflicting to him?"

"Then wouldn't he be killing more men?" asked Daniels.

"Obviously, his issues are mainly with women. Cue me when I got on his case and publicly called him out. I epitomize the strong woman he hates."

Daniels considered the obvious. "Then let me ask the obvious. Why not kill you? Why taunt you instead with phone calls and photos?"

Rem hung up and listened.

Jacobs picked up her mug and took a sip of coffee. "We wondered about that in Seattle. What is it about me that keeps his interest? The likely answer is that I remind him of someone. Maybe I look like his mother? Or maybe there's something about me that's different from the others? I don't know."

"But if you reminded him of his mother, wouldn't that make him want to kill you even more?" asked Rem.

"Yes, and no," she answered. "Maybe it's because I got in front of the cameras and gave him the attention he desperately craves. I suspect though, that after he has his fun, then he'll want to kill me too. But right now, he's enjoying lording his power over me. Showing me who's boss. In his eyes, I made myself a public figure. Of all his victims, maybe he sees me as the strongest, and by terrorizing me, it makes him feel powerful. He likes that. And as long as he feels he has the upper hand, and I continue to play along, he'll keep the game going."

"But you stopped for two years," said Daniels. "Why not kill you then?"

"I don't know." She tapped her mug. "He had plenty of opportunity. The only reason I can think of is in his own warped mind, he likes me."

"You mean he's attracted to you," said Rem. He sat forward. "Maybe he thinks you like him too."

She nodded. "That's possible. By playing along, I validate him. Give him a reason to keep going. Murdering these women and using it against me is exciting to him. He probably saw his victims as potential sexual conquests, and when he perceived that they ignored or rejected him, he took their life. Same with Craig Lester. Maybe Craig ignored the killer or debased him in some way."

"But you didn't ignore him. You called him out, on TV," said Daniels.

"I did. And I'd hoped that would have been a trigger for him. I expected to be next on his list. We were waiting for that. But he didn't stick to the game plan." Jill rubbed her neck.

"And what about the makeup?" asked Daniels. "Why does he do that?"

Jacobs put a paper on her desk. "The makeup defiles them. Puts them in their place. In his mind, they act like they're better than him, and they're pretending to be something they're not. He's showing what he really thinks of them and how he depicts them, and probably more important, how others should view them."

"Why red lipstick and blush?" asked Rem.

Jacobs shook her head. "Good question. It obviously reminds him of someone he didn't particularly like. Could be his mom wore it or even a woman who rejected him. Maybe he frequented prostitutes who wore a lot of makeup and that's how he sees women."

Daniels sighed. "Unbelievable." He looked at Rem. "What'd the lab have to say?"

"Nothing much," said Rem. "No DNA found at our latest crime scene. They did find some online profiles of men Schein had connected with through a dating service. They're going to send us their information."

"Maybe we'll get lucky," said Daniels.

Jacobs flipped through a file. "There is something interesting though."

Rem dug through a bag of cashews on his desk and popped a few in his mouth. "What's that?"

She held up a paper. "The first victim in Seattle, Giselle Varella, was an aspiring musician. She sang in a band. Our first victim here, April Smith, was a bartender."

Daniels took a last bite and threw his banana skin away. "What's the connection?"

"There was a guitar case at April's place. I remember seeing it. Did she play the guitar?"

Daniels stopped in mid-chew.

"That's a good question," asked Rem.

Jacobs put the paper down. "And your second victim, Daniella Oberon, waited tables at the wharf between acting gigs. Our second victim in Seattle, Alice Dumont, was a single mom with a full-time job."

"But she waited tables for extra money," said Daniels.

"Exactly," said Jacobs. "And the third victim, April Denison was a dental assistant…"

"And Nicole Schein was an X-ray technician." Rem sat back. "Shit. He's not just following a script, he's looking for women like the ones in Seattle."

Daniels whistled. "If that's the case, then our next victim could be an accountant?"

"Maybe," said Jacobs. "At least something professional, possibly in finance of some kind."

"Well, that narrows it down," said Rem, rubbing his temples.

"What about the last vic in Seattle? Officer Henderson," asked Daniels. "I get what you're saying with the other victims, but that one feels out of place. The timetable is off. He killed Henderson only days after Lester. And why kill a cop? I understand you were getting in the killer's face, but you'd been doing that since the beginning. What triggered it? How well did you know Henderson?"

Jacobs picked up her coffee again, her fingers white with the grip, and took a sip. Her face took on a pinched look, and Daniels caught the tension in her body.

"What's different about Henderson?" asked Rem. When she didn't answer, he made eye contact with Daniels and Daniels knew he was picking up on the same cues. "Jacobs?" he asked.

The phone on Jacobs' desk rang, and Jacobs startled in her seat. She put down her mug, looking almost relieved. "Who's calling me? Does someone have this number?"

"That phone rings occasionally. Could be the desk downstairs," said Daniels.

"There's one way to find out," said Rem.

She frowned and picked up the phone. "Jacobs."

She listened for a moment, before her face went flat, she closed her eyes and sighed. "Hey, Dad."

Daniels raised a brow at Rem, and he went back to his files, trying not to listen, but doing so anyway.

Jacobs spoke. "No. I'm fine." She paused. "Yes. I know." She paused again. "Dad, listen…"

Daniels couldn't help but look up.

Jill stood and paced at her desk. "I realize that. That's not what I want. But I can't just—" She bit her lip and ran a hand through her hair.

Rem was trying to look engaged in his work but was failing.

"I don't think that's a good idea," she said. "No. I can't. I really think…If you would just listen for two seconds…" She stopped. "Dad?" She groaned and dropped the receiver back down. "Shit," she said, sitting down.

"Everything all right?" asked Rem.

She pulled her hair back into a messy bun and wrapped a hairband around it. "That was my father."

"Jailtime Jacobs?" asked Daniels.

She huffed. "You've heard of him?"

"His reputation proceeds him," said Daniels.

"I sense you two don't get along," said Rem.

"You should be a detective," said Daniels.

Rem raised his coffee. "Thank you."

"Dad can be a difficult man," said Jill. "They don't call him 'Jailtime Jacobs' without a reason. He's tough in a courtroom, but that didn't stop at the bench. He's pissed I'm working this case."

"You didn't tell him?" asked Daniels.

"Hell, no," said Jacobs. "I heard enough when I was in Seattle. He didn't want me to be a cop in the first place, which is probably why I became one. Dad's always wanted me to follow a more traditional path."

"Husband and kids?" asked Daniels. He reached over and grabbed a handful of cashews from Rem's stash.

"Exactly," said Jacobs. "I think he thought once I left the force that I would finally give him what he wanted."

"He wants grandkids," said Rem. "Most dads do."

"He's got grandkids. My older brother is married and has two children. He's an attorney. He followed the path my dad wanted, and my father can't stop lathering praise for Brian. Brian this and Brian that." She held her head. "I'm just not built that way. Nor is my younger brother. Neither one of us is in Dad's good graces."

"Younger brother?" asked Rem.

"Dylan," she said. "He's worse than me. He's a nomad. Never sits in one place for too long. Drives Dad nuts."

"They're both in Seattle?" asked Daniels.

"Brian is. Last I heard Dylan was hiking the Appalachian trail."

"Sounds fun," said Daniels.

"I suppose," said Jacobs.

"You close to them?" asked Rem.

"Dylan and I are. We're more alike. Brian and I get along, but he's more like Dad."

"What did they think of what happened in Seattle? Did they support you?" asked Rem.

She sighed and sat back. "They were encouraging at first, although concerned about me. Once things escalated, though, Brian wasn't too thrilled. He had a family, and he worried about their safety. We put a detail on their house, but he kept his distance from me during that time. Understandable." She played with her fingers. "Dylan was off in Europe, trouncing through Germany and France. He'd occasionally check in, make sure I was still alive."

"That was nice," said Rem, popping another cashew.

"He came home after…after I quit the force. We spent some time together before he got fidgety and took off again."

"When did your mom pass?" asked Rem.

She reached over and grabbed a cashew. "You mind?"

"Help yourself," said Rem.

"She died when I was three. Dylan was one. Had heart problems, and one day, she didn't wake up. Dylan and I don't have many memories of her, but Brian does. He says everything changed after Mom died. Dad sort of switched off somehow, and he's never been able to switch back on." She ate a cashew and stared off.

"Losing someone you love can do that to you," said Rem.

Daniels looked over at his partner. "Doesn't mean you can't love again."

Rem caught the look. "You're just saying that because you've got a lovely lady with a baby on the way."

"Baby?" asked Jacobs. "You're having a baby?"

Daniels smiled. "Well, my girlfriend is doing all the work, but yes. She's due in six weeks."

"That's great. Congratulations," said Jacobs.

"He's gonna be a great dad," said Rem.

Daniels pointed. "Don't think you're getting out of diaper duty by buttering me up."

"The only way you're getting me on diaper duty is bribery. I take food and money."

Daniels rolled his eyes. "I already have one kid on my hands. Don't know why I'm worried about a second."

Jacobs smiled as the squad door opened. Daniels looked to see Delgado enter.

"Oh, Lord," said Rem.

"Look busy," said Daniels under his breath, turning toward his desk.

Delgado approached. "Hi, Detectives." Like before, he wore his uniform and held his hat.

"Delgado," said Rem. "What brings you here?"

"I don't mean to bother you again. I know you are busy. I was just curious to know how things were going. Are there any new leads? After I talked to Miss Schein's roommate, I was hoping…"

"…that she would provide a clue that would bust the case wide open? No such luck," said Daniels.

"I've been working extra hours to help with the tip line. Following up on the more interesting information. I'm hoping that will help."

"Every little bit does," said Rem.

"If I find something, I'll let you know."

"Thanks," said Daniels.

He held out his hand. "You must be Officer Jacobs. I'm Ethan Delgado."

Jill shook his hand. "I'm not officially an officer. Just a consultant assisting with the case. Nice to meet you…"

He shifted on his feet. "I'm applying for a promotion to detective. It would be my dream to work on this with you."

She took back her hand. "Be careful what you wish for."

"I'm hoping to hear something soon. Maybe next week." He fiddled with his hat. "Maybe we'll be working together."

Jacobs nodded. "Maybe."

He paused. "I heard you worked on the Seattle case. I've studied the Makeup Artist. I'd love to sit and pick your brain some time. If that's okay with you."

Daniels detected a slight blush on the man's cheeks.

"We're pretty busy right now, Delgado," said Daniels. "Not a lot of time for visiting."

He raised his hands. "Oh, I get it. I don't want to stop you guys from working. I just thought I'd ask."

"To be honest," said Jill, "I'm currently eating, sleeping and drinking the Makeup Artist right now. The less I can talk about him, the better."

Delgado nodded and studied his feet. “Of course. I understand. You’re dealing with a lot. I don’t blame you for not wanting to talk about him any more than you have to.”

Jill shifted forward. “But I’ll make you a deal. We crack this case and catch this guy, I’ll share a coffee with you and you can ask away.”

Delgado’s face lit up, and Daniels half expected the man to jump up and down.

“That’s great,” said Delgado. “You’ve got a deal. We’ll catch him. I know it.”

“I hope you’re right,” said Jill. “The sooner, the better.”

Delgado nodded and played with his cap.

“Better go hit up those tip line leads,” said Rem. “Maybe you’ll find something that takes us right to the bad guy.”

Delgado shot out a thumb. “I’m headed out now. A woman called who said she saw a suspicious jogger in the park near the neighborhood where our latest victim died. I’m going to go talk to her.”

“That’s great,” said Daniels. “Every little bit helps.”

Delgado nodded and put on his cap. “I’ll let you know about the promotion.”

“Sure,” said Daniels.

“Good luck,” said Jacobs.

Delgado offered her a shy smile and a wave, before he turned and left. Seeing him leave, Jacobs furrowed her brow. “Who was that guy?”

Daniels groaned. “Hopefully, not our new partner.”

“He won’t get the promo,” said Rem. “Nobody makes detective on their first try.”

“We did,” said Daniels.

“So did I,” said Jacobs.

Rem threw out a hand. “But we’re exceptions to the rules. Would you compare him to us?”

“He’s helping follow up leads on the tip line now. Probably working on his own time too,” said Daniels. “You know he’s making an impression.”

"Following up on a jogger in a park? If you had dozens of leads to follow, is that the one you'd choose?" asked Rem. He grabbed the bag of cashews. "You want anymore?" he asked Jacobs. She waved him off, and he put them in his desk drawer. "The bosses will see right through him."

"I like your optimism, but I'm not convinced." Daniels tilted his head toward Jill. "He likes her though."

"What?" asked Jacobs.

"Maybe he can partner with her," said Rem, grinning.

"The guy asked me for coffee to talk about the case," said Jacobs.

"Oh, he doesn't just want coffee. He likes you," said Daniels.

"A lot," said Rem. "I think you have an admirer on your hands."

Jacobs huffed. "I have enough as it is. I don't need another. I thought he was just being shy." She sighed. "Or maybe I hoped he was being shy." She glanced back toward the door.

"What is it?" asked Daniels. "Worried he'll come back?"

Jacobs shook her head. "No." She wrung her hands. "It's just..." She rubbed her head.

"Something wrong?" asked Rem.

She stared for a second more, then turned back to her desk. "It's nothing." She sighed and went back to the file on her desk. "Where were we?"

CHAPTER ELEVEN

Rem stopped at the head of the stairs on their way into the station. "I'm going to the head."

"Sure," said Jacobs. Her weary eyes barely looked in his direction as she pushed the door and entered the squad room.

Rem paused and waited. Watching through the glass panel on the doors, he could see Daniels sitting at his desk, writing something. He looked up as Jill sat and glancing back toward the doors, saw Rem. Rem motioned with his head and Daniels raised a brow and stood. Rem walked down the hall, out of sight.

Daniels stepped out a few seconds later, joining Rem in the hall. "What's up?" he asked. "Why are you standing out here?"

"I want to talk to you."

"Something wrong?"

Rem groaned. "It's Jacobs. This past week has been hell. She's barely slept in the last few days. I got up this morning, and she was at the kitchen table, looking at a file. Said she had a nightmare. I'm all for her helping us, but at the rate she's going she's going to collapse before the end of the week. I tried to say something, but she blows me off, and to be honest, it's getting harder and harder to hold my tongue."

Daniels expelled some air. "I know. She bit the head off the guy at the lunch counter in the cafeteria yesterday because he gave her potato chips instead of french fries." He crossed his arms. "The longer we go on this, the more stressed she gets. It's been two weeks since Schein, and I know she's acutely aware that the Artist will hit again soon. It's obviously getting to her."

"I'm guessing that's what her nightmare was about last night. She muttered something about he's watching. That she could see him watching." He put his hands on his hips. "I don't know how she can function with so little sleep and mostly coffee to keep her going. Plus, dreaming about what this guy might do next. I don't know how she held up as long as she did in Seattle."

"She said she could see him?" asked Daniels.

"Yeah. Not him exactly, but it's like she has a window through his eyes. His view is her view. I don't know whether to believe her or think she's ready for the looney bin. To be honest, just between you and me, if this is how intense she was in Seattle, I can see how others might have thought she'd lost it."

Daniels thought about it. "What do you want to do? You want to talk to Lozano?"

Rem glanced back toward the doors. "No. Not yet. If anything, we need to speak to her first. Maybe we can talk her down. I want to give her the benefit of the doubt. We need her help, but I don't want this to take her sanity, or mine, at the same time."

"You know if we want to catch this guy, she's the key. We lose her, we lose him too."

Rem sighed. "Yeah. I know." He rubbed his face. "Maybe I'm just overreacting. I haven't slept well either. We're all exhausted, and our nerves are shot."

"And she's got the most at stake," said Daniels. "Once he strikes again…"

"I know. Then things start ramping up. Especially if we stick to his script."

"Doesn't mean we can't talk to her though. Maybe she could use some support."

Rem frowned. "If she keeps snarking at me, I'm going to bite back. Support or no support, there's only so much I can take."

Daniels nodded. "I get it, but you two arguing with each other is the last thing we need right now. So do your best to show her your charming side. You've put up with me during some not so great times. I know you have it in you."

"Yeah, well, I'm stuck with you. I don't have a choice. Besides, breaking in another partner would take too much time. It took months to get you up to speed."

Daniels' face dropped. "Not only is your hair funny looking, but so is your memory. Come on, let's go or she will have another reason to snark at you."

Rem patted his head. "What's wrong with my hair?"

They walked back into the squad room, and Daniels returned to his desk and Rem sat at his. Jacobs held a cup of coffee and loomed over a file.

"You two done talking about me?" she asked without looking up.

Rem glanced at Daniels. He debated being honest or just making a joke. "We are," he answered.

There was a pause. "You want me to go?" she asked, still looking down.

"No," said Daniels. "Do you want to go?"

"No," she answered. "Not yet, anyway." She sipped her coffee.

Daniels nodded. "Okay."

Rem debated saying more but chose not to. Now wasn't the time. "Okay."

Lozano burst through his office door. "We've got another one. East side of town."

They all stood. "Where?" asked Rem.

"I'll text you the address. Just keep me informed."

Nodding, Rem followed Jacobs and Daniels out the door.

**

Arriving at the scene, they saw the press vans.

"Shit. They're already here," said Daniels, parking beside a police cruiser.

Jacobs surveyed the scene. A small crowd of onlookers had gathered in front of a yellow-framed house with white shingles and a small picket fence around the yard. Police officers were putting up tape to keep onlookers back as the three of them exited the car. Her heart thumped as her memories swirled, recalling the case in Seattle when she'd first made an appearance. It was much like this, a cute house, press converging, and people watching. It was an eerie sensation to step into, and she took a second to center herself. Stepping onto the curb, she walked over, and flashing her credentials to access the scene, she studied the house. This would be her first foray back into an active crime scene since Seattle. It was one thing to view a place where a previous crime had occurred, but another to step into a location where the victim still lay, and where the perpetrator had been, possibly only hours before.

Approaching the home, she stopped at the bottom of the stairs. Police milled about outside, careful not to disturb the area. The forensics team had arrived, and she could see them inside, taking pictures. She thought about the fourth victim in Seattle and steeled herself.

"You need a minute?" asked Rem, standing beside her.

Some part of her wanted to tell him to stop babying her, that she was just fine, but she hesitated. She'd been pushing herself so hard the last couple of weeks, dreading this eventual moment, and she'd taken out her frustrations on him. "I'm fine. Let's go."

She followed them up the stairs. Someone gave her a pair of gloves and coverings for her shoes, and she put them on.

"Check that out," said Daniels, as he put on a glove.

Jill saw Ethan Delgado down near the crowd. He was talking to another officer, but he was staring up at the house.

"Back again," said Rem.

"He's persistent," said Daniels.

"Guess he didn't get the promotion," said Rem.

A man stepped out onto the porch. He wore a wrinkled suit and had puffy eyes. "What we got, Bill?" asked Rem.

"She's in the hallway, just outside the kitchen. Same thing as before. Stabbed, make-up on her face, body posed."

"Got an ID?" asked Daniels.

He pulled out a pad. "Melanie Dentz. Thirty years of age. Married. One child, a son, ten years old. Was staying at his grandparents for the weekend. Husband was away on a business trip. Found her this morning when he got home."

Jill glanced inside the house. "Where is he?"

He scratched his stubbled jaw. "I had Tony take him to the station. I didn't want the press getting in his face. And he needed to not be here."

Jill nodded. "Do we know what she did for a living?"

Bill checked his pad again. "Husband said she was a financial analyst. Worked for a firm downtown."

"Not an accountant, but close enough," said Rem.

"Married, too, just like the Rebecca Molina in Seattle," said Jill.

"Who?" asked Bill.

"The fourth vic in Seattle," said Daniels. When Bill frowned, Daniels waved him off. "Never mind."

Bill stepped aside. "It's all yours. Be careful where you step. Oh, and there's more writing in the john."

Rem entered with Daniels and Jill followed. Flowered curtains and a yellow sofa sat against a soft green wall in the front room. Pictures on the coffee table depicted a smiling man and woman, with a little boy standing with them in front of a mossy waterfall.

There was a small dining area to the left with framed artwork on the walls. The kitchen extended beyond the dining room. A plate with crumbs sat in the sink, and there was a fork and knife beside it. Jill stepped beyond the kitchen and saw the hallway. On the ground lay the body, posed as all the others. Blood discolored the walls and carpet and her blood-spattered dark hair was splayed out behind her. Her arms were crossed over her chest and red lipstick and blush were crudely painted on her lips and cheeks.

The impact of the scene hit Jill in the chest, and she sucked in a breath. She recalled her nightmare from the previous night. With her own eyes, she'd seen herself stalking this woman. She hadn't been able to recall the specifics, but seeing the victim now, it came back in stark detail. This woman had been getting ready for bed, and he'd been watching. Jill had seen it, and she'd been unable to stop it.

She moved closer, hating every second, but doing it anyway. Flashes of the victim's pain and fear tore through her, and her anger rose. How could anyone derive a moment of satisfaction from doing this to someone?

"Hell," said Daniels.

"How is he doing this?" asked Rem. He looked around. "No signs of struggle, just like the others."

Jill steeled herself, her stomach gurgling. "He's already in the house. He's waiting." She recalled her dream. "He watches her get undressed. He knows she's alone. He's in no hurry. She takes a shower, puts on a nightgown. Maybe comes out here to get a late-night snack or watch some TV, and he strikes. She barely has time to scream." She stepped away from the body, closing her eyes and trying to breathe normally before opening them again. "I need to see the writing."

The hallway led to the bathroom down the hall. A technician stood outside taking photos, and he moved aside as Jacobs entered. The bathroom was small, but it had a shower with a tub. The curtain had been pulled aside, and Jill saw the rose first, laying in the tub, beneath letters scrawled in blood. *I see you, JJ.* And beneath that, *It's time to play.*

Jill stood beside the tub, staring at the ugly red letters. Some part of her wanted to reach out and touch the blood, smearing it with her fingers. Would that help her find him? Would it somehow provide her with the elusive connection that would lead her to the killer?

Realizing she was only feeling what the killer felt as he wrote the words, she ignored the urge. But the bathroom suddenly felt intensely small, and the nausea bubbled up in her belly. “Excuse me.” She pushed past Rem and Daniels and went back down the hall and out onto the front porch, breathing gulps of fresh air. She needed to clear her head. The energy had been thick with the killer’s presence, and she had an intense feeling that he’d been in her head, too, watching her as she’d watched him, and she had to get him out.

Her stomach settled, and she sat on a chair on the porch, wondering what to do next. The crowd had increased out front as had the press, but the officers had pushed them further back. She didn’t see Delgado. Hearing footsteps, she turned to see Rem and Daniels join her on the porch.

“How are you?” asked Rem.

“Better,” she said. “It was getting a little claustrophobic in there.”

“No kidding,” said Daniels. “Hard to breathe.”

Rem scanned the crowd. “What do you want to do now?’

Jacobs rubbed her forehead. “I don’t know. Maybe grab a drink. Something stronger than a soda.”

Rem made a half-smile. “Tempting.”

“You gonna do what he wants?” asked Daniels. “You gonna play the game?”

Jacobs knew what he meant. It was after the third victim in Seattle that she’d given her heated interview to the press that had resulted in garnering the killer’s attention. She hadn’t done that for the third victim here, so she didn’t doubt that the killer would expect it now. The closer he could get her to the script, the better. She closed her eyes.

“We’ll do whatever you want to do. It’s your call,” said Rem.

Jill opened her eyes, seeing the news vans and reporters. All she had to do was walk down the stairs, cross the street, and find a microphone. But what would that accomplish? It hadn’t worked in Seattle, and there was no reason for her to believe it would work here. Why should she play his game?

She stood. “You guys see enough?”

“All I care to see for a while,” said Daniels.

She nodded. “Me, too. Let’s go.” She walked down the stairs and passed the press.

“Any comments, detectives? Can you confirm it’s the Makeup Artist?” She heard the yelled inquiries, but she ignored them.

“You sure about this?” asked Rem.

She kept walking. “I am. He wants to play this game? Let him, but I don’t have to play along. He can go f- himself.” With one last glance at the reporters, she got in the car.

CHAPTER TWELVE

They spent the next three days learning all they could about Melanie Dentz. They talked to neighbors and friends, tracked her movements prior to her death, and interviewed her husband. They'd even called local florists to see if they could determine the origin of the red rose. Like the others, nothing stood out that provided a major clue. The lab was still working on the evidence gathered at the scene, but they had no reason to believe they would discover anything new.

After grabbing a quick lunch, they returned to the station, tired and disappointed.

Daniels threw his jacket over his chair. "Anybody check in with Georgios? He and Titus were going to talk to Dentz's sister and coworkers today."

Rem popped open a bottle of aspirin. "Nope. Not a word." He dropped two tablets in his palm and offered the bottle. "Anybody else?"

Jacobs reached for it. "Please."

Rem handed her the aspirin and popped the pills in his mouth, following it with some water. "I am exhausted. I can barely see straight."

Daniels headed for the coffee machine. "I'll make a fresh pot."

"Thanks," said Rem. "You want to talk to the Cap now or later?"

"What's the point?" asked Jacobs. "We have nothing new to tell him. This case has stalled just like before. We're going in circles." She sat and rubbed her temples.

Rem paced behind his seat. "This is crazy that we can't get a single thing on this guy." He stopped and looked at Jacobs. "You still think it was a good idea not to do the interview with the press?" asked Rem.

Jacobs flattened her hands on the table. "What does that mean?"

Daniels added the grounds to the filter and flipped on the coffee machine. He stifled a yawn. "There's no point in second guessing anything at this point."

Jacobs' eyes widened. "You're saying I should have done it?"

Rem picked up a file. "I'm simply asking if *you* think you should have."

Jacobs tensed. "It sounds like you're saying a lot more than that."

"Guys, c'mon…" said Daniels.

"I'm just thinking if you had done it, maybe…" Rem dropped the file back on his desk.

"Maybe what?" asked Jacobs.

Rem ran a hand through his hair. "I don't know. Maybe he'd keep playing. If you don't play, then he won't either. For all we know, he'll go off script, and we won't know what to expect."

"You think knowing what to expect will make any difference?" asked Jacobs, her voice pitching higher. "We knew what to expect with Melanie Dentz. I don't see us cracking this open based on that."

The coffee percolated. "Listen," said Daniels. "We're all tired—"

"How do you know what would have happened?" asked Rem. "If you'd gone up there, gotten in his face, said something to piss him off, maybe he would have reached out—"

"Rem…" said Daniels.

Jacobs dropped her jaw. "Is that what you want? You want him to start that shit with me? Is that what you're waiting for?"

Rem shoved his chair into his desk and it banged against the top drawer. “I don’t know what I’m waiting for,” he yelled. “Anything other than this bullshit.”

Jacobs yelled back. “You think I like this bullshit any more than you? You brought me back into this bullshit. If it hadn’t been for you…”

Rem pointed a thumb at himself. “I didn’t do shit. You didn’t have to do anything you didn’t want to do.”

Lozano stepped out of his office.

“Guys,” said Daniels.

Jacobs narrowed her eyes. “You son-of-a-bitch.”

Her phone rang, but she ignored it. “What happened to ‘We’ll have your back no matter what?’” She snorted. “I guess that was only as long as Rem got his beauty sleep.”

Rem slapped his hand on his desk. “Don’t talk to me about beauty sleep. I bust my butt just as much as anyone else.” He pointed a finger. “I just wonder about you and your decision making. Maybe there is something to those stories—”

“Rem,” yelled Daniels and Lozano at the same time.

The phone kept ringing. Jacobs stood there, breathing hard, her face red, but flat. When the phone rang again, she swiped at it, picking it up. “What?” she snapped.

Rem cursed and shot out a hand, knocking a pencil and some papers off his desk.

Lozano walked up. “What the hell is going on here?”

Daniels stepped closer. “We’re okay. Just a little frayed with fatigue. Right?” He stared at Rem, who seemed to be pulling it together.

Rem closed his eyes, took a breath, and blew it out. He opened his eyes. “Sorry, Cap. I lost it. I…” He stopped, his eyes alert.

Daniels looked to see what had his attention and saw Jacobs, listening into the phone, her face now pale. She pointed to the receiver. “I’m here,” she said, her voice quiet. Sitting, she bit her lip. “What do you want?”

Rem grabbed for the phone on his desk and hit some numbers. He listened for a second until someone picked up. "Charlie. I need a trace on extension 7001. Now."

**

Jill focused on her breathing. Everything had gone ice cold when she'd heard the familiar voice, and her mouth was so dry it was hard to speak. Although some part of her had known this time would come, she still was not mentally prepared for it. Memories of Seattle swirled.

"Did you miss me JJ?" he asked. "It's been a long time." His voice was deep and scratchy, and she'd never known if that was his way of disguising it, or if it was his real voice.

She steadied herself. "No. I didn't miss you."

"You sound nervous. Why? We've known each other a long time now."

She saw Rem on the phone. He grabbed a piece of paper and started writing. "I wasn't expecting your call." Rem handed the paper to Daniels.

He chuckled, and chills broke out on her skin. "I know. The game says I don't call until after number five. But you didn't play by the rules, so neither did I."

She swallowed. She had a vague awareness that Daniels was dictating to Dispatch the address that Rem had given him. They would send police to the location.

"I didn't want to play by the rules," she responded. Rem circled his finger, indicating to keep him on the line. "I played by the rules last time and look where it got me."

Rem reached over and hit the speaker button, so they could hear the call. She put down the headset. Her fingers trembled, and she squeezed them into a fist.

His voice traveled into the squad room, which was luckily quiet. “You weren’t playing by the rules then; you were making them. You’re the one who started this. Now you need to play.”

Her body felt like a block of ice. “I’m here, aren’t I? I don’t have to be.”

She could hear his breath over the line. “You are wherever I want you to be. Don’t you know that by now?”

She bit her bottom lip so hard, it surprised her it wasn’t bleeding. “I don’t have to stay.”

He paused. “I don’t have to play either. I could walk away. But I won’t. Because I like you JJ. And I’ll follow wherever you go. But I need you to play by the rules.”

Her stomach constricted. “What if I don’t?”

He sighed. “You won’t like the consequences. You know what I’m capable of. By the way, I like the new digs. Is Officer Remalla a good roommate?”

She held her breath, feeling the blood leave her face, and offered a worried glance at Rem, who nodded, encouraging her to keep going. “I don’t want to talk about that.”

“Then play by the rules,” he said, his voice curt. “I’d hate for something to happen to another policeman. You understand?”

She didn’t know how to respond.

“Do you understand?” he asked curtly.

“I do,” she said.

“Good. It was nice to hear your voice, JJ. I look forward to talking again soon. And please offer my hellos to your partners listening in. I look forward to playing with them too.”

There was a click, and the line went dead.

Daniels remained on the phone as he waited to hear what happened as the patrols arrived on the scene.

Jill let go of a held breath, trying to stay calm. She sat and put her head in her hands. She’d forgotten how frightening it was to talk to him. Her hands continued to shake.

"You okay?" asked Rem.

"No," she said. "And please stop asking me that."

"A patrol is at the address," said Daniels, listening. "It's a corner drugstore on a busy street. They're checking it out."

"Tell them to check the trash cans outside the store," said Jill. "He uses burner cells and dumps them when he's done. Then he walks away."

Daniels paused, but then repeated her instructions over the phone. They waited to hear the outcome. Jill wanted to go to the bathroom and throw up, but she pushed through it.

After a few minutes, they patched Daniels in to an officer at the scene. Daniels spoke to him and hung up. "They got nothing. He's gone. They found a cell in the trash on the corner. They'll grab it for fingerprints."

Jill stared off. "They won't find any. They never do."

"I'm requesting a detail to watch your house," said Lozano to Rem. "I want somebody out there around the clock."

"Cap…" said Rem.

"Don't argue with me," said Lozano. "I'll have that phone call pulled. They should have recorded it. And I'll make sure that extension gets traced, so we'll be ready next time he calls."

Jill barely heard him. She rose from her desk. "I'm getting out of here, Cap. It's been a long day." She pulled her purse out of a drawer.

"That's fine," said Lozano. "You all need a break. Go home early. I'll send Mel and Garcia to the drugstore."

"I'll get the car," said Rem. "Pick you up out front."

Jill held out a hand. "No thanks. I'll get my own ride." She turned.

"Jacobs—," said Rem. "Listen…what I said…"

She looked back. "Forget it."

"I was pissed," he said.

"You got what you wanted. He called, and I'm back on the radar. You should be happy. You and Daniels can pop some champagne. But forgive me if I don't celebrate with you."

"You going home?" asked Daniels.

"Home?" she asked. "I wouldn't call it that, but no I'm not going to the house." She pushed the door to the squad room open. "I'm just getting the hell out of here."

"You need to tell us where you'll be," said Daniels. "You know he could be watching."

She stopped and turned before the door closed. "What does it matter, as long as I'm playing the game, right?"

They didn't answer, and she turned and left.

CHAPTER THIRTEEN

Rem sat on the couch, looking at his watch for the hundredth time. It was after ten o'clock, and Jacobs had not yet returned. He understood she needed some space, and his behavior earlier had not helped, but she was the object of a serial killer's attention, and she should have checked in by now. He'd texted her, but she hadn't answered.

He'd had dinner with Daniels and Marjorie, over at Daniels' place. Marjorie waddled and held her belly like she could deliver at any moment, but she still had a few weeks to go. Rem hadn't stayed long. He wanted to be home when Jacobs returned. He needed to apologize and know she was okay.

Thinking of the phone call from the killer, Rem stood and looked out the window. The police cruiser sat on the other side of the street. It had arrived about an hour ago, and although Rem didn't think they were any safer, there was still some comfort in knowing someone was watching. It made Daniels feel better, too. The phone call had unsettled them both and had given Rem a little more insight into what Jacobs had dealt with in Seattle, which made him feel like an even bigger jackass after his outburst.

He was about to step away from the window when headlights flashed. A car drove up the driveway and Rem watched as Jacobs got out, closed the door, and the car backed out and left. Relief flooded through him.

He went back to the couch and sat, glancing at the TV. An old western was on and the sound was low, but Rem could still appreciate John Wayne galloping on his horse across a stark but beautiful landscape.

The front door opened and closed, and Rem saw Jacobs throw her purse on a table in the entry. She glanced over at him.

"Glad you came back," he said.

"It's been a long day. I'm going to bed," she said, as she turned away.

"Hey, wait a minute."

She stopped, her back to him. "What?"

He stood. "Can you come here for a second? We need to talk."

She hesitated. "There's nothing to say. Let's just forget about it."

"I don't want to forget about it. That's not how I work." She didn't move. "Five minutes. Give me that much. If you still hate me then, I can live with it."

Her shoulders raised as she sighed. "Fine." She turned and walked to the couch.

Rem noticed her red-rimmed and puffy eyes. It was obvious she'd been crying. He sat beside her. "I'm a gigantic idiot."

She shook her head. "No, you're not. You're frustrated and—"

"Shut up and let me finish. I got angry, and I took it out on you, the last person who needs it. I should have punched Daniels instead." He swiveled toward her. "I apologize. What I said was cruel. I told you I'd back you up no matter what and I will, but I get a little hot-headed sometimes."

She hung her head. "I haven't exactly been easy to deal with either. I've been on edge, knowing he was getting ready to strike again and expecting the worst. I know I haven't been an easy roommate." She squeezed her temples. "I can be a little tough to deal with when I'm stressed."

"You have every right to be upset. I couldn't really appreciate what you'd dealt with until today, so I'm sorry for what I said and did."

She nodded. "Apology accepted."

"You're sure? You're not just saying that to get me out of your hair?"

She sniffed. "No. I'm not. We're good."

"Great. Thank you. But now I'm going to bitch at you for going off on your own like that and not telling us where you were. I texted you several times and so did Daniels. You've got a serial killer after you, in case you've forgotten. I almost called Lozano to send out the cavalry. Where the hell did you go?"

She stared at her shoes. "The Artist is not going to touch me. Not yet, anyway."

"I don't care. You don't go off on your own. You should know better. You have no idea what he might do next."

Tears sprang into her eyes.

Rem leaned closer. "What's wrong? Did something happen?" He reached over and grabbed a tissue off the box on the side table. "Here."

She took it and dabbed her eyes. "I'm fine."

"No, you're not fine. What is it? Did he contact you again?"

"No." She wiped her nose. "Nothing like that." She pushed her hair off her face. "When I left, I just walked for a while. After our argument and the phone call, I didn't know what to think. I considered leaving again, but then changed my mind. I found a bar and did two shots of tequila, but they made me sick and I couldn't keep them down." She wiped a teary eye. "I sat in a booth and ordered some French fries, but I couldn't eat. I started looking around, wondering if he was watching me, thinking he probably was. The more I thought about it, the more upset I became. I ended up calling my dad."

"You called your father?"

She nodded, and her lip quivered. "I don't have much in the way of friends after Seattle. No one likes to hang around a stalked woman, no matter how well you know her. I just needed to talk. Tell someone what was happening. I don't know why I thought dad could help."

"He's your father."

She played with the tissue. "He's not the touchy feely type. He got mad at me. Told me I'm the one that got myself into this mess, and I should have listened to him years ago. If I had, I wouldn't be dealing with this."

A tear trickled down her cheek, and Rem fought the urge to wipe it away. "I take it back. He's the idiot, not me."

"I hung up on him, and called my older brother, Brian. He wouldn't take my call." Her breathing hitched, and fresh tears spilled from her lashes. "My own family has pushed me away." She dropped her head and held it.

Rem's heart ached for her. He slid close and put his arm around her, then pulled her into him. Her head fell into his shoulder, and he let her cry.

"What am I going to do?" she said between sobs.

"What about your younger brother?"

She sniffed again. "I can't reach him."

He rubbed her arm. "Well, screw them. I know I didn't exactly help things earlier, but you can talk to me or Daniels. We're always available to listen. Especially now."

She wiped her face. "I don't want to burden you with my problems. We're already so strung out as it is."

"Don't worry about that. We're all going to need to be here for one another. If you have to listen to me bitch, I can certainly let you cry it out once in a while. My shoulder can handle it."

Her breath caught, and she sobbed against his neck. His heart sinking, he held her closer.

Gaining a little composure, she cleared her throat. "I promise I won't do this every day."

He chuckled. "Good. My shoulder will be fine, but I don't know about all that snot on my shirts. That's a lot of laundry." He heard her laugh softly, and she seemed calmer. "You feeling a little better?"

She pulled back and dabbed her wet cheeks with the tissue. "I still don't know what to do."

He considered what to say. "I'll tell you what we'll do. We'll take it one day at a time." He made sure to emphasize *we.*

She shook. "I can't ask you to risk your life for me. I did that once, and it cost me everything."

"I signed up to catch a killer. Just like you did. That's our job. If we don't do it, who will?"

"But if I don't do what he says…" A fresh sob bubbled up.

"He's pushing your buttons. Forcing you to do what he wants. You need to decide how you want to handle it."

"I don't know if I can."

"Then we'll help. Daniels and I will talk it through with you. We're a team, remember?"

"I wasn't sure after today. I thought you might want me to leave."

He closed his eyes, angry at himself. "I'll be honest. It wasn't my first outburst and it won't be my last. I'm going to have my moments on this case, just like you. But I will never turn my back on you. You got that? No matter what."

"You don't know that. You heard him on the phone. He mentioned you. If something happens…"

"If something happens, then we'll deal with it. Anyone of us could lose our lives in this job. It could be because of the Makeup Artist, a domestic violence call, or chasing a perp down the street. And if it did, I wouldn't blame the abused spouse or the guy who got robbed. Daniels and I have just as much choice in this as you. We wouldn't stay if we didn't want to."

She remained quiet, but the crying had slowed. "I'll be honest. I'm not sure how much of this I can take. The first time was bad enough."

He rested his elbows on his knees. "I get it. And I know the pressure will only mount the further we go on this thing. Which is why it's important we talk to each other. If it's getting to be too much, let us know. I promise to do the same. We can't afford to snipe at each other. That gives him the edge."

"He knows it too."

"Which is why we can't let him get to us."

She sighed deeply. "So we take it one day at a time."

He reached over and took her hand. "One day at a time."

She squeezed his fingers. Her eyes were red, but the tears had stopped. They stared for a second before she glanced back at the TV. "Don't tell me. You're a John Wayne fan, too?"

"The Duke? Who's not a fan of the Duke?"

She smiled. "*True Grit* is a favorite of mine."

He raised a brow. "Then there's still hope. All is not lost." Feeling the warmth of her hand in his, he let go of her and sat back. "This is *Rio Bravo*. Have you seen it?"

"No."

He picked up the remote and hit pause. "Well then, if you're up for it, we'll watch for a bit, before we crash for the night. Have you eaten?"

"No."

He stood. "Then go get your butt comfortable. I'm making hot dogs and popcorn."

"Didn't you eat already?"

He checked his watch. "That was three hours ago. I'm due for my snack."

"You don't have to—"

He headed toward the kitchen but stopped. "Don't argue with me. You need to eat. Now go wash up and change and I'll meet you back at the sofa."

"Rem," she said as he continued and flipped on the kitchen light.

He turned back and saw her standing beside the sofa. "What?" he asked.

She walked into the hallway. "Thank you," she said. "For pulling me back from the edge. I was close to falling off."

As she stood there looking at him, with her hair ruffled and tear-stained cheeks, his heart thumped, and he winked at her. "Anytime." He flexed a bicep. "I've got strong arms, so I'm good at holding on."

She smiled. "Sorry about the snot on your shirt."

He glanced at the damp fabric. "Nothing a little detergent won't fix." They held the glance for a second. "Go get changed. I'll start the dogs."

She nodded, and he watched her walk away.

CHAPTER FOURTEEN

The next morning, Jill sat in Lozano's office with Rem and Daniels on either side of her. They were due to meet with him, but he'd been detained at a meeting. Wishing she'd caught more sleep, she yawned.

"What time did you two finally hit the hay?" asked Daniels. "Don't tell me you pulled an all-night John Wayne marathon."

"We were in bed by eleven. We barely made it to the end of our hot dogs," said Rem. He glanced at Jill. "I even told you to sleep-in a little. Did you get any rest?"

Jill swallowed a sip of fresh coffee, trying to wake up. "I fell asleep fine until the dreams started."

"You have another nightmare?" asked Rem.

Jill shook her head. "Not so much a nightmare, but still unsettling. Makes it hard to sleep. It's happened before. The deeper I get into this, the more I dream."

"About what?" asked Daniels. He cracked open a green juice bottle he carried.

"Sometimes it's nightmares. I become the victim and I'm attacked. Or it's me in my home being chased by the killer. Those are the worst. But there are others that are less intense, but almost just as disturbing. Like last night, I dreamed about faces."

"Faces?" asked Rem. "Just faces?"

Jill put her cup on the arm of the chair, remembering. "Yes. I see victim's faces, my family's faces, yours, Lozano's. They all swirl around and it's like I have to watch all of them, not let any disappear, which is hard enough, but there are other faces, too."

Daniels leaned forward. "What others?"

Jill rubbed the bridge of her nose. "I don't know. I don't recognize them. But yet they're important." She paused. "I think it's victims."

"Victims?" asked Rem. "You mean others he's killed?"

"No," she said, sighing. "I think it's his future victims. That's what's so hard. I think I'm seeing their faces. I think I see his face, too."

Daniels face furrowed. "Have you had this dream before?"

"Yes. I had it in Seattle. More than once."

"You're sure it's future faces?" asked Rem. "How do you know it's not a victim from his early years?"

"Because," she picked up her coffee, "when I see them, they're alive and well. They're laughing and smiling. Happy. When I dream about past victims, they're already dead."

"You ever thought about going to a sketch artist? Getting the image on paper?" asked Daniels.

"That would be great," said Jill, "if I could remember them. I wake up and they're a distant memory. I can't recall any detail." She moaned. "It's incredibly frustrating."

Daniels sat back, rubbing his jaw.

"What about hypnosis?" asked Rem. "I've heard that's helped others remember things."

"Tried it," said Jill. "Nothing happened. All I saw was pizza and beer while the shrink talked. Guess I was hungry at the time."

"Or maybe you were seeing Rem in your future," said Daniels, drinking his juice. "Was he holding any Mallomars?"

"Or hot dogs?" asked Rem.

"Not that I recall," said Jill.

"Lord, help me," said Daniels, capping his drink.

Rem grimaced. "He'll need to after drinking that green stuff." He scanned Lozano's desk and the floor. "Where's my chocolate milk?"

"You left it on the desk," said Daniels. "But I'll share my juice with you."

Rem stuck out his tongue in disgust. "I'd rather be Delgado's partner."

"That can be arranged," said Daniels.

Lozano stepped into his office, munching an apple. "Sorry I'm late. The chief held me up. The latest bank robbery yesterday added more to the plate."

"How's the teller?" asked Daniels. "I heard he was injured."

"Took a shot to the shoulder," said Lozano. "He's stable though. Should be fine."

"These robberies are getting more frequent, and the robbers are getting bolder," said Daniels.

Lozano sat at his desk and wiped his brow. "They are. We need to catch these guys soon before they kill someone. Between them and the Artist, I may end up divorced - again." He took another bite of his apple.

"Back on the diet, Cap?" asked Rem.

Lozano frowned while he chewed. "I never went off it."

"That's funny," said Rem. "I swear I saw you eating a—"

Lozano swallowed. "And I swear you told me you were gonna get that hair of yours cut last month. Regulation says it needs to be above your collar. I could write you up now if you'd like, or would you rather talk about my food?" He put the apple down and crossed his arms.

Remalla slunk down in his seat. "Do I have to choose?"

"I think he'd rather talk about this case," said Daniels. "We can worry about food and hair later."

"Excellent idea," said Lozano, grumbling. "Now, where are we?"

"No fingerprints on the burner phone, but we're trying to track down where it was bought. Forensics is studying the phone call, seeing if there's anything on it that might provide some clues," said Daniels.

"But he didn't give us his address, so that's a bust," said Rem.

"Georgios and Titus are at the drugstore, asking around again to see if anyone saw anything yesterday," said Daniels.

Lozano swallowed the bite of apple. "What about you?" he asked Jill. "You decide how you want to handle this?"

Jill remembered the phone call. "You mean do I want to play by the rules?"

"Yes."

She thought about it. "I don't know. On one hand, if I do, then we have a better sense of what's coming, what to look for. It's more predictable."

"Safer, I suppose, if we know what to expect," said Rem.

She nodded at him, remembering crying into his shoulder. "Yes."

"Nothing wrong with that," said Daniels.

"But if I don't go along, then it forces him outside the box. It pushes his buttons. Makes him angry. Which means it's more likely he'll screw up and make a mistake."

"But it's more dangerous," said Rem. "He could go off the reservation."

"Exactly," said Jill. "If I piss him off, there's no telling what he could do, or where it could lead. He already made a veiled threat when he mentioned Rem in that call."

"Don't worry about me," said Rem. "I can take care of myself."

Jill tensed. "And that's exactly what leads to your death. You get cocky, and he takes advantage."

"I'm not cocky. I'm confident," said Rem. "There's a difference."

Jill's heart pounded, and she held a hard stare at Rem. "That's exactly what Henderson would have said."

Daniels tapped his fingers on the arm of his chair. "I don't like it."

Rem broke the look with Jill. "I don't like it either, but maybe that's what we need. Maybe we need to push him. See what happens when we don't stick to the script."

"You have an idea?" asked Lozano. Picking up the apple, he took a last bite and threw the core into the trash.

Rem leaned forward. “I think he mentioned me for a reason. I don’t think he likes that Jill moved in with me. Maybe we should up the ante.”

“You mean make it look like you’re more than roommates?” asked Daniels.

“Absolutely not,” said Jill, standing.

“Why not?” asked Rem. “Maybe if he gets provoked enough, he’ll stop killing women—”

“And kill you instead,” said Jill. “No. No way.”

“What do you think?” Rem asked Daniels. “You think it has merit?”

Daniels gripped his juice. “I don’t like you making yourself a target, but I see your point.”

“What makes you think he’ll go for you at all?” asked Lozano. “He may not care that you’re living with Jacobs. He’s probably just using that to get to her.”

Rem tipped his head. “Maybe. Maybe not. But something tells me I’m not his favorite right now.”

“There’s no way I’m going for this.” Jill paced, waving her hands. “Not after...” Her throat stuck, and she couldn’t form the words.

“Not after what?” asked Daniels.

She didn’t answer, but her mind whirled. Images of Seattle flashed through her mind. Coming home late, rose petals on the floor. The smell of cologne. Then the blood. All the blood.

“Jacobs?” asked Rem.

The door opened, and Georgios stuck his head in. “Sorry to interrupt, Cap, but we got a lead.”

Lightheaded, Jill sat in her chair, thankful for the interruption. She could feel Rem’s stare on her, but she didn’t look up.

“What is it?” asked Lozano.

“Talked to a lady walking by the drugstore yesterday. She saw a guy on a cell outside the store about the right time as our call. Said she noticed him because she admired his jacket. Thought her grandson might like it, but when she went to ask him where he bought it, he blew her off. She got a good look at him though.”

“Can she meet with a sketch artist?” asked Daniels, swiveling in his seat.

“Pierce is already on his way. She’s sittin’ outside the squad room, waiting. I got her a coffee.”

Jill took slow, steady breaths and tried to put Seattle out of her mind.

“That’s great work, Georgios. When will Pierce get here?” asked Lozano as he stood from his desk.

“About thirty minutes.”

“What’s her name?” asked Rem.

He studied a notepad in his hand. “Sonia Vandermere. Interesting lady.”

“How so?” asked Daniels.

“She’s a bit of a gypsy. Wears a lot of robes and jewelry. Makes her own creams and lotions. A little out there.” He paused. “You’d probably like her, Jacobs.”

Jill heard the sarcasm, but she let it go. She stood, feeling stronger. “She sounds interesting. I hope she has a good memory.”

“How did you find her?” asked Rem.

Lozano put on his jacket. “I’d like to meet her.”

“Just good ole’ detective work,” said Georgios. “Hitting the pavement. That’s typically what solves cases in the long run. Don’t you think?”

Jill caught the slight again. This man obviously did not like her. She reached for her coffee cup. “I know I think you’re an asshole,” she muttered under her breath.

“What was that?” asked Georgios, his brow rising.

Jill straightened. “I said I think that’s wonderful,” she replied, as Daniels smiled. She glanced at the Cap. “I’d like to meet her too.”

Georgios frowned, but she walked past him, following the Captain. Stepping outside Lozano’s office, they walked through the squad room. Once outside the station’s door, she saw an older woman, probably around sixty, sitting in a chair. She was as Georgios described. She wore a printed purple dress that reached her ankles. A sash cinched the dress at her slightly round waist and long necklaces with various stones of different colors and sizes hung from her neck. Large rings with similar stones were on her fingers, and a hair band held back her shoulder-length, black-dyed hair with a hint of silver at the roots. She wore no makeup, but her blue eyes were bright and shiny, and she smiled as the Captain approached.

Georgios made the introductions. The woman stood and shook everyone's hand. Reaching Jill, she paused slightly, keeping her hand in hers.

Jill felt a strange tingle in her fingers. "Do I know you, Ms. Vandermere?" she asked.

The woman let go of her. "Oh, no, dear. We've never met. But I'm glad we have now. And please, call me Sonia."

Jill nodded, wondering about the woman's strange vibe.

"We just want to thank you for your time, ma'am, and appreciate you coming down here to help," said Lozano.

"I certainly hope I can," said Sonia. "Your detective seems to think the man on the phone outside the store may be of some importance. Did he do something illegal?"

"We think so," said Rem. "It's important we find him as soon as possible."

"What did he look like?" asked Daniels.

Sonia played with a necklace. "He was a nice-looking man. Sort of a brooding Edward Norton, but taller, and not quite as attractive."

"Edward Norton?" asked Lozano.

"He's an actor, Cap.," said Rem.

Lozano grunted. "I see."

"All I wanted to know is where he got his jacket. It was this lovely chocolate brown leather, with a pop-up collar. Very James Dean."

"He's another actor, Cap," said Rem.

"I know James Dean, Remalla," said Lozano.

"Is there anything else we can get you while you wait?" asked Daniels. "Our sketch artist shouldn't be more than thirty minutes."

She threw out a ringed hand. "Oh, poo. Don't worry about me. And don't worry about the time. I've don't have to be anywhere important." She eyed Daniels' gray leather jacket. "Now that's nice too. You look very Steve McQueen."

"That's another ac—" started Rem.

"Be quiet," said Lozano, with a grunt. "Unless you'd like me to call my barber. I can get you an appointment within the hour."

Rem's face dropped.

"Ma'am…I mean Sonia," said Jill, peering down the hall. "Why don't we have you wait somewhere else instead of the hall." She spied an empty interview room. If this woman really knew what the killer looked like, she wanted to keep her safely tucked away where they could keep an eye on her. "I think you'll be more comfortable there."

"I agree," said Lozano. He gestured down the hall. "You can take this one here."

"Oh, I'm comfortable anywhere, but all right." She picked up her large, purple and white fabric purse, and followed Lozano to the closest room. Jill noticed she left her coffee behind. She picked it up and brought it into the room.

"Have a seat, Ms. Vandermere," said Rem, pulling out a chair. "Are you sure we can't get you something while you wait? There's an excellent candy machine down the hall. I can personally vouch for the Heath Bar."

She stopped before sitting. "You're so sweet," she said. "You're more the Errol Flynn type, aren't you? Dashing and handsome." She eyed Daniels. "Don't you think so?"

"I was thinking more like Mr. Bean," said Daniels, his face flat.

Rem smirked. "You're just jealous, McQueen."

Sonia clasped her hands together. "Oh, I loved Mr. Bean. I watched him on that British TV station every weekend. He was so funny and entertaining. I bet you are like him, aren't you, Detective?" Sonia asked Rem.

"Oh, Lord," said Daniels. "I can't win."

"We'll be with you as soon as we can," said Lozano. "We'll be right outside." He walked to the door and Jill followed Rem and Daniels behind him. She still held the coffee, but had the impulse to throw it out. Without thinking, she dropped it in the trashcan beside the door.

Sonia sat. "Dear," she reached out her hand toward Jill. "Would you mind sitting with me for a while? I'm not a fan of being by myself."

Jill paused. "Sure, I'd be happy to stay with you." She sat in the seat beside Sonia.

"We'll let you know as soon as we're ready," said Daniels.

"Thank you, dear," said Sonia with a wave, and Daniels closed the door behind him and Remalla as they left.

Jill fidgeted in her seat and started to ask a question when Sonia reached over and touched her on the wrist. "So, tell me, my dear," she said. "How long have you had the sight?"

CHAPTER FIFTEEN

A chill crept up Jill's spine. "Excuse me?" she asked.

"The sight," said Sonia. She patted Jill's wrist. "You know what I mean."

Jill narrowed her eyes. Who was this woman? For a moment, she wondered if this was an elaborate joke put on by Georgios and Titus. Would they go that far?

Sonia shook her head. "No. I'm not joking. I wouldn't be that cruel." She sat back. "But unfortunately, sometimes people like us have to put up with cruel people. I'm sure you know what I mean."

Jill bit her bottom lip, uncertain of what to say. She'd learned to be careful of whom to trust.

"I could sense it the moment I touched your hand. You see things you don't want to see. Feel and know things about others you'd rather not know. You've done a good job of denying it for a long time, but you can't deny it any longer." Sonia put her hands together, studying Jill. "You doubt yourself. You should open up and rely on your instincts," said Sonia. "Stop fighting your abilities. You're making it very hard on yourself." She cocked her head. "Just take a moment and listen. Stop thinking. You're too much in your head."

Jill wanted to say something. Her immediate reaction was to get up and leave. This woman was getting way too personal and hitting too many buttons. But something kept her in her seat. "How do you know this about me? You're just someone who witnessed a man on a cell phone on the street."

Sonia picked up her purse and began to rummage through it. "Oh, dear. Why do you think I tried to talk to him?" She pulled out some Chapstick. "It wasn't by accident."

"What do you mean?"

She applied some balm to her lips. "The minute I walked past him, I knew he was bad news. I could sense it." Her body shook, and she grimaced. "I can still feel it." She paused. "He's done some bad things, hasn't he?"

Jill swallowed, feeling a dark cloud settle over her. "If he is who we think he is… Yes, he has."

Sonia put the Chapstick back in her purse. She leaned in, her elbows on the table, and sat still for a moment. Jill had the distinct feeling she was being studied.

"Interesting," said Sonia.

Jill didn't like it. Without thinking, she closed off.

Sonia grinned. "Good. Very good. You should learn to do that more often."

Jill frowned. "I don't understand how you know all this." She stood. She again debated leaving but couldn't do it. If this woman was messing with her, she was doing a good job. But some flicker of insight told her Sonia was the real deal. There was an energy about her it was hard for Jill to explain. It felt as if she was talking to someone she'd known all her life.

"How long have you had it?" asked Sonia.

"Had what?"

"The sight, dear. The sight."

Jill paced, debating how to answer. "I really don't know what you mean."

"Oh, Detective. I've lived too long to play silly games. I know you can see things. You're probably doing it right now without even realizing it. Why do you think you threw out my coffee?" She paused. "You can see him, can't you? You can see through his eyes." She closed her eyes and shook her head. "You poor dear. The things you've witnessed."

Jill's chest constricted, and she gripped the back of a chair. "I don't…I don't understand."

"You're clairvoyant, dear. What's not to understand? He probably is too, to some degree. Many people are. And you two have made a connection."

Jill took a deep breath. The room began to feel small. "I don't want to be clairvoyant."

"Why ever not, dear? It's quite helpful. In most circumstances."

Jill sat and put her head in her hands. "Not in my case."

"I can see that."

Jill popped her head up. "Do you know me? How do you know about this…this…sight?"

"Because I have it, too. Since I was a child. I can sense it in others, which is probably why I felt it from him, and how I knew the minute I took your hand. For most though, it's hard for me to detect. Those who have it don't know it either. But others have a rare ability. They can sense things. Visions. Future events. Other's thoughts and feelings. Some have a mixed bag. You fall into that category, much like me. You just need to learn how to control it. That's all."

Jill almost checked for cameras to see if she was being filmed. This was straight out of *The Twilight Zone*. Another one of Rem's favorite TV shows. "How do you control something like this? It feels very uncontrollable."

"Practice, dear. Like anything else." She rummaged through her purse again. "Would you like a mint?" She pulled out a small metal canister. "I didn't have the heart to tell that nice detective I don't like coffee. Now it's all I can taste."

"No, thank you," said Jill. Had she really picked up on Sonia's distaste for coffee?

She popped a small white square into her mouth. "Suit yourself."

Jill put her head in her hands. "You can feel what I feel?"

She tossed the mints into her purse. "Not exactly. I've been at this game a while now. I've mastered what I allow in, and what I don't. But I've been there. I know how it feels to be in someone's head you don't want to be in. It can be a personal hell."

Jill raised her head. "How do I get him out?"

She adjusted a necklace. "It's simple, really. You just refuse him entrance. What's harder is learning to stay away from him."

Jill made a sad chuckle. "That shouldn't be hard at all. I can think of a million other places I'd rather be."

"Then why haven't you done it?"

Jill started to answer but stopped.

"Detective?"

"I'm not a detective."

Her brow furrowed. "Doesn't look that way to me."

"I don't have a badge."

"It's not about the badge, dear."

Jill's head started to pound. "I stayed away for a while. But I came back." She sighed. "And I let him back in."

"And he was waiting."

Jill nodded.

"He's a smart one, isn't he? He's manipulating you. He knows your weaknesses."

Jill thought of the phone call. "He does."

She crossed her arms. "So, at what point do you turn the tables? Start using his weaknesses against him?"

"He's willing to kill people, and I'm not."

"Strength has nothing to do with force. Those with the most power require the least effort. He only has power because you give it to him."

Emotion flooded her, and Jill found herself close to tears. "I don't see it that way."

Sonia leaned forward and touched Jill's forearm. "You're as strong as he is, dear. You just don't believe it. Your connection intrigues him. That's his weakness. His need for you could be his downfall."

Jill let go of a deep breath. "I'm so tired."

"That's because your energy is scattered. He sucks it right from you. You must learn to protect yourself." She reached for one of her necklaces and pulled it off. It was a long black cord with a large black stone. "Here. Take this. It's a black Tourmaline. It's a powerful protection stone. I want you to have it."

Jill waved her hand. "I can't take that."

"Don't argue, dear. Take it. I insist. Learn to accept help when it's offered. That's the first step to gaining your power back."

Jill studied the stone and then reached out and took it. Holding it in her hand, it had a calming effect, like honey on a sore throat. She placed it around her neck. "You wouldn't know the second step, would you?"

"That's easy," said Sonia, sitting back. Her gentle demeanor shifted, her eyes narrowed, and she pointed. "Stop taking his shit. You're a woman. We all have a badass bitch inside us. It's time you showed him just exactly what you're made of." She tipped her head. "And don't let those boys out there tell you otherwise. Men can sometimes feel threatened by strong women." She leaned in. "Although that dark-haired one is interesting, don't you think?"

Jill couldn't prevent a blush, but she didn't answer.

"I thought so." Sonia relaxed, reached into her purse again, and pulled out a small tube and opened it, squeezing a dab of cream onto her hands, her sweet persona returning. "Would you like some lotion, dear? My hands are so dry."

Jill couldn't help but smile.

**

Rem sat his desk, tapping his pencil on an empty glass. He stared down the hallway.

"If you keep banging that, I may have to shoot you," said Daniels.

Rem dropped the pencil. "Sorry. It's been an hour. How long does it take to sketch someone?"

"It takes as long as it takes," said Daniels. He held out a piece of paper. "Here. Sign this."

Rem took the paper. "What am I signing?"

"It's your manifesto," said Daniels. "Detective Aaron Remalla. My Life, My Journey." When Rem scowled, Daniels rolled his eyes. "It's the expense report. They're paying for our meals while we're on overtime, so unless you want to pay for your own Taco del Fuegos, I need your John Hancock."

Rem sighed. "Got it." He signed the paper but monitored the hall.

"You mind handing it back?" asked Daniels.

"Oh, yeah," said Rem, returning the expense report.

Daniels paused, glancing back toward the hall and back at Rem. "You like her, don't you?"

"Who?" asked Rem. "Sonia? She's a little old for me."

Daniels chuckled, and Rem smiled. "Is it obvious?" asked Rem.

"Maybe to me. I notice you're smiling more, despite this grim case."

"I smile."

"Not that much, and certainly not with me." He picked up some folders and straightened them.

"You're not pretty," said Rem. "Maybe if you grew your hair out."

"Careful," said Daniels, pointing. "You're talking to Steve McQueen here." He put the folders on the side of his desk. "Just be careful, okay, partner? She's got a lot to deal with and we have no idea how this case is going to end." He rested an arm on his desk. "You've been through a lot yourself. I don't want you to get hurt."

Rem met his gaze and sighed. "I know, and I will." He picked up the pencil. "Thanks."

Daniels nodded, and Lozano's door opened, and Georgios and Titus stepped out. They approached the detective's desks.

"Anything?" asked Titus.

"Nothing," said Daniels. "Still waiting."

"Jacobs is in there with her?" asked Georgios.

"Yeah," said Rem.

"Maybe they're in there conjuring spells together," said Georgios. "Mirror, Mirror, on the wall. Show me the Artist down the hall."

Titus snorted. "Don't quit your day job, George. You suck at rhymes."

"Amongst other things," said Rem, under his breath.

"What?" asked Georgios, frowning.

The squad doors opened, and Daniels saw Ethan Delgado, in his customary uniform, enter the room. Normally, he'd try to look busy, but now he was glad for the distraction. "Delgado, what can we do for you?" He made eye contact with Rem, sending a silent communication to keep his cool.

"Hi, Detectives," said Delgado. "Sorry to interrupt, but I heard the news. Is there a witness?"

Rem and Daniels scowled at Georgios and Titus. "So much for keeping it a secret," said Rem.

Titus threw out his hands. "We may have told a few guys on the way in. No big deal. It's not like no one's going to figure it out once we distribute the sketch."

Daniels shook his head. "You going to tell that to Sonia if she becomes the next target? It would have been nice to keep her identity safe."

"He's not coming after her," said Georgios. "For all we know, she's giving a description of Big Bird."

Rem dropped his pencil. "The only Sesame Street character around here is you, Georgios. You wouldn't know your ass from your partner." He glanced at Titus. "Although Titus looks like an ass, so I might give you some leeway."

Georgios' face dropped. "You should know all about ass, Remalla. I hear you're getting plenty of it at your place."

Rem came out of his chair at the same time as Daniels. Daniels moved faster though and stood in front of Georgios just as Rem approached.

"You better watch your mouth, Georgios," said Daniels. He put up a hand to keep Rem from launching himself at Georgios.

"Or what?" asked Georgios. "You gonna do to me what you've done with this case so far? Absolutely nothing?"

Titus put his hand on Daniels' shoulder. "Come on, guys. We're just goofin'. No harm intended."

"Watch your hands, Titus," said Rem. "I'd hate to mistake your fingers for Georgios' face."

Titus let go of Daniels' shoulder.

Rem pointed at Georgios. "You better hope we don't meet outside of here. Because if we do, I'm gonna do to you what I do to every cockroach I see. I'm gonna stomp the living shit out of you."

Georgios glared, and Lozano's voice boomed from behind them. "What the hell is going on out here?"

The four detectives stared at each other. Delgado was the first to speak.

"Captain, sir. Apparently, Detectives Georgios and Titus let it slip about the witness, which upset Detectives Daniels and Remalla. Then Detective Remalla said something about Titus looking like an ass, and Detective Georgios made a very inappropriate sexual innuendo about Detectives Jacobs and Remalla, to which Daniels and Remalla are now reacting."

Lozano paused, before he boomed again. "Georgios. Titus. In my office. NOW."

Daniels and Rem continued to stare back at Georgios and Titus.

"We're not done here," said Rem to Georgios.

Georgios narrowed his eyes. "I'm looking forward to it."

Lozano yelled. "Move!"

Georgios finally broke eye contact, and he and Titus headed toward Lozano's office. They entered, and Lozano slammed the door behind them.

Daniels turned toward Rem. "You all right?"

Rem scowled. "I'd be better if I could have punched him."

"Then we'd be in there right now."

"It'd be worth it."

They could hear Lozano's angry voice travel through the glass.

"You sure about that?" asked Daniels.

Rem took a breath and his shoulders relaxed. "Thanks for backing me up."

"You mean thanks for saving your ass…again."

"I hate that guy. He deserved it."

"Uhm…Detectives?"

They finally noticed Delgado, who stood there looking like he'd just walked into the wrong dinner party.

Rem walked back to his seat. "Thanks for helping us out, Delgado."

"We appreciate it," said Daniels.

"I just told the truth, although I may have left out the part where Detective Remalla told Detective Georgios about not being able to find his own ass."

"Minor detail," said Rem, waving it off.

"So, there is a witness?" asked Delgado.

Daniels hesitated. "She's talking to a sketch artist now. But let's try to keep that to ourselves. At least until we can get her out of here."

"I think that cat's out of the bag," said Rem. He rubbed his head. "Idiots."

"But if that's true, then you may catch this guy," said Delgado.

"Maybe," said Daniels. "We're hoping for the best."

"If you need my help in distributing the sketch or talking to witnesses, let me know," said Delgado.

"What happened to your promotion?" asked Rem. "Did you hear anything?"

Delgado played with the flashlight on his belt. "Not yet. Apparently, they're delayed. I haven't heard 'no' though, so that's a good sign."

"With all the attention this case is garnering, plus the latest bank robbery, they've probably got other things on their minds. They'll get to it eventually," said Daniels.

"Well, until then, just let me know what I can do." He looked around. "Where's Detective Jacobs?"

"She's in with the witness," said Rem.

"Oh, well, tell her I said 'Hi,'" He fiddled with his belt some more.

Daniels hid a smile. "Will do, Delgado. I'm sure she'll be sorry she missed you."

"You think?" asked Delgado. His eyes lit up. "I'd still love to talk to her about this case."

"If this witness sketch pans out, maybe you'll get to," said Rem. "We'll let her know you stopped by."

Delgado nodded. "Thanks. I guess I'll head out. I don't want to be late." He shot out a thumb. "Oh, I almost forgot. Don't let Jacobs forget her flowers."

Daniels popped his head up. "Flowers?"

Rem's brow furrowed. "What flowers?"

Delgado gestured toward the hall. "They're outside the door. They're roses. I was curious and peeked at the card. They're addressed to Jacobs. Didn't she see them?"

Daniels shot a look at Rem and they headed toward the hallway. Outside the squad room, Daniels eyed the two chairs near where Sonia had been sitting. Lying on the small side table sat a bouquet of red roses. A card poked out from the stems. Looking closely, Daniels could read the scrawl on the card. *For Jill Jacobs.*

Rem saw it too. "When the hell did those get here?"

"That's a good question," said Daniels. He raised a brow at his partner. "You thinking what I'm thinking?"

Rem's eyes widened. "You don't think…? How the hell…?"

“I don’t know,” said Daniels. He studied the flowers. “Delgado, you want to make yourself useful?”

Delgado had followed them, and he answered. “Yes. What can I do?”

Daniels grunted. “Call Forensics. Get ’em down here. We may have a delivery from the Artist.”

CHAPTER SIXTEEN

Jill studied Sonia's card. It had her name and phone number on it. "Call me dear," the older woman had said before leaving, "if you ever need to talk."

Sonia had provided a detailed sketch of a man who appeared to be in his early thirties, with short brown hair and brown eyes. He was clean shaven with a narrow face, heavy brows, and a strong chin. Sonia had even recalled a small scar on the man's right hand.

Before she'd left, Lozano had offered Sonia a protective detail, but she'd refused it, saying the Artist wouldn't come looking for her. She wasn't his cup of tea. Despite Jill's concerns, she'd smiled, patted Jill on the wrist, told her everything would work out, to remember what she said, and then gone home.

Jill tucked the card in her pocket and returned to the squad room. Rem and Daniels hadn't been around when Sonia had left, but they were there now.

She sat at her desk. "You guys getting the sketch distributed?" She'd been hesitant to be hopeful prior to seeing the image, but now she couldn't help but feel a glimmer of excitement that they had a lead, even though the picture was fairly generic.

"Lozano's working on it," said Daniels. "We'll get it out to all the precincts."

"What about the news stations?" she asked.

"Likely them, too," said Rem. "It'll be on the evening news, I'm sure." He sat on the edge of his desk and watched her.

Daniels leaned back in his chair, tapping his finger on the desk, and he watched her too.

Jill squirmed in her seat. "What is it?" She wiped at her cheek. "Is there something on my face?"

"You got a delivery while you were in with Sonia," said Rem.

"Delivery?" asked Jill.

Daniels held out his phone. She leaned in and saw a picture of a bouquet of roses. Cold fear hit her in the pit of her stomach. Daniels swiped to the next photo, and she saw a picture of the card with her name hand-written on it.

Jill went still. "Where did you find it?"

"Out in the corridor. Near where Sonia was sitting. About an hour ago," said Rem. "Delgado found it."

She nodded and took a deep breath. "You read the card?"

Daniels answered. He read from a piece of notebook paper. "Thinking of you, Jill. So ready to play again. Don't disappoint me." He put the paper down. "Forensics has the original. They're checking it for prints and DNA."

She studied the floor. Everything felt like it was closing in on her. "Shit," she said. "How the hell did he get it there?"

"We're wondering the same thing," said Daniels.

"He, or someone else, somehow walked in after Sonia left the hallway and before Delgado arrived. There was about a ninety minute's span of time in between."

"Nobody saw anything downstairs?" asked Jill.

"There'd been a bar fight. A lot of arrests. There was a lot going on. Guy walked right by," said Daniels.

"We're pulling the video though. Guy can't get by that," said Rem. "If we're lucky, we won't need the sketch. We'll have him on tape. Bastard won't escape the camera."

"He may not have been the delivery boy though," said Jill. "He might have paid someone to bring them. They were always sent by messenger in Seattle."

"We'll find out soon enough," said Daniels.

Jill rested her face in her hands. "He's ramping things up. First the phone call. Now flowers."

"Is that what he did in Seattle?" asked Rem.

Jill thought back. "Yes. Only not so close together. There was more time between them."

"What's his hurry?" asked Daniels. "Why so soon?"

"I don't know. Maybe because I didn't play by the rules, he's going off script." She thought of Sonia. "You think he knew there was a witness?"

"The timing is uncanny," said Daniels. "He shows up with flowers at the same time as someone is describing what he looks like? Seems a little coincidental."

"I think we're giving him too much credit," said Rem. "Guy's not a mind reader."

Jill wondered about that. "I hope not," she said. She sighed and sat back. "You think Sonia's safe?"

"Probably," said Rem. "We already have the sketch. Killing her isn't going to take it back."

"He'd do it just for fun," said Jill.

"But that would mean he's gone off script," said Daniels.

"Considering we have a picture of him now," said Rem. "We're already playing by different rules. How do you think he'll handle that?"

Jill shook her head. "I don't know. I'd still feel more comfortable if we kept an eye on Sonia though."

"Which is why Cap is putting an unmarked car at her house," said Daniels.

"But she declined protection," said Jill.

"What she doesn't know won't hurt her," said Rem.

Relief coursed through Jill. "Did you guys have something to do with that?"

Rem shrugged. "We may have guided Lozano in a certain direction. It wouldn't look too good if our only witness became the next victim."

"No, it wouldn't." She sighed. "Thank you." Jill didn't want to admit that Sonia could be at risk because of her new association with her. It was one more person to worry about.

"But if he sticks to the rules, what happens next?" asked Daniels.

"He's killed four," said Rem. "That leaves three more. Another woman and two men."

"And what happens after flowers?" asked Daniels.

Jill groaned. "Photos. He'll send photos."

"Of you?" asked Rem.

"Yes."

"I don't suppose there's any way to prevent that," said Daniels.

"We could put you in a hoodie," said Rem. "You like hoodies?"

"Doesn't matter," said Jill, pushing her hair back.

"Why not?" asked Daniels.

"Because he's already been taking them. Probably has been since the beginning." She pulled her hair up in a bun and wrapped a hair tie around it. "That's his M.O. When I got pictures in Seattle, some of them were from not long after that first press conference."

Rem frowned. "Well, that's freaking me out. Why the hell aren't we planning for that?"

"What would you like to do? Put a bubble around me?" asked Jill.

"We could be more vigilant. Be aware of anyone taking pictures," said Daniels.

"We did that in Seattle. We detained a few wedding photographers and almost got sued by a nature photographer when we screwed up a shot of a rare butterfly, but never found our killer."

"Doesn't mean we can't still try," said Daniels. He made a note on a piece of paper.

"Our resources are thin enough as it is," said Jill. "I doubt assigning someone to look out for creepy photographers will be at the top of Lozano's list."

"We can ask," said Rem. "Maybe Delgado's available."

Daniels chuckled. "I'm sure he'd do it. If it meant hanging out with Jacobs."

"Best to keep him out of this," said Jill.

The phone rang on Daniels' desk, and he answered it.

Jill stood and paced behind her chair.

"How are you doing?" asked Rem. "You hanging in there?'

"I need a drink."

"I could get you a soda."

"Add a little vodka, and you're on."

He watched her as she paced. "We've got a sketch now. You didn't have that before. We're going to catch this guy."

"I'll believe that when he's dead or in custody." She hugged her arms.

"You hungry? You didn't eat breakfast."

"Not really no."

"You want something? My treat."

She stopped pacing. An image of them sitting on his couch, aiming popcorn into an empty hat, while John Wayne fired his gun came to mind. "You should stop being so nice to me."

His face furrowed. "I didn't realize that was a problem."

She stepped closer. "You don't get it, do you? You said it yourself. One woman and two men. You could easily be one of those men."

"We already had this discussion, remember?"

She studied the tile, and for a moment, allowed her shield to drop. "I don't want anything to happen to you."

He pushed off his desk and moved closer. "Nothing will happen to me. I promise."

His nearness made her body heat bloom, and she wanted to step back and away from him. This was the last thing she wanted or expected.

Instead, she held her ground and his gaze. She noticed as his eyes traveled over her face and to her lips, and she wondered if they'd been alone, if he would have pulled her in, and kissed her.

Daniels hung up the phone. "That was the lab. They got nothing on the video. Not a damn thing. Guy avoided all the cameras. Can you believe that?"

CHAPTER SEVENTEEN

Jill awoke with a scream, sweat slick on her skin. Remembering where she was, she took deep breaths, trying to acclimate. The dream still vivid, she searched with shaky fingers to find the light switch on the lamp but knocked over her water glass in her haste. The glass hit the floor and shattered on impact.

Startled and tense, Jill cursed. Light illuminated from around the door frame and she heard a knock. It opened, and Rem stuck his head in. "You okay?"

Jill searched for the light and turned it on, seeing Rem's worried face. "I knocked over a glass."

"Stay put. I'll get a broom." He disappeared.

Jill tried to pull it together. The clock on the nightstand read four am. Her heart still raced, and her hair stuck to her neck and face. She pushed it back and exited from the other side of the bed, avoiding the glass with her bare feet. Putting on a robe, she stood as Rem returned.

"Be careful. I don't want you to step on anything." He swept the glass fragments into a pile. There had been little water in the glass, so the puddle was small.

"Were you up?" asked Jill, her voice raspy.

"I was on the couch. Trying to sleep. I kept thinking about how the Artist may have been in our precinct today, right outside the door, and nobody saw a damn thing. Freaks me out." He swept the shards into a dustbin. "You have another nightmare?"

She rubbed her arms. "Is it obvious?"

"Slightly. I heard your scream and the crash."

"Sorry if I scared you."

He stood and dumped the debris into a small wastebasket in her room. "Rosemary's Baby is on. Care to watch?"

"Who's baby? Is it a documentary?"

He snorted. "No. It's a horror classic."

She rolled her eyes. "Is that a wise choice when you're trying to sleep?"

"Maybe not, but it's a wise choice when you're trying to get your mind off things."

Her heart rate had stabilized, but her fingers still shook. "I suppose a few minutes of horror couldn't be any worse."

He carried the broom out, and she followed, noticing he wore long pajama pants and a T-shirt, but no robe. He went into the kitchen with the broom, but she headed into the den.

Sitting on the couch, she saw Mia Farrow, with her short pixie haircut, holding a baby in a blanket. The sound was so low, she could barely hear it. She held her hands, still feeling shaky. Recalling the dream, she shut her eyes. The images returned, and she shivered.

"You want to talk about it?"

She opened her eyes to see him standing there, holding a shot of clear liquid. She didn't think twice, took the glass, and shot it back. Warmth traveled down to her belly, and she took a breath, trying to relax. "Thank you."

He took the glass and put it down, sitting next to her. "Was it like the last one?"

"Worse." She tucked her hair behind her ear. "I think the sketch did it. I could see him. He was in the house. I knew he was here, but I couldn't find him. He came after me, and…and…I couldn't move. I couldn't scream. He laughed and he—." She found it hard to continue.

"Take your time," said Rem.

She nodded. "I'm not sure you want to hear the rest."

"I'm watching Rosemary's Baby at four o'clock in the morning. I'm tougher than I look."

She gave him a skeptical look. "He came after you. You were in the house but didn't know he was there. I was trying to warn you, but you didn't hear me. I screamed, and screamed, but he got a hold of you, and he had a knife and…" She stopped and took a shuddered breath. "It was awful."

He paused for a second, then picked up the remote. "On second thought, perhaps there's a better choice." He flipped the channel and a cartoon of Bugs Bunny and Elmer Fudd played on the screen. "Much better."

"Sorry."

"You had to live it. I just had to hear about it." He put down the remote. "You feeling better?"

"A little."

"If you want, we can skip town, go rob banks, and disappear to Mexico."

She chuckled, feeling the fear lift. "Tempting, but I'll leave that to you and Daniels."

He rested his foot on the coffee table. "He's got a baby due any day, and something tells me Marjorie might not go for it."

"You're probably right. Being nine months pregnant sort of squelches the need for sudden life changes."

"Crazy," he said.

"I agree. Mexico is lovely this time of year."

He smiled. "Maybe one day."

"Yeah." She picked up a couch pillow and held it in her lap.

They were quiet for a moment as Elmer chased Bugs through the woods before he spoke. "You ever think about the future?"

She tensed, staring at the pillow and playing with its frayed edges. "Not in a long time."

"Why not?"

"What's to think about?"

He shifted to face her. "Oh, I don't know. Marriage. Kids. You want that?"

Her stomach knotted. "I thought I did."

"Not anymore?"

"Before the Artist, things were different. Now…well, now I don't know if I'll live long enough. It's hard to see beyond the next day, never mind the next year."

"We'll get him. I can promise you that."

"I hope you're right." He had his elbow on the back of the couch and the light of the TV played across his face. "I just don't want him to take anybody else when we do. He's done enough damage as it is." She studied his eyes, telling herself she needed to go to bed, but her mind wouldn't listen, and she had a brief image of him in bed with her. Her face warmed, and she hoped the low light in the room kept him from noticing.

His expression told her he may have been thinking the same thing. His gaze held hers and warning bells flared. *Get up, Jill*, they blared. *He's going to kiss you*. Her heart thumped, but her body wouldn't move. "You ever think about the future?" she asked, hearing a little tremble in her voice.

"Oh, yeah. I do." His gaze moved to her lips. "I'm thinking about it right now." He leaned closer, and he brought his hand up to her chin and he stroked her jaw. "But it's about something a lot more fun than marriage and kids."

He shifted closer and his leg touched hers. No matter what her inner voice was shouting at her, she couldn't make it out. As much as she wanted to leave, she also wanted to know what it would feel like to have him against her, touching her, tasting her, stroking her. Her heart rate jumped, and she tried to breathe. "Rem…" she whispered.

His lips hovered over hers and the caress of his fingers against her skin made everything tingle. Leaving her inner voice in the dust, she leaned in to meet him. Her body was like a magnet drawn to his, and his mouth descended over hers. The kiss was slow and delicate, as they took their time to enjoy that first intimate contact. His lips were soft, and she savored the feel of them. His fingers brushed down her cheek and traveled to the back of her neck where he pulled her closer. The kiss became more insistent, and her breathing escalated as he opened his mouth over hers, and she joined him. His tongue delicately touched her own, and the intensity exploded. Her heart thudded, and she brought her arm up and around his neck, pulling him against her. Feeling his breath against her cheek, she fought to stay in control. It had been so long. Could she risk this again?

They kissed like that for a while. She had no concept of time, before his other arm went behind her, and she felt herself being lifted as he pulled her up, and she swung her leg over and straddled him. His hands cupped her butt, and he pushed against her. The pajama pants left only a thin layer of protection and she felt everything. The sensation was explosive. Everything fired at once. Her whole body was a torch set ablaze, and she knew there was no stopping now. She wanted him. All of him. She'd deal with the consequences later.

And then the phone rang.

**

Rem heard his cell, but his mind didn't want to engage. The feel of Jacobs' body over his and her lips slanted and moving over his own had him on full alert. The sensation was electrifying, and he wanted to taste and touch every inch of her. But the damn phone kept ringing.

"No, no, no," he kept hearing and then realized it was him.

Jacobs pulled back, breathless. "You should answer it."

He stared into her darkened eyes. "I don't want to. I want to stay right here."

She gave him a quick but heated kiss and spoke against his lips. "Me, too. But we can't. We're on call 24/7."

"Shit." He moaned. "Okay."

She slid off him, and he groaned with the sensation, grabbed for his cell phone, and saw it was Daniels. He cursed again. "Yeah. I'm here," he answered. "Everything okay?"

He listened to his partner, incredulous. "You're kidding. When?" He looked at Jacobs, who gave him a concerned look. "Son-of-a-bitch. I don't believe it." He rubbed his eyes. "Yeah, we're on our way." He hung up.

"What is it?" asked Jacobs.

He stood. "There's another victim."

Her jaw dropped. "What? That's way too soon."

"I know. Come on. We have to meet Daniels, and I need to take a freezing cold shower."

**

The crime scene was a madhouse. Police on the scene had kept the press at bay, but their flashbulbs popped, and Jacobs squinted. The sun had yet to come up. They were at an apartment complex, and she followed Rem to the second-floor where Daniels stood outside a door where other police waited, his expression grim. A dog barked from a nearby apartment.

"What have we got?" asked Rem.

"Sorry to wake you guys," said Daniels. He wiped his tired eyes. "I know we had a long day yesterday."

"Don't worry about it," said Rem, glancing at Jill. "We were watching TV."

"How long have you been here?" asked Jacobs.

"Not long. But I got a few details. Victim is Veronica Johnson. She's a chef at a local restaurant. Came home late. Neighbor heard noises. Called the cops."

"Are we sure it's the Artist?" asked Jill. "This is way too soon. Could it be a copycat?"

"I don't think so. There's writing on the wall. I haven't seen it yet, but nobody knows about that."

"Can we go in?" asked Rem.

"I'm just waiting for the okay. It's not a big apartment. Forensics arrived not long ago. Apparently, the neighbor's dog wouldn't let anybody near the place, so it took them a while before they could enter."

"What?" asked Rem, frowning. "The neighbor's dog? Is that who's barking?"

"I think so. The dog got out and wouldn't let anybody close. The neighbor finally got it under control and back inside. I heard it's a German Shepherd, and obviously very protective."

"Terrific," said Rem. "That's all we need. Why couldn't the dog have stopped the killer instead?"

"We should be so lucky," said Jacobs.

Just then, a burly man with tousled hair stepped out. "You guys can go in. Just cover yourselves." He handed out the protective gear.

Jill, putting on gloves, tried to think. "Why would he strike so soon?"

"Just be warned," said the man. "It's pretty gruesome."

Once they were ready, they stepped inside. The first thing Jill saw was the blood. Dark splatters darkened the walls in the living area. There was a small kitchen and dining area. An overturned chair lay across some scattered mail on the floor along with a broken potted plant. Walking further in, Jill noticed a wet, bloody handprint on the kitchen counter. Then turning toward the bedroom, Jill saw the victim's legs. She had one shoe on and there was blood on her feet. Moving closer, Jill recognized the posed stance, and the coarsely drawn makeup on the woman's face. There were multiple stab wounds in her chest, and blood saturated the floor and walls around her.

"Jesus," said Rem.

Jill immediately felt the hit. Her chest ached with sharp pains and she heard the woman's screams in her head. Only now, she saw the man in the sketch, raising a knife. But this time, the woman didn't go down easy. There'd been a struggle. Clenching her hands, she thought of her own dream that night. Had she somehow tapped into this murder? Her nightmare had been just as gruesome, but this woman had not been at the end of the knife. Thinking of Rem, she took a breath and tried to remember Sonia's words. She just needed to gain control. "Something went wrong. Something he didn't expect. This woman fought back."

"Maybe because he struck so soon after the last one, he didn't have time to prepare like he would've for the others,' said Daniels. "He made mistakes."

"So maybe he finally left something behind," said Rem. "Or maybe our victim got some DNA from him."

Feeling lightheaded, Jill practiced Sonia's advice and tried to close off. Something told her the killer was enjoying seeing her reaction through her eyes, and she didn't want to give him the satisfaction of feeling her pain. As the lightheadedness eased, she reluctantly headed for the bathroom.

"Careful," said the burly man. "Our guys haven't made it in there yet."

"Got it," said Daniels.

Jill took a tentative step inside and sucked in a breath. Streaks of blood covered the walls. It was like the killer had put his hands in the victim's blood and ran them down the tile.

"What in the hell?" asked Rem. "Has he done this before?"

"Never," said Jill. Watching where she walked, she stepped over to the tub and pulled the shower curtain back and froze. Plastered on the back wall, in big letters written in blood, were the words. "Play or Die. Tell your friends, JJ." Four red roses were in the bathtub.

"He's losing it," said Daniels. "He's definitely off script now."

Jill stepped back. She understood his threat. Do what he wanted, or he'd kill her and those around her. People she cared for. Taking a chance, she allowed herself to drop her shield, wondering if she would feel his presence. She didn't want to, but Sonia had told Jill to remember that she was in charge. She only needed to assert herself more.

Jill opened up, letting him in, and his presence reared up immediately. She reached out, touching the wall to stabilize herself. Pure rage enveloped her, and she had to hold on. Focusing, she heard him speak to her with threats of violence. His voice echoed in her head, and she could see him as he attacked, but in his eyes, as he stabbed Veronica Johnson, he saw Jill's face, not the victim's. And then she saw him place the roses, and she realized who they were for. Feeling his menace and anger, she allowed herself to stay in it for as long as she could until she had to shut down again. She wondered how she was still standing when she realized that Daniels and Rem each had a hold of her, keeping her up.

"Jill, you there?" asked Rem, his brow furrowed. "You all right?"

She shook her head, trying to come fully back. Her fingers shook.

"What happened?" asked Daniels. "Where'd you go?"

Trying to steady her breath, she studied the tub. "I know why the four roses."

"Why?" asked Daniels. "It doesn't make sense."

"Unless they're for us," said Rem.

Gaining strength, she stood on her own power. But still unsteady, she held on to Rem. "They are. There's one for each of us. But he's planning another. There's someone else on his list." She looked back. "If we don't do what he wants, he'll kill us all."

CHAPTER EIGHTEEN

Jill walked out of the apartment, her senses in a tailspin. She stared out at the press and growing crowd, wondering what to do. Something told her the Artist was out there amongst the onlookers, watching. Pulling off her gear, she scanned the area, looking for anyone matching the sketch. The sun was rising, and she could see better. Unfortunately, the sketch looked like a lot of men, and there were no less than a half a dozen males in the crowd who might match it. She recognized Delgado down at the barrier when he held up a hand to push a reporter back. Even he matched the sketch, but then so did a few other cops she knew. They couldn't suspect everyone. She'd heard how the tip line had exploded with calls once they had released the picture and finding the killer based on that alone would be a long shot. She could only hope that in his anger he'd left some evidence at the crime scene.

Rem came up behind her. "You think he's here?"

She shook her head. Since she'd dropped her guard and let him in, it had been hard to reestablish her boundaries. But getting away from the scene had helped. Her mind was a little clearer. "Probably. If nothing else, he's watching the coverage on TV."

Daniels, pulling off his gloves, leaned on the railing. "He's waiting, isn't he? To see if you'll play along. Although he's deviated off script, so what does it matter?"

“He doesn’t see it that way. He just wants me to do what he expects. He wants control.”

“And maybe he’s out there now to see if he’s got it,” said Daniels.

“Most likely,” she said.

“What do you want to do?” asked Rem.

She shook her head. “If I do what he wants, he might relax, and settle back into his pattern. If I don’t, he’ll get angrier. God knows what happens then.” She pointed back toward the apartment. “He left a hell of a mess here.”

“Something’s going on with him,” said Rem. “He’s unraveling. Based on this scene, he may very well have left his DNA behind. We might know who he is in a few days.”

“Or not,” said Daniels. “In which case we’re back to square one. Unless someone saw something.”

“Mel and Garcia are here. They’re talking to the neighbors,” said Rem. “We’ll find out soon enough.” The dog continued to bark from next door. “Maybe that dog alerted someone in time to see something.”

“There’s another option,” said Jill turning. “I could still leave.”

Rem shook his head. “You know that won’t work. He’ll only follow and pick up somewhere else.”

“Not if I keep moving.”

“You really think that’s the answer?” asked Daniels. “Running for the rest of your life?”

“I may not have a choice,” she said.

“You always have a choice,” said Rem.

She held his gaze, remembering his lips on hers. “I know I sound like a broken record, but if I stay, he might kill you both. You saw the roses.”

“And if you go, he’ll kill others,” said Daniels. “What’s the difference?”

“Like you said, we’ve had this conversation before. We need to stay the course. I told you we’ll catch him,” said Rem.

Jill ran a hand through and pulled on her hair, trying to think. Her mind jumbled, she thought of Seattle and all that had happened there, and all she'd lost, and she thought of Rem, and what she was potentially starting. But then Sonia's words returned. *Show him who's boss.* Could she do that? And how would she start? Where would it lead? She didn't know, but she realized it couldn't be any worse than where she was. If the killer had left a clue behind, he might be behind bars before next week, but if he hadn't… She studied the crowd, recognizing a reporter from one of the local news stations.

Taking a second to consider her options, she handed her gloves and shoe covers to Rem. "Here. Take these." Taking a deep breath, she walked around him and took the stairs down.

"Jacobs?" he asked. "Where are you going?"

"I think she's made up her mind," said Daniels from behind her.

Jill kept moving, pushing past the fear, thinking she was crazy, but feeling strangely empowered.

As she approached, the reporter held out her microphone. "Detective? I'm Laura Saunders from RLTS News. Can you confirm if this is the Makeup Artist?"

Jill paused, reconsidering, but then walked up to the microphone. "I'm actually not a detective. I'm a consultant from Seattle. And yes. I can confirm this is the Makeup Artist."

"Can you tell us the name of the victim?"

"No. Not until the family has been notified."

"When did it happen?"

"In the early morning hours. We'll know more when Forensics finishes their report."

"Was there a witness?"

"Not to my knowledge, but we're still interviewing neighbors."

"Who reported the crime?"

"I don't know that either."

"You say you're from Seattle. Do you have some connection to the crimes there?"

Jill hesitated. "I do. I worked on the case as a detective in Seattle."

"You guys weren't able to catch him there. Do you think you'll be able to catch him now?"

"Yes. I do."

"Why? What's different?"

Jill stared at the camera, debating her next move, but finally deciding. "What's different is that he's not the same. There are aspects of his personality that have changed. He's made mistakes, which is not like him. There's a sketch of him now, which means he screwed up. And there are signs at this scene that he's devolving. He's not his normal calm, cool self."

"Is that why he murdered this victim so soon after the last?"

"Exactly. His control is slipping. He's allowing emotion to shade his decisions. It's the classic sign of a possible mental breakdown. It's just a matter of time before he does something that brings him to justice."

"So you're confident you'll catch him before he kills again?"

"I'm confident that we're much closer. In fact…"

"Yes?" asked the reporter.

Jill straightened. "I think he's watching now, and I'd like to let him know that if he has a beef with me, then come and get me."

The reporter stared, and Jill looked directly into the camera, her eyes like lasers. "But you know what I think? I don't think you have the balls. You never did. You're scared. You've always been scared. Especially of women. Which is why you think you need to kill others to validate yourself. You're a sad and pathetic man, trying to show me and whoever else you want to impress how strong you are when you're actually weak. Strong people don't have to prove a thing. You'll always be weak, no matter who you murder." She paused, considering her next words. "I think…no…I know you like me, but you know what? You will never have me." Setting her jaw, she paused again. "You may think you're in charge because you kill, but you will always be a coward." She almost walked away but stopped to add, "Play with that, you bastard."

Nearby reporters had caught what she'd said, and they scrambled closer with their microphones, shouting questions, and bumping Laura Saunders, who seemed uncertain of what to ask next.

"I have no further comment," said Jill, before she turned and walked away.

CHAPTER NINETEEN

Jill held her aching head and stared blankly at her computer. It had been several hours since her impromptu news conference, and all hell was breaking loose. News channels were calling repeatedly to get a statement, and the phones were ringing off the hook. Other police officers were giving her strange looks, and Detectives Georgios and Titus wouldn't speak to her when they arrived at the station. Lozano had been on the phone all morning, presumably talking to the higher ups. He didn't look happy.

None of them had eaten breakfast, and her stomach growled. They'd spent a good part of their morning talking to neighbors, trying to learn if anyone had seen or heard anything. The neighbor that had called the police had only heard the scuffle and a scream but saw nothing.

Sadly, it had taken the police fifteen minutes to arrive, and then the neighbor had come out and the dog had derailed them. By then, the killer had long since disappeared. It had been so close. Five minutes sooner, and no dog, and they may have had him.

Hearing laughter, she raised her weary head toward the coffee machine, seeing Georgios. "Hey, Jacobs. Got any more surprises up your sleeve?"

She ignored him. Having dealt with this in Seattle, she knew she shouldn't engage. Georgios nodded toward Lozano's office. "I hear he's getting his ass chewed for your little stunt. My guess is you'll be out on your own ass by the end of the day." He filled a mug with coffee. "It's about time."

She sighed, wondering where Daniels and Rem were. They'd gone down to the cafeteria to grab some breakfast. Her stomach growled again. "Georgios," she said, knowing she should keep her mouth shut but ignoring her own advice. "Has anybody ever told you what a great detective you are?" His brow furrowed. "I didn't think so." She paused. "Probably because you're as dumb as you look."

Scowling, he put his coffee down. "I don't need some second rate, has-been detective from Seattle telling me anything. How about you deal with your shit first, and then you can talk to me."

Jill straightened, tired of these assholes. "And what exactly is my shit, and what makes you think your pile is any less shitty than mine?" She put her elbows on her desk. "You seem to have an issue with females in authoritative roles. You and the killer have a lot in common." She narrowed her eyes. "Do you secretly admire him from afar? I bet you put his sketch on your bedroom wall. God knows you've dealt with rejection, just like him." She scoffed. "Your mother probably did a number on you, or you did a number on her. I can't decide which."

The squad door opened, and Rem and Daniels walked in.

Georgios' face dropped. "You stupid bitch."

Jill stood. "The only stupid bitch in this room is you. If you have a problem with me, then go whine about it to someone else. We've got bigger issues to deal with other than your damaged ego. Jesus, just get over yourself."

Georgios pointed. "If I wasn't—"

"What," said Daniels, approaching. He glowered. "A man?"

Rem approached, standing next to Georgios. "You got a problem with Jacobs?"

Georgios looked between the three of them. He pointed at Jacobs. "You deserve to be out. You've done nothing but make this worse."

"Gee," said Jill. "Maybe you should call the cops."

"Get lost, Georgios," said Rem. "Your breath alone is making this worse. I don't know how Titus stands it. Ever heard of toothpaste?"

"You're a funny guy, aren't you Remalla? You won't be laughing when I kick your ass."

"Better be prepared to kick mine, too," said Daniels, his face stony. "Don't threaten my partner." He looked at Jill. "Or partners."

Georgios fumed, his voice raising. "She's gonna get you both killed. And when that day comes—"

"Georgios! Shut your damn mouth." Lozano's voice shook the squad room, and everyone, including the phones, went quiet. He stood outside the door to his office. "We've already had this talk once. Do we need to have it again?"

Georgios deflated. He glared at all three of them, took his coffee and walked away.

Lozano glared too. "You three." He pointed at them. "In my office."

Rem eyed Georgios as he left and spoke to Jill. "Sorry about that."

"Not your fault," said Jill. "It just stuns me how stupid people can be."

He handed Jill a bag. "Hopefully this will help. I got you some donuts. Best not to face the firing squad on an empty stomach."

"I told him to get you a protein bar," said Daniels.

"Are they chocolate?" asked Jill, glad to get her mind off Georgios.

"With sprinkles," said Rem.

Daniels groaned.

She rubbed her temples. "I don't suppose they could sprinkle them with aspirin, too?" she asked.

"I didn't think to ask," said Rem. He opened his drawer and pulled out a pill bottle. "Here."

"Save me some," said Daniels.

"I didn't say tomorrow," yelled Lozano from his office door.

"Sorry, Cap," said Rem. "We're comin'." He held another white bag as Jill doled out pills to her and Daniels, picked up her coffee and followed Rem and Daniels into Lozano's office. She shut the door behind them.

"I got you a donut, Cap. Jelly," said Rem, placing the bag on Lozano's desk.

"Sit down," said Lozano. He did not smile.

They all sat. Jill wanted to eat her donut but waited. Her stomach grumbled again. She popped the aspirin in her mouth and took a sip of her coffee.

Lozano stood at his desk, his eyes narrowed. "If you think a donut is going to get you out of the mess you're in, think again. I've been on the phone with the Chief for two hours after he'd been on the phone with the mayor. Your little performance, Jacobs, has been picked up by every major news station in the country. What the hell did you think you were doing?" he asked, frowning at Jill.

"Her job," said Daniels.

"Isn't that what you brought her here for?" asked Rem.

Lozano shoved his chair into the back of his desk with a bang, and Jill jumped. "Don't be a smart ass. I brought her here to help catch a killer, not get in his face, belittle and publicly call him out. Plus, she's a consultant working on a case, for crap's sake, not a detective." He spoke to Jill. "You didn't have the authority or the approval to make a statement like that, and the chief is asking for your dismissal and wants a public apology." He paced behind his desk. "So before I go to bat for your butt, you better give me a damn good reason why I should keep you here."

"Cap…," said Rem.

"Be quiet, Remalla. I'm not talking to you." He picked up the bag. "And you know I'm on a diet.

Remalla went quiet.

"I told him, Cap…," said Daniels.

"You be quiet, too," said Lozano. "I'll deal with you two later for going along with this, but first I want to hear from her." Lozano pointed at Jill.

Jill stared at her coffee. "He wanted me to do it. I played along. We talked about that."

Lozano narrowed his eyes. "I know about the whole Seattle thing, but you went above and beyond on this one. Calling him out is one thing, but you deliberately taunted, almost begged him to kill again. That wasn't part of the script."

She paused. "I made a decision."

"You better have more for me than that," said Lozano.

She looked him in the eyes. "You didn't see the crime scene, Captain. You didn't see what he did to her or what he wrote on the walls of that bathroom. He's on a spree. He's pissed I'm not doing what he wants. I had a choice. I could either do nothing or give a subdued comment to the press, which would make you and your Chief very happy, but would do very little to solving this case. I just did it my way, instead of his. I'm tired of playing by his rules." Anxious, she stood and walked to the window. "Yes. I pushed his buttons. But I had to. Don't think for a second I didn't know what I was getting into. It was similar in Seattle. Yes. The world went nuts for a day or two, but then people moved on. The world continued to turn. But he continued to kill."

"What makes you think this will be any different?" asked Lozano.

"Because this time I made it personal. I told him the truth. That he could never have what he really wants." She crossed her arms. "Me."

"What makes you think he won't get worse? He already killed someone within days of the previous victim. His spree is escalating," said Lozano.

"He escalated because Jacobs didn't cooperate," said Daniels. "Now she cooperates, and you guys jump down her throat. What do you expect her to do?"

"You brought her here to help catch this guy. If it means stirring the pot, then that's what we'll do. And since when does the Mayor not like press coverage? He should be eating this up," said Rem. He took a bite of his own donut.

"When that press coverage makes him look like a fool," said Lozano.

"He won't look like a fool when we catch the Artist," said Daniels.

Lozano grunted. "I fail to see how this helps us catch him. It will only make him angrier."

She sighed. "I agree. It's a big risk." The aspirin was not kicking in, and her headache bloomed. "Believe me, I know how this looks, and I know the pressure on the department and know how I put everyone in the crosshairs. If this goes bad, it's on me."

"If this goes bad, it's on all of us," said Rem.

"What do you think he'll do?" asked Daniels.

Jill leaned against the windowsill. "I don't know. He's got another victim on his list, but I don't know if that will change after my show today. If he stays the course, it won't be long before he'll strike again. He took a lot of risk speeding up his timeline. He almost got caught and he may have left evidence behind. My guess, or my hope, strange as it is, is he'll do what I did. Make it personal."

"He'll come after us," said Daniels. "Maybe leave the other victim for later?"

"Or forget him or her all together," said Rem.

She massaged her neck. "Maybe. Probably. It's what I feel from him. He wants to make me hurt. If he can't have me, no one can."

"Who would be his other victim, though? Outside of us?" asked Rem.

"There's no way to know. But maybe Jacobs' show will keep him or her safe for now," said Daniels.

"Then maybe we push his buttons some more. Draw him out," said Rem. "He reacted once, let's make him react again." He held the last half of his donut. "Jacobs fired a shot across the bow. Let's fire another."

"You mean flaunt a relationship in front of him," said Daniels. "You and Jacobs."

"Exactly," said Rem, eyeing Jill.

Remembering straddling Rem that morning made Jill's stomach clench. "I still don't like it," said Jill.

"I know you don't, but I don't think we have a choice," said Rem. "Let's keep his attention on us, rather than another victim."

Jill pulled on the blinds and stared out at the street, watching the pedestrians walk by. Maybe they were on their way to work or an appointment, or maybe to pick up their children. She wished she was one of them and envied their problems. They didn't know how easy their lives were. It had been so long since she'd had a normal existence. There'd been a time when she'd walked to the store or her job, feeling good, or even feeling lousy, but only because she'd stayed up too late the previous night or because she'd had an argument with her dad. Those days were long gone. Now she had to consider losing someone else, and she wasn't sure she had the strength. But what Rem said was true. What other choices were there, other than to leave? And she wasn't sure if that would save anyone. She hung her head, thinking of Sonia and her advice.

"We can keep an eye on you both," said Lozano. "If he makes a move, we'll be there."

Jill heard the words, and knew they sounded good, but she also knew the killer. He would find a way. "You need to watch out for Daniels. He's in this, too." She watched a jogger run by. "He may be escalating, but remember, the last two victims are men." She looked back. "If we do this, that makes you two prime candidates. Roses or no roses."

Rem and Daniels stared at each other.

"You could take early leave," said Rem. "You've got a baby on the way."

"And I won't be able to look my child in the eye, or myself, if I walk away," said Daniels. "We're all in this together."

Jill's heart swelled with the weight of those words, and she prayed they were making the right choice.

"I'll take it to the chief," said Lozano. "See what he says. I'll see if I can get him to hold off on any action for now. But I won't beat around the bush. Another stunt and we may all be out."

"Promise?" asked Jill.

He grunted and started to reply when his phone rang, and he answered. Jill went back to her seat and picked up her donut bag, but now she didn't feel so hungry. This plan didn't feel right, but she had no idea what to do about it.

"Eat your donut," said Rem. "You need your strength."

Daniels snorted. He leaned forward. "How about I treat you two to an egg and bacon breakfast? Anything other than that crap you're eating."

Weariness descended over her. Her shoulders may as well have had barbells tied to them. Her stomach churned. "Sure. Why not?" She didn't think she could handle food, but she wanted to get out of the office. She couldn't help but wonder if the decision they'd just made had doomed them all.

"Your treat?" asked Rem, his eyes widening.

"My treat," said Daniels. He pointed. "But that means one entrée, not three."

Rem's face fell. "Spoilsport."

Lozano hung up the phone. "You have a friend downstairs," he said to Jill.

Jill looked up. "A what?"

"A fellow officer from Seattle. He's downstairs. Said he wanted to see you. He's on his way up."

Jill's mind whirled. Who would want to see her from Seattle? She hadn't spoken to anyone other than Merchant since she'd left. Images of officers from the past flipped through her head, but no one stood out who she would expect to visit her. Standing, she glanced out Lozano's glass window into the squad room. "Who is it?"

"Said his name was Detective Thomas Fitzpatrick. His credentials check out."

Jill froze, and she felt the color drain from her face.

"Somethin' wrong?" asked Rem, standing.

Jill walked to the Lozano's door and opened it. Her heart thumped, and she swallowed. Seconds later, a man entered the squad room. He wore pressed brown pants and a button-down long-sleeved light blue shirt with a tie. A badge on his belt reflected the overhead light. His short blonde hair was combed back, and he looked as crisp and clean as she recalled. She took a step out of the office when he saw her.

Words temporarily left her, but she made herself talk. "Hey, Fitz," she said.

He stood silently, and she could feel his appraisal.

"Hey, Jill," he answered.

CHAPTER TWENTY

They stood for a second, neither one speaking. Shocked to see him, Jill bit her lip, a million thoughts flooding her mind. What was he doing here? Their last encounter had been an ugly one, and she wondered if his opinion of her had changed.

She heard a throat clear behind her and remembered she wasn't alone. Turning, she saw Rem and Daniels standing behind her. "God. Sorry. Uhm, Rem, Daniels this is Officer Thomas Fitzpatrick from the Seattle P.D."

Rem and Daniels walked over and met Fitzpatrick with a handshake.

"Fitz, this is Detectives Gordon Daniels and Aaron Remalla," she said, noticing she was wringing her hands, and she stopped.

"I'm Detective Fitzpatrick now. They promoted me not long after you left," said Fitz.

"That's great," said Jill. "Congratulations."

"What brings you to this neck of the woods?" asked Daniels.

"I heard about your troubles. Thought I'd check in and see how it was going. I talked to Merchant. He said Jacobs was down here helping." He put a hand on his leather belt. "I heard about the latest victim this morning. Looks like you're having as much difficulty as we did." He made eye contact with Jill.

"It hasn't been easy, that's for sure. But Jacobs has been a huge help," said Remalla. "We're lucky to have her."

His face flattened. "Really? That's interesting."

Jill's heart thudded. "Fitz..."

"Because there's a few cops back in Seattle who might disagree." His quiet demeanor became more rigid.

Jill held her breath. "Why don't we go talk. There's a room off the hall."

Fitz hesitated, but then held out a hand. "Sure. Why not? Let's talk."

Jacobs could feel the curious stares of Rem and Daniels, but she wouldn't look at them. As she started to leave, Rem took her elbow. "You all right with this guy?" he asked.

She nodded. "Yeah. I'm fine."

Fitz watched as she passed him, and he followed her into a small interview room down the hall. He closed the door behind them.

"Looks like you got yourself a nice setup here," he said. "Do they know what happened in Seattle?" It was obvious his anger had not faded.

She tried to stay calm. "They know my story, yes. It's why I'm here."

He sat, leaning back in his seat. "I mean, do they know *all* of your story? Not just the ones you or Merchant told them."

Jill took a breath and her heart hammered. "They know enough."

He chuckled. "I figured."

"Why are you here? The last time we spoke, you said you hated me. I can tell this isn't a friendly visit."

He sat up and put his hands on the desk. "I may have been a little harsh the last time we spoke. I'll be the first to admit I can be a little too black and white. Henderson always said that was one of my worst traits."

At the mention of Henderson, the painful weight of the memories almost broke her. She wasn't sure how much more her shoulders could carry. "Yeah, well. He was always honest."

"To a fault. It's why I loved the guy."

She nodded, sitting in the chair beside him. "I know." She bounced her leg.

They were quiet for a moment. "I have a new partner now," he said.

"You do?" she asked.

"Name's Billings. Young kid, but smart. He just got promoted himself. Sort of like you. He impressed a lot of people and rose quickly in the ranks. Some sort of superstar." He made quote marks with his fingers.

"You like him?"

"He's all right. It takes time though, to form a partnership. Good ones are hard to find."

She nodded. "I get it."

"Do you?"

She looked over. "I lost him too, you know?"

His face hardened. "Believe me, I'm aware." He swiveled and put his elbows on his knees, clasping his hands. "I wish I wasn't."

She heard the hurt in his voice, but there was nothing she could do about it. Apologizing a million times in Seattle hadn't helped, and she'd accepted his accusations and anger. But it had been two years. "What do you want? Please don't tell me you came to heap more guilt on me, because you can't possibly heap more than I do on myself."

He studied her. "I wanted to see you. Did you know Merchant was planning to send me down to help here? Until you showed up." He paused. "It just amazes me that despite everything you've done, you always find your way back in." He shook his head. "I'd really like to know your secret."

She shook her head. "I don't have any secrets. I never did. I'm not exactly sure how I ended up here either. I never planned on it. Thought I'd be on the other side of the country by now."

"But yet, you're not. You're back on the very case that almost destroyed you. I find that so curious."

Jill set her jaw. "What's so curious about it, Fitz? I don't like it either, but what choice do I have? Running from it will only draw it out.

I'll never be rid of him if I don't confront him. No matter what he's taken from me…and you."

He studied a fingernail. "Believe me, if I could make you understand what you did…"

She put her hands on the table, her voice raising. "What I did? I did what any cop would have done. How could I have known—"

He stood. "How could you not have known? You're doing the same thing here you did in Seattle. It's all over the news. You took risks back then you knew could end in tragedy, and you cost Henderson his *life*…"

She stood, too. "You don't think I realize that? You don't think I think about it every night before I shut my eyes. His smile, his kindness, his devotion. Everything. I question every move I made. I wonder what I could have done differently. But I can't go back. I have to live with myself and the choices I made. It's been damn miserable."

He pointed at her. "I can see how guilty and miserable you are. You're back doing the same thing. Messing with something you have no business messing with. Whose lives are you risking now?"

Her voice rose higher. "I'm doing what I have to do to catch this guy. He killed Rick, a man we both loved dearly. I have to bring him to justice. He has to pay for what he did."

He made a derisive snicker. "You couldn't do it before, and I doubt you'll do it now." He nodded toward the door. "Those two detectives out there. Do they realize the danger they're in? What associating with you could cause?"

She ran a nervous hand through her hair, pulled it back and wrapped it up in a messy bun. Sweat popped out on her skin. "Stop it. I don't have to explain myself to you."

Frowning, he smacked a palm on the tabletop. "Oh, yes, you do. You already got one cop killed. And now you might get others killed. How can you live with yourself?"

Anger bubbled over. "Because I have no choice!" She shoved her chair, and it smacked against the wall. "He followed me. He'll keep killing until we either catch him or he kills me first. That sort of makes me involved. So you coming here to berate me more is pointless. I can't keep apologizing to you. You're a cop. So was Rick. Rick understood the risks. So should you."

"I don't think Rick realized he would be giving his life for you," he yelled.

"He risked his life every day as a police officer. Just like you. I have a stalker. Everyone in Seattle went along with the plan to push this guy's buttons to catch him. Even Rick. None of us knew the extent to which it would go." She held her head. "I can't do this anymore. You can hate me forever. I don't like it, but I can live with it."

"That's nice. Funny how you keep on living and everyone else keeps on dying."

She dropped her hands, her jaw dropping. "What are you saying?"

"There were whispers back in Seattle. I didn't believe them, and Rick backed you to a fault, but looking back now, sometimes I wonder."

Her heart still thudded, but now it was from pure disbelief. "I think we've said enough. You came here to yell at me again. Fine. You yelled. You're still pissed. I get it. We're done here."

"Your two new friends out there should know what's at stake. It's nice for them to say they're willing to give their life, but those are just words. I told Rick repeatedly…" He shook his head.

"You told him what?"

He paused. "I told him you weren't worth the risk. I told him that there was something fishy about your connection with the killer. Something didn't add up. I warned him, but he didn't listen to me. Our last words were in anger. If he'd just listened…" His voice thickened.

She hung her head, understanding his regret. "I can't give you what you want. I can't bring him back. I'll accept all the blame, but I can't bring him back."

"That's not what I want," he whispered.

She sighed. "What then?"

He straightened, his quiet evaporating. "I want everyone to stop giving you a second chance. To stop thinking you're some sort of wunderkind. You screwed up in Seattle, and they bring you here to screw up again. You know what will happen, don't you? He'll kill someone you care about, probably one of those two good detectives, probably the one you like the most…"

She flinched, and he caught it. His eyes widened. "You like one of them, don't you?" He chuckled sadly. "I don't believe it. Who is it? Don't tell me. The dark-haired one, right? What's his name? Remalla? Jesus, you really are a piece of work."

She didn't know what to say, but the words pierced her. Was he right? "I think you need to leave."

"What? Did I strike a chord?"

She walked to the door and opened it. "You've said your piece. Now get out."

Pausing, he frowned. "Fine. I'll leave." He stood and stepped out of the room. She followed, happy to see him out, but instead of turning down the stairs to exit, he pushed opened the doors to the squad room.

"Fitz…" She ran over and pulled his elbow, but he ignored her.

"Detectives," he said and Rem and Daniels, who were sitting at their desks, looked over.

"Yeah," said Rem.

"Did she tell you about Officer Henderson?"

"Fitz, please don't…" Her stomach flipped.

"Yes, we know about him," said Daniels, swiveling in his seat. "Officer in Seattle, who was the killer's last victim."

"Did you know she was in love with him?"

"Fitz, please," she said, finding it hard to breathe.

Rem and Daniels' faces fell.

"He wanted to marry her. I told him he was a fool. But he ignored me. He was my partner. He should have listened. Instead, he got slaughtered. In her apartment, while he was waiting for her to come home, because she was too busy on this damn case, even after Merchant had pulled her off, thinking she was Wonder Woman. So be very careful, detectives, about helping her out. Especially you, Remalla. You've been warned."

Her emotions unraveled, and she held her stomach, as hot tears escaped and ran down her cheeks.

Fitz pulled away from her. "Now they know the real story." He turned and hurried down the stairs.

Jill stood stunned in the hallway. Everything seemed to be crashing down around her as the memories rushed in and she couldn't keep them out. Coming home that night in Seattle, seeing rose petals on the floor and smiling. Seeing the candles lighted. Calling out to him, but he didn't answer. Stepping into the bathroom and seeing him, lying in a tub of water, his throat slit, makeup on his face, blood everywhere.

The room spun, and there was a hand on her arm.

"Jacobs?"

Her stomach gurgled, and she blinked, seeing Rem and Daniels beside her. She struggled to find air.

"Sit down," said Daniels.

"No." She wasn't sure who spoke, but realized it was her.

"You're as white as a sheet," said Rem. He pulled her arm.

"I have to leave," she said.

"It's okay," said Rem. "Just sit before you fall over."

She pulled away from him, still seeing Rick in the bathtub. "Stop being so damn nice to me."

"Jacobs, listen…" said Daniels.

She held her ears. "I can't listen anymore."

Rem took her elbow. "It doesn't matter."

She swiped at a tear. "Of course, it matters. How can you say it doesn't matter? I loved him, and I killed him. I lost him." She nodded toward the stairs. "Fitz is right. I screwed up. And now I'm doing it again."

"You're not—," said Rem.

The anger erupted. "What would you know about it? You don't know what I'm dealing with. What it's like to lose someone you love because of something you did. You don't know how I feel. The misery I put myself through. How I try to go on living this life when I hate myself. I hate what I did. You can't possibly understand. So please stop trying to help me. Just leave me alone." She swiped at her nose as tears streamed down her face. "I…I can't do this. I have to get out of here." She headed toward the stairs.

"Jacobs, wait," said Daniels.

She turned, barely able to see. "I'm moving out of the house tonight." Then she fled down the stairs.

CHAPTER TWENTY-ONE

Daniels headed up the steps and walked into the squad room, carrying a bag and two cups of fresh coffee. He pushed a door open with his foot and stepped inside, seeing Rem at his desk, holding a small Winnie the Pooh stuffed animal.

He held the bag out with the coffee. "A fresh cup, plus a treat."

Rem held the bear. "You got me a treat?" His eyes widened like a little boy's. It was that childlike nature that Daniels could always appreciate about his partner. Through all the nasty cases and ugly people they experienced as detectives, his partner's eyes could still light up at a tasty snack.

Rem took the coffee and opened the bag. "You got me a cookie." He smiled. "Is it chocolate?"

"What else?"

"You're the best."

"What are partners for? Since we didn't get our breakfast, I threw a protein bar in there too. You need some sustenance. That cookie won't hold you."

Rem put the bag down. "Thanks for thinking of me. I'll tell Lozano to ignore my transfer request."

Daniels chuckled and sat, drinking from his own cup of coffee. "I'd appreciate that." Despite Rem's humor, Daniels noticed he didn't touch the cookie, but continued to hold the bear. "I didn't know you kept the bear here."

Rem stared at Pooh, looking lost in his thoughts. "I brought it up here, you know, not long after…" He sighed. "I guess it helped. I put it in the drawer, and it sort of got shoved in the back. I forgot it was in there."

Daniels nodded. "She won it at the carnival, right?"

"No. I won this and gave it to her. She won the giant polar bear. We gave it to her niece. Thing could have had its own bedroom."

"That's right," said Daniels. "I remember you carrying that bear around. You could barely see around it."

"I almost didn't get it in the car," he smiled wistfully. "She was so excited though. Said she'd never won anything before." He held Winnie.

Daniels put his coffee down, watching his partner. That day at the carnival had been their last double-date together. "You know Jacobs didn't mean anything by what she said, right? She doesn't know—"

Rem held up a hand. "No. I know." He put Winnie down. "It just stirred a few things up. She's not the only one dealing with memories."

Daniels frowned. "I know, partner." Thinking about it, he realized why Rem may have felt more vulnerable. "Jennie's birthday is coming up, isn't it?"

Rem touched Winnie's paw. "Yeah. Next week." He ran a hand through his tousled hair. "Hard to believe."

Daniels remembered Jennie's last birthday before her death. Rem had thrown a surprise party for her. He'd planned it for months, but Jennie had known the whole time, and confided in Daniels. He'd played along, never telling his partner that Jennie knew anything. To his knowledge, Rem never found out. Jennie didn't want to spoil his partner's fun. He wasn't the only one who'd appreciated Rem's childlike nature. Daniels played with a pen on his desk, thinking back. He missed her, too. "You want to do something?"

Rem sat Winnie on his desk. "What, now?"

Daniels rolled his eyes. "No, bonehead. For Jennie. For her birthday?"

Rem let go of a breath. "Don't know what, the way this case is going. We're a little overwhelmed."

"We can go have a drink for her. Toast her with a pink lemonade."

Rem chuckled. "She did like her pink lemonades." He picked up the bear again, his eyes sad.

Daniels waited. "Hey," he said.

Rem looked up, his eyes haunted.

"You okay?"

Rem's eyes shone with unshed tears. "Yeah. I'll be all right." His voice was gruff. "Sometimes it just hits me, you know?"

Daniels wished there was more he could say, but there wasn't. "I know," he said, knowing time was the only answer.

They sat for a second, as the activity in the squad room buzzed around them. It had quieted since Jacobs left, but the phones still rang. They didn't seem to stop since the early morning news shows aired. Daniels straightened and picked up his coffee. "What do you want to do about Jacobs?" He hoped maybe a change in subject would help.

Rem stared at the bear for a second before taking a deep breath, opening his drawer, and putting it back. "I don't know." He closed the drawer. "I've texted her. She's not answering."

"Me, too," said Daniels. "That asshole didn't help anything."

"Some partner," said Rem.

"What do you think about the whole Henderson thing? At least now we know why she's so quiet about it."

"I think she's got a shit ton of guilt bearing down on her. And now we're dealing with the same crap again."

"And she's worried about you," said Daniels, seeing his partner's face fall. "What?"

"Well," Rem said, playing with the label on his coffee cup. "I wanted to tell you…"

Daniels narrowed his gaze. "Tell me what?"

Rem sat back and groaned. "Things got a little heated between me and Jacobs last night." He rubbed his eyes. "Or I should say early this morning."

"Heated?" asked Daniels. "Heated how?" He paused. "Anger or sex?"

Rem lifted a brow. "It wasn't anger."

Daniels nodded, widening his eyes. "I see."

"We didn't sleep together. Your phone call stopped everything in its tracks." He shifted in his seat. "Much to my discomfort."

"Sorry about that." He leaned forward. "Can't say it surprises me though." He took a sip of his drink. "You're sure about this? Starting something with Jacobs?"

Rem stared at his fingers. "I know. It sounds crazy. She's a mess, and I'm not exactly a completed puzzle."

"But you like her. And she likes you."

He nodded. "I think so. Somehow, our missing pieces fit. Although now she's dealing with survivor's guilt." He tapped his finger. "Maybe me too."

"You've been with women since Jennie."

"Yeah, well, nothing serious. This is the first time I've felt…" He gripped his cup.

"A connection?" asked Daniels.

"Yeah. As much as I tell myself to run and hide, when we're together, I just, well…I kinda feel that same zing I felt with Jennie." He closed his eyes and sighed. "Is that bad?"

Daniels knew how hard that was for Rem to admit. "No. That's not bad. That's called healing, partner." Rem opened his eyes. "Just know that Jacobs may not be in that same space."

"I know. I know." He picked up his phone. "At this point, it may not matter. After that mess with Fitzpatrick, she may not come back. I'm gonna try her again."

"You think she'll move out?" asked Daniels.

Rem shrugged. "Have no idea. She could be moving now for all I know."

"Unlikely," said Daniels. "Her purse is still here. All she has is her phone."

Rem listened and hung up. "Damn it. She's not answering. I know she's pissed but she should get in touch."

"That's another thing to consider," said Daniels. "After last night, you guys aren't exactly posing anymore. You've made yourself a bigger target."

"Well, I don't know how that's going to be an issue. I'm always with you or Jacobs and either here or at home where there're cameras and a patrol car outside. Guys gonna have to be Spiderman to get to me." He picked up the cookie bag and reached inside.

Daniels thumped a pen against his coffee cup, thinking. "I wonder if that's what Henderson thought, too."

Rem, biting his cookie, stopped and stared at this partner.

**

Jill walked down the street. A cool wind blew, and she closed her jacket against it. She'd been gone for hours, ignoring the calls and texts from Rem and Daniels. When it had started to rain, she'd stopped in a coffee shop but realizing she'd forgotten her purse, she'd could only sit and watch the pedestrians walk by. She thought of everything Fitz had said, and kissing Rem, and then thought of Sonia. The words and images racked her brain, and she didn't know what to do. All she knew is that she was tired of thinking. Her brain hurt.

She wished she could just walk away from it all. Leave the case, Rem, Henderson, the killer and Seattle all behind. She could start a new life, but that was not possible. As much as she hated it, she'd have to stay and face her issues. And she owed Rick. He deserved to have his killer brought to justice, but she wanted to do it without anyone else dying.

She thought again of Rem and their kiss. How serious was she about him? Was he just a way to forget for a while? Her heart thudded, and she knew it was more than that. There was so much about him that reminded her of Rick. His humor, kindness and that male machismo combined with an impish grin made her stomach flutter. God, this was the last thing she needed. But man, the feel of him against her…

Someone dropped a glass, and she'd jumped, pulling her out of her reverie. Staring out the window, she saw the rain had stopped, and she'd resumed her walking, knowing she'd have to return to the station get her purse, plus prevent Rem and Daniels from physically searching for her. Stopping in front of a retail store, she eyed a pair a red high-heeled shoes in the window. Thinking back, she tried to remember the last time she'd dressed up, putting on a dress, makeup and sexy shoes. The memory surfaced and fresh tears threatened. It had been her last dinner with Rick. Looking away from the shoes, she was about to leave when she caught a reflection in the window. She stood still, narrowing her eyes. Behind her, across the street, stood a man wearing a baseball cap and sunglasses. He held a camera, and he was taking photos.

CHAPTER TWENTY-TWO

Jill held her breath, and her heart rate jumped. Could it be him? Had she caught him taking pictures of her? Continuing to watch his reflection in the mirror, she considered her options. She could call for help. She had her phone. But she discarded that option. It would take too long for them to show, and she worried that making a phone call could tip him off. He seemed to be aware of every move she made. Her mind swirled. If she didn't call, then what?

Deciding, she entered the retail store. A mannequin wearing a blue pantsuit and holding a yellow handbag greeted her with an empty stare as a saleswoman approached. "May I help you?" she asked.

Jill walked and pointed, seeing the array of shoes toward the back of the store. "I love those pumps in the window."

The woman smiled. "Oh, yes. They are beautiful, aren't they?" They headed back and Jill saw various shoes lined up on shelves. The woman paused. "What size do you need?"

Jill shot a look back toward the entrance and saw that she was no longer in eyesight of the entrance. "Actually," she said, "I need your help. Do you have a rear exit in this place?"

The woman's eyes widened. "Yes. Why?"

"Where?" asked Jill.

"Just back there," the woman pointed. "It goes to the alley, but why—"

"Thanks," said Jill, heading for the exit. She walked through the back door, seeing a storage area of boxes and retail items. Beyond that was another door, and she opened it and stepped out, squinting in the sun.

She closed the door and jogged down the alley to the next side street, turned and headed back up toward the street she'd just left. Reaching the end, she stopped and peered around a brick wall, looking back toward where she'd just stood a moment before. The man with the camera was still there, and the camera hung from his neck, and he leaned against a tree. He appeared to match the height and build of the man Sonia had described.

Jill stepped back behind the wall, breathing hard. She stooped and lifted her pant leg, pulling out her small caliber weapon. She checked it and put it back. Then stepped to the wall and looked again. The man was checking his camera. After a few seconds, he put it up to his face and appeared to take a few shots near the retail store she'd just entered. There was the sudden blare of a horn and the screech of brakes at the light at the corner, and Jill saw the man turn and she darted across the street.

Reaching the corner, she made it to a thick tree and stood behind it. She took a steadying breath, trying to pace herself. He could walk away and she couldn't afford to lose him. Closing her eyes, she said a silent prayer and stepped out from the tree. The man was maybe thirty feet from her, facing away, and aiming his camera. Coming up behind him, she reached low, pulled out her gun and kicked him in the back of the knee. His leg buckled, and he yelled as he went down on his knees. She put a hand on his neck and held the gun on his head. "Police. Put down the camera. Now."

The man froze. "What is it? What did I do?"

Jill shoved him. "I said put down the camera. Now."

His hands shaking, he put down the camera. "Here. Take it. You can have it. Just don't kill me."

"Why are you taking pictures of me?" asked Jill.

The man stuttered. "Pic…pictures of you? What…what do you mean?"

"I saw you. You were taking pictures of me across the street. Why?" The man started to turn. "Don't move. Keep your hands where I can see them. Get down on your belly."

"But…but…I didn't do anything."

"I said get on your stomach." Jill gave him a shove with her foot and he shakily dropped to his hands and went flat on the sidewalk. A small crowd began to gather, but Jill ignored them. She couldn't get distracted. "Answer my question. Why are you taking pictures of me?"

The man raised his arms. "I am not taking pictures of you. I'm an art student at the community college. I'm taking photos of the street and the people on it. That's it. I promise."

Jill hesitated. The small group of people was growing, and she pulled out her credentials. "Nothing to see here. I'm a cop, and I'm questioning this man for suspicious activity." She figured telling them she was a consultant would be less effective.

The people studied her before slowly moving on. Jill turned back when she heard a woman shriek. "What are you doing?" A thin woman with long blonde hair and a knitted cap ran up. She held two ice cream cones. "Roger? What's happening?"

Roger yelled back. "I don't know. Ask the crazy cop lady. I was taking pictures, and she came after me."

Jill kept her weapon trained on Roger but held up her hand at the blonde woman. "Stop right there." The woman didn't move and the ice cream began to drip down her fingers. "Who is he and why is he taking photos?"

The woman's face fell, and she stammered.

"For God's sake, tell her Sheila," said the man from the ground.

Sheila looked as white as her ice cream. "He…He's Roger Bailey. We're students at Dayton Community College. We're working on a photography project together."

Jill studied the woman. Her hands were shaking as the ice cream dripped. She was no more of a threat than the kids in the nearby park. Jill put her credentials back in her jacket pocket, reached down, picked up the camera and held it out. "Show me."

Sheila eyed the camera and her ice cream, seeming unsure.

"I'd suggest you drop the ice cream, Sheila," said Jill.

"Come on, Sheila," said Roger, his voice high-pitched. "Show her."

Hearing Roger, Sheila seemed to snap out of it. She dropped the ice cream cones into the grass and reached for the camera. Jill still held her gun but pointed it toward the ground.

Sheila hit some buttons and the back of the camera lit up. Jill stepped closer and watched as Sheila flipped through the photos. They were all scenic shots of the street and random people, all in black and white. There were a few shots of the park, and one of the retail store Jill had just been in, but it was a picture of the unique sculpture of a Native American man that stood in front of the neighboring storefront that was the focal point. Jill was not in the photo.

Jill's heart slowed but her chest constricted. What the hell had she just done? Pulled her weapon on an unsuspecting art student and his pretty girlfriend. She holstered her weapon. "You can get up, Roger."

Roger seemed uncertain, but finally he took some shaky movements and got to his knees. Sheila ran over to him. "Are you all right?" She helped him stand.

He grimaced at Jill, wiping at his shirt and pants. "What the hell is the matter with you? I should call your captain and complain."

Jill bit her lip, feeling like an idiot. "I apologize, but there's a serial killer on the loose, and he's been taking pictures of victims."

"And you thought I was him?" asked Roger angrily.

"I had to take precautions," said Jill. "You fit the profile."

Sheila handed Roger the camera. "Are you talking about the Makeup Artist? The one that's been on the news?"

Jill nodded. "I am."

Roger checked his camera. "I don't care. I could sue you and your whole department for harassment. This is outrageous."

Jill's shoulders dropped and extreme weariness crept in and almost made her cry. Clouds had rolled back in and rain threatened once more. She stared up at the sky and wondered how she had gotten here. It had been a hell of a long ass day and it seemed to be getting worse. "You know what, Roger? You do that. That's the least of my problems right now." She regarded Sheila. "Sorry for the trouble." She turned and walked away as a light rain began to fall.

"Trouble?" yelled Roger. "Trouble? You pulled a gun on me."

Jill heard Sheila answer. "Oh, shut up, Roger. It's the most interesting thing that's ever happened to you. Too bad you didn't get a picture."

Jill kept walking. She passed the playground, seeing the kids jumping on the jungle gym and laughing on the swing set. She tried not to think. It didn't help and had only caused more problems. The rain fell lightly, but she didn't care. She didn't know how long she walked or where she was going, until paying closer attention, she found herself back at the station. Her head was clearer, and she was calmer, but her incident with Roger and Fitz played in her head. Should she be on his case anymore? She hadn't arrived at any clear decisions. If Roger called and complained, then it may be out of her hands. Rick's voice popped into her head. *Just take it one day at a time*. Rem had told her the same thing. Maybe that was all she could do.

Entering the building, she wondered what she would face. She'd been a little hysterical when she'd left and said some things she didn't mean. Plus, the guys wouldn't be happy that she'd ignored them. All she wanted to do was get her purse and leave. Maybe if she was lucky, they'd be gone. She didn't think she could handle any more talking about her problems.

Entering the squad room, she paused when she saw Daniels typing at his desk, but Rem was not around. Standing there, she debated leaving but told herself to get over it. She walked over warily. "Hey," she said.

He stopped working. "Hey. Welcome back." He frowned. "Were you out in the rain?"

She touched her damp hair. "I guess so." She sat at her desk, feeling a little sheepish. "I forgot my purse."

"Did you also forget how to text?"

Her shoulders drooped. "I'm sorry. I just…I just needed a breather. I was a mess, and Fitz…well, he brought up a lot of things I…I really wasn't prepared to face."

He swiveled in his chair. "Did your breather help? You feeling better?"

Jill picked up a pen and played with it. "Honestly, I'm wondering if I should even be here."

Daniels didn't speak for a second, but then he cocked his head. "Your friend, if you can call him that, is an asshole."

"He lost his best friend and partner."

"You did too. And it doesn't give him the right to be cruel."

She paused. "What he said about Henderson…"

"Is something you should have told us earlier, but we're not judging you for it."

She rubbed her arms. "Why not? I do."

He leaned forward. "That's obvious and understandable. But how could you have known what would happen?"

She shook her head. "I've had this conversation a million times with Merchant. But it doesn't help. I'll always feel guilty. I'll always wonder…what if?"

Daniels sighed. "At some point, you will have to forgive yourself. You were in an impossible situation."

She thought of Rick and their last night together, and what he'd asked her. "Maybe."

He studied her. "You moving out of Rem's place?"

She closed her eyes, coming back to the present. "Oh, god. I threatened to move out, didn't I?"

"Yes. You did."

Opening her eyes, she fiddled with the pen. "It's probably a good idea. Now that Rem knows about Rick, he'd probably prefer it."

"Then you don't know Rem very well."

She put the pen down. "He's foolish. He'll want me to stay and risk his life."

"You think leaving will risk either of you any less?"

She considered that. "No. Not really." She looked over. "Is he here?"

"I sent him home. His day wasn't much better than yours."

She hung her head. "I'm sorry. That's my fault."

Daniels paused, as if considering what to say next. "It's nobody's fault, but you should know, you're not the only one who's grieving."

Jill peered up.

"He lost someone, too, much like you. About eighteen months ago. Her name was Jennie. He was crazy about her, but a drunk driver killed her coming home late one night. Rem was supposed to be with her, but he got caught up at work, so she went out with friends instead, and never made it home."

Jill's breath caught in her throat. "He never said anything."

"And he probably never will, until he's ready."

She didn't know what to say.

"He's a tough guy on the exterior, but he'll crumble like a cookie on the inside, and he can hide pain like a prizefighter. So go easy on him, okay? He's been through the ringer and back." He paused. "And be careful with his heart. It's tender just like yours."

Jill shared a gaze with Daniels and realized how much Daniels loved his partner. She wondered if Rick had felt the same about Fitz. Partnerships like that were unique but not rare. It came with risking your life with someone every day. She'd never worked with a partner long enough to develop that bond, and now she wished she had. It would be nice to rely on right now.

Daniels pointed with a pen. "And don't think I haven't had this talk with him too, about you. We both know what you're going through."

Jill smiled softly, thinking about partnerships. Maybe she had what she was looking for. "He told you, didn't he? About our little tryst last night?"

"He did. Sorry I interrupted."

She groaned. "Maybe it was for the best."

"Maybe. Maybe not. You two could be good for each other."

"The timing sucks."

"Since when does everything come together perfectly? Life never works that way."

"I wish it did."

"Me, too." He picked up a folder and tossed it on a pile. "What are you going to do?"

She stared up at the ceiling. "I have no idea. But I don't think I'm going to move out."

"Good. I'm glad. You should go home and tell him. Have a good talk. You could both use the opportunity to tell the whole truth to each other."

She nodded. "It couldn't hurt."

"It would probably help. You've both had a hellish day."

Jill thought of Roger. "You could say that. I accosted a student photographer today. Thought he was taking pictures of me. He wasn't pleased."

Daniels raised a brow. "Sounds like you had a fun afternoon to go with your fun morning."

Putting her elbow on the desk, she rested her head in her hand. "If he calls and complains, that'll be the nail in the coffin."

"Did he get your name?"

"No. I flashed my pseudo badge. Told 'em I was a cop, which isn't great either. The girlfriend seemed cool though."

Daniels waved a hand. "Don't worry about it. He didn't get a picture, did he?"

She couldn't help but snort. It all seemed so ridiculous. "Sadly, no."

"It'll be fine. If he calls and complains, he won't know who to complain about. And if he does, we'll deal with it. Like we always do."

She studied him. "You're a good cop, Daniels. Rem is lucky to have you."

He threw his pen in a drawer. "We're all lucky to have each other. That's the way I see it." He smiled slightly. "But I agree. I don't know what Rem would do without me."

She straightened. "Can I quote you on that?"

"Please do. He can't deny it. About time he heard the truth."

Ready to go back to the house, she started to rise but stopped. "Rem and I rode together. I don't suppose you could give me a ride?"

"Lozano took him home. Rem left his car keys here, so you'd have transportation. We figured you'd be back for your purse. The keys are in the drawer."

She reached and pulled the drawer open. "He's gonna let me drive his car?"

"Now you know he likes you."

She took the keys. "What about you? You need some help here?"

"Nah. I'm just finishing up paperwork. Told Rem he could buy me dinner for finishing his too. He actually agreed to it. That's how I knew he was spent."

Feeling her fatigue, she found her purse. "Thank you for helping with the reports, and for telling me about Rem."

"You're welcome."

Standing, she flipped her purse over her shoulder and started to leave, but hesitating, she turned back. "If something happens to him, I'll never forgive myself. Rick and Fitz. They were close. I know you don't believe this, but if something were to happen to Rem, I'm not sure you would act any differently toward me than Fitz."

His face went flat. "Let's try not think the worst. I honestly don't know how I would react."

She raised a brow. "Now who needs to tell the truth?"

He didn't answer, and she picked up her phone from her desk and walked away. "Good night, Daniels."

CHAPTER TWENTY-THREE

Rem flipped through the photo album. It was probably a bad idea, but he did it anyway. There were pictures of him and Jennie after their first date, the time they went to the zoo, their first weekend away together. Sighing, he wondered if there would ever come a time when he would stop thinking about her, but he doubted it.

The microwave dinged, and he closed the book. He'd gotten home about an hour earlier and had jumped into a hot shower, hoping to ease his tension. It had helped a little. Between his kissing Jacobs, the early morning crime scene, the encounter with Fitzpatrick, Jacobs' outburst, and his memories of Jennie, it had been a tough day.

The smell of the frozen meal filled the kitchen and his stomach growled. His lack of food intake was catching up to him. He pulled the food out of the microwave and sat down to eat. He knew Jacobs had returned to the station and was on her way back because Daniels had texted him. Remembering what she'd said, he wondered if she'd decided to move out, and if she had, how would he handle it?

He didn't wonder for long, because he heard a key in the lock and the door opened. Blowing on his food, he peered around the wall and saw Jacobs return. She put her purse down and glanced over at him.

"Hey," she said.

"Hey," he answered, holding his fork. "Glad you came back. We thought you'd jumped ship."

She crossed her arms. "I considered it. Sorry about not getting in touch."

"We talked about this. You need to stay in contact. Now more than ever."

"I realize that. I just had a moment. I promise I won't do it again."

He nodded and picked at his food. "You okay?"

"I'm still alive. That's about all I can offer." Entering the kitchen, she put his keys on the table. "Thanks for the ride."

He took a bite. "You're welcome. My car intact?"

"Yes. I only hit two trees and three curbs on the way over."

He stopped mid-chew.

"I'm kidding. Your car is fine."

He swallowed. "You should never kid with a man about his car while he's eating."

Frowning, she pointed at his meal. "You call that eating? What is that?"

"It's Salisbury Steak with potatoes."

"It looks gross."

"Well, the pantry isn't exactly brimming with options."

She nodded. "I know." She checked her watch. "I realize we're beat and this day has been worse than one of my nightmares, but how about we order a pizza, have a beer, and talk?"

"Talk?" he asked.

"Yes. I think we need to discuss a few things, don't you think?"

He poked at his meal, studying it, before dropping his fork. "Sounds good to me."

"Great. Large pepperoni?"

"With mushrooms."

"Perfect." She pulled out her phone and ordered the pizza. After the phone call, she pointed to her room. "I'm going to take a quick shower."

Rem tossed his so-called steak in the trash. "Okay."

She disappeared, and he felt fairly certain she wasn't planning on moving out, at least not tonight. Comfortable in his sweats, he settled himself on the couch, flipped on the TV, and was pleased to find a Godzilla movie. Yawning, he hoped he didn't fall asleep before the pizza arrived.

Twenty minutes later, she returned, wearing a robe. Her hair was up, and loose, damp tendrils framed her face. Something stirred inside him, and he recalled their encounter early that morning.

Sitting beside him, she glanced at the TV. "Godzilla? Really?"

"What's wrong with Godzilla?"

She smiled. "Nothing. It's a classic, isn't it?"

"Sure is."

Getting comfortable, she picked at her robe. "We've got a few minutes before the pizza gets here."

"We do," he said. "You said you want to talk?"

She nodded. "I wanted to apologize for what happened today, with Fitz."

"There's no need."

"Yes, there is. I said things I shouldn't have said. And if I hurt your feelings, I apologize."

He sat up. "You didn't hurt my feelings. That jerk said things he shouldn't have said."

"They were all true though."

He shifted to face her. "He told his version. Why don't you tell me yours?"

Her face fell. "I've wanted to. It's just not an easy subject for me to talk about."

"I get it. But it will help. I get the feeling you haven't been able to talk about it with anyone."

"Not really."

"Now's a good time to start."

Looking uneasy, she glanced over. "If I tell you about Rick, will you tell me about Jennie?"

He went still for a moment. "Daniels told you?"

"Yes."

He took a breath and blew it out. "Deal. You show me yours and I'll show you mine."

Still playing with her robe, she reached into her pocket and pulled out a small black-and-white photo. "Okay." She sat cross-legged on the couch and held the picture out. It was Jacobs and a dark-haired man in one of those photo booths, making funny faces at each other. She held it out, and he took it. "I met Rick when I was an officer. We hit it off immediately. You know. One of those strange connections."

Rem knew all too well. "I get it." He studied the picture and thought of Jennie.

"We didn't advertise it. Technically, it was frowned on to date a co-worker. Only Fitz knew and my partner but that was it." She paused. "Not long after we became serious is when the killings began. Long story short, they promoted me to detective and assigned me the Makeup Artist case. It was a lot of long hours and hard work, plus having to deal with the killer's attraction. It would have been an easy reason for Rick to break up with me."

"But he didn't."

She smiled softly. "He was the opposite. He couldn't have been more supportive and understanding. I missed a lot of dinners and dates. I know it was hard on him, but he never complained."

She quieted, and Rem sensed her emotion rising. "Take your time."

Jill cleared her throat, and continued. "As the pressure mounted to catch the Artist, I pushed back, and maybe took risks I shouldn't have. Sort of like today." She sighed. "I thought I knew what I was doing. I had a sense of this guy. I felt like I knew him. Not personally, but through some odd connection. I was sure his need for my involvement would be his undoing." She rubbed her forehead. "I was wrong."

"You were doing what you thought was best."

She clenched her hands together. "I knew many people thought I was nuts. I knew things I didn't understand how I knew. There was talk

I was in cahoots with the killer. Rick ignored it all. He knew what I was up against, and he never failed to back me up. Fitz on the other hand, I sensed he'd told Rick otherwise. Rick ignored him, too."

"Sounds like Rick was a stand-up guy."

She nodded. "To a fault." She wiped at her eye. "If he'd listened…"

He let her have a second. "What happened next?"

She collected herself. "That last night I saw him, we had dinner. He took me out to a nice place. I was late. I'd gone home to get cleaned up for once. But he didn't care I was late. He had this look in his eye and I knew something was up." She paused and swallowed. "We had a lovely meal. He bought champagne, and we toasted, and that's when he got down on one knee." Tears threatened, and she shook her head, pushing her hair back.

Rem grabbed a tissue and handed it to her.

"I'm not gonna lose it," she said.

"It's okay if you do," he said.

She fanned her face. "I've never told anyone this before."

He understood the remorse she carried. "It's about time you did."

She took a moment but then kept going. "He proposed in the restaurant, and I said yes."

"That's great," he said.

Nodding, she wiped a fallen tear from her face. "We decided not to tell anyone. He may have told Fitz, but I don't know. I doubt Fitz would have approved." She dabbed at her cheeks with the tissue. "We didn't even have a ring. He wanted to look for one after the case was over, when we had more time to find something we both liked."

"Sounds smart."

She held her forehead. "It didn't matter though. Three days later, I came home after a late night at work. I wasn't supposed to be at the station. Merchant had taken me off the case. Told me to take some time off, but I'd ignored him. Rick was at my place, making dinner. I told him I was on my way, and that I loved him. Those were my last words to him." Fresh tears fell.

Rem sighed. "Tell me what happened."

She took a shaky breath. "I came home. There were rose petals on the floor, the table was set, soft music was playing, and candles lit. I didn't see him, though." She bit her lip. "I saw the bathroom light on, so I called him, but he didn't answer. I went in…and found him." She closed her eyes. "He was in the bathtub. His throat was…was…slit, and there were rose petals in the tub and writing on the wall. It said, 'I did this for you.'" Her voice was a whisper.

Rem had read the report, which was horrible enough on its own, but now he saw the devastation in a new light. "I'm so sorry."

Holding the tissue to her eyes, she cried softly. "I was in shock. I don't really remember what happened after that. The next thing I recall is sitting on the couch with Merchant beside me. He had to tell me what had happened because I'd blocked it completely."

Rem shifted and moved closer, putting the picture down on the coffee table, and pulled her into his arms. "Come here," he said, and she wrapped around him and her hot tears slid down his neck. Sniffing, her crying slowly ebbed, and then the doorbell rang.

"Pizza's here," he said. "Think you can handle some food?"

She pulled back and made a sad smile, dabbing her cheeks. "I'm starving."

"Then stay put. I'll be right back." He left the couch and ran to the door. He took it from the delivery guy and headed back to the couch. Seeing she was more composed, he put the pie down. "I'm getting us some beers and napkins."

She nodded and opened the box.

He ran into the kitchen and got what he needed, and they spent the next fifteen minutes wolfing down most of the pizza while Godzilla roared and breathed fire as he battled Mothra. Rem was glad to have a moment of quiet. Her story was difficult to comprehend, and he marveled at her strength. Plus, he needed some sustenance before he started talking about Jennie.

Jacobs sat back, holding her stomach. "I can't eat another bite."

He wiped his mouth with a napkin. "Feel better?"

"Yes. Much." She took a swig of her beer.

"Good." Taking the last bite of his crust, he closed the pizza lid. He glanced at the TV as Godzilla roared again.

Jacobs sat back and tucked her feet up on the couch. "You ready?"

He knew what she meant. Crumpling his napkin, he threw it on the table. "I guess so." Sighing, he relaxed against the cushions, holding his beer.

"Tell me about her."

He picked at the label on his glass, not sure where to begin. "We met on a blind date."

"Really?"

"Yeah, well, she wasn't my date. She was the other guys."

"Whoops."

He smiled. "I know. I'd been dating a girl for a few weeks and she wanted to go out with her friend. So we did. Her friend was Jennie, and much like you and Rick, we hit it off immediately. We talked a good portion of the night while the other two stared at each other. My date broke it off before we even made it to the car. I went out with Jennie the next weekend. It was love at first sight. We, to the point that we were able, considering our work schedules, were inseparable after that. I'd never met a woman who could put up with me so well. She even liked my cheesy movies."

"That's remarkable."

He half-smiled. "What that she liked me or my movies?"

"Your movies are a little cheesy, but there's nothing remarkable about liking you. You're easy to like."

"That has not always been my experience with women."

"Then you were dating the wrong women."

"Apparently so." He took another swig of his beer.

"Continue," she said.

"Right." Picking at the label some more, he kept going. "There's really not much more to say. We dated for a year. I loved her. Daniels loved her. That was another great thing about Jennie. The life of a cop isn't easy, and Daniels and I go back a ways. We're like brothers and spend a lot of time together, but she loved both of us. And she never had an issue with my career choice, even when I came home with a bruised face or a story of how I ran down a perp or fired my weapon. She didn't like it, but she accepted it."

"What did she do for work?"

"She managed a chain of daycares. Her hours weren't so great either. But she loved seeing kids every day." His breath caught. "We always talked about having a couple of our own. She wanted to be a mom." He gripped the bottle, thinking back.

Jacobs put her beer down and reached over and took his wrist. "I'm sorry."

He waved her off and put his own bottle down. "It's okay." He spoke softly.

"No. It's not."

He nodded. "Life happens."

"Life sucks."

He chuckled. "And then you die." She slid her hand into his and he took it. Taking a deep breath, he pushed forward. "Anyway, things were going great. We'd been entertaining the thought of marriage, but neither of us were in any rush. We were just enjoying our time together. We thought we had a lot. Until…we didn't."

She squeezed his fingers. "What happened?"

He groaned, wishing he could wipe that night from his memories. "We had plans to go out. I canceled because Daniels and I were caught up in a case. She went out on a girl's night and got hit by a drunk driver doing eighty on a forty mile per hour road. She likely never knew what hit her." He closed his eyes, biting back the swell of emotion and pain.

"My God."

He paused, clearing his throat. "I got the call from a patrol and rushed to the hospital. But she was DOA." The tears surfaced, and he wiped them away.

"Rem…"

He rubbed his eyes. "Like you, I remember little from that night. Only that Daniels had to pull me away from her. I identified the body, and I couldn't leave her side."

Jacobs reached over and grabbed a tissue for him and kept one for herself. He saw her wipe her cheeks.

"The next few days were a whirl. Her funeral, the eulogy. I couldn't do it, so her brother did. I was a wreck. Daniels wasn't much better, but he kept it together for me. He got me through it somehow."

"He's a good man. He loves you."

He nodded, trying to compose himself. The tears flowed down his face, and he sniffed. "I wouldn't have survived it without him."

"How long have you two been partners?"

His tissue crumpled, he wiped his face with his shirtsleeve. "Nine years."

"That's a long time. I think he still worries about you."

He sighed. "I know he does. It's his nature. But I do the same. He's had his own challenges, which is why I'm glad he found Marjorie."

"You like her?"

"I do. She's good for him. Plus, she puts up with me."

"That's good. He seems happy."

He looked at their clasped hands, feeling comfort from her touch. "He is, but I think he tries to hide it, and I wish he wouldn't."

"He doesn't want to make you feel bad about losing Jennie?"

"It's ridiculous, and I told him so."

"Did he listen?"

"He did, but he's still working on it."

She nodded and wiped her nose. "I guess we all need time."

"They say it heals, but has that been your experience?" He studied her with shiny eyes.

"Not yet."

"Me either. I just learn how to bear it better."

"Me, too. Until you have those days where you can't bear it at all."

He thought of that afternoon. "Those days suck."

"Yes. They do."

He rubbed his thumb over the back of her hand. "Thank you for listening."

"Thank you for sharing."

Her thumb moved over his and his body warmed.

Shifting on the couch, she flapped the corner of her robe. "It's getting a little warm in here."

Rem smiled. "A little. It must be the beer."

She gave him a dubious look. "I'm sure."

His eyes traveled over her, and he remembered their early morning kissing.

Biting her lip, she said, "Maybe we should talk about this too."

"Talk about what?"

"The way you're looking at me right now."

"How am I looking at you?"

"Godzilla's not the only one shooting fire." She pulled on her robe and it came partially open. He saw her nightgown beneath, and his body heat flared.

"All this sharing will do that," he said, turning to face her. "But if you want to talk about it, that's fine."

She rested an arm on the back of the couch. "You really think it's a good idea?"

"What? Sharing?"

"Very funny. You know what I mean."

He grinned, feeling better as his mind shifted from Jennie to Jacobs. "I know what you mean." Looking at her hair, he wanted to pull that pin out and see it spill over her shoulders. "And I know there's a lot to consider."

"We're in the middle of a serious case, and our lives could be at risk. And we're both still grieving the loss of two of the most important people in our lives." She rested her forehead in her hand. "I'm afraid we're biting off more than we should be chewing."

Rem thought about it. "Are you attracted to me?"

Her eyes widened. "That's a silly question. I almost jumped your bones last night."

"Just checking. I'm attracted to you too, by the way."

She rubbed her forehead. "Are you attracted to me in the 'she's cute and I need to blow off some steam' way, or in the 'she's beautiful and I can't wait to be with her' way."

The question surprised him, but it was fair. "Listen, Jacobs. I'm not saying I don't think we can't have some fun together, because we can. This case is sucking the life out of us and blowing off some steam might be a little stress relieving. But does that mean once this case is over, I'm done?" He squeezed her hand. "No. Not for me at least. I like you. I'd like to spend time with you and get to know you, and I hope once this case ends, we can do that. But I know you've got a lot to deal with and things to work out, so maybe it's you that needs to just blow off the steam and then move on after the case. But I get it. I'm not asking for you to give me more than you have. I think if we're honest with each other, we'll be fine. We're both adults here."

She let out a deep sigh. "I think our hearts are tender right now. I don't want one of us to get hurt."

Rem paused. "If you want to wait, that's fine. I understand. You won't get any pressure from me. I can stay in the friend zone."

"You're sure?"

"Doesn't mean I won't have lewd thoughts." He wiggled his eyebrows.

Smiling, she moved her thumb over his hand again. The sensation was distracting. "I may have a few of my own."

"I hope they're colorful and creative."

She met his gaze. "They are."

Looking into her eyes in the low lighted room, he wanted to reach over and pull her back into his lap. "Good."

She raised a brow. "So, we're okay?"

"We're more than okay."

"Good." She was quiet for a moment. "I guess we should probably go to bed. It's been a long day. And it will be a hard one tomorrow. Assuming I'm not fired."

"You won't be fired."

"You didn't hear about the photographer."

Rem raised a brow. "What photographer?"

Jacobs waved. "Doesn't matter. I'll tell you tomorrow. Again, assuming I'm still employed."

"You will be."

"If you say so."

"I say so." He met her gaze, and they stared until Jacobs roused herself.

"I'm getting up now." She let go of his hand and stood. He stood with her. "Thank you for talking tonight," she said. "You're a good talker. A lot of men aren't."

"I'm not a lot of men." He was close enough that he could have reached out and pulled her in.

She nodded, and he could see her flushed cheeks. "No. You're not."

Her robe had come open and he could see a long white nightgown beneath. He took a steady breath. "Good night."

"Good night."

Standing there, she held eye contact and didn't move. He didn't move either, and he wasn't going to.

He waited. "What time do you want to get up tomorrow? You want me to wake you?" His voice was gruff.

"No. I'll set my alarm," she said, but her eyes shifted, and he saw her study his face and then her gaze fell on his lips, and his whole body reacted, but he stayed still. Time slowed and almost stopped.

"Oh, what the hell," she said, taking a step closer. Reaching out, she put her hand on his chest and moved it up to his neck. "Let's blow off some steam." Her fingers moved into his hair and she pulled him in.

Rem needed no more invitation. Letting himself be pulled, he reached around her waist, and drew her close as his lips descended over hers. The same electricity as the night before sparked, and he didn't feel the need to be delicate. He kissed her hungrily. She matched his hunger, slanting her mouth over his. Their breathing escalated rapidly, and he moaned, gripping her back. Loosening his hold, he let his hands travel upward and he yanked her robe off and it fell to the ground. Seeing her sleeveless nightgown, he trailed his fingers over her soft shoulders, his body tingling from the sensation. Still kissing her, he heard a soft keening from her as she gripped at his shirt and he stepped forward as she traveled backward. Her back hit the living room wall, and he pressed against her, loving the feel of her body against his. His desire mounting fast, he forced himself to slow down. If he didn't, this moment would be over way too soon. But she felt so damn good.

Her tongue roamed over his, and her fingers were in his hair until they moved back to his shirt, where he felt her tugging on it. Pulling back briefly, he yanked it off, and then she pulled him back, but now her fingers were on his bare skin, and he groaned as she explored his chest. His hands moved to cup her backside, and he pushed against her. Her head fell back, and he kissed her neck, savoring the taste of her skin.

Gathering her nightgown in his hands, he pulled it up, and she raised her arms as he took it off. He gasped when he saw she was naked beneath it. Her body in the soft light of the TV was glorious. My God, how was he going to survive this? All he wanted to do was ravage her, but he forced himself to slow down and stay in control.

Breathless, she watched him take her in, and reaching out, she pulled him back against her, and she spoke into his ear, her raspy voice tickling his skin. "No more Mr. Nice Guy. Take me now and don't be gentle. I want you. Desperately."

His heart almost burst out of his chest and it was all he needed to hear. He reached low and picked her up as her long legs encircled his waist. Carrying her, he took her to her room while she peppered his neck with kisses and ran her hands down his bare back. Closing the door behind him, he spoke into her ear, his heart racing and his voice rough. "Your wish is my command, sweetheart."

CHAPTER TWENTY-FOUR

Daniels studied the file. He'd come in early to review a few things. Since learning more about Jacobs' relationship with Henderson, he wondered if that might shed more light on the case, and maybe help shake something loose he hadn't noticed before.

Hearing the squad door open, he turned to see Rem and Jacobs walk in, both looking relaxed and far better than they had last night.

Rem held a bag and handed it to him. "Mornin' partner. I got you some breakfast."

Daniels took it. "Please tell me it's not a jelly donut."

"Nope." Rem raised his own bag. "That's for me. You got a bran muffin." He frowned and made a choking sound. "I don't how you eat those things. They taste like dust."

Daniels smiled. "It's called popping it in your mouth and chewing. Something you are very familiar with." He pulled out the muffin. "Thank you."

"You're welcome."

"How long have you been here?" asked Jacobs.

"I got here about an hour ago. Wanted to check a few things," he said.

"How's Marjorie?" asked Rem.

"She's great but getting tired of carrying the little fellow around. It doesn't make sleeping too comfortable."

"I bet," said Rem.

Daniels looked between the two of them. "How are you two doing after yesterday?"

They glanced at each other. "We're great," said Rem.

"Yes. I'm feeling much better," said Jacobs.

"You get some sleep?" asked Daniels.

Jacobs smiled shyly, putting her purse away. "Uh, sure. Slept fine."

"Me, too," said Rem, offering a similar smile and arranging papers on his desk. "Like a baby."

Daniels narrowed his eyes. "Good. Glad to hear it." Focusing on his partner, it suddenly became clear why Rem looked so sheepish. "You two needed the rest." Something had happened between the two of them.

Rem met his gaze. "We did."

Daniels nodded, saying nothing else.

"Am I still employed?" asked Jacobs, looking toward Lozano's office.

"As far as I know," said Daniels, seeing Lozano through the glass window. "He's been on the phone since he came in about thirty minutes ago."

"You'll be fine. Don't worry about it," said Rem.

"I appreciate your positive outlook. I wish I shared it," she said, staring at the squad room. "At least the phones have quieted a bit."

"I'll take that any day," said Rem.

Jacobs glanced at Daniels' desk. "Is there something from Seattle that we missed?" she asked. "Which victim are you looking at?"

He held up the folder. Although much of it was on digital, sometimes printing it on paper helped him to review it better. He paused. "Henderson's."

She stopped for a second. "Why his?"

"Something interesting?" asked Rem.

"I wondered since we know his relationship to Jacobs maybe something would stand out that didn't before." He looked at Jill. "If you'd rather not review it, I can talk about it with Rem."

She stared at the file. "No. It's okay."

"You're sure?" asked Rem.

"There are crime scene photos," said Daniels.

She nodded. "It's fine. I'll step away if it gets to me."

"Okay," said Daniels. He pointed at the paper. "This has always bugged me before. Henderson's throat was slashed. He wasn't stabbed, and he wasn't posed. Plus, the writing was different. Instead of 'I see you' he wrote, 'I did this for you.' Why?"

"He had the makeup though," said Rem.

"And it was applied accurately," said Jacobs. "The press didn't know the details. It's specifically blush and lipstick. Both red. We did have a copycat in Seattle. Guy put blue eye shadow and mascara on the vic."

"So the makeup fits, but why the slashed throat?" asked Daniels.

Rem sat on the edge of his desk. "Henderson's a cop. He's not going to go down easy. If our killer approaches from the front, he might have a fight on his hands. If he comes from behind, it's an easy kill."

"But there's no blood except in the bathtub," said Jacobs.

"Yes, there was," said Daniels. "Forensics found evidence of blood on the bathroom floor and walls."

"What?" asked Jacobs. "But I didn't see…"

"The killer had cleaned it up," said Rem. "Our guy probably didn't want you to know what you were walking into. Henderson's getting ready for you to come home. He's doing his thing, making dinner, dropping rose petals, leans over to prep the bath, and the killer comes up from behind him."

"He never saw it coming," said Daniels.

"Killer gets Henderson in the bathtub, cleans up the bathroom, leaves his note, and disappears, knowing how you'll find him," said Rem.

Jacobs' face fell. "I never reviewed the file. I never went back to work after he..."

"It's understandable," said Daniels.

Jacobs closed her eyes.

"You hangin' in there?" asked Rem.

Opening her eyes, she nodded. "What else?"

"The writing," said Daniels. "'I did this for you.' What does it mean?"

"My guess is the killer thought he was doing me a favor by removing Rick from my life," said Jacobs. She set her donut bag to the side of the table. "I need some coffee. You want some?" she asked Rem.

"Please," said Rem.

"So, Henderson's out of the way, which means you have no one left but him," said Daniels.

Jacobs poured two cups of coffee from the pot on the counter. "That sums it up."

"Makes sense," said Rem, taking a coffee from Jacobs. "Thanks."

"But he did nothing about it," said Daniels. "He disappeared when you did."

Jacobs brought her coffee to her desk. "I know. That was his last murder in Seattle."

"But why not come after you?" asked Rem. "You were alone and vulnerable."

She sat. "Because as much as he hates me, in his own mind, he idolizes me too. He thinks maybe he loves me? It's why he didn't come after me. He wants me alive, but he's too scared to do anything else."

"You keep him going. He likes the game," said Daniels.

"Exactly," said Jacobs, blowing on her coffee. "As long as we play, he won't kill me."

"What happens when the game goes awry? Or we learn who he is?" asked Rem.

"I don't know," said Jacobs.

"Once the game's up, and you're no longer able to play, or he loses interest…" said Daniels.

"Then the jig's up," said Rem.

Jacobs sipped her drink. "Maybe. Hard to say what could tip him over the edge. Something's going on, though. He acted impulsively with our latest victim. Was it because I wouldn't follow the rules or something else? It could be a sign of worse to come."

"Maybe it's the beginning of the end," said Rem.

"Of us or him?" asked Jacobs.

"Him, of course," said Rem, sipping his coffee.

"There's something else," said Daniels. "After Henderson's death, they searched his place and found a laundered jacket. It had been sent to the same laundromat owned by Craig Lester, the vic prior to Henderson."

"What?" asked Jacobs, sitting up.

"I saw that in the file. It's the only known time we have a connection between victims," said Rem.

"How did I not know that?" asked Jacobs.

"You didn't study Henderson's file," said Rem. "It's the only one you don't know backwards and forwards."

"Did you ever take his clothes to the laundromat?" asked Daniels.

Jacobs stared off. "No. Never."

"Well, at some point he took a jacket to Lester's laundromat, but we don't know when. There was no date on the tag, and they didn't find a receipt," said Daniels.

"But it's not a coincidence that Lester died," said Rem. "Why him though? Why would the killer care about who laundered Henderson's suits?"

"Did you ever hear Henderson mention anything about Lester?" asked Rem. "Did he somehow befriend him?"

"No. I'd never heard of Lester prior to his death," said Jacobs. "And Henderson didn't mention it to me when Lester died."

"Maybe he never met Lester," said Daniels. "Guy owned the place. Doesn't mean he worked the front desk."

"Then why kill him?" asked Jacobs.

Daniels closed the file. "I have no idea. It makes no sense."

The door to Lozano's office opened and Lozano stepped out, holding his jacket.

"Mornin' Cap," said Rem.

"Remalla. Jacobs," he said, as he walked by. "I've got a meeting. I'll be back." By the look on his face, he was all business.

"Sure thing, Cap," said Daniels.

"See you when you get back," said Rem.

Lozano pointed at them as he left. "And don't do anything stupid while I'm gone."

"We'll try, but don't expect miracles," said Rem. "I can't be responsible for Daniels."

Lozano frowned and disappeared out the door.

"Who was he pointing at?" asked Rem.

"Probably me," said Jacobs.

"So, back to Lester," said Daniels. "Why target him?"

Rem rubbed his face. "Well, maybe a little food will help." He reached into his bag and pulled out a jelly donut." He looked over. "You two going to eat?"

Daniels reached for his muffin when Rem's phone rang.

Rem reached over in mid chew and answered. "Remalla speaking."

He listened for a second before his face dropped and he put his donut down. Licking his fingers, he said, "Yeah. We'll be right down." He hung up.

"What is it?" asked Daniels.

"Delivery boy. Downstairs. He's got a package for Jacobs."

Jacobs stood. "Hell."

Daniels put down his muffin. "He's waiting?

Rem nodded, heading for the door. "Said he couldn't give the package to anybody but Jacobs."

Daniels followed, and they headed down the stairs.

**

At the lobby entrance, the officer at the front pointed them toward a skinny kid in tattered jeans with a tattooed sleeve on his arm and a ring in his nose. Jill noted he couldn't have been more than twenty. He held a manila envelope.

Rem walked up to him. "You holding a package for Officer Jacobs?"

The kid sat up. "Sure am. You him?"

"Nope," said Rem, shooting out a thumb. "It's not a him, it's a her."

The kid appraised Jill. "Cool." He stood and held out the envelope.

"Just a second," said Daniels. He stepped up to the front counter. "Shorty, you got a pair of gloves?"

A tall officer with a narrow face reached under the counter. "Here you go." He handed him a box of blue latex gloves.

"What's your name?" Rem asked the kid.

"Tommy. Tommy Douglas."

"You work for a delivery service, Tommy Douglas?" asked Rem.

Daniels put on a pair of gloves.

"No," said Tommy.

"Who asked you to deliver the envelope?" asked Jill.

"I was coming off my shift at the drug store. Some guy stopped me and asked if I wanted to make fifty bucks. Said all I had to do was deliver a package."

"What did he look like?" asked Rem.

"I don't know," said Tommy, shrugging. "A guy."

"Think about it," said Rem.

"Is anybody going to take this?" Tommy asked, holding the envelope.

"I'll take it," said Daniels.

"It's supposed to be for her," said Tommy.

"You have my consent to hand it to him," said Jill. "But we need to know what the man looked like."

"He was tall." He gave the envelope to Daniels.

Rem grunted. "Fat or thin?"

"Thin."

"Muscles?"

"I don't know dude. I wasn't checking him out."

"Long or short hair?" asked Jill.

"Short, but he was wearing a baseball cap, so who knows."

"Clean shaven?" asked Rem.

"He had a mustache, and he was wearing sunglasses, so don't ask me his eye color."

"Where do you work?" asked Daniels.

"Not far from here. At the Corner Drug."

"And he just walked up to you and asked you to deliver a package?" asked Rem. "You'd never met or seen him before?"

"Don't know the guy."

"Didn't you think it was a little strange?" asked Daniels.

"Man, it was fifty bucks. What do I care about strange?"

"He pay you in cash?" asked Jill.

"Sure did."

"You got it on you?" asked Daniels.

Tommy patted his wallet. "Safe and sound."

"We're gonna need it," said Rem. "Evidence."

Tommy's face fell. "Dude, you're not taking my money."

"We'll pay you back," said Rem. He spoke to Shorty behind the desk. "Shorty, this guy's got fifty dollars cash. I need you to bag and tag it." He looked back at Tommy. "I need you to go over and give all your info to Officer Benson behind the desk. The money too. Fill out some paperwork and the department will send you a check."

Tommy huffed. "Man, I don't have time for this."

Rem pulled out his wallet. "Here's an extra twenty for your efforts. That's seventy bucks, kid. Not bad for an hour's work."

Tommy eyed the money, then took it. "Fine."

"Right over there," said Rem.

Tommy, his shoulders drooping, walked to the desk and pulled out his billfold.

"Thanks, Shorty," said Daniels. "Will be back for it."

Shorty waved and pulled out some papers. "Sure thing."

Daniels held out the envelope. "What do you want to do?"

"Let's take it upstairs," said Jacobs. "I'd rather not open it down here."

They headed back up to the squad room, where Daniels laid the envelope down on an empty desk. Rem took some pictures of it with his cell. There was no writing on it, but it was sealed.

"You think he was stupid enough to lick the envelope?" asked Daniels.

"Unlikely," said Jill. Her heart thudded. She had an idea of what to expect, and she held her breath as Daniels broke the seal with his gloved hand.

Once opened, he looked inside.

"What is it?" asked Rem.

Daniels tipped the envelope and photos spilled out onto the desk.

"Shit," said Rem. "He's been busy."

Jill walked closer as Daniels moved the pictures around the table. There were photos of Jill walking down the street, holding her jacket closed against the wind. She remembered that day. Pictures of her at the beach at the trailer park. Pictures of her with Rem and Daniels as they entered the station. And pictures of her and Rem entering Rem's house. There were dozens of them.

Jill had to sit down.

"My, God," said Daniels. "How long's he been following you?"

Rem stared at the pics. "Looks like he never stopped."

Daniels moved another picture and noticed one with a sticky note on it. "What's this?"

Jill looked closer. The sticky note said. "Tsk. Tsk. You should know better." Daniels pulled off the note, and it was a picture of Jill straddling Rem on his couch, kissing him. It had been taken from the living room window.

Jill felt the blood leave her face. "No."

Rem went still. "How in the hell?" He straightened, his face furrowed. "Where in the hell was the patrol out front?"

"I don't know," said Daniels, holding the picture. The light was low, but the image was clearly visible. "He had to have taken it without a flash. You would have seen it otherwise."

"He was right outside the door," said Jill.

"But how is that possible?" asked Daniels. "He killed Veronica Johnson around the same time. How is it that he made it to your place?"

"Maybe he didn't take the photo. Someone else did," said Jill. "Like Tommy Douglas downstairs. He pays somebody to watch and if he gets a good photo, pays even more."

Daniels dropped the photo back on the desk. "Or, if we think about the timeline, it's possible he could have made it to your place." Daniels thought about it. "He kills Veronica Johnson. Neighbor reports it. Cops take a while to respond, and then it takes even longer before they can get past the guard dog. By the time they figure out she's a victim of the Artist, and the call comes to us, it's at least an hour, probably longer. Plenty of time to head to your place and snap a few photos."

"Jesus," said Rem. He turned and kicked a nearby desk. "This guy is making us look like fools and I'm getting tired of it."

"Maybe. Maybe not," said Daniels.

Rem rubbed his neck. "What do you mean?"

"Cameras, partner. You've got cameras at your house." He dropped the photo. "Maybe this time, if we're lucky, and he did his own dirty work, we got him on video."

CHAPTER TWENTY-FIVE

They weren't that lucky. Jill leaned over Rem's shoulder as he reviewed the video on his cell from that night and saw a man in a knitted cap, bulky dark sweatshirt and jeans briefly pass by the camera, but his back was to the frame. The man had stepped outside of the video's range when taking the photo from the window. It was as if he knew exactly where to place himself to stay out of view.

"Who the hell is this guy?" asked Rem. "Houdini?"

"He knows where the cameras are," said Jill. "He knows what he's doing."

Rem smacked a fist on the table. "Son-of-a-bitch."

Daniels hung up from the phone call he was on. "Anything?"

"Nothing," said Rem. "What's the point of having cameras if they don't catch anything?"

Daniels scowled. "I just talked to Monroe. He and his partner were on duty that night outside your place. He doesn't recall seeing anything, but when I pressed him, he admitted that they may have dozed off for a bit."

Rem grunted. "Wonderful."

"Probably for the best," said Jill. "If they'd seen anything, he could have killed them."

"Or they could have caught him," said Daniels. "If it was him."

“There’s a thought,” said Rem. He tossed his cell phone on the table in frustration. “Now what?”

“We’ll send the envelope and photos to forensics. See if they can get any fingerprints or DNA from them,” said Daniels.

“We know how that will go,” said Rem. He stood and paced beside his desk.

“I’ve asked Mel and Garcia to check out the drugstore where Tommy works. Maybe our guy got the pictures printed there, and he picked him up, which is how he may have found Tommy. They’ve got video too.”

“It’s a long shot,” said Jill. She sat and put her head in her hands.

“Probably, but that photo of you two is recent, which means he would have been there within the last forty-eight hours, which helps narrow the timing down,” said Daniels.

“Have we heard anything from the lab about Veronica Johnson, our latest victim?” asked Jill.

Daniels sighed. “No fingerprints that matter. They’re still working on DNA.”

“Shit. We can’t seem to catch a break.” Rem continued to pace. “The rate we’re going, this guy will outlive us all from old age.”

“Better than the alternative,” said Jill.

Daniels tapped his pen on his desk. “Yeah.”

Lozano walked into the squad room, returning from his meeting.

“How’d it go, Cap?” asked Rem. “Hopefully better than it’s going here.”

Lozano stopped at their desks. “I need to see you all in my office.”

Jill straightened as they all looked at each other. Lozano kept going, sliding off his jacket.

“That sounds serious,” said Jill.

“I hope not,” said Rem. “This day’s not going too well as it is.”

“Let’s find out,” said Daniels.

They filed into Lozano’s office and sat. “What’s up, Cap?” asked Rem. He threw an ankle over his knee.

Lozano threw his jacket over his chair and took a seat. "I've been talking to the chief most of the morning and then met him for a cup of coffee. The fallout from this is not good. Your little news conference brought attention to the department they didn't need or desire. They don't want what happened in Seattle to happen here."

"Don't you think it's a little late for that?" asked Daniels.

"Not in their minds," said Lozano. "They think Seattle lost control of the situation and let a killer dictate to them the course of the investigation, and a detective got caught in the middle of it because they gave her too much leeway."

Jill rubbed her jaw, prepared for the worst.

"That's ridiculous, Cap," said Rem. "Seattle was doing its best. Just like we are. You're just making Jacobs a scapegoat."

Lozano lowered his eyebrows. "That's their opinion. Not mine. But I have to answer to them, Remalla."

Rem leaned forward. "You're going to fire her? After we asked her to come help us. You're going to throw her to the wolves?"

"That's not fair, Captain," said Daniels.

Lozano smacked his hand on his desk, and Jill jumped in her seat. "Nobody said anything about getting fired. Just keep your shorts on."

Rem and Daniels went quiet.

Lozano eyed Jill. "No more press conferences, you got that?"

Jill nodded.

Lozano continued. "I had to do some fancy talking and a lot of convincing, but you're still on this case, provided you see a department psychiatrist."

Jill wasn't sure she heard right. "Excuse me?"

Rem threw up a hand. "A shrink? Are you kidding me?"

"Nobody needs a shrink, Captain," said Daniels. "Jacobs is only doing—"

"Nobody's asking what you think," boomed Lozano, his voice angry. He pointed. "I got the chief down from throwing Jacobs out on her ass to staying on this case as long as she sees a psychiatrist. I'd say you owe me a thank you instead of a lot of whine with that cheese."

"I'm not crazy, Cap," said Jill, feeling defeated.

"Nobody said you were," said Lozano. "But we have to make a few concessions if we want to keep you on this. The department doesn't want any loose cannons, and unfortunately, they think you are one, and they're questioning your ability to stay on this thing. The only way I could convince them was to have you check in with a shrink." He huffed. "I know you don't like it. Hell, I don't like it either. But that's the deal. Take it or leave it."

Jill slunk in her seat. She could see where this was going, but could see no way out, unless she left.

"You realize what you're doing?" asked Daniels. "They're setting her up to take the fall again."

"Just like Seattle," said Rem. "This goes bad, then guess what? That crazy lady from the department who got in front of the cameras botched the investigation. We tried to help, which is why she was seeing a shrink, but ultimately the damage was done."

Lozano sat back in his seat with a groan. "That's the best I can do. I don't like it, but that's all I got for you." He studied Jill. "You have a choice. Hang in and play along. Go see the shrink. Humor them. Just stay out of the public eye. Or you can leave. It's up to you."

"She's screwed either way," said Rem.

Lozano stood and leaned over, his hands on his desk. "That's one way to see it, Remalla. The other way is to go out and *catch* this guy. Then you won't have to worry about it." His eyes narrowed, and his voice lowered. "You got a problem with that scenario?"

Jill's heart thudded at Lozano's menacing tone. She could see now how he'd become Captain, and it wouldn't surprise her at all if one day he sat in the chief's chair. "I'll stay," she said. "And I'll see the shrink."

Lozano relaxed, his voice quieting. "Excellent." He eyed Rem and Daniels.

"Whatever you say, Cap," said Daniels.

"Okay," said Rem. "I hear you."

Lozano sat back at his seat, his face less stony. "Good. Now that we're all on the same page, why don't you catch me back up to speed with this case? What's the latest?"

**

Not long after, they filed out of the office and returned to their desks. Jill sat back and stared up at the ceiling, wondering what the hell she was doing with her life.

"Hey," said Rem. "Don't worry about it. They made me see the shrink too after…" He paused. "It's no big deal."

"We may catch him before that anyway, so you may not even have to deal with it," said Daniels.

"Sure," said Jill. "No big deal." But she knew how it would look to the rest of the department. Like Rem said, they'd take it and deem her 'Crazy Jacobs' and the rumors would swirl. Then whispers of why she was on the case at all would begin. Shades of Seattle. And if they didn't catch him, she would be an easy mark. She sighed and closed her eyes. Did anything ever change? The anchors that had lifted slightly from her shoulders after her night with Remalla returned. It was becoming obvious that they might never leave.

"Hang in there," said Rem, and she looked over at him. "You go down, we go down, too. We won't leave you hanging."

She sat up. "That's sweet, but I don't expect that. There's no need for all of our careers to get flushed down the toilet."

"Nobody's career is going down the toilet," said Daniels. "Listen to us. It's like the guy's already won."

Rem nodded. "You're right. We've been sideswiped but we're not down. I said it before and I'll keep saying again. We'll catch him." He caught Jill's eye. "Okay?"

"Sure," said Jill. But she'd been on this road before and she knew where it led. Her only hope now was to keep Remalla and maybe

Daniels alive. If she could do that, then she could live with whatever happened afterwards.

Rem's phone rang, and he sighed. "Now what? Maybe for a change we could get some positive news."

"Cross your fingers," said Daniels.

Rem reached over and answered. "Remalla speaking. Tell me something good."

Jill played with a pencil on her desk but sensed the shift in the air. Glancing over, she saw Rem's eyes widen. "Daniels," she said.

Rem snapped his fingers and pointed at the phone. "No," he said. "To what do I owe the pleasure?"

Daniels quickly made a separate call, asking someone to trace Rem's phone. Jill stood in shocked silence.

"Why?" asked Rem. "Don't you enjoy talking to me?" His face was pale. "No. Just wait." He put the receiver to his shoulder. "He wants it on speaker."

"Keep him talking. They'll have his location in a second," said Daniels.

Rem hit a button and put the receiver down. "Okay. You're on speaker."

"Thank you, detective," said the same raspy voice Jill recognized from before. "Jill, are you there?" he asked.

Jill's throat was dry, and chills broke out on her skin, but she spoke. "I'm here."

"Detective Daniels, too?"

Daniels brow furrowed. "I'm here."

"Excellent. I have all of you. So nice."

"I doubt you called to catch up," said Rem.

"That's correct, Detective. There's no need. I'm all up to speed. Did you have a nice evening last night?"

Rem looked over at Jill. "It was great. How was yours?"

"Oh, not near as interesting, I'm sure. Jill? How about you? Did he help you forget Henderson for a while?"

Jill closed her eyes as the bile rose in her stomach. Had he been watching last night too? "What do you want?" she asked.

"That's a fair question. I appreciated your performance on TV the other day. Not quite what I was expecting."

"You wanted me to play. I played," she said.

"Oh, you know what you did. You're testing me, as usual. The question is how will I respond?"

"How about turning yourself in?" asked Daniels.

"The game will end soon enough, Detective," said the voice.

Rem leaned in. "Since we're speaking of responses, why'd you kill Veronica Johnson so soon?" asked Rem. "You rushed it. Took risks. That's not your style."

Daniels whispered. "Patrols are on their way."

"Don't presume you know me, detective. I did what I had to do to get Jill's attention. Have I got it now, Jill?"

Jill held her breath. "Yes."

"Good. Did you like the photos? I especially like the one of you and Remalla. You look remarkable in the soft light. It really illuminates your skin. Don't you think, Detective Remalla?"

Jill held her stomach and tried to breathe slowly. She thought of Sonia.

Rem set his jaw. "What I'm thinking is how much you'll enjoy maximum security when we catch you. They love guys like you."

There was a soft laugh. "Nice threat, but you know I'll never be caught. At least not alive. But that's not the question, is it? The question is, will you still be alive? What do you think, JJ? Should I let him live?"

Jill straightened, and anger sparked. "Why don't you come after me?" she asked. "You love to throw your weight around and threaten others to mock and intimidate me. But why not just confront me? I think I know why. Maybe you wish you were Remalla. That you wish you could have what he has. But you're just too timid to come and get it." There was silence on the phone. "What's wrong? Cat got your tongue?"

There was another pause. "We'll see what I am and am not afraid of," he said, his voice clipped. "Very soon. And I look forward to meeting you, too, Detective."

"Can't wait. Bring some wine. We'll catch up," said Rem.

"And congrats on the baby, Daniels. I'm sure you'll make an excellent father."

Daniels' face froze as the line went dead.

Jill let go of the breath she was holding as Rem sat. "Son-of-a bitch." He frowned at Daniels. "Anything?"

"They're approaching the scene," said Daniels.

"Where?" asked Rem.

Daniels sighed. "The airport."

Rem's face fell. "Great."

Jill groaned. "There's no way they'll find him in a crowd. He'll blend in and disappear."

"Unbelievable," said Rem, kicking the side of his desk.

They sat and waited for a few minutes before Daniels spoke into the phone. "Yes. I got it. Keep me posted. Thanks." He hung up and held his head.

"Don't tell me. They caught him chatting up a waitress, watching the shopping network in the airport bar," said Rem.

"Close," said Daniels. "Only there's no waitress, bar or shopping network." He rubbed his shoulders. "They're looking, but nothing so far."

"He probably is sitting at a bar, laughing as they search," said Jill.

"They have the sketch," said Daniels.

"That looks like every Tom, Dick and Harry," said Rem.

"I know," said Daniels. "It doesn't look good."

"It sucks," said Rem, scratching his head. "The question is what will he do next?"

"What do you think he meant by saying 'the game will end soon enough?'" asked Daniels.

"It scares me," said Jill. "He threatened both of you."

"But there was a fourth rose, so someone else is on his list," said Rem. "But who?"

"I don't know," said Jill. "He's planning something."

"He certainly doesn't like you two being together," said Daniels.

Jill clenched her hands together. "You think he was watching again? Last night?" she asked Rem. Her heart thudded at the thought.

Rem met her gaze. "I don't know. We were lax in closing the front blinds, but with the bushes I didn't think it was a big deal. Could be he's just messing with our heads."

"I think you both should go into a safe house," said Daniels. "Today. We should talk to Lozano."

Rem raised a hand. "Hold up. Let's think about this. Maybe if we keep our routines, we'll make him comfortable. If he likes to look, why not lure him in? We'll just make damn sure our patrol isn't snoozing outside."

"It doesn't matter," said Jill. "He won't be anywhere near the house. At least not tonight. He knows we'll be on alert now. And I don't think a safe house would make any difference. Merchant tried it in Seattle. The guy sent a photo of me in front of it. I moved home after that. If he's determined to kill us, a safe house won't stop him."

"What about Marjorie?" asked Rem. "Maybe you two should go somewhere safe."

Daniels' brow furrowed. "She's due any day. You want me to ask her to go to a safe house?"

"It's unlikely he'll target her," said Jill. "He's just trying to instill fear and doubt. Throw us off our game. But if it makes you feel better, you could add a patrol to your place."

"A lot of good that did us," said Rem.

Daniels sighed and gripped a paper weight. "I'll talk to Lozano about it."

"Jacobs is right though," said Rem. "He wants us scared. If we're busy worrying about safe houses and patrols, it keeps us from thinking about the real threat, which is when he'll strike next."

“And who he’ll strike next,” said Daniels, eying Rem.

“Again,” said Rem. “It won’t be easy. I’m not exactly an unsuspecting target, especially if I’m expecting it.”

“If that’s his plan, then he’ll need a diversion,” said Jill. “Something that makes you vulnerable.” She tried not to think of Rick waiting for her at home that last night in Seattle.

“Then we need to be ready,” said Daniels. He pointed at Rem. “And I know you. Don’t go off half-cocked on some wild goose chase. You don’t go anywhere without me or Jacobs with you. You got that? We need to know where you are at all times.”

Rem raised his hands. “Who me?”

“Yeah, you,” said Jill and Daniels at the same time.

CHAPTER TWENTY-SIX

Jill awoke with a scream stuck in her throat, another dream vivid in her mind. She'd been running, sweat pouring from her skin. The killer was near, but she couldn't see him. His laughter traveled though, and she couldn't determine where it was coming from. Everything around her was fog, dense as mud. She called out, asking for help, but no one heard her. In the distance, she thought she saw Rem, but the faster she ran toward him, the more he faded away. She screamed, and another figure appeared in the distance. Terrified, she raced toward him. Getting close, she saw that it was a man lying on the ground. Desperate for help, she rolled him over and saw Rick, eyes glazed over, and throat slit, blood running down his neck.

That's when she'd come awake. Kicking back the covers, she sat up, breathing hard.

"You okay?" asked Rem in a groggy voice from beside her.

Her hair stuck to her face, and she pushed it back. "I'm fine. Go back to sleep."

He sat up and the sheet slid down to reveal his bare chest. "Bad dream again?"

She nodded. "I just need some water."

Leaning behind her, he reached over to her side of the bed and grabbed her glass. "Here." She took it. "You want to talk about it?"

"No. Not really." She sipped the water.

Once they'd come home after another miserable day where they'd accomplished little, they immediately closed the blinds to every window in the house. They'd picked up some food on the way home and picked at it, neither of them particularly hungry. Then Rem had taken her in his arms and held her, and she'd responded, needing to feel his touch again, and they'd made their way back into the bedroom, eventually falling asleep in each other's arms.

"Did those photos trigger it?" he asked.

"They didn't help."

He sat up, raised a knee and put an elbow on it. "You sure you don't want to go to a safe house?"

"No," she said. "I'd rather stay. It's familiar here. If he shows, at least I know the layout."

"You think he will come here? Is that how he'll end this thing?"

"I don't know. But I have a feeling that's his plan. He'll end this game on his terms, and I think he's getting ready for the grand finale."

He nodded, his face grim in the darkness. "And what do you think that is?"

She rubbed the edge of her glass. "You sure you want to know?"

"I wouldn't ask otherwise."

She studied him. "If what I'm feeling is accurate, he'll kill you to torture me, and then he'll kill me, and disappear into the sunset, ready to play again with someone else when the opportunity presents itself."

"You're sure about that?"

She sighed. "Not a hundred percent, but my instincts are usually accurate. I just can't predict the when, or the where, but the most likely place would be here."

He paused, studying his fingers. "You know, we've never really talked about this sixth sense of yours."

She paused. "No. We haven't. I guess it's not something I bring up in casual conversation."

"How long have you had it?"

She fluffed the pillows and sat back. “I guess the first time I noticed something was weird was right out of college. I wanted to join the police academy, much against my father’s wishes. We had a raging fight, and we didn’t speak for two months. Not long after, I got sick. I ended up in the hospital with pneumonia and Dad came to see me. I remember him sitting beside me and I had this visual in my head of him in the hospital, too, with heart monitors and a nose tube. I felt this horrible pain in my chest, and somehow, I knew my dad was on the verge of having a heart attack. I guess the stress was getting to him too.”

Rem shifted to face her. “Were you right?”

“Once I was out of the hospital, I encouraged him to see a doctor immediately. He admitted he hadn’t been feeling well and made an appointment. Within a week, he was in surgery for a nearly blocked artery. Surgeons told him if he’d waited much longer, he could have died.”

“Did he ever say anything to you about how you knew?”

“Never. Dad never wanted to talk about it. He’s a black and white, by the book, science-based man. If it doesn’t have a research paper proving it, it doesn’t compute to him.”

“He could at least acknowledge you saved his life,” he said.

“He told me he was planning to see the doctor anyway, so either way, he’d have caught it.” She played with the edge of the bedsheets.

“Your old man doesn’t seem like an easy guy to deal with.” He scooted back and sat beside her.

“I try to give him some leeway. After Mom died, he was never the same.”

“She died when you were little, right?”

Jill nodded. “Yes. I was three. I remember little about her, but I recall Dad losing his smile. We didn’t see it much after that.”

“He never remarried?”

“No. Never seemed interested.” She glanced over. “What about you? Your parents alive?”

“My mom is. Dad died five years ago. He went to take a nap and never woke up. Doctor said it was an aneurysm.”

"I'm sorry."

"It's all right. It was tough, but he had a good life. My mom took it hard, but she's better. She moved to Florida a couple of years ago and she's even dating."

"Good for her."

Rem went quiet, then cocked his head. "You know, you make me think of my Aunt Maggie." He took her hand. "She had abilities, too."

Jill shifted, getting comfortable. "Really? What abilities?"

Rem traced his fingers over hers. "She would know things. She read people's palms in the neighborhood. My dad thought she was cuckoo, but my mom knew better. Said Margaret had a gift."

"What did you think?" asked Jill.

"She told me when I was seventeen that I'd be a cop. At that point, I was just a pain-in-the-ass kid who'd toilet-paper other kid's homes and steal candy from the grocery store. I thought she was nuts."

"But here you are," said Jill, trying not to get distracted as Rem ran his fingers over hers.

"Here I am, Detective Remalla, lying in bed with a beautiful woman."

She shook her head. "Who's being stalked by a serial killer, and who could be endangering your life by your association with her. Maggie didn't see that one coming." She went back to studying the bed sheets.

"That's not the way I see it. I see a woman who's stronger than she thinks and has the cajones of a bullfighter."

Jill half-smiled. "I've never heard myself described that way." She made a sideways glance at him. "You like my cajones?"

His fingers trailed up her arm. "They look a little different than mine, but, yes, very much." Even though the nightlight in the bathroom provided the only illumination, she could picture his eyes getting darker. "Before we talk about your delicious body though, my aunt gave me some good advice once, and I wonder if it might help you."

She turned toward him. "What was that?"

"I asked her once about her skills and how she handled it, knowing things she didn't always want to know. I knew it stressed her out."

Jill put her hand on his sheet-covered leg. "What did she say?"

She heard him take a breath. "She told me that when she felt overwhelmed and she needed to relax, she would go still. She'd find a quiet place where no one could disturb her and turn it all off. She'd let her mind and thoughts go silent. She'd sit for as long as it took until the peace she sought came over her." His fingers traveled up to her shoulder and chills popped up on Jill's skin.

"You mean she'd meditate?" she asked, her breathing picking up.

"Yes. She said it helped a lot. It kept her sane in an insane world. Have you tried it?"

Jill sighed, thinking back. "I tried it once. It didn't work much better than hypnosis. My mind just bounced all over the place. I didn't find it very calming."

His hand went to her neck, and she moved her palm up his thigh.

He made a small groan. "Well, maybe you should try it again. You never know. It might help. If things get crazy, and you need a break, try quieting your mind."

Her heart rate escalating, she nodded. "Okay. Maybe I'll try it again sometime." Her hand moved higher, and he moaned. "But right now, I'd like to focus my energy on you."

He sucked in a breath as her fingers teased him. "Jesus," he said. His other hand found its way under the bedcovers, grazed up her thigh and she gasped. All thoughts of quieting her mind disappeared, and he offered her a lecherous grin. "I'll show you mine if you show me yours." Tugging on the sheets that covered her, Rem pulled them away. "Let's see those cajones."

**

The next morning, Jill checked herself in the mirror. She tucked her hair back, smoothed her jacket, and yawned. Despite her nightmare and sexual escapades with Rem, she'd managed some decent sleep and her eyes looked fresher than they had in weeks. Leaning over, she double checked the gun in her ankle holster. She knew Lozano wouldn't approve her carrying her personal weapon while on the job, but she never left the house without it. She'd be damned if they found the killer and she had no way of protecting herself or shooting him between the eyes if she had the chance.

Satisfied, she flipped off the bathroom light and left the bedroom. Rem had been up earlier to take a shower and was making coffee. Smelling the brew, she couldn't wait for a cup.

Entering the kitchen, she saw Rem filling two mugs. He handed her one.

"Thank you," she said.

"You're welcome. Feel better this morning?"

She sipped her coffee. "Yes. I do. How about you?"

"Can't complain. Of course, I got to wake up next to you. That helps."

"Sure. Puffy eyes and morning breath. I'm sure that's attractive."

He leered at her. "Don't forget those gorgeous cajones."

She smiled. "Yours aren't so bad either."

They stared for a second before he looked away. "Don't tempt me, or we're never gonna make it to work on time."

Feeling that familiar rush, she agreed. "Much less make it to work." Feeling the caffeine hit, she thought about her day, and the mental weight returned. "I think I'm going to have to see that shrink this afternoon." She sighed.

He leaned against the counter. "I know. It sucks, but just do your best to get through it. He's a nice guy though. Easy to talk too."

"Did he help you?"

He nodded. "He didn't hurt. Sometimes it helps to get things off your chest."

"As long as it doesn't give them a reason to pull me off this thing. I'm afraid that's what they want."

"Maybe don't talk about your visions. That might help."

She shook her head. "Yeah. I know. I learned that the hard way in Seattle."

He put his coffee down. "Just keep it to the basics. Hopefully, you'll only need a few sessions and they'll back off." He pointed. "Come here. I want to show you something before we leave."

Jill recalled the previous night. "I thought we didn't want to be late for work."

Rem raised a brow at her and half-smiled. "Not that. We'll save that for later. Something else."

She followed him into the den. "What is it?"

Moving around to the coffee table, he raised it so she could see the underside. "I thought about what you said last night. This is just a precaution and hopefully not needed, but just in case."

She saw a gun taped to the backside of the wooden table. "Is that yours?"

"Yes. I keep it upstairs. But I thought it wouldn't hurt to have it down here. In case we need it."

"But to the bottom of the table?" she asked.

He nodded. "This guy knows we carry weapons. If he catches us without them, or he takes them, we have an ace up our sleeve. It's unlikely that we'll need it, but if you're right and he comes here, you and I both know where it is."

She stared at the gun, sad that it was necessary but realizing it wasn't a bad idea. "Okay. Got it."

He lowered the table. "It's fully loaded, so no children in the house."

"Of course." She sipped her brew and stared at the table as Rem retrieved his coffee from the kitchen. A chill ran through her and she rubbed her arm with her free hand.

Rem spoke from the kitchen. "We'll leave in five minutes."

Still staring, she shook her head to clear it. "Okay," she said, and turned and walked away.

CHAPTER TWENTY-SEVEN

Lozano hung up the phone and rubbed his neck. Mentally exhausted, he found some aspirin and popped them in his mouth and took a sip of his water. Looking out the glass window, he saw Daniels, Rem and Jacobs at their desks, and wondered how he would share the latest news from Merchant. Picking up the phone, he made another call to the department shrink, asking a quick favor. The psychiatrist wanted to see Jacobs a little later, but Lozano asked to move the timetable up. He needed Jacobs out of the office. The doctor agreed to make it work and Lozano hung up.

Tapping his pen on his desk, he thought for a second and then stood. He walked to the door and opened it, sticking his head out. "Jacobs," he said. "It's time for your appointment."

She popped her head up and checked her watch. "I thought I had an hour."

"I just got a call. He needs to see you sooner. Something came up."

Jacobs squinted. "Why didn't he call me?"

Lozano threw out a hand. "Don't ask me these questions. I don't know." He waited as Jacobs hesitated. "Better go now. Don't keep him waiting."

"You know where to go?" asked Rem.

She stood, getting her purse. "The next building over, right? Suite 200."

"Yup. You want me to walk you?" asked Rem.

Lozano opened his mouth to argue, but Jacobs answered first. "No need. I'm a big girl."

"You come straight back afterward. No wayward errands, okay?" asked Daniels.

Jacobs nodded. "No problem with that. I've no wayward errands to run."

"Good luck. I know you'll do great," said Rem.

"I hope so," she sighed. "See you in about an hour." She walked away and exited the squad room. Lozano gave it a few seconds to ensure she didn't return.

"Everything okay, Cap? You forget something?" asked Rem.

Satisfied she wasn't returning, Lozano shot out a thumb. "I need to see you two in my office."

Rem and Daniels gave each other a look before standing and heading over. Lozano let them pass and he closed the door behind them as they sat in front of his desk.

"What's up?" asked Daniels.

He sat and rubbed his face. "How's it going out there? Anything new to report?"

Daniels shook his head. "I wish. Our guys have talked to all of Veronica Johnson's friends, family, neighbors, and coworkers. Nobody has much to add that we don't already know. We're still waiting on DNA results."

Lozano huffed.

"I've been wondering something though," said Daniels.

"What's that?" asked Rem.

Daniels leaned forward, his elbows on his needs. "Going through the reports, I had this thought. The Artist is always one step ahead of us. He covers his tracks and leaves nothing behind." He paused. "What if he's a cop?"

Rem groaned and scratched his temple. "You know, I had the same thought. I just didn't want to take it seriously."

"Did Merchant ever say anything to you, Captain, about that? Did they ever wonder the same thing? I didn't see anything in the files to indicate that they did," said Daniels.

Lozano sat back. "Not that I know of. But just because the killer's smart doesn't mean he's a cop. You can do an internet search and learn all you need to know."

Daniels studied his hand. "Maybe. But it's something to consider."

"There's something else," said Lozano. "I just got off the phone with Merchant."

Rem frowned. "Something new?"

"Yes," said Lozano sitting up. "He just got some information. He hasn't shared it with Jacobs, for obvious reasons."

"Really? What reasons are those?" asked Daniels.

"Jacobs' brother. You know about him?" asked Lozano.

"She's got two. Which one?" asked Rem.

"The younger one," said Lozano. "Dylan."

"He's the nomad, according to Jacobs. Tends to wander and do his own thing," said Rem.

"There may be more to it than that," said Lozano. "The case in Seattle is still under investigation for obvious reasons. Merchant still has eyes on it. His detective brought up a theory that has merit and has led to some interesting developments."

"What's that?" asked Rem.

"Dylan Jacobs is more than a nomad. He's been in jail," said Lozano.

"Jail? Since when?" asked Daniels.

"About fifteen months. He was arrested not long after Officer Henderson's murder. Assault charges. Jacobs has no idea. She thinks he's been hitchhiking around the country."

Rem's brow furrowed. "Are you kidding? Nobody told her? What about her dad? He had to know."

"I can't speak for that. All I know is what Merchant has told me." He picked up a paper and read from it. "Dylan Jacobs assaulted a man in a bar. Beat him up pretty bad. Prosecutor came down hard on him. Apparently, it wasn't his first brush with the law. But because of who is dad is, he got off easy a few times."

Rem rubbed his head. "What are you saying, Cap? He's got a temper. So what?"

"Apparently, a couple of the earlier complaints against him were from women. They never pressed charges though. But Merchant's man has been putting two and two together. They always wondered if the killer was someone who knew Jacobs. Once they started digging deeper, they think the timeline fits. He went to jail three months after Henderson's death and got out about five months ago."

"That's a broad timeline. Doesn't make him a murderer," said Daniels.

Lozano dropped the paper. "No. But it's enough to make him a suspect. But there's something else."

"What?" asked Daniels.

"They started going through Dylan's background. Looking at his whereabouts during the Seattle murders. They checked his credit card charges. Turns out he was a customer at the bar where Alice Dumont, the second victim, worked."

Rem shook his head. "I'm sure there are plenty of people who've patronized that bar who have bad tempers and have done jail time."

"I know, but based on that information and his history, they got a search warrant to check out a storage unit he has in Seattle. They went in this morning."

"And?" asked Rem.

"No smoking gun, but they found something close. Alana Stenham, the fifth vic in Seattle? They found her business card in his things. That's a second connection to a victim. Based on that, they've issued a warrant for his arrest."

Rem's jaw dropped. "Are you serious? They think Jacobs' brother is the murderer?"

"That's the view of the Seattle P.D. They want us to be on the lookout. They think he's in the vicinity."

"You mean they think he's killing here, too?"

Lozano grunted. "Basically, yes."

Rem ran his hands through his hair. "Shit. I don't believe this."

"And Jacobs doesn't know?" asked Daniels.

"No," said Lozano.

"Still doesn't make him our guy," said Rem. "They're gonna need more than that to get a conviction."

"Believe me, they're looking, but they want to find him first. See what he has to say. Problem is they don't know where he is. Merchant gave us the choice on how we want to tell Jacobs."

"Wonderful," said Rem. "So we get to tell her that her brother is the main suspect and might be the Makeup Artist?" He shook his head. "This makes no sense, Cap. Why would her own brother stalk her?"

"When you catch him, you can ask him," said Lozano. "Hopefully they're barking up the wrong tree."

"Or they're not," said Daniels. "In which case we've found the killer."

"We're screwed either way," said Rem. "Jacobs' brother is the killer, or he's innocent in which case the killer's still on the loose." He sighed. "This sucks."

"I don't like it either, but it is what it is," said Lozano. "So…do you want me to tell her or do you?"

Rem stood, his eyes weary. "We'll tell her." He put his hands on his hips. "Anything else?"

"Nope," said Lozano. "I think that covers it."

Rem nodded and left the office.

Lozano watched him walk out and pointed. "What's up with him and Jacobs? Something I need to know?"

Daniels stood. "Nope. Nothing." He turned to leave.

Lozano huffed. "I thought you were a better liar than that."

Daniels raised the side of his lip. "You caught me on a bad day," he said, shutting the door on his way out.

**

Daniels watched his partner sit at his desk and hold his head. He approached and leaned against the wall. "What do you think?" he asked.

Rem groaned and dropped his hands. "What do I think? I think this is the worst possible scenario. How are we supposed to tell her that one of the people she trusts most in the world may be the one torturing her, and may be the one that's killed twelve people, including her lover?" He let go of a deep breath. "It'll kill her."

"We have to tell her though. She needs to know," said Daniels.

"I know that."

Daniels crossed his arms. "Doesn't mean he did it. Seattle could be wrong. Everything they have is circumstantial. Our killer could still be on the loose. Which means we still have to stay on guard. We can't assume anything."

Rem shrugged. "Yeah. I guess. I just hate to give her one more thing to deal with."

Daniels studied his partner. "You two are getting close."

Rem played with a paperweight. "Yeah, maybe."

"She's got you to lean on. She'll be okay."

Rem gave him a sideways glance. "You think it's a bad idea?"

"What? To tell her the truth?"

"No, you bonehead." Rem rolled his eyes. "Us. Me and her."

"Why would I think that? You like her, don't you?"

He studied the paperweight. "I do."

"Then I'm all for it. It's the first spark of light I've seen in your eyes in a while."

Rem put the paperweight down. "Does that mean you'll stop down-playing your happiness with Marjorie?"

Daniels pushed off the wall and went to his desk. "I don't know what you're talking about."

"Uh, huh," said Rem. "Of course, you don't."

Daniels made himself look busy. "We've got bigger fish to fry though. She'll be back soon. How do you want to tell her?"

Rem picked up his empty coffee cup. "I find the direct approach usually works best." He put the cup down. "We need something stronger than coffee."

Daniels opened a drawer and put away a file. "If we have found the killer, then I'll take you and Jacobs out for a few drinks. We're all going to need 'em."

"Marjorie's due any day, partner. Your late nights are about to get limited."

"Then let's hope we caught him now."

Rem sighed and sat back. "Is it bad to hope it's not her brother?"

Daniels felt for his partner. "No. Of course not."

The squad door opened, and an officer walked in. Daniels recognized him as Doug Parsons, Delgado's partner. Parsons looked around and approached their desks.

"Can we help you, Parsons?" asked Daniels.

"Hey, detectives," said Parsons. "Sorry to bother you, but I'm looking for Delgado."

"You lose him?" asked Rem.

"Apparently." He held his hat. "We're due out on patrol and he hasn't shown up. I know he's come up here before and was just wondering if he'd wound up here again, especially since his promotion came through."

Daniels sat up. "His what?"

"Yeah, you didn't hear? He found out this morning."

Daniels looked at Rem.

"Well, the news just keeps getting better and better," said Rem. "He made detective?"

"Sure did. I think he starts in two weeks," said Reynolds. "I guess with all the workload between the Makeup Artist and the bank robberies, they need the help. I'm applying too. Hoping I get lucky."

Rem shook his head. "That's great. Just great."

Daniels waved a hand. "Well, we haven't seen him. I assume you tried calling?"

"Yeah. No luck," said Parsons. His radio squawked to life, and he grabbed it.

Daniels heard the call. Another bank robbery was in progress. All units in the vicinity were to respond.

"Crap," said Parsons. "I've got to go and no partner." He clicked the radio and answered.

"Maybe he'll hear the call and head that way," said Rem. "Who knows? Maybe he lost his phone, or the battery died."

"Maybe," said Parsons. "He's been so preoccupied lately. All his work on this case and all."

Daniels cocked his head. "Excuse me?"

"What do you mean, working on this case? You mean the Makeup Artist?" asked Rem. "He's not on this case."

Parsons headed toward the door. "Yeah. I'm surprised he didn't tell you. He's been working it on his own, in his free time. He's sort of obsessed with it. Ever since he left Seattle, he hasn't been able to leave it alone."

Daniels froze, unsure he heard correctly. "Ever since he left where?"

Rem leaned forward. "Did you say Seattle?"

"Yeah, sure," said Parsons. "He transferred from the Seattle P.D. I think it was about six months ago." The radio squawked again. "I got to go. If you see him, let him know to get his ass back to work." He opened the door and disappeared.

CHAPTER TWENTY-EIGHT

"What the hell did he just say?" asked Rem.

Daniels shifted back in his seat to face Rem. "He said Delgado worked in Seattle."

"I heard. I don't believe it. Why didn't Delgado tell us that?"

Daniels rubbed his jaw. "I agree. He's told us everything else."

Rem scratched his head, thinking. "Plus, he's investigating the Artist on his own? Why?"

"I guess he's bored." Daniels stared off, but his brow furrowed.

Rem shook a finger. "What's that look? I know that look. Something's going on in that head of yours."

"I don't like it," said Daniels.

"You don't like what? Officers from Seattle showing up here not long before the murders start, who strangely have a unique interest in those same murders, and in the former detective who's investigating them. What's not to like?"

Daniels squinted at him. "It's pretty thin. Delgado's a stand-up cop."

"But he's a cop. He knows what he's doing," said Rem. Daniels eyed Lozano's office. Rem looked too. Lozano was on the phone. "You want to take this to him?"

Daniels picked up his phone. "No. Not yet." He dug through some papers, and finding what he was looking for, dialed a number.

"Who you calling?" asked Rem.

Daniels listened. “Merchant. I want to find out about Ethan Delgado.” He spoke when someone answered, and he asked for Merchant. “I’ll hold,” said Daniels.

Rem’s own desk phone rang. He stared at it, wondering if it might be the killer.

Daniels watched him. “You thinking what I’m thinking?”

Rem reached for the phone. “If it’s him, should I come right out and ask if he’s Dylan or Ethan?”

Daniels shrugged while waiting for Merchant. “Can’t hurt.”

Rem answered. “Remalla speaking.” He let out a breath he didn’t realize he was holding when he heard someone else speak other than the Artist.

“Rem? It’s Garcia. Is Mel there?”

Rem shook his head at Daniels, who sat back, still waiting. “Since when are we lost and found for missing cops?”

“What?”

Rem rolled his eyes. “No, Garcia. He’s not here, nor do I know where he is. What’s up?” He heard Daniels speaking, but Garcia responded. “I broke down on the damn freeway. The tow truck’s stuck in traffic. Everyone’s responding to that robbery. I need Mel to come pick me up.”

Rem eyed the squad room. It did seem oddly empty. “No one’s here, Garcia.” He checked his watch. “Where are you?” Garcia told him his location. He was only about ten minutes away. “Sit tight. I’ll come get you.”

Garcia thanked him, and he hung up.

Daniels spoke on the phone. He was asking about Delgado and his tenure at the Seattle P.D. “Yes. I’ll hold again.”

Rem stood, grabbing his car keys. “Garcia’s car broke down. I’m going to go pick him up. You call when you know something.”

Daniels put his hand on the receiver. “They transferred me to another department. I’ll know more in a minute. And don’t stray. We still don’t know what’s going on here.”

"I won't stray. Just keep me posted." He picked up his jacket and jogged out of the room.

**

A few more transfers, and several minutes later, Daniels wrote the information the Seattle officer provided on a pad of paper. Thanking the officer, he hung up. Staring at what he'd written, he tried to think. Delgado had started work at the Seattle P.D. one month prior to the beginning of the murders in Seattle. He was a good cop, had good scores from the academy, and had no red flags. But something nagged at Daniels, and he recognized that nudge when his gut was talking to him. Something wasn't right, and he didn't like it.

Looking into Lozano's office, he saw Lozano still talking. He guessed the latest bank robbery was taking the Captain's attention. He tapped the pad of paper with a pencil, thinking, when his phone rang.

He answered. It was Rem. "Hey," said Rem. "I picked up Garcia, but the tow truck just showed, so I'm headed back. You find out anything?"

Daniels stared at the paper. "Actually, yes." He stood. "Don't come back here. Meet me at Delgado's place. I'll send you the address." He figured before they started accusing cops of crimes, maybe they ought to do a little checking first.

"Got it," said Rem. "I'll meet you there. You be careful."

"You too," said Daniels, as he hung up.

Daniels grabbed his cell and started to head out when Jacobs returned.

"Where's the fire?" she asked, as he headed for the door.

"Potential lead. I'm checking it out with Rem. How was your appointment?"

"Fine. Not as bad and quicker than I expected. Let me go with you."

"You can't."

Her face fell. "Why not? Does this have to do with the Makeup Artist?"

"It does. Which is why you can't go. I'll fill you in when we get back." He pushed the door open.

"Daniels…"

He held up a hand. "You're a consultant. Not a cop. Trust me. We'll be back soon. Just stay put and wait to hear from us." And he headed out the door.

**

Jacobs stared blankly, unsure what to think. What had happened in the last hour for a sudden lead to appear? She returned to her desk, wondering about what to do. Eyeing Lozano's office, she wondered whether to ask him, but he was on the phone.

Thinking about her appointment, she helped herself to some stale coffee, but grimaced after tasting it and threw it away. The doctor visit had gone well. She'd talked about a few things to show her willingness to be open but had stayed away from any discussion about her extrasensory abilities. She considered that a success. Maybe she could get through this without getting thrown off the case.

Her desk phone rang, and she hesitated. Could it be him again? And what would she do or say if it was? It rang again, and she cursed and picked it up. "Jacobs," she said, holding her breath.

"Jill, is that you?" asked a familiar voice. The connection crackled, and she heard noise in the background.

She couldn't believe her ears. "Dylan?"

"Hey, sis."

She held her opposite ear. "Where are you? I can barely hear you."

"At the bus station. Sorry about the interference. I'll try to move to a better place that's less busy." Jill continued to hear static, but she could make out his voice. "You know you're a hard person to track down. Long time, no talk. How are you?" he asked.

Jill could only groan. "That's a long story and will require a long meal and a stiff drink. How have you been? Where have you been? I haven't talked to you in forever. And don't you have my cell phone number?"

"Hell. I lost my phone a while ago. Someone stole it in Paris. You know me. I lose more crap than I keep. And yes, I've been traveling. Went to Europe for a while and checked out the locals. Had some fun. Came back to the states and went to Canada. The usual."

"Are you back in Seattle?"

"Better. I'm here."

Her heart thumped with excitement. "Here? You're in town?"

"I am. And I need to see you."

"That's great. I would love that. How about dinner tonight? Would that work?"

"No, Jill. It's kind of important. I need to see you now. Some place private. Can you get away?"

Jill surveyed the squad room. Rem and Daniels were out, and Lozano was still on the phone. They wouldn't like her leaving, but she could let them know where she was. "Of course. Is everything okay?"

"We'll talk when I see you. Where can we meet?"

Considering it, she gave him Rem's address. "I can be there in about fifteen minutes, actually make it twenty." Since Rem had left, she'd have to get a car service to drive her.

"Perfect," he said. "I'll see you soon." He paused. "I missed you, sis."

An unexpected well of emotion rose and her throat constricted. It had been too long since she'd confided with a family member, and she hadn't realized how much she needed it. "I missed you too, Dylan. See you in a few." She hung up, grabbed her purse, and headed out the door, eager to see her brother.

CHAPTER TWENTY-NINE

Rem pulled up the long driveway of the small house. It was an A-frame with a red roof and dust colored brick with one window on either side of the front door. Not much to look at and driving up he saw the front yard was bigger than the back. A parked car sat in a standalone garage, but he didn't know if it belonged to Delgado. He stopped and killed the engine and within a few minutes, Daniels pulled up behind him. They both got out.

"Anything?" asked Daniels.

"I just got here. Don't know if that belongs to him." He shot a thumb at the parked car.

"We can find out. Let's knock."

"After you." Rem held out a hand and Daniels headed toward the front door. Rem followed. Reaching it, Daniels rapped his knuckles on the door. They stood, listening, but heard nothing. He tried again.

"Delgado. It's Remalla and Daniels. Open up," said Rem. Still no answer.

Daniels walked to one of the side windows and peered in.

"What do you see?" asked Rem, heading to the opposite window.

"Not much." He leaned closer. "Furniture. TV. What about you?"

Rem looked through the opposite window. "Small kitchen. No Delgado."

Daniels came back to the door. "What do you want to do?"

Rem shrugged. "Good question. How seriously are we worried about this guy?"

Daniels glanced at the door. "Worried, but we don't have much to go on. There were no red flags from his time in Seattle. And we don't have a warrant and we don't have probable cause. Basically, all we have is a hunch."

Rem scratched his head thinking. "Well, we could—"

Daniels' cell rang, and he pulled it out of his pocket. "It's Marjorie. Hold that thought." He answered. "Hey, babe."

His face dropped. "Okay. You're sure?" He looked at Rem, who frowned. "No. Don't worry. I'm sure everything's fine. Yes. I'll be there as soon as I can." He listened. "I love you, too." He hung up.

"Everything okay?" asked Rem.

Daniels paled. "This might be it partner. She's headed to the hospital."

"Really?" He paused. "Then why do you look worried?"

Daniels put his cell away. "She says something feels weird. She saw some blood. I think she's worried something's wrong."

"First babies. I'm sure everything's fine."

Daniels nodded, but he looked a little ill. "You're probably right." He stood there, looking uncertain.

Rem watched him, waiting. "Well?"

Daniels stared back, as if wondering why Rem was speaking to him. "Well, what?"

Rem raised an eyebrow. "You gonna go?"

Daniels eyes widened. "God, yes. I need to go."

"What are you waiting for?" Rem hid a smile. His partner was definitely flummoxed.

"I have to go," said Daniels. "To the hospital."

"Yes. You do." He pointed. "That's your car. You have keys. You put them in the ignition and you drive."

Daniels face fell, and he pulled his keys out, but then stopped, his eyes sharp. "Don't you dare do anything while I'm gone, you got it?"

Rem held out his hands. "What would I do?"

Daniels pointed. "Don't give me that innocence crap. I know you. You stay away from this until I'm back." He gestured toward the house. "You stay away from Delgado and no wild goose chases. You got that?"

Rem snorted. "Would you go? Marjorie is waiting."

"Rem…"

Rem put his hand over his heart. "I promise. I won't do anything stupid."

Daniels stared for a second. "I wish I believed you."

"Would you stop worrying? Go be with Marjorie. You're about to be a dad, for God's sake. Go to the hospital and keep me posted." He cocked his head toward the house. "There's not much going on here, anyway."

Daniels paused, as if he wanted to say something else, but then nodded and headed toward his car. "You go back to the station and I'll call you when I know something." He got to the car and opened the door.

"Hey partner," said Rem.

Daniels stopped before getting in.

"Congratulations. You're gonna be a great dad."

Daniels hesitated, then nodded. "Thanks partner." Then he slid into the seat, closed the door, started the engine, and drove off.

**

Jill entered the house, turning off the beeping alarm. It was quiet, and her brother had not yet arrived, but knowing him, he'd make a detour or two on the way over and be twenty minutes late. She threw her purse in a chair and went to the kitchen. She still wanted that cup of coffee and put on a pot to brew. Anxious, she found it hard to sit. She hadn't seen Dylan in a while, and there was a lot she hadn't told him about her life. She wondered how much she should reveal. Knowing Dylan, he'd likely be in town for a day or two and then disappear again. It was like him. He never stayed in one place for too long.

Listening to the coffee percolate, she again thought back to her earlier appointment with the shrink and couldn't help but worry. If she continued to see him, would she reveal too much? Would it get her kicked off the case? Glancing out the window, she saw the patrol car in front of the house. She'd waved at the officers when she'd been dropped off, but she didn't know their names. Maybe she'd bring them a cup of coffee.

Sighing, she considered the mess she was in. The shrink, the Artist, the department, her brother, her family, and Rem. It all seemed so overwhelming.

She paced with nervous energy and then sat on the couch, remembering what Rem had told her about his Aunt Maggie. How when things seemed out of control, she would quiet her mind and go still. She thought of Sonia, wondering if she'd done the same thing.

Deciding she had a few minutes, she thought about giving meditation a shot. It couldn't hurt. The house was quiet, and no one would interrupt her. Plus, it might help settle her thoughts before she spoke with Dylan. Sitting on the couch, she kicked off her shoes and sat cross-legged. Closing her eyes, she breathed deeply, letting her mind go still. Her thoughts lingered, but she slowly let them dissipate, letting each float away with every breath. The longer she sat, the more relaxed she became, until her mind began to clear. Everything wound down, and her body softened as her muscles released the stress they'd been carrying for weeks. Time faded, and she found herself in a void world, where she could exist unhindered, and it was a satisfying place to be.

Gradually, pictures coalesced in her mind's eye, and curious, she allowed the visions some leeway, staying behind the scenes, acting only as a bystander, to see where they would lead. A heavy fog framed the images, making them hard to see and as she waited, she noticed a presence. Someone was with her in the fog. Staying calm, Jill let the vision play out. One presence became two, and then three, all standing with her. She saw no faces, but one was a woman, and the other two were men. They stood in the fog, faceless, yet somehow connected.

Jill wanted to reach out, but something held her back. She knew these people, but she didn't know how. Watching from her safe place, she waited to see what would happen. A short time passed, she couldn't be sure how long, when one of the female presences stepped forward, as if she'd realized Jill's presence. She reached out her hand, and Jill, desiring that connection, also stepped forward. Their fingers almost touched when a powerful force, like a wave from a turbulent sea, slammed over them, and Jill was shoved back violently, and her eyes opened. She blinked, trying to understand what had just happened. Who were the people in the fog, and why had their connection ended?

Shaking her head, she checked her watch, surprised to see that it had been almost an hour since she'd sat to meditate. Her brother was still not there.

**

Rem stared up at the house. Daniels had just driven off, and he'd been about to get in his car to leave, when he thought twice. What would be the harm in checking the back yard? If he found something, he could call in for back-up.

Daniels wouldn't like it, but Rem didn't see the problem. It made perfect sense. Leaving his car, he headed toward the back gate. It was rusty and needed paint, and it creaked when he pushed it open. Heading toward the back porch, he passed another small window and peered inside, seeing a small dark hallway. It looked tidy and neat, and he saw nothing out of the ordinary.

The yard was nothing fancy. Just uncut grass, a forlorn tree, and a bench sitting on a small cement patio. There were two more windows on either side of the back door, and he peeked into the first one. He saw the back end of the kitchen and a small breakfast nook with a little table and two chairs. There was a plate and fork on the table, and a coffee cup and newspaper. The paper was open as if it someone had been reading it.

Rem stepped back and wandered over to the other side of the patio. He swung the screen door open and knocked again. "Hey, Delgado. It's Detective Remalla. You in there?" he asked. There was no response.

He headed over to the other window and leaned in, his eyes up to the glass. He squinted to focus, unsure of what he was seeing, but it soon made sense.

Newspapers covered the walls, and a desk was littered with file folders and paper. This room differed from the others. It was dirty and cluttered. Looking more closely, he could make out a headline on one of the papers. It was about the Makeup Artist, and it was an article from the local paper. That was just one of several articles strewn about the room. Rem's heart rate picked up. Who was this guy? Still scanning, his eyes centered on a small couch, which was also littered with papers and trash but something else caught his attention. Spotlighted by the sun as it streamed through the window was a picture of Jill.

That changed everything, and in Rem's mind, gave him probable cause. He reached into his jacket and pulled his weapon from his holster. Moving slowly, he walked across the patio and swung open the screen door. It creaked just like the gate, and staying to the side of the door, tried the knob. To his surprise, it was unlocked. He opened it and pushed the door in. Some part of his mind chattered in his partner's voice to call for backup, but Rem didn't listen, focusing instead on the house, all his senses on alert.

Peering around the corner, he looked inside. It was quiet and the only things moving were the tiny dust particles in the air that caught the light. He held his gun at his side and with the voice still nagging at him about calling for backup, he stepped into the house instead.

**

Jill got up from the couch, wondering where her brother was. Since she didn't have a contact number for him, all she could do was wait.

Peering out the window, she didn't see Dylan, but she saw the patrol car, still sitting in its place.

She thought of the coffee long since brewed. Deciding she'd wait a little longer before giving up and returning to the station, she went into the kitchen. If nothing else, the time would give her an opportunity to ponder that strange vision. Who were the people in the fog? And why did she feel she knew them? Grabbing a cup out of the cabinet, she looked for some aspirin. A slow pressured throb was building in her head, and she wanted to ward off the oncoming headache. Not finding any, she knew she had some in her bathroom. She put down the cup and went to find it.

Entering her bedroom, something on the bed caught her eye, and she stopped cold. Staring, Jill didn't move. Her stomach clenched and chills popped out on her skin. Lying on the comforter, below the pillows, was one red rose. Her body went numb, and for a moment, she couldn't breathe. Forcing herself to act, she snapped out of it, and quickly reached for the gun in her ankle holster. Grabbing her pant leg, she had a brief realization that she wasn't alone before something hard came down on her head, her knees buckled, and she fell to the floor, losing consciousness.

**

Rem's focus was the room to the right. Listening intently, and sensing nothing and no one, he walked carefully toward the cluttered room. The door was open, and he entered, now seeing the crazy amount of newspaper articles taped to the walls, all of them appearing to be about the Artist. It was like a bizarre wallpaper. The desk was a mess, but he moved toward the couch and the picture of Jill, and that's when he saw the open door to the bathroom, and two bare feet on the ground sticking out of the entry.

Starting to sweat and his heart thudding hard, he held out his weapon and moved swiftly, double checking behind him. Still assured he was alone, he approached the bathroom door. It was partially closed against the legs, and using his foot, he pushed it open. There was total silence, and he swung around the corner, his gun out, and froze. Blood covered the bathroom, and Delgado lay posed, makeup on his face, and stab wounds in his chest.

Rem tried to take it in. It was a grisly scene, but his eyes caught sight of the bathroom wall across from him. Smeared in blood were more words, only these differed from before. This time it read, *Game over, JJ.*

CHAPTER THIRTY

Rem holstered his gun and grabbed his cell. He called dispatch. His heart thudded and his fingers shook. A woman answered, identifying herself as Linda. He identified himself. "This is detective Aaron Remalla. I've got an officer down. I need all units to respond." He gave her the address.

The woman paused. "You said an officer down?"

"Yes. I need immediate assistance."

"Be advised, Detective. We have a bank robbery in progress with another officer down and a hostage situation. I'll send whoever I can."

"You have another officer down?" He couldn't believe it, but he recalled Parsons' radio call earlier that afternoon about the robbery in progress.

"Yes, Detective. I'll get the call out. We'll send as many as we can."

Rem realized Delgado was beyond saving, but he was still a cop murdered by a serial killer. "At least get Crime Scene over here, if you can. I'll stay at the scene and secure the area."

"Ten-four, Detective."

"Thanks, Linda." He hung up in disbelief, wondering if he should call Daniels, but chose not to. But he needed to call Jacobs. She was out of her appointment by now and was probably wondering where they were.

He rang her cell, but she didn't answer. Then he called Lozano. He could tell him about Delgado and have Lozano convey the message to Jacobs. Lozano's phone rang a few times and Rem almost hung up when someone answered. "Officer Benson speaking."

"Shorty?" asked Rem, recognizing the officer's voice from the front desk. "It's Remalla. I'm trying to reach Lozano."

"He's on the phone. The call transfers here when he doesn't answer. It's crazy around here." Rem could hear muffled voices in the background. "Have you heard about the bank robbery? One of our guys is a hostage. All hell is breaking loose."

"What?" asked Rem. He shook his head. "Is he all right?"

"Don't know, Detective. You want me to get a message to Lozano?"

Rem thought about it. "No. He'll find out soon enough. Just transfer me to Jacobs' desk, please."

"She's not here."

Rem perked up. "She's not there? Where is she?" Something cold moved through his belly.

"She left not long after you and Daniels. Said something about meeting her brother at your place."

Rem's heart stopped. "You're kidding."

"Nope. Why? Something wrong?"

Rem's mind whirled. "Shorty, I need you to get on the horn. Call the patrol in front of my house. Find out what's going on. I'm on my way over. And I may need backup." He left the house and headed for his car.

Shorty paused on the phone, and Rem heard the distant sound of a grainy voice traveling over the line and realized he was hearing Shorty's radio squawking. "Jeez, there's a call coming in. There's another officer down?" asked Shorty.

Rem got to his vehicle and opened the door, realizing Linda was getting the word out. "Yeah. I know. We're stretched thin."

"I'll do what I can, but it may be awhile before I can get another black and white over to your place."

"Just do your best. Thanks." He hung up as he sat and hit the ignition. The engine roared to life, and he put it in reverse and shot down the driveway.

**

Jill blinked, unsure of where she was, but fully aware of the pounding in her head. It felt like someone had taken a jackhammer to it. Blinking again, she tried to focus, but it was hard to see. For a moment, she wondered if she was blindfolded, but then realized it was blood. It was running down her face and was in her right eye. She tried to clear it and shook her head, but instantly regretted it. Sharp pain flashed through her skull, and her stomach threatened to revolt. A cloth was stuffed in her mouth, so she couldn't throw up without dire consequences. Breathing deeply through her nose, she tried to calm down, but as her focus sharpened, she saw she was sitting in the living room on one of the kitchen chairs. Her hands were bound behind her and her feet were tied with plastic zip ties. Moving her hands, she assumed it was the same around her wrists. Gagged and hog-tied, she felt certain she had a concussion, if not a skull fracture.

Trying not to panic, she eyed the room. Nothing seemed out of place, except for her, but she didn't see her gun or phone. She wondered about the patrol outside. Had they seen anything? And her brother. Where was her brother?

She wriggled her wrists, but the bindings were tight. She wasn't going anywhere soon. Feeling something sharp though, she recalled what Rem had told her about this chair. Moving her arms, she found the rusty nail that protruded from one of the rails that his uncle had never fixed. A small kernel of hope blossomed as she positioned herself to use the sharp nail to saw through the plastic bindings.

Footsteps sounded, and her heart pounded. Whoever this was who'd made her life a living hell was here, and he was about to show himself. She swallowed, trying to control her fear, and not choke on the gag at the same time. Her mind raced. She had to keep herself alive long enough for help to arrive.

The footsteps neared, and a man entered the room. Jill froze, eyes wide and completely stunned. She blinked, unsure she was seeing correctly.

"Hello, Jill," said Thomas Fitzpatrick, Rick's former partner. His body language was cool and relaxed, as he seated himself on the sofa, but his eyes held a manic look. "Surprised?"

She tried to control her breathing, and tears sprung into her eyes.

"I know. It's a shock, isn't it?" He put his arms up on the couch cushions and Jill saw the glitter of a knife in his waistband. He had it hooked under his belt.

Her stomach rolled again, but she forced herself not to get sick. *How could this be possible?* A tear escaped and rolled down her cheek.

"I know you're wondering why, and I'd love to explain. I've been wanting to for a long time, but it just took you forever to figure it out." He paused. "Oh, wait. That's right. You never did figure it out, did you?" He chuckled. "All those so-called visions and how you connected with the killer. Just a bunch of lies to get attention. You do like attention, don't you?"

Jill shook her head, her mind searching for ways to get out of this, but no ideas appeared.

"Although I will admit that sometimes I think you were right. I had these odd moments where I felt like I was in your head too, the same way you claimed to be in mine. It was an odd sensation, but not disagreeable." He picked up a pillow and tossed it aside. "It was short lived, but it told me something that I've always known. I'm smarter than you. I've always been smarter than you. You just can't see what's right in front of you, can you? That's a weakness of yours."

She struggled to understand. He wasn't making sense.

He played with the fringe on a small throw pillow. "Did you know that when you initially joined the department in Seattle, you were supposed to be paired with me?" He raised the side of his lip. "But there was a glitch. And you ended up with someone else, and Rick and I became partners, and then you met Rick, and blah, blah, blah." He set the pillow aside and eyed her instead. "But I always wondered what if? What if they had partnered you with me? What would have happened?"

She tried to hold eye contact with him to show some courage, but she failed.

Fitz scooted closer. "Maybe you would have fallen for me instead. It's possible. In fact, even probable. I used to imagine that, you and I together." He stared off.

Oh, God. Help. Please, somebody help me. She struggled against her bindings and tried to keep up a slow shredding of the plastic against the nail, praying he wouldn't notice.

His far-off look returned to her. "I expected you to break up with him. I mean, he was a great guy, and I loved him, but he was never the one for you. I expected you to see that, but you never did." He leaned in with his elbows on his knees. "I could have been so much better for you. Don't you see that?"

A strangled sound escaped her throat and more tears fell.

"I would have been good for you. I protected you. Kept an eye out. I would have never let anyone hurt you. You were never like the others. The ones who like to pretend they're so high and mighty. Like they are better than everyone else. My mother was the same way. She never saw me." His eyes went soft, and he went somewhere else.

Terror made her chest constrict, and Jill thought her heart was going to pop out of her chest. Her breathing came in harsh spurts through her nose.

His eyes refocused. "But you were different. You spoke to me with truth, and you weren't afraid. I think we had a connection. Somehow I think you knew it too."

He reached over and touched her knee and she jumped, wishing she could pull away. From what she could tell, she wasn't bound to the chair itself, but there was no way she could hop to safety.

"I just don't understand why you didn't want me too." He squeezed her knee. "But now we will make it all right. Won't we Jill?"

Fitz touched the knife at his waist, and if it weren't for the gag in her mouth, she would have screamed.

**

Remalla raced down the road, the light on the roof flashing and his siren on. He rushed through two stop signs and ran a red light. Luckily, the traffic wasn't heavy, and he was making good time.

He prayed that Jill's phone was only dead or lost, and he hoped their theory about her brother was wrong, but the more he considered it, the more worried he became. Rem thought of Delgado and the writing on the wall in his bathroom. Had Delgado figured out the identity of the killer? Is that why he was targeted? And what did the killer mean by *Game Over*? Was Jill next on the killer's list? The fears mounted, and he punched the accelerator, hoping he was overreacting.

He thought again of calling Daniels but chose not to. His partner needed to be present for the birth of his child without worrying about Rem. Rem just didn't want Daniels to be blindsided when everything was said and done. But there was little he could do about it now.

Reaching his neighborhood, he turned onto his street as the tires squealed and the wheels burned rubber onto the cement. Racing past the homes, he flipped off the siren as he reached his house and was shocked to see no patrol car in front. Where the hell were they?

Screeching to a halt in front of the house, he grabbed his phone. Had Shorty managed to call the patrol? He hit a button and called again. The home was quiet, and the blinds were closed, but Rem hadn't opened them since they realized they'd been watched.

The call transferred again, and Shorty answered. "Detective Benson speaking."

"Shorty. It's Remalla. Did you manage to get a hold of the patrol in front of my house?"

"Sorry, Rem. It's crazy here. I didn't get a chance to call you back. They said they got called off and told to assist at the bank robbery. That's where they're headed."

"What the hell are they talking about? Nobody reassigned them," said Rem.

"Apparently, someone did."

"Shit." Rem stared at the house. Was it a mistake, or had they deliberately been reassigned to get them away from his home? "Listen, I still need back-up. Any progress there?"

"I put a call in. There's a team dispatched to the second officer-down call. The hostage situation is still in play downtown, so unless you've got an emergency, you might just need to wait before you go in."

Something told Rem that he didn't have time to wait. "Just keep trying, okay?"

"What about Daniels?"

"He's at the hospital. His baby is on the way, so don't call him. You got that?"

"Remalla…"

"Get a hold of Lozano when you can. Tell him what's going on."

"Don't do anything stupid. We don't need another officer casualty today." Remalla heard another phone ringing and people shouting in the background. "I got to go," said Shorty. "I'll get the word out. Stay put if you can." And the line went dead.

Rem thought of Daniels, who would have offered the same advice as Shorty. Unfortunately, he didn't have a choice. If Jill was in danger, he couldn't leave her alone. Putting his cell in his pocket, he pulled out his weapon, checked it, and returned it to its holster. Then he opened his door and got out.

**

Fitz stood, and Jill froze in fear. Would he kill her? Would she die in this chair, left to be found by Rem, posed with makeup on her face and blood pouring from her chest? She gulped in air as he approached her, but then he kept going. He passed by her, brushing her legs, and she pulled back, not wanting to be touched by him.

He stood next to the wall. "I should tell you, I killed Delgado this morning."

His words stunned her. Did she hear right? Delgado was dead? She shook her head and moaned.

"I know you're wondering why." He leaned against the door frame, his fingers on the knife handle. "Did you know he worked in Seattle?"

Jill held her breath, not moving.

"Before he came here, he was on the Seattle P.D. Apparently, the case struck a nerve with him, as it did you. He liked you." His fingers tapped on his belt. "It seems a lot of men do."

She'd stopped sawing at her bindings, not wanting him to notice. When he glanced off again though, she started again, keeping her movement as minimal as possible. Her fear almost stopped her, but her survival instinct kept her going.

Fitz seemed to drift off again, lost in some strange world, before a few seconds passed and he returned. "Tell me about Remalla."

Fresh tears welled in her eyes. A low keen escaped her throat and she silently prayed again for help.

"Why do you pick men who can't possibly give you what you need? What you *deserve.*" His face tightened, and it was his first display of anger with her. His fingers tightened on the knife handle.

Her fear ramping up more, she started to ramble, although the gag prevented her from communicating. Her stomach bubbled again, and her head throbbed. Blood continued to drip down her face and down her shirt. It was beginning to sink in that she was going to die.

His face softened, but his grip on the knife did not. "Maybe I've misjudged you. I've told myself over and over to just kill you and get it over with, but I could never do it. I just wanted you to see me the way I see you. I thought if we played the game, you would understand. That you would come to appreciate and understand my work, but you never did." He straightened and pushed aside the blind, peering out the front window. "You still don't, do you? Even now."

While he looked out, Jill again dragged her plastic binding over the nail. She felt a wet sticky warmth on her wrists and she knew her skin was abraded and bleeding. Hearing a siren approach, she stilled, but then it abruptly stopped. Had the patrols called for help? A small kernel of hope blossomed.

Fitz squinted, as if seeing something of interest. "It appears we have some company." He dropped the blind, and she prayed the cops were there. "Remalla is here to save you."

Her heart skipped. *No. No. Please no*. If that were true, Remalla was going to walk right into this, and Fitz would kill him, probably while she watched. She yelled through the gag, but it made little difference.

"I was hoping he would show. And it appears he's alone. Too bad. This would have been perfect if Daniels were here." Fitz left the room briefly, and she continued to moan, but feverishly worked on breaking the plastic on her wrists. She eyed the coffee table, knowing what was taped beneath it. If she could get to it…

Fitz reappeared, and she froze again, and tried to speak, making only muffled sounds.

"Shut up," he said, pulling out the knife.

Jill shrieked into the cloth, and he walked behind her and grabbed her hair, bringing the knife to her throat. "I said shut up," he whispered harshly into her ear.

Closing her eyes, she went quiet, her rapid breathing the only sound in the quiet room. *What was Fitz doing? Would he slit her throat?* she wondered, feeling the cold steel against her skin. *Where was Rem?* And then she heard the front door open.

CHAPTER THIRTY-ONE

Rem approached the house, holding his gun close to his side. He had no idea what he was walking into. Jacobs could be in the house napping, having coffee with her brother, or she could be…he pictured Delgado's corpse in his mind. He refused to believe that Jacobs could also be a victim, lying dead in his guest bathroom. The thought made him physically ill. Having already lost one great woman in his life, he couldn't imagine losing another.

Since he was on his own, he didn't have many options. Reaching the front porch, he cursed when he realized he'd forgotten there were cameras around the house. He could check them now to see who may have accessed the home. Why the hell had he not thought of that before?

Still holding his gun, he pulled out his phone and quickly accessed the app. He punched a button and cursed when he saw nothing. The video was off line. That usually meant he needed to reboot the system or his phone, but he didn't have the luxury of time to deal with technology issues. Sliding the phone back into his pocket, he stepped quietly to the front door and considered his options. Walk right in? Check the perimeter of the house? His mind whirled to determine the safest course of action for him and for Jacobs. Sweat popped out on his skin.

He decided if he went slowly, and entered from the front, his gun out, he would be ready for whatever confronted him. Some part of his brain shot out warning signals, but he didn't think stalling, and coming in from the back was any better. Daniels voice rang in his head. *Wait for back-up, dummy*. But he shut it out. He'd always trusted his gut before, and he figured now wasn't the time to stop. Reaching out, he tried the knob, and turning it, realized it was open. His heart raced. He knew Jacobs would not have left it unlocked. The image returned of her lying bloody on the bathroom tile, but he shook his head, focusing on the task ahead. Thinking the worst served no one.

The door opened, and he pushed it in, staying to the side, waiting. He heard nothing. The house was quiet. Peering inside, he saw the front entry. Nothing seemed out of place, and he leaned further in, his gun still at his side.

Seeing into the kitchen and dining area on his right, he noticed nothing unusual, other than a chair missing from the table. He tried to think if he or Jill had moved it, but he couldn't recall. If Jacobs' brother was here, was she entertaining him? Did she realize the danger she was in? Moving further in, he held out his gun. If they were really sitting on the couch having coffee, they were about to get a hell of a shock.

Taking another step, he moved past the door and swung his gun around the front entry. The staircase was empty, and the door to Jill's room was open. There was a side table against the wall that separated the foyer from the living room, and he noticed Jill's purse laying on it.

Then he swung further and faced the living area, just as the couch and TV came into view, and taking another step, he stopped dead. A man stood beside the sofa, holding a knife against a bound and gagged Jacobs' throat.

**

Daniels checked his watch.

"You know you've done that three times since you got here," said Marjorie, as she sat back against a pillow.

He shook his head. "I'm sorry." He was sitting on the side of the bed with her and he scooted closer. "How are you feeling? Anything?"

Marjorie huffed. "Nothing. Not a thing." She waved at the monitor beside the bed. "I literally call you, and everything stops. This machine is basically recording my gas pains."

Daniels chuckled. "The doctor will appreciate that." He held her hand. "And you're sure everything's okay with the baby?

She nodded. "Yes. Everything's fine. All normal. I just got nervous." Sighing, she closed her eyes. "I was so sure this was it."

"Honey, it's our first baby. You've never done this before. Cut yourself some slack."

"I know, but I called you and you came racing down. I hope I didn't pull you away from something important. You didn't leave Rem in a ditch or something did you?"

Daniels smiled but couldn't help but worry. He'd left Rem at Delgado's, and although Rem had promised Daniels not to do anything stupid, Daniels knew the likelihood of Rem keeping his promise was slim, especially with an important case. His partner was infamous for being impulsive.

"What is it?" asked Marjorie, lifting her head from the pillow. "Did you leave him in a ditch?"

"No, no ditches." He fought the urge to check his watch again.

"Something's bothering you though. I know that look."

Squeezing her fingers, he thought of Rem saying the same thing earlier. "Never mind me. You're the one in the hospital bed. Rem's a big boy. He can take care of himself."

Her brow furrowed. "You and I both know that you count on each other to stay alive. One without the other is like a blind puppy. Are you sure he's okay?"

Something nagged at Daniels, and he wanted to tell her his worries, but the door opened, and the doctor entered the room.

"Hi, Marjorie. Detective. How are you two doing? Are we getting ready to have this baby?"

Marjorie sighed. "I thought so, but now I'm not so sure. Everything's gone quiet."

"Not unusual for a first baby. Let me examine you, and we'll see what's going on." She grabbed some gloves.

Daniels stood, but Marjorie tugged on his hand. "Why don't you go call him," said Marjorie. "Ease your mind." She cocked her head at the doctor. "I'm not going anywhere."

Daniels nodded, amazed by how well she could read him. "I think I will. I'll be right back." He leaned over and kissed her. "Take care of her, Doc."

"Will do, Detective." She snapped on a glove.

Daniels stepped outside and pulled out his cell. The antsy feeling he'd been feeling since he'd arrived at the hospital crept up his spine. If he could talk to Rem and realize everything was fine, then maybe he could attribute the feeling to becoming a father. That was making him just as nervous.

He held the phone to his ear as it rang and went to voicemail. The feeling didn't go away. Instead, the hair on his neck raised. Why didn't Rem answer? He was supposed to go straight back to the station. He hung up and tried Jacobs instead. One of them should pick up. Her phone did the same though. Straight to voicemail. Alarm bells rang in his head. Something wasn't right.

Turning, he walked back into the room as the doctor scooted back from the end of the bed, removing her gloves.

"It's confirmed," said Marjorie. "Nothing's happening. No baby today."

"Soon though," said the doctor. "You'll continue to experience contractions, but it will probably be another two to three days." She patted Marjorie's knee. "Don't worry. This time next week, you'll have a beautiful baby in your arms, and you'll be exhausted and sore as hell."

Marjorie moaned. "I'm already incredibly uncomfortable and exhausted, but at least I'll finally be able to see that little bundle I've been carrying around all this time."

The doctor picked up a tablet and typed on it. "I'm discharging you. A nurse will be in soon to disconnect you from everything and you can go home."

Marjorie frowned at Daniels. "Everything all right? You look a little pale. How's Rem?"

Daniels walked closer. "You sure she's okay, Doc? No last-minute surprises?"

"She's fine and so's the baby. In perfect health," said the doctor.

"Great." He put his hand on Marjorie's shoulder. "Honey. I have to go. Do you have a ride home?"

She shifted on the bed. "Yes. Katie drove me. Remember?"

Daniels nodded. He'd forgotten Marjorie's sister had brought her to the hospital. She'd gone down to the commissary to get some coffee and a snack. "Sorry. My mind's elsewhere."

"Something's wrong, isn't it? Rem did something stupid."

"I don't know, but I have to find out." He leaned in and kissed her. "I'll call you as soon as I know. You're sure you're okay?"

"I'm fine. I'm so fine, I'm boring. Go. Check on Uncle Aaron. We need him to change diapers."

He touched her face, then turned, and headed for the door. "See you tonight. Love you."

"Love you, too," she said as he left. Making a slow jog, he headed toward the elevators and grabbed his phone again when it rang. He saw that it was Lozano and answered.

"Captain?"

Lozano's voice boomed over the phone. "Daniels. Where the hell are you?"

An icy finger of dread ran down his spine. "I'm leaving the hospital. We thought Marjorie was ready to deliver, but it's going to be a few more days."

"Everything okay? No problems?" asked Lozano.

"She's fine and so's the baby. Where's Rem?"

"I'm calling to ask you the same thing. Have you heard from him?"

The elevator had still not arrived, and Daniels saw the sign for the stairs. He headed for it. "No. I haven't. I left him at Delgado's, but Delgado wasn't home. Rem was going back to the station."

The captain grunted. "Why the hell was he at Delgado's?"

"What's going on, Cap?" Daniels raced down the stairwell.

"What's going on? All hell has broken loose, and it's raining down on us. Delgado's dead."

Daniels almost tripped on the stairs. "What?"

"And I've got a bank robbery in progress with an officer down and a hostage situation. And to top it all off, someone just called in a bomb threat at the station. The building is evacuating, and dispatch is operating on one staff member. It's a zoo."

Daniels exited the stairwell and accessed the lobby. He ran through it and out into the parking lot. "Who found Delgado?" He got to his car and opened the door.

"From what I've heard, your partner did. He called it in."

"Where did he go from there? And where's Jacobs?"

"Shorty says they went back to Rem's. Jacobs' brother showed, and she went to meet him. Rem called in and was headed that way. Said something about needing backup. But now he's not answering, and neither is Jacobs. What the hell is going on? Did you tell her about what we learned about her brother? Did she know?"

Fear made Daniels' chest constrict. He started up the engine and backed out of the space. "Cap. I think they're in trouble. I'm headed there now. Can you send anybody?"

"I'm standing out here in a parking lot while dogs are sniffing my office. Dispatch is down to one officer, and all 911 calls are getting diverted to the neighboring county. I'm a little short-handed myself."

Daniels shot out of the parking lot and onto the street. An annoyed motorist honked at him and he flipped on his lights and siren. "I think the Artist may have Rem and Jacobs, Captain. When I get there, I'm going in alone if I have to. I'm not hanging around and waiting to see who may or may not show up."

There was a pause on the line. "Damn it," said the Captain. "I'll do what I can to get somebody over there. I'll come myself if I have to, if I can get my damn car out of the lot." His voice raised, and Daniels heard him yell at somebody on the other end of the phone. "You be careful," said Lozano, returning his attention to Daniels.

"I will, Cap. I got to go." He raced through a light and heard another horn as he hung up the phone.

**

Blood and tears ran down Jacobs' face and dripped down her shirt as the man held the steel against her throat. Rem didn't move, but something clicked in his head that this man was familiar. He'd met him.

"Hello, Detective," said the man. "Close and lock the door and put down your gun."

Fitzpatrick, thought Rem. It was Henderson's former partner. Seeing the knife against Jacobs' throat press harder, he heard her whimper. A slim red crease appeared on her skin. He held out his hands, letting the gun go loose in his fingers. "Just take it easy."

"Close the door and drop it," he repeated more forcefully. "Or I'll slice her open right in front of you."

Rem didn't hesitate. Fitzpatrick's eyes held a wild look, and Rem didn't doubt for a second that he would do what he said. His fear making his heart race, he kicked the front door shut with his foot, leaned back and locked it, and carefully laid his weapon down on the floor, his hands visible.

"Now kick it into the dining room."

Rem hesitated.

"Now." He pulled on Jacobs' hair and Jacob whimpered again. She had a nasty cut on her scalp and her shirt was soaked in blood. The gag securely in place, she was breathing hard through her nose.

"Okay," he said softly. He moved his foot and kicked his gun into the dining area.

"Now get on your knees."

Rem's adrenaline levels were sky high. His fingers were shaking as he held them out. "Listen—"

Fitz yanked on Jacobs and pressed the knife deeper. Jacobs choked and a thicker trickle of blood ran down her neck. Rem got on his knees, keeping his hands up. He would have to look scared and vulnerable to keep this guy calm. It wouldn't be difficult.

Jacobs' breaths became more labored. "I think she's having a hard time breathing. You need to take out the gag," said Rem.

Fitzpatrick, seeing Rem comply, eased his hold on Jacobs, but the knife was still on her throat, and her tears ran down her pale but bloodied, face.

Rem lowered his voice and spoke softly. "Fitz, listen to her. She's struggling to get air. She's crying, and her nose is running. Take out the gag, or she's going to die from suffocation."

Fitz blinked, as if unsure where he was, and lowered the knife. He eyed Jacobs. "Maybe that's what I want. She's made me suffer, now it's her turn."

Rem scrambled to think. How was he going to reach this guy? "If she dies right in front of you, it will be a relief for her. You'll be putting her out of her misery."

Fitzpatrick hesitated, his face impassive. Rem prayed he was getting through and not making it worse.

A few slow seconds passed until Fitz stepped back, reached around, and yanked the tape off Jacobs' face, and pulled what looked like a scarf out of her mouth. Jacobs gasped and coughed, her face constricted as she sucked in air.

Fitz grabbed her by the hair. "Don't think for one second I'm taking it easy on you. You scream, and I'll cut him, and then I'll cut you. You understand?"

Jacobs nodded and sputtered. "Yes," she said gruffly. He let her go.

Rem relaxed slightly, relieved to see Jacobs' breathing when his cell phone rang. He kept his hands out. "It's probably the station, checking in on me. They know I'm here."

Fitz waved the knife at Jacobs again, and she flinched. "Take it out, slowly," said Fitz.

Rem did as he asked, sliding his phone out of his pocket, seeing it was Lozano calling. He put the phone on the floor.

"Slide it away. You won't be needing it," said Fitz.

Rem did as asked, not wanting to upset Fitz further, and shoved the cell away and into the foyer.

"You came alone?" asked Fitz. "Where's your partner, Daniels? It would have been nice to have you both here."

Rem thought fast. "He's out back. Calling in the cavalry, I'm sure." He met Jacobs' gaze, trying to reassure her.

The room went quiet as the phone stopped ringing. Fitz chuckled. "You're a liar. Nobody's out back. If he were here, you wouldn't have entered without him." He waved the knife. "That's why you walked in, because you weren't even sure I was here." Fitz narrowed his eyes. "Oh, and I know about your cameras. I'm not an idiot. I ripped the video out of the wall, so no one will know of my entry, or yours."

Rem eyed the coffee table, thinking of the gun taped beneath it, and then looked back at Jacobs. Her gaze, despite her fear, told him she was thinking the same thing. "You sure about Daniels not being here? You're pretty cocky." he said. "And if you're wrong? You better get the hell out while you still can."

Fitz lowered the knife. "I'm damn sure I'm right. You forget who you're talking too. I'm a cop too, and I know how it works. I've always been one step ahead. I know exactly what I'm doing. I'm sure you noticed the missing patrol car. Who do you think sent them away?"

"You sent them away?" asked Jill. She shifted in her seat and Rem wondered if Fitz had tied her to the chair.

"It was easy. Two bored cops sitting outside a house while a hostage situation is playing out with an officer down. All they needed was a nudge, and they couldn't leave fast enough. All I had to do was flash my badge." He studied the tip of his knife. "Just goes to show you how everything works out for me. The moment I was outside Delgado's house, I heard about the robbery. It was perfect. They would send every cop in the city in that direction. It's making my day so much easier. I just added another diversion to the mix to ensure that interruptions are kept to a minimum. Bomb threats work well for that." He lowered the knife at Jill. "I'd like to take my time while I'm here. Especially now that Remalla has joined us."

Bomb threats? Rem didn't know what he meant, but he decided to change the subject. "Why'd you kill Delgado?" asked Rem. "Was he getting too close?" He had to keep this guy talking.

"Delgado was stupid, just like the rest of them. He thought he could impress her if he found me. Well," he looked at Jacobs, "are you impressed?"

Jacobs bit her lip and Rem saw her take a quiet breath. "No," she said.

Fitz squatted next to her. "That's right. Because he's not the one. And neither is he." He pointed the knife towards Rem, and Rem saw Jacobs tremble.

Jacobs sniffed, but held her head up. "Why Henderson? Why did you have to kill Rick?" Another tear slid down her cheek.

That question seemed to ruffle him, and he stood. "Don't play stupid with me. You and I both know what happened to Rick."

Jacobs narrowed her eyes. "You killed him. In my apartment. You slit his throat." She let go of a sob. "You killed your best friend and partner."

Fitzpatrick eyed her, his eyes like concrete. "You're smart, blaming me. But it won't work. I know what you did." He moved the knife back toward her, and she shied away from it. "I was angry at first, but then I understood. You had to do it. It's why I admire you. You do what needs to be done. Rick was in the way. I wasn't strong enough to do it, but you were."

Rem frowned, as he watched Fitz's words affect Jacobs. It sounded like Fitz was accusing Jacobs of killing Henderson. Had the man blocked it from his mind?

Jacobs' jaw dropped. "I didn't kill him."

Fitz's eyes clouded over. "Yes. You did."

She shook her head. "No. I didn't. You did."

"Stop lying!" he yelled, and Jacobs jumped in her seat. He brought the knife up again. "I should have killed you before. Why didn't I? I would have saved myself such misery."

"Why'd you kill Craig Lester?" asked Rem trying to divert the subject. "We couldn't figure that out."

Fitz turned his attention back to Rem, his eyes wide. "Craig Lester?"

Rem's phone rang again. Fitz cocked his head. "You sure are getting a lot of phone calls."

"They want to be sure I'm all right. They probably want to talk to you too," said Rem.

"I turned Jill's cell off. You should have done the same. Nobody's talking to anybody. I know the drill. You will both die here today. There will be no rescuing." He looked at Jacobs. "Do you know what I wrote on Delgado's wall?"

Jacobs didn't move.

"Game over, JJ," he said.

The phone stopped ringing.

CHAPTER THIRTY-TWO

Daniels cursed as the railroad arms came down. He was seconds away from crossing, but the train was coming faster. He slammed his hand on the steering wheel and considered alternate options but knew there weren't any. He would have to wait.

His cell rang, and he saw it was Lozano. He answered. "It's me, Cap."

"I got a hold of Georgios. He's going to meet you at Rem's. You almost there?"

"Georgios? You're serious?"

"Daniels," Lozano yelled. "I don't need your smart-ass comments. You need back-up. He's a cop. He'll do his job no matter who's in trouble. So don't give me shit about it. Titus is on his way, but he's on scene at the bank and Mel and Garcia are on scene with Delgado. I can send them, but it will take longer for them and Titus to get there. Georgios is the closest."

Daniels rubbed his head as the train lumbered by. He knew he didn't have a choice. He needed help if he hoped to save Rem's and Jacobs' life. "I hear ya."

"Don't you do a damn thing until he gets there, you got that?" asked Lozano.

The train passed, and Daniels nudged as close to the rail arms as he could as they opened, and he shot by them. "Sorry, Cap. I got to go." He heard the captain yell an expletive before he hung up.

**

Jacobs made slow movements, trying to work on her restraints while Rem distracted Fitz. Now that she could breathe without the gag, her mind had cleared somewhat, and she was less panicked, but no less fearful. Fitz was on the edge, and anything could set him off. She needed to move fast. If she could get to the gun, then they would have a chance.

Rem kept talking. "You didn't say anything about Lester. Why him? He's not an obvious target."

Fitz snickered. "Lester made his own bed. Henderson told me he'd once used Lester's laundromat to dry clean a suit, so I went one day to drop off some clothes. Lester was there. His TV was on and they were showing her," he cocked his head toward Jill, "on the screen. You were talking to a reporter." He gripped the knife handle. "He started making lewd comments about you. What he'd do if you were alone with him. The man was a pig. I decided then that he was next on the list."

Jill couldn't believe Fitz was calling Lester a pig and had to ask the obvious. "If Lester was a pig, what does that make you?"

Fitz stilled. "This is why I like you, Jill. Despite your circumstances, you always step up to the challenge." He wiped a finger through the blood on her scalp and rubbed his fingers together as Jill pulled away. "I wonder what I will write on your bathroom wall?"

"You've murdered thirteen people," said Jill, wincing. Her arms ached from pulling on the restraints. "At least Lester didn't kill anyone."

"That you know of," said Fitz, wiping his fingers on his jeans. "You want to know what was on his home computer? Never mind the drugs he took. I did society a favor."

"You could have arrested him," said Jill.

Fitz reached out and grabbed Jill's face by the chin. She tried to pull away, but he held tight. "I wonder what it will be like when I put the makeup on your face?" he asked. He squeezed, and Jill grimaced.

"What about Jacobs' brother? Dylan?" said Rem. "It's not a coincidence that a victim's business card was found in his stuff, was it?"

Fitz let go, and Jill blinked, trying to clear her vision as fresh blood dribbled down her face. She wasn't sure she heard right. "What's he talking about? What does Dylan have to do with this?"

Rem sat back on his heels, his hands still raised. "Your brother's been in jail. Seattle P.D. found evidence in his storage locker that linked him to the Seattle crimes. They think he's the murderer."

Fitz chuckled. "He's the perfect scapegoat." He tapped the knife on Jill's shoulder, and she held her breath, not moving. "I'll disappear after this, and all anyone will know is that you came here to meet Dylan. I leave a few crumbs of evidence, and he goes to prison for the rest of his life."

"That will never work. Dylan wouldn't kill anybody," said Jill. "A little detective work would prove that."

"It's a good distraction," said Rem. "But you know it's thin. It's gonna take more than a business card to put him away. Besides after today, they'll know it was you."

Fitz stepped back from the chair. "Nice try, detective. But you know that's not true. No one suspects me. I'm in Seattle, on a nice quiet fishing trip. I can kill you both and walk away and never be a suspect. If I plan it right, and you know I will, Dylan the wanderer will be the killer and I'll move on to whatever comes next. It's sort of my final masterpiece. But I admit, it leaves me feeling a little sad." He traced the knife along Jill's shoulder. "My last three years have all been about you Jill."

Jill shuddered. "It won't work. Dylan could be somewhere right now where a million people could vouch for his whereabouts."

"Oh, but he's not. I invited him, or should I say you did. He drove in this morning and is currently camping in some park. Nobody knows he's here, and he's expecting you to arrive tonight. No alibi, no witnesses." He shook his head. "Poor man. He won't know what hit him."

"But I talked to him on the phone. He was on his way here," said Jill. Her shoulders ached, and it felt like wires were slicing through her wrists.

Fitz grinned. "How are ya sis? Long time, no see. I've missed you. Want to meet?"

Jill couldn't believe it. Fitz sounded like Dylan. How could she have missed it?

"That's right," said Fitz. "It was me. Add in a little background noise, and a poor connection, and you were easy to fool. I do a mean Jack Nicholson, too. Want to hear?"

Jill widened her eyes. "It doesn't matter. They'll figure it out. What about the other victims?"

He leaned in, his voice threatening. "Haven't you learned by now, Jill, that I usually get what I want?" He held the knife in front of her face. "Does it really matter, anyway? They'll spend so much time trying to prove that Dylan's the killer that they won't be looking for anyone else, especially not me." Jill clenched her jaw as he brought the knife to her chin.

"How did this all begin?" asked Rem. "Why kill women? What did they do to you?" He caught Jill's eye, and she knew he was drawing this out. They had to keep him distracted.

Lowering the knife, he straightened, taking his attention off Jill. "You ask a lot of questions. I know what you're doing. But it won't work." He smiled. "But since you ask, and we have the time, I'll humor you." He stood beside Jill, the knife never far away. "The first was Giselle. We went out once, but she did what so many other women do. She thought she was better than me. And when I told her so, she argued, and I got angry. And I showed her who she truly was and showed the world too. She deserved it. It felt so calming, and it was easy. I made her see the truth and stopped her from spreading her lies."

"What lies?" asked Rem.

"The lies she was projecting to other men. The men she believed to be less than her. It was the same with the second one. She needed to learn her place, as well."

"Alice Dumont," said Jill. "She was a mother."

"I did her kid a favor," said Fitz. "He's better off."

"Then why not me?" asked Jill, continuing to saw at her bindings when she had the chance. "How am I any different from these women?"

Fitz started to pace beside her, his agitation growing. "Because you're smart, beautiful, and you liked me. If you'd been partnered with me, you would have seen me, too, the way I see you. But the department screwed up. I couldn't blame you for that. But I remember you brought me a cup of coffee one day, and you told me you looked forward to working with me and Rick. I knew that you were special. You weren't like the others."

Rem began to scoot forward in small movements on his knees, inching toward the coffee table. Jill kept up her attempts to break through her bindings, being careful to keep Fitz from noticing. Her fear raging, she kept talking, trying to keep her voice steady. "But I started to date Rick. Did that make you angry?"

He stepped back and put his hand on the wall. "By then, I was too invested in the murders. I was having fun, and you were getting more involved with the case. It was like you and I were playing our own game. I wondered secretly if you knew it was me, and that you looked the other way, because you wanted to play too." He touched the tip of the knife against the wall, putting a small nick in it. "Plus, Rick was my friend. I knew eventually you would break up with him when you realized he wasn't the one." He paused. "But then he told me he wanted to propose."

Rem stopped moving. "What did you think of that?" Fitz glanced out the blinds and Rem moved a couple more inches. He was within three feet of the table.

"I was angry," said Fitz. "I was wondering when you would tell him, Jill, that it would never work. But you never did." He switched his grip on the blade, facing the steel downward.

Jill tensed in her seat. Sweat trickled down her back.

"I wonder why?" He dropped the blind and stepped away from the wall. "Did you want to marry him?" He approached Jill, the knife raised. "Did you ever want me? Or were you just like all the rest?"

"Fitz—" said Jill, leaning back.

He grabbed her by the hair. "Is that what you were doing all along? Did you play me for the fool?" His brief calm had vanished, and he sneered at her.

"Fitz, please. No." Jill tried to pull away but shrieked as Fitz, his back to Rem, brought the blade up. Jill knew Rem would not have time to reach the gun before Fitz sliced her open like a fish.

"Should I stab you or slice you, like you did Rick?" he asked. His face twisted, and Jill braced for the piercing impact.

As the knife descended, Rem shot forward, grabbing Fitz from behind, knocking him off balance, and lunging for the knife which narrowly missed Jill. Fitz stumbled but turned at the last minute, preventing his fall to the ground. His knee came up, catching Rem in the side. Rem grunted but held on to Fitz, and both men toppled to the floor. Jill and the chair fell sideways to the carpet and Jill scrambled to sit up. Her legs still bound together, her best hope was to get her hands free. Finding the nail again on the chair, she furiously sawed at her restraints as both men fought for control. Fitz had the upper hand as he loomed over Rem who held the knife at bay.

Jill prayed the zip tie would break loose, but it didn't budge. Her wrists were slick with blood as the plastic cut into her skin. The coffee table was in front of her as Rem shifted and Fitz toppled to the side. But as Rem shoved upward and battled for the knife, Fitz got a hand free and wrapped it around Rem's throat. Rem grabbed at Fitz's wrist, just as his hand slipped from his grip on the knife, and Fitz plunged the knife upward and into Rem's midsection. Jill screamed.

**

Daniels pulled up to the house and came to a screeching halt, tires squealing behind Rem's car. He'd turned off the siren a block away to prevent announcing his arrival. The car rocked back and forth as Daniels hopped out, staying behind and squatting low, and viewed the house as he pulled out his gun.

The home was quiet. The door was closed, and the blinds pulled. He couldn't see anything inside. Remembering the cameras, he accessed the video feed on his phone, but saw nothing. The cameras were offline. He cursed and put his phone away. Shifting toward the backside of the car, he was about to dart to the front of the house when another car turned onto the street at a fast pace and came to a hard stop across the street. Daniels recognized the driver. It was Georgios.

Daniels watched the house as Georgios joined him, running up and squatting beside him. His clothes rumpled and his hair disheveled: he held his gun.

"What we got?" he asked. "Is he in there?"

"Did you sleep in those clothes?" asked Daniels.

Georgios waved his gun. "I can shoot with a wrinkled jacket. I assume that's okay with you?"

Daniels checked his weapon, knowing it was fully loaded, but it gave him reassurance. "Just so long as you don't miss."

"I won't miss," said Georgios. He studied the scene. "You want me to take the back?"

Daniels started to answer when they both heard a high-pitched scream, and they both took off running toward the house.

**

Jill's shriek reverberated through the room as Rem groaned and continued to fight. Fitz yanked the blade out, but weakened, and blood oozing from his side, Rem could not ward off another assault. Fitz raised the knife again just as Jill's restraints broke free and her hands came apart. Frantic, she scrambled toward the coffee table, but with her legs still bound, she had to push with her knees. Breathing hard and shaking with terror, she made it to the table. Glancing back, she saw that Fitz had realized she'd escaped, and he turned toward her and away from Rem, who clutched his side, his fingers red with blood. Within a few steps, Fitz loomed over her, knife raised.

"Where do you think you're going?" he asked.

Panicked, she rolled to get beneath the table, but a sharp sting beneath her shoulder made her cry out. Her momentum kept her going though, and she turned on her back and saw what she was looking for – the gun. She reached for it, grabbing it just as Fitz seized the side of the table and lifted it, tossing it roughly aside. But she'd pulled the gun free and held it, pointing it upward, and cocked it.

Gripping the knife, his eyes went wide, and he froze.

Holding her breath, she shot him a dead stare. "Now the game's over you son-of-a-bitch." And she pulled the trigger.

**

Daniels and Georgios reached the front door, each on either side of it. Georgios tried the knob, but it didn't turn.

"You realize we're breaking every protocol, don't you?" asked Georgios, breathing hard and sweating. "We should wait and get a hostage negotiator out here."

Daniels took a deep breath, trying to stay focused. "You want to go wait by the car, then go ahead. But my partner's in there. And waiting will get him and Jacobs both killed."

Georgios paused for a second and then nodded. "Okay. Just want to be sure we're on the same page." He looked up at the door. "On three?"

Daniels nodded. He shifted to get a better position. "On three."

And then two shots rang out.

**

Jill held the gun, hands shaking, as two rivulets of blood began to dribble down Fitz's chest, but he stood unmoving as if in disbelief. Jill blinked as a wave of dizziness hit her and her arms wavered and shook.

Fitz wobbled, but still prepared to fight, raised the knife once more, his face frozen in hatred, and she fired again, only the shot went over his shoulder and into the ceiling.

Determined to take her with him, Fitz released a guttural yell and arced the knife down once more just as Jill heard a loud crack and a crash and the front door slammed open. Fitz had a brief chance to look toward the sound and never completed the swing of his knife before Jill emptied her rounds and the furious sound of gunfire erupted from the foyer.

Fitz jerked and, hit multiple times, fell sideways onto the couch, then slumped over, and rolled onto the floor, eyes open but lifeless, blood seeping from the wounds in his body.

Jill, seeing his collapse, went limp but still held the gun. Fitz had fallen beside her, and feeling him against her, she pushed back and away from him. Shaking and bleeding, she had a vague awareness of two men in the house, but all she could see was Rem, lying on the floor, bleeding from his side.

**

Daniels rushed into the living room. Georgios ran to the killer who Daniels recognized as Detective Fitzpatrick, Henderson's former partner. Georgios kneeled and checked his pulse, confirming he was dead, and tossed the knife to the side.

Jacobs, bleeding heavily from her head, held a gun, her wrists and hands bloody. Her eyes were wild and unfocused. "Rem. How's Rem?"

She dropped the gun and tried to move closer, but her ankles were bound.

Daniels found Rem lying on the ground, holding his side, blood pooling onto the carpet. Daniels did a quick once over of Jacobs. From the front, she was a mess. Her hair was sticky and matted and her face and blouse red with blood, but he didn't see any fatal wounds. "Jacobs. You okay?"

Dazed, she nodded, and he made his way over to Rem, who was pale but conscious and squatted beside him. He spoke to Georgios. "Georgios, we need an ambulance." He pointed at Jacobs. "And she's tied at the ankles."

Georgios pulled out his phone. "Got it." He reached into a back pocket with his other hand and took out a pocketknife. He opened it and cut Jill's bindings as he spoke into the phone, requesting medical assistance.

"How is he?" asked Jill, coming closer now that she was free to move.

Daniels, his heart thumping, checked Rem's wound. "Hey, partner. How you doing?"

Rem blinked. His breathing was short and labored. "Hey, Daniels. Did the baby come? You a dad?"

"Not yet," said Daniels. "Couple more days, at least." He grabbed a throw pillow on the couch and put it against Rem's injury. He had to slow the bleeding. "Looks like he got you. What happened to those ninja-like reflexes, huh?" His voice shook.

Rem made a pained smile. "This? It's no big deal. Minor injury." He grimaced as Daniels applied pressure to the gash in his side.

"Easy. Take it easy," said Daniels. He kept his face calm, but inside, he feared the worse.

Jill crawled closer. Tears streaked down her face. She touched his arm. "Don't you dare die."

"I'm not planning on it," said Rem. "You okay?" he asked with a wince.

Daniels looked over his shoulder. "Georgios, go get some linens in the hall closet."

Georgios nodded. "Ambulance is on its way." He disappeared around the corner.

Rem groaned as Daniels continued to push.

"Sorry, Buddy. I got to stop the bleeding. Hang in there," said Daniels.

Rem nodded, looking paler. Sweat slid down his neck. "I'm all right. I'm tougher than I look." He eyed Jill. "Did you get him?"

Jill nodded, her voice raspy. "It's over. He's dead." Her head bobbed, and her words trailed off.

Daniels noticed her wobble slightly, and she briefly closed her eyes but reopened them. "Jacobs, you okay?"

"Jesus," he heard Georgios say as he came back around the corner. Daniels followed his stare and as Jill fell forward, he saw the growing circle of blood on her back.

"Shit," said Daniels. "Jacobs? Georgios. Help her."

Georgios ran over.

"What's wrong?" asked Rem, lifting his head. "Jill?"

Georgios balled up a sheet and kneeling beside Jacobs, applied pressure to her back. "Jacobs, you hear me?"

But Jacobs had gone silent.

CHAPTER THIRTY-THREE

Lozano sat in the hospital waiting room and checked the clock on the wall. He'd arrived an hour earlier, after the chaos of the long day had finally wound down. The bank robbery and hostage situation had ended in success, resulting in the serial robbers' apprehension, and one police officer with a gunshot wound to the leg.

Delgado's body was at the coroner, and the crime scene was being processed, although they no longer needed to hunt for his killer.

And after never finding a bomb, the bomb squad had allowed him back into his office, only for him to learn of what had happened to Rem and Jacobs. At the first opportunity, he'd headed to the hospital. Daniels had kept him informed, telling him they were in surgery.

Once he'd arrived and made it past the slew of press that had also learned of the Makeup Artist's death, he'd found that Jacobs was in recovery and doing well. Daniels was speaking to the doctor and waiting for news on Remalla. Lozano had called Merchant in Seattle, giving him the details. Merchant could barely speak in disbelief but told Lozano he would handle things on his end and would notify Jacobs' family.

He called his own wife, telling her the situation and that it would be a late night. Lozano had to ensure his officers were in the clear before his day would end. They'd already lost one that day. He didn't want to lose another.

Sighing, he pulled out a handkerchief and wiped his forehead. His stomach growled, and he realized it was close to ten o'clock, and he hadn't eaten since breakfast. It had been a hell of a day.

A door opened to the surgical waiting room, and Daniels entered, looking tired but relieved. He sat next to the captain. "He's okay," he said, rubbing his eyes.

"Out of surgery?" asked Lozano.

"Yeah. Doc said he's doing fine. Just need to keep an eye out for infection. He's lucky, though. Said it could have been a lot worse." He hung his head.

"You all right?" asked Lozano. "You look like you could hang meat from the bags under your eyes." He patted his detective on the knee. "Why don't you go home. Get some rest. I can hang out here for a while."

"Nah, I'm okay, Cap. I talked to Marjorie. Told her I'd be late."

"You sure? It's been an awful day."

"For you too." He sighed, leaned back and closed his eyes.

Lozano watched him. "He scared you, didn't he?"

Daniels popped open a weary eye. "It was damn close, Cap."

"Yeah. I know. But that's how your partner plays it." He paused. "Much like you."

Daniels glanced over. "I guess we take a few risks. But this…"

Lozano grunted. "Comes with the territory. You know that. But this is how you two work, and sometimes, it comes with a price."

Daniels sighed. "Makes me wonder. I'm about to become a dad."

Lozano understood. He'd been in a similar position as a younger detective. "Don't freak yourself out. Thankfully, cases like these only come around once in a blue moon. Hopefully, this is the worse it will get." Daniels nodded and stared off, deep in thought. "You sure you don't want to get out of here? Conserve your energy? You're going to need it soon."

Daniels made a tired moan. "Don't I know it. Between my partner and this new baby, I may not make it through the year."

Lozano lifted the side of his mouth. "It's not gonna be easy with two kids, is it?"

Daniels shook his head. "I just hope I can handle the little one."

"Rem or the baby?" asked Lozano with a chuckle, trying to lighten the mood. His detective needed to get his mind off things.

Daniels smiled. "Rem I can deal with. Just give him food, and he'll be okay."

Lozano nodded, studying his detective. "You'll be a fine dad, Daniels. Don't worry so much."

Daniels sat up and studied the floor. "You think? Sometimes I have my doubts. This job…" He waved a hand.

Lozano put his handkerchief away. "The job is what it is. You'll make it work. We all do. You're not the only one with kids." He snorted. "You and your partner just need to stay out of trouble."

Daniels massaged his neck. "I can only ask for so many miracles, Cap. I may have used them all up."

"Well, you got a few this afternoon. You may have more than you realize."

"You might be right. But it was a little too close for comfort."

"Close, but you all survived. And that's all that matters."

"Delgado didn't survive."

Lozano laced his fingers together. "I know. He was a good cop."

"Yeah."

The door opened again, and Georgios walked in carrying two cups of coffee and a bottled water. Lozano had Garcia and Mel helping with Delgado's case and Titus working on wrapping up the bank robbery, but they all planned to stop by soon to check in. Despite the late hour, other cops in blue milled about in the lobby.

"Here, Cap." Georgios handed Lozano the water and Daniels one of the cups of coffee.

"Thanks, Georgios," said Daniels. "They're both in the clear. I just talked to the doctors. You can get out of here if you want."

Georgios sat. "Nah. I'll just hang out if you don't mind. Titus is on his way. He wants to check in on us." He checked his watch. "I'll go later. The reports aren't going anywhere."

"No, they're not," said Lozano, and he sat back. "By the way, based on what I've heard, you two broke the rules today. You should have waited for back-up. You could have gotten killed."

Daniels and Georgios regarded each other. "I suppose so, Cap," said Georgios.

Lozano cracked the seal on his water. "But I won't tell anybody, if you don't." He took a sip of his drink.

**

The fog returned, swirling and churning around Jacobs. It was hard to see, but she kept moving, as if she knew where she was going. It was quiet and peaceful, and Jacobs sensed no fear in the mist, only a strange calm, and she knew she'd been here before. The fog shifted slightly and thinned, and she realized the two other presences were back. Their silhouettes framed against the soft light appeared in the distance, and she walked toward them, eager to meet them. Sensing they were important to her, she picked up her pace. Getting closer, she could tell it was the same man and woman, but she could see no distinguishing features. They were anxious to meet her too, and they approached, arms outstretched, but faces still obscured.

Jill stretched out her hand, but before they could touch, that same wave of oppression came between them, physically pushing them back. The fear, which had dissolved, bubbled up, and Jill sensed the inherent danger in the new presence. It was a man, and he didn't want the three of them in the fog to connect.

Reaching out, he grabbed for Jill before she could contact the others, as if his touch would set the tone and determine all that would happen afterwards.

Jill sensed that his connection would be harmful to all of them, and she turned and ran, frightened and eager to distance herself. But she heard his footfalls from behind, and when she glanced back, he was there, grasping for her, his face only a black mask.

"Jill," she heard him say in a raspy whisper, and she ran faster.

Gasping, she came awake with a start. The fog cleared, and she blinked, looking around, wondering where she was. The dream faded, as did the masked man.

"Hey," said a voice. "You're awake."

Her eyes focusing, she saw Daniels sitting by the side of her bed. She heard the soft sounds of machines in the room and saw the tube hanging from her arm. She was in a hospital.

Swallowing, she relaxed her head back against the pillow. "Hey," she said, her voice gruff. Her throat was dry, and she tried to clear it.

"Have some water," said Daniels, holding a jug with a straw.

She lifted her head and took a sip. The cool liquid felt soothing, and she sighed in relief.

"Better?" he asked, putting the jug down.

She nodded, and then the memories returned. The house, Fitz, the knife, the gun, Rem. She sat up or tried to. "Rem. Where's Rem?" Her head ached, and something pulled in her back, and she winced.

Daniels put his hand over hers. "It's fine. He's fine. He's across the hall. I just saw him. He's resting comfortably."

"You're sure?" she asked.

He held up three fingers. "Scout's honor."

She carefully leaned back, wondering why her shoulder hurt so much. "What happened?"

He raised a brow. "You don't remember?"

Everything was jumbled, but then her mind cleared. "I remember shooting Fitz, and Rem getting hurt, but then it all goes blank."

"You've got twelve stitches in your head, a concussion, and he stabbed you beneath the left shoulder. They did surgery to repair the damage. You were lucky. Doctor doesn't know how the knife missed your lung. You lost a lot of blood though, but you'll make a full recovery."

She nodded, wanting to scratch her stitches but trying not to. "And Rem?"

"He had surgery too. Had some intestinal damage. There's a lot of doctor speak, but they basically removed a couple of Taco del Fuegos and a jelly donut. As long as he can avoid infection, he should be fine. He's lucky too. Could have been much worse."

Jill studied his face. The fatigue and worry lines were evident. She didn't know who'd been through the worst of it. Him or her and Rem. "You look exhausted."

He rubbed his face. "I was about to go home. Just wanted to check in on you guys one last time before I left. Make sure there weren't going to be any surprises."

Jill found the clock on the wall. It was close to one o'clock in the morning. "I think visiting hours are way past over. Go home."

"They gave me a little leeway since we're cops, but you're right. I need to go home."

"I'm not a cop. I'm a consultant."

He found and squeezed her fingers. "You call it what you want, but I'd take you as a partner any day of the week. You're a brave lady."

Her heart swelled. "Don't tell Rem."

He smiled. "That's just between you and me."

"Deal," she whispered. "Now go get some rest." Her own eyes were heavy, and she yawned.

He yawned in return and stood. "I'll be back in the morning."

"Take your time. We're not going anywhere."

Daniels walked to the door. "Your brother was here earlier, but he left to meet your dad at the airport. He took a red eye. They'll be here in the morning."

Jill rubbed her eyes. "Okay. Thanks."

"Get some sleep."

She nodded, her eyes closing, as he left the room.

**

Jill didn't sleep well though. Images of Fitz and his knife assailed her. The memory of Rem lying on the ground, bleeding from his side, would not abate. She couldn't help but think how close they'd come to dying. If she hadn't broken through her bindings…maybe Daniels would have been there in time, but she doubted she'd have escaped with only a shoulder injury, or if Rem would even be alive.

The shock of it only wound her up more, and the occasional nurses' visit to ensure she still knew her name hardly bothered her. The quiet made her uncomfortable and having someone in the room helped. The moment they left though, the anxiety returned. The slightest noise made her turn to look to ensure it was harmless.

She realized this was normal. She'd just shot and killed a psychopath who'd stalked her, broken into Rem's home, and almost murdered them. It would take time for her to feel normal again. Maybe a lot of time.

She did manage to doze fitfully, until a memory would spark, and she'd be back on the living room floor, holding the gun, and pulling the trigger. The boom would echo in her ear and she'd be fully awake.

A nurse came and went again, and Jill checked the clock. It was close to four o'clock in the morning. Rubbing her bandaged wrists, she wondered about Rem in the other room. Was he going through the same thing?

Sighing, she threw back the covers, and using the remote, brought the bed up to make it easier for her to sit. Once it was fully upright, she leaned forward, feeling the pull on her back. It hurt, but it was bearable. The nurse had offered her drugs for the pain, but she'd declined. She didn't want to feel foggy and lethargic. It made her too vulnerable.

Biting her lip, she slid her legs over to the side of the bed and put her feet on the ground. She took a second to get her bearings, ensuring she wouldn't get dizzy. Taking her time, she put weight on them and stood. She wore only the hospital gown, but it covered her sufficiently. She was only going across the hall.

Shuffling and taking her time, she pulled her IV stand along with her and made it to the door. Reaching it, she grabbed the handle and opened it, peering into the hallway. It was quiet at that time of the morning. The nurse's station was further down, and one nurse faced a monitor, but she was looking in another direction.

There was a door across from her, and Jill hoped it was Rem's. Daniels had said that's where he was, but if she was wrong, she could just turn and leave. Simple enough.

Taking careful steps and trying not to rush, she moved into the hallway and over to the opposite door, and slowly pushed it open. Poking her head in, she saw a bed with a man in it. Rem's dark head of hair rested against the pillow. Satisfied, she entered the room, and let the door close behind her. Wheeling the IV stand, she approached the side of the bed. Rem rested comfortably, his eyes closed.

Something in her relaxed, as if seeing him solidified that he was okay, and it wasn't a dream. She searched for a chair, needing to sit. Her achy shoulder and head were taking its toll, and she didn't know how much longer her legs would hold her.

"Jacobs?" She heard the whispered words and saw Rem staring up at her. He blinked and spoke in a groggy voice. "Is that you?"

She nodded, suddenly feeling emotional. "Hey. Yes. It's me."

"What are you doing in here? You okay?" He shifted in the bed and winced.

"Don't move. You've had surgery."

He rested back against the pillow. "So have you."

Jill suddenly felt silly standing in the room. "I'm sorry. I shouldn't have woken you." Turning to leave, she put her hand on the bed when a wave of dizziness hit her, and she wobbled.

"Whoa," said Rem. He took her hand. "You're not going anywhere. Sit down before you fall over."

Taking a few breaths, she sat beside him on the bed, and her head slowly cleared.

"You all right?"

"Better." She studied his face and felt bad that she'd bothered him. "I should go." She started to stand.

"Wait a minute. Don't leave. Now that you're here, you might as well stay a while."

"You were resting. He stabbed you for God's sake. The last thing you need is for me to keep you awake. I've done enough as it is."

He frowned. "What are you talking about? This isn't your fault. You didn't stab me."

Jill recalled the horror of the previous day. "You should have never come into the house by yourself. What were you thinking?"

Rem touched her damaged wrists. "It's not my style to play it safe. I wasn't going to leave you in there alone."

"He almost killed you." The memory of the knife slicing into Rem rushed back. She shook her head to try to forget.

"Then blame me, not you. I went in there knowing what could happen."

"I can't stop thinking about it. What he almost did to you, to me. He was insane. How could I not have known…?" She closed her eyes, still seeing Fitz and the knife.

His fingers trailed over her arm in reassurance. "There's no way you could have. How could you have suspected Fitzpatrick? Nobody else did." She didn't answer, and it was quiet for a moment. "How's your shoulder?" he asked. "Daniels said you had surgery. And you have a concussion. How did you even make it over here?" He shifted in the bed, with a groan. "Come here. Lie down."

Her fatigue and emotional distress were catching up to her and the thought of lying next to him was appealing. Mindful of his own injuries, she carefully moved to his side. Her shoulder caught a few times, but she lay next him on the opposite side of her wound.

Feeling his body warmth against hers, she finally began to relax.

"Feel better?"

"Yes. Are you sure you're okay?"

He rested his head against hers. "This is way better than any medication. I have to admit, I woke up a few times thinking someone was in the room. It takes me a second to get my bearings."

"Me, too. Every time I close my eyes, I see him."

She heard him take a breath. "Maybe we can both rest now, at least until the nurse comes and chases you out."

Jill closed her eyes for a second, feeling her nerves relax, when another thought occurred to her. "Rem?"

"Hmm?"

"Do you remember what Fitz said? About Henderson?"

Rem paused. "When?"

"He said he didn't kill him. He thought I killed him. Why would he think that?"

Rem shifted to look at her. "Because he'd unraveled by then. It's one thing to face the murders you've committed against innocent women, it's another to own up to killing your best friend. He'd probably blocked it completely and put it on you instead. It was his mind's way of coping."

Jill nodded. "I guess."

He kissed her forehead. "How's your head? Still have all your brains?"

She smiled. "As far as I know. It's sore but I'm okay. I hear the doctor took out a couple of Taco del Fuegos from your gut."

He smiled back, closing his weary eyes. "Yeah well, no big deal. I'll replace them soon enough."

Jill snuggled closer to him. "I'm glad you're okay," she whispered in his ear.

He whispered back, "I'm glad you're okay too." He found her hand and held it. "Now get some rest, Detective."

Finally letting go, she drifted off to sleep.

CHAPTER THIRTY-FOUR

Dylan pulled her suitcase from her hand. "I'll take it," he said. "You're not supposed to be carrying anything heavy."

"Thanks, Dylan," said Jill. "I'll meet you out by the car."

Dylan picked up her overnight bag and headed outside. "Take your time. No rush."

"Thanks." Jill adjusted her left arm in the sling. It had been two weeks since she and Rem had left the hospital after a four-day stay. They were both still recovering and on medical leave, but the doctors had cleared her to travel.

"You have everything?" asked Daniels. He rocked the car seat at his feet. Baby boy Joseph Preston Daniels had been born two weeks earlier. Daniels looked fatigued, but in a good way. He'd taken a few weeks off and had been able to enjoy being a new dad, as well as keeping an eye out for Rem and Jill.

"I think so," said Jill.

Rem came down the stairs, holding a box. He was managing much better and his doctor thought he could return to work in another week, provided he stayed at his desk for a while.

Reaching the bottom, he handed her the box. "Lozano wanted me to give this to you. Said to tell you to claim it whenever you want." She took the box and opened it. Inside was a plastic detective's badge. "Whenever you're ready for the real thing, so is he," said Rem.

Jill's chest tightened. She didn't think going home would be this hard. "You tell him I may take him up on his offer. I just need some time. But I'd be happy to have him for a Captain, and to work with my two favorite detectives."

Daniels stood and walked over. "The offer stands however long it takes."

Jill nodded. "Thank you. I appreciate that."

Daniels pointed towards the front door. "Dylan seems like a nice guy. I'm sorry we didn't get a chance to hang out some more."

"Yeah, well, you've got some other things to deal with, Dad," said Jill.

"He's a good kid," said Rem. "Makes a mean hamburger."

Daniels frowned. "You are supposed to be eating healthy."

Rem face dropped. "I added lettuce and tomato."

Daniels rolled his eyes. "You better not have had any Taco del Fuegos."

Rem held up a hand. "I plead the fifth."

Daniels opened his mouth to complain when Jill interrupted, returning to the subject. "Dylan is a great guy. He's got some issues to work out, and we've got a lot to talk about on the drive home."

Daniels took his eyes off Rem but not before giving him the look that their discussion was not over. "You ever ask him about why he never told you about being in jail?"

"That's one of the topics on my list. Although I knew he was in jail. Brian told me. I kept his confidence though because Brian had been sworn to secrecy."

"Sounds like it's going to be a fun car ride home," said Rem.

"He'll love it," said Jill. "But I hope he's ready to talk. I think with everything that was happening to me before, he didn't want to burden me with his problems, but now maybe he'll open up."

"How's your dad doing?" asked Daniels. "He excited you're coming home?"

Jill shook her head. "That's a whole other matter. It's one reason I need to go back. I need to see if we can talk things out. Before…well it was hard to talk about the future and what it held. But now, I don't know. Maybe he can be more flexible."

"Or he'll want you to go into flower arranging. I hear it's much safer," said Rem.

Jill smiled. "He'd like that, although I'm sure he'd prefer it if I went to law school, but that will never happen. That's Brian's area of expertise." She sighed. "Brian and I have a few things to work out, too." She rubbed the top of her head. The stitches had come out a few days before and it itched. "It's been a long three years."

The baby stirred and began to cry. "That's my cue," said Daniels. "It's about time for a feeding and diaper change." He raised a brow at Rem. "You ready to give it a try, partner?"

Rem's face paled, and he held his side, making a sad groan. "I'm still a little weak and achy. I think I need to sit this one out. Maybe next time."

Daniels furrowed his brow. "Uh-huh. I figured."

Rem grinned. "Besides, I need to walk Jacobs out."

The baby cried louder, and Daniels walked to the car seat and picked him up. "Come on, little man. Let's get you something to eat."

"Tell Marjorie I said goodbye," said Jill.

"I will," said Daniels, holding Joseph. "She wanted to come, but she was up a good part of the night last night feeding little JP here. He's got an appetite like his Uncle Rem. I told her to rest."

"I can't wait to give him his first taco. He's gonna love it," said Rem.

Daniels accessed a bottle from a bag and popped it into Joseph's mouth. He spoke to the baby. "I'm apologizing now for your Uncle Rem, but there's not much I can do about it." The baby quieted as he ate, and Daniels looked up. "Take care, Jacobs. Don't be a stranger."

Jill waved, feeling her chest constrict again. "I won't be." She paused. "And thank you, Daniels. For everything."

He held her gaze. "You're welcome."

Her eyes watered as she nodded and headed out the door. Rem followed, and they stood on the outside porch as Dylan waited in the car.

"You gonna be okay?" Rem asked, facing her.

"I don't know," she said. "Are you?" She glanced at the house. "They cleaned the house up, but it still holds some disturbing memories. Are you going to stay?"

He shrugged. "I think so. It's not like me to get pushed out of my home by some madman. Besides, I like this house. And I don't want to move." He waved at the door. "It will be weird for a while, but it will fade. Besides, I have other memories here, too." He grinned. "Some really good ones." He took her hand.

She smiled and squeezed his fingers. "I know. I won't be forgetting those anytime soon."

"Whenever you want to relive a few…" He paused. "Well, I'll be here."

She nodded. "I know." She took a breath. "And don't think I don't want that. I just need some time. It's been so long since I've had any normalcy in my life. I need to see my family and figure things out."

"I get it. You'll get no pressure from me. Just know that when you're ready, and if you're up for it, I'll be here. And if you ever need to talk, I'm only a phone call away."

Her tears surfaced again. She raised a hand and touched his cheek. "You're a good man, Remalla. I think much better than I could have ever expected for myself."

A tear fell from her eye, and he brushed it away. "Then you should raise your expectations. Don't sell yourself short, Jacobs. You've got some cajones. You should be proud of them. I know. I've seen 'em."

She smiled, and her breath caught. "I'm going to miss you."

He nodded and his own eyes watered. "I'm going to miss you, too."

"This is not goodbye though. I promise."

"I know. When you're settled. Let me know. Cap has a place on the lake. We'll go for a weekend. Take some time for us."

"I'd like that." She sniffed.

They stared for a moment until he brought a finger to her chin and lowered his mouth to meet hers. Their lips met, and they kissed softly, holding the contact, until he pulled back. “Take care, Jacobs.”

She nodded, as tears clouded her eyes. “I will.” She bit her lip and paused, unable to leave. “But we need to do better than that.” Raising up, she kissed him again, wrapping her good arm around him, not caring if Dylan was watching. He kissed her back hard, holding her for several seconds, before she broke the contact and slid her arm down and took his hand one more time. Squeezing his fingers and finally letting go, she walked away.

**

The couple in the car across the street watched the exchange between Remalla and Jacobs on the porch.

“You think she’ll come back?” asked the man behind the wheel.

The woman in the passenger seat arranged her large stoned necklaces, so they sat properly on her neck. “Of course. Do you see the way they look at each other? They won’t be separated for long. They have a future together.”

The man watched Jill walk to the car idling in the driveway and get in. “What kind of future, considering what we know.”

“That all depends. She’s made it this far.”

The man tapped the wheel. “When do we intervene? She still doesn’t know what really happened to Henderson.”

“At this point, there’s no need for her to know. Our objective here is to find the problem. She’s only the first steppingstone.”

“And the others?” the man asked.

“We can only wait and see. Jill survived her ordeal with the Makeup Artist. Now we just have to see what happens next.”

The car backed out of the driveway and left, as Remalla waved and went inside. “It seems like a long wait. Who knows when he’ll strike again?”

"We don't have a choice. They want us to find him, but we can't do that until he makes another move."

"That could take a while," said the man. "He may not pop up again for months."

The woman pulled a small plastic bottle from her purse and opened it, dispensing some lotion on her fingers. She rubbed the cream into her skin and the car filled with the smell of flowers. "No. He won't wait long. It's not his style. Jill was just the beginning." She put the lotion back in her purse.

The man's phone rang, and he answered. "Yes?" He listened in disbelief. "Really?" He looked over, his eyes wide. "I got it. Thank you." He hung up.

"What is it?"

"You're on the money, as usual. There's been more activity. Another death. A husband. Up at Secret Lake, about an hour away."

Sonia Vandermere stared off, turning a large amethyst ring on her finger. "Oh, dear. I know where that is, and I know who that is."

"You do?"

"Yes. It's the next steppingstone. Hopefully, the one that will lead to him." She sighed. "Come on. Let's go. There's more work to do."

Wondering where this next murder would lead, he started the car and drove away.

ꝏꝏꝏ

Want more from J. T. Bishop? Sign up for her newsletter at jtbishopauthor.com and get her first book, *Red-Line: The Shift,* and future books for **free**, including the Daniels and Remalla novella, *The Girl and the Gunshot*, and a *First Cut* missing scene!

Did you enjoy *First Cut*? Then get ready for *Second Slice*. There's still a killer on the loose and he's got a new target. Daniels and Remalla are on the hunt, but will they catch him before he moves on to his next victim? An excerpt of *Second Slice* follows below. *Third Blow* and *Fourth Strike* continue the *Family or Foe* saga, so put your reading hats on.

After *Family or Foe*, jump straight into Daniels' and Remalla's own series with *Haunted River*. This standalone involves the ghost of a woman whose murder remains unsolved. When another woman turns up dead years later, are Daniels and Remalla next? This book is followed by *Of Breath and Blood* where our detectives investigate a cult leader and will have to rely on each other to survive. *Of Body and Bone* continues the story arc and *Of Mind and Madness* is available for pre-order.

And, in case you like light sci-fi/urban fantasy with a dash of paranormal and a delicious romance thrown in, then check out Bishop's first series, *The Red-Line Trilogy*, or the sister series to the Red-Line trilogy, *The Fletcher Family Saga*. Either can be read first. Take your pick. Boxsets are available, too!

And get ready for a spin-off series from Detectives Daniels and Remalla. *Lost Souls,* the first book in *The Redstone Chronicles* featuring paranormal PI, Mason Redstone and his sister Mikey, introduced in *Of Breath and Blood*, is now available. *Lost Dreams*, part two in this series, follows and *Lost Chances* is available for pre-order.

A NOTE FROM J.T.

I love to hear from my readers about their experiences with my books, and I'd love to know what you thought about *First Cut.* This book was my first foray out into the world of crime, after completing my *Red-Line* series. I wanted to delve more into murder mysteries and the thriller side of things and this book opened up an exciting storyline featuring two awesome, bantering detectives. The story of *First Cut,* where a former detective makes a psychic connection with a serial killer, was banging around in my head for a while and it was time to get it on paper. Did you ever watch *Profiler* or *Medium* on TV? It's kind of a combo between the two series. I added Detectives Daniels and Remalla, plus additional characters to develop the story arc, and the *Family or Foe Saga* was born. If you don't know me or my work just yet, I love to add a touch of the supernatural to my books. I think it creates an extra layer of fun and keeps my characters on their toes.

Reviews are a huge plus and big help for an author, and potential readers. I would love it if you could please take a couple of minutes to leave a quick review for *First Cut.* Add if you'd like, please leave a few comments, too. I'd love to know what you think.

As always, thank you for your time and readership. It is deeply valued and appreciated.

Now, on to the next book!

BOOKS IN CHRONOLOGICAL ORDER

Although not required, in case you like to read in order…

Prelude to The Shift, a short story (free at jtbishopauthor.com)
Red-Line: The Shift
Red-Line: Mirrors
Red-Line: Trust Destiny
Curse Breaker
High Child
Spark
Forged Lines
The Girl and the Gunshot, a novella (free at jtbishopauthor.com)
First Cut
Second Slice
Third Blow
Fourth Strike
Haunted River
Of Breath and Blood
Lost Souls
Of Body and Bone
Lost Dreams
Of Mind and Madness
Lost Chances

ENJOY AN EXCERPT FROM J.T. BISHOP'S NEXT BOOK, *SECOND SLICE*

A murky fog obscured her vision and she blinked to see, but it didn't help. Holding her hands out, she walked through the soupy mix, careful not to walk into anything. She saw and heard nothing.

Squinting, she stopped, focusing as the fog swirled and turned, and figures became visible. There were three of them. They were only silhouettes, but she could see enough to tell one was a woman and the other two men. They didn't move, but just stared back. There was something about these three that intrigued her, and she took a step closer. The fog swirled, and as she reached out, she saw the woman reach out as well. But before their hands could touch, the fog thickened, a gust of wind blew, and she was shoved backward.

Madison opened her eyes. The stars greeted her. Blinking, she sat up, holding her chest. Her heart thudded, and she could still see her hand reaching out to the other, when something had stopped them from connecting.

Everything was still. Nothing moved on the lake. She had no idea how long she'd been asleep. The boat had drifted, but not far. Shaking off the strange dream, she stood and hit the ignition. The engine rumbled and she steered herself quietly back home. Within a few minutes, she approached her dock. She cut the engine, and as the boat floated slowly toward the pier, she jumped out, grabbed the side rail, and pulled the pontoon closer. It bumped softly against the wooden deck, and she tied it to the posts.

The boat secured, she turned back toward the house. The kitchen light she'd left on was now off, and it was dark. She supposed Donald had gone back to the kitchen. The glow of the moon though gave her sufficient light, and she walked down the dock to the patio. Reaching for the door, she paused, hearing something. It was faint, but in the quiet, it was easier to detect. She thought it sounded like a footfall, and maybe someone moving through the brush. Her heart rate jumped. She saw nothing, just the bushes along the side of the cabin, but something cold moved through her and the hair on the back of her neck raised. Sliding the glass door open, she stepped inside, and closed the door behind her. Locking it, she scanned the area, but there was nothing other than the distinct feeling she was being watched. Rubbing her arms, she shook her head. Karl's murder had spooked everyone around the lake. It had always been a place where everyone had kept their doors unlocked, and neighbors came and went. But now everyone thought twice about keeping their doors open.

Taking a deep breath, and telling herself she was overreacting, she went into the kitchen and got a glass of water. She kept the light off, and after getting a drink, she realized she needed some things from her bathroom before going to sleep in the guest room. She didn't know if Donald really thought he was punishing her by forcing her to sleep elsewhere, or if he, like her, just preferred to sleep alone. Considering how often she slept there, she should have just stocked the bathroom with her toiletries. She made a mental note to do that in the morning.

Moving slowly down the carpeted hallway, she stopped at the door to the master and quietly opened it. She had no doubt that Donald would yell at her if she woke him, so she tiptoed into the bathroom. All she could make out in the dark room was the curve of his body beneath the sheets. Entering the bathroom, a soft night light gave her enough illumination for her to see what she needed. She grabbed a few things and opened a drawer to get her moisturizer when she kicked something on the floor. It clattered as it slid against the tile. Squinting, she tried to make out what it was, but couldn't see well enough. She found the shower light on the wall and flipped it on. The shower brightened, and the bathroom came into sharper view.

Finding the object, she froze, uncertain of what she was seeing. Her eyes widening, she stepped closer. It was a knife. She recognized it specifically as the knife she'd used earlier that evening to cut the brownies. She's rinsed it and put it in the drainer next to the sink.

Her mind tried to comprehend why it was there. The knife was red with blood, and as her eyes looked around, she saw drops of blood in the bathroom. She followed their path and saw they led from the bedroom.

She stopped breathing, but her heart took a sudden leap in her chest. Everything went still and a cold horror settled over her body. Her skin prickled. Where did that knife come from? Why was it in the bathroom? Why was there blood on it? Whose blood was it?

She tried to call for Donald, but nothing escaped her throat. She couldn't utter a word. She thought of the noise on the patio and wondered if someone had been, or was still in the house. Could he be waiting for her? Her hands shaking, she dropped what she held back onto the counter. She had to get out of the bathroom and get to a phone. Her cell was still in her purse that sat in the dining chair. There was a landline in the bedroom though. She had to get to it and call for help. And what about Donald? Was he okay? She had to warn him too.

Forcing herself to move and breathe, she took tentative steps backward, watching the knife, as if it might jump up and stab her at any moment.

Quivering, she made it to the bathroom door and pushed it open. Visions of someone standing there, waiting, made her almost throw up. But no one was there. The bedroom was dark though and she was terrified she wasn't alone. The fear was so intense, she began to cry and tears ran down her cheeks. Forcing herself to move, she raced to the side of the bed, desperate for light, and flipped on the bedroom lamp. She began to reach for the phone, when she saw Donald in the bed.

Nothing in the bathroom had prepared her for this. His lifeless eyes stared upward, and blood covered the headboard and the white sheets. His mouth was open in a silent scream and his throat was sliced open, the wound raw and seeping.

A scream caught in Madison's throat. The scene was horrifying and indescribable. She couldn't think. This was Donald, in their bed, murdered. She stepped back, and stepped into something warm. Looking down, she saw it was blood. The shock finally hit her, her throat unlocked, and she let loose a blood curdling shriek. The sound of it catapulted her out of the room, and she ran. Expecting at any moment for the assailant to step out of the shadows and assault her, she managed to make it to her purse. Grabbing it, she fell to the floor, her back against the wall, as tears ran down her face. Her hands shook so hard, she could barely grasp the phone.

Crying and shaking, she dialed 911.